TRANSMISSION

TRANSMISSION

RAGNAROK TRILOGY

Book 2

JOHN MEANEY

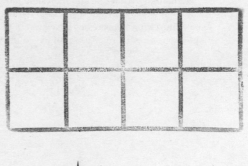

The right of John Meaney to be identified as the author of this work has
been asserted by him in accordance with the
Copyright, Designs and Patents Act 1988.

First published in Great Britain in 2012 by
Gollancz
An imprint of the Orion Publishing Group
Orion House, 5 Upper St Martin's Lane, London WC2H 9EA
An Hachette UK Company

This edition published in Great Britain in 2012 by Gollancz

1 3 5 7 9 10 8 6 4 2
A CIP catalogue record for this book is available
from the British Library

ISBN 978 0 575 08537 4

Typeset by Input Data Services Ltd,
Bridgwater, Somerset

Printed in Great Britain by
Clays Ltd, St Ives plc

The Orion Publishing Group's policy is to use papers that
are natural, renewable and recyclable products and
made from wood grown in sustainable forests. The logging
and manufacturing processes are expected to conform to
the environmental regulations of the country of origin.

www.johnmeaney.com
www.orionbooks.co.uk

To John Richard Parker: the best of agents,
true gentleman and friend.

A note on Norse names:

In English, the letter combination *th* has two pronunciations –
compare 'this'll' (as in *this'll be good*) with 'thistle'.

The following words have a hard *th* as in 'this' or 'other':
Óthinn, Heithrún, Davith, Ingrith, Autha, Jorth, *seithr* (dark
magic), Asgarth (home of the gods). These names have a soft
th as in 'thistle' or 'thing': Thórr, Thórrvaldr, Arrnthórr. Mixing
both, the first *th* of Thórthr is soft, while the second is hard,
correctly written as Þórðr.

Also, the *ý* in Týr is pronounced like the *u* in French *tu*, or *ü*
in German *Glück*.

ONE

Poor Roger. That was the sentiment in their obsidian eyes, those few Pilots who knew him: poor bereaved Roger, his parents famously dead, he a nobody (in a city-world that remained bounded yet infinite) who lacked the training that Labyrinth-dwelling Pilots were immersed in for years; while as a mudworld-raised youth-turned-man, what could he actually *do*?

And those eyes! As he walked the endless Borges Boulevard and saw only strangers, each was without disguise: so many pairs of all-black eyes, glittering jet and hard to read, even for him, whose own eyes matched; for in this place, only a Pilot could remain sane.

In the midst of Labyrinth, the air was never free of the faintest of amber glows, or the prickling feel of layers-within-layers of reality, the tactile sense of other geometries accessible with a gesture or a thought; for this was mu-space, the ur-continuum, a universe no ordinary human could comprehend or live in.

In front of him, the air curved, pulled into a rotation; and he knew it was Jed Goran even before Jed stepped through. He was lean and hard-looking, grinning now.

'Roger.'

'Hey, Jed.'

They shook hands – Jed's grip stronger than Roger's – in another ritual, newly familiar. Back on Fulgor, at least in Lucis City and the surrounding province, politeness had dictated the bumping of fists with acquaintances old or new. Just one more human behaviour extinguished when the Anomaly subsumed that world.

For the place of his childhood was gone: Fulgor, now a hellworld ruled by a global collective mind, the Anomaly, each former human a component in a vast gestalt whose properties and processes were emergent, therefore *different* in the way that human cognition bears no relation to a single neuron's chemical cycles.

'Are you busy?' asked Jed.

'Well . . . I've been trying to study in the Logos Library, but' – with an asymmetric shrug – 'I can't get into it.'

'No rush, pal. You've got to rest up, get used to things, you know?'

They were at the head of Feigenbaum Alley, home to shops run as part-time hobbies, often by families. Here Roger might buy some story- or study-crystals from his Admiralty-granted allowance. A part of his awareness noted the successive diminishing of shop dimensions along the alley's length, like some odd, straightened-out Nautilus.

Everything was different, even perspective.

'Are your parents still alive, Jed?'

'Sure. Not around much, but they're fine.' Jed glanced at the shopfronts, then: 'Med Centre are shipping out the first batch. Did you want to watch?'

'I don't really—'

'You won't be able to see her, though. I asked.'

'All right.' A memory whipped into Roger's awareness but he pushed it back, flattening the mental image and twisting it into a vortex, trying to blur the fat naked man over Alisha's body, to forget how the brothel stank. 'Shit.'

With an effort, he flung it all away.

'Maybe I should've told you afterwards.'

'I can watch,' said Roger. 'And I need to see more ships in operation, don't I?'

'With me, then.'

Jed summoned another fastpath rotation, a skill that remained beyond Roger's power; then the two of them stepped inside – everything whirling, the axes of reality transforming –

and came out onto Archimedes Avenue, facing an abyssal drop beyond which rose a cliff-like city wall, Med Centre blossoming upon it. Closer by, a shoal of white drones floated in the air, ready for wholesale movement towards the internal docks where ships were waiting with empty holds. The visual pattern would have been beautiful were it not for the similarity to coffins, and the knowledge that each med-drone contained a traumatized survivor, their present coma a prelude to waking in realspace, to remembering how their world had died.

'Is Alisha in this batch?'

'I don't know,' said Jed. 'I haven't seen *my* manifest yet, never mind anyone else's.'

'Manifest?'

'I'm flying one of the loads to Molsin.'

Of all the human worlds, Molsin had turned out to be the one most receptive to refugees. The others were scared, and it was hard to blame them. Who knew whether the Anomaly might replicate elsewhere? What if an infectious seed resided in one of the refugees' minds?

'It's going to be a one-leg flight for me,' Jed went on. 'But most ships are stopping off at a dwarf-star orbital for interview. They're going to wake the poor bastards up to question them.'

In case of Anomalous infection. An extra layer of precaution, and sensible enough.

'So why aren't you stopping off?' said Roger.

'I'm taking the ones that they daren't wake up, not without medics present.'

'I— So Alisha's one of them, is that what you're saying?'

'As I said, my manifest hasn't arrived.' Jed held up his turing. 'But there's a good chance she's on my list, don't you reckon?'

En masse, the floating drones began to move.

'Do you think—?' Roger tried to work out what he wanted to ask, then let the words fall out anyhow. 'Could I come with you to Molsin?'

'That's why I showed you this.'

'You think I should go?'

What he meant was, should he be there when Alisha woke up? But Jed had never known Alisha properly, for she had been unconscious during the Fulgor rescue and ever since.

'Actually, my friend . . . I don't.'

'You think I should stay in Labyrinth?'

'I think you should have the choice. But if I were you, I'd stay on here. Keep communing with your other girl.'

Jed's words produced an echo in Roger's memory: something he said once to Dad, about the other love in *his* life.

'Excuse me?' called Jed. 'Did you want something?'

A wide-shouldered Pilot was watching them. At Jed's challenge, he gave the tiniest of starts.

'Sorry. My name's Dak Stilwell.' He stepped closer. 'I didn't want to interrupt, Pilot Blackstone. But I did want to pass on my sympathies.'

'That's all right,' said Roger, not sure of the man. 'Did you know my parents?'

'I met your father briefly, in fact. But I'm with the Med Centre, and we offer many services, including simply talking.'

'You're a counsellor?' asked Jed. 'You don't look like one.'

Stilwell raised his hand. The knuckles were shiny and enlarged.

'What do counsellors look like? I teach close-quarter combat in my spare time.' He turned to Roger. 'When you're alone and feel like talking, call Med Centre and mention my name. At absolutely any time.'

'Thank you,' said Roger.

'Then I'm off.' Stilwell gestured for a fastpath rotation. 'Take it easy.'

He stepped inside and was gone.

'Counsellor, my arse,' said Jed.

Beyond the boulevard, the shoal of autodocs continued to move, heading for the ships that would take the refugees away

4

from Labyrinth, where no realspace menace could reach, but where ordinary people could never wake up to continue their lives, to experience joy or hardship or anything else.

The man who called himself Dak Stilwell exited the rotation at the centre of a long, clear chamber whose defences were invisible. In front of him, a holo figure stood.

'Identify, please,' it said.

'I'm Zeke Clayton, beta team leader, section 7.'

'Confirmed.'

As if loosening a heavy backpack, Clayton shrugged his ursine shoulders, then walked straight through the holo to the next chamber, where shielded doors curled out of existence, allowing him to pass inside. Pavel Karelin was waiting: narrow-bodied, narrow-eyed, quietly spoken.

'I'm going in with you,' he said.

'It's only Colonel Garber.' With another shrug of Clayton's big shoulders: 'I'm not exactly scared of him.'

'Of course not. You're a loyal officer.'

Was that a faint stress on *you're*? A hint about Garber's loyalty? Clayton was trying to figure a way to frame an inno-cent-sounding question when a doorway folded in on itself, revealing Garber.

'Come inside,' he called.

Pavel entered alongside Clayton.

'I'm sitting in,' he said. 'Given our overlapping areas of operational responsibility, Colonel, it seems best.'

'Very well.' Garber gestured for flowmetal chairs to rise from the floor. 'Sit down, both of you.'

'Roger Blackstone knows nothing.' Clayton knew better than to begin with chitchat. 'That's the short version. Maybe Analysis can find something in my logs, but for my money, every indicator says Carl Blackstone kept his family separate from his work. Trained his son in a few good habits, kept him clear of operations.'

'Uh-huh. Blackstone senior has already had the posthumous

medal.' Garber's tone was tight and cold. 'Now we can pick apart the reality.'

'Understood, sir. But the son has made no attempt to contact anyone, and he's said nothing to indicate special knowledge. Poor lad hasn't got to grips with the basics of spatiotemporal manipulation, so even a simple dead-letter drop is out of the question.'

Pavel said, 'That's natural, for someone raised in realspace.'

'Yes, but he's not motivated to do anything about it,' said Clayton. 'That's my point. It's natural for someone who's, er, grieving, but not for a clandestine operator. If the father cached anything in Labyrinth, it won't be out in the open.'

Garber changed position, his chair adapting.

'So you're persisting in the notion that Carl Blackstone was clean?'

'Sir, I'm not presenting an opinion either way. What I *do* think is Roger Blackstone lacks all operational knowledge of his father's work.'

'Very well. Present the full report now.'

'OK.' Clayton manipulated his tu-ring. 'Done.'

Garber checked his own tu-ring, nodded, then looked at Pavel.

'Molly-coddling your team is hardly to anyone's credit, Colonel Karelin.'

'I couldn't agree more, Colonel. I've softened them so much, they can't take the cut and thrust of memos and meetings in the dangerous corridors of power.'

No tightening of facial muscles betrayed Garber's feelings, but his voice flattened.

'I'm glad we share the same analysis. Thank you both for coming.'

Clayton stood up a tenth of a second before the flowmetal subsided to the floor. Pavel was already on his feet.

'Always a pleasure,' he said.

He led the way out, and Clayton followed.

*

Sitting in the study carrel, Roger found it impossible to concentrate. Around him the Logos Library contained effectively infinite knowledge; but the amount he felt capable of absorbing hovered between infinitesimal and zero.

'This is impossible.'

He shut down the display, then gestured for the crystal array to fold back into its designated pocket of fractal reality. It took three attempts before the crystals were tucked away. At this rate, he would soon have the capabilities of an eight-year-old.

I'll never have a place here.

As he left the carrel, it rotated itself into a fist-sized holding-shape; but he could take no credit: the process was automatic.

'Been studying?' asked an olive-skinned woman.

'Uh, trying.'

'It never gets any easier, does it?'

She smiled, her face triangular and feline, then twisted away and was gone.

Bloody hell.

Behind him, a young female Pilot said: 'She *spoke* to you.'

'Er— What?'

'You've just been visited by a living legend. Don't you get it?'

'I don't . . . No, not really.'

'Oh, for—'

Her fastpath rotation tore the words away, leaving silence in the infinite corridor.

I'm getting out of here.

But he would have to do it the hard way, by walking.

Roger considered Jed a friend; yet it would have been nice to utilize a route of his own devising instead of this one, constructed by Jed. It took him to a chamber off Poincaré Promenade. Once there he had only to stand still: the chamber itself moved fast, a bubble through flowmetal. By logical deduction and feel, he decided it was following a horizontal path across the cliff-like series of edifices that became Ascension Annexe.

This was one of the most notable sections of Labyrinth, one that an observer might expect Roger Blackstone to view from a distance and admire, but not to enter.

Great panes of energy swivelling in mid-air, along with the golden lightning flickering across walls, indicated this was a secure area. Internal itching grew in every organ of Roger's body as deepscan fields passed through him. Then they were gone, and he felt himself grinning as he walked fast through building-high doors that folded back, allowing entrance to a huge hangar space.

Far too vast for her.

I'm here.

A small shape moved, some ten metres above the ground. Black, mostly: a convex triangle webbed with scarlet and gold that only emphasized how dark her body mostly was. She turned in the air.

Roger!

Warmth more than verbalization flared in his brain. He opened his arms as she flew towards him; then she stopped, quivering, to hang level with his face. She was growing bigger: no longer could he reach all the way across her triangular width. Twin differentiating folds were visible, where her lateral extremities would grow into delta wings.

When she became a big girl.

Play now?

For the first time since the catastrophe, he laughed without sadness.

Race you!

He broke into a sprint, moving in a fast straight line then dodging, breaking right then left, throwing himself through a shoulder roll and coming back to his feet, while she swooped around him, tumbling through aerobatics: never touching him at speed except to brush his clothing; and all they felt was warmth and love as they played until they were tired and then they stopped. Afterwards, Roger sat on the soft floor, and she settled beside him so her nose was on his lap, and his hand was upon her dorsal hull that felt so warm and strong. Though ships and Pilots alike possess a fine-grained sense of time, neither could have said how long they held each other like this, so fully absorbed, so filled with love and rightness.

Knowing they belonged together.

TWO

EARTH, 1941 AD

To be a Nazi in Tokyo was ... interesting. The Reich and Imperial Nihon might be allies but their cultures were different; while to be a *pretend* Nazi, like Dmitri Shtemenko, meant every day was filled with pervasive threat, the good and the bad of it: nervous fear yet a sense of life on the edge. There were recurring icons: blades, blood and a fascination with suicide by sword, the hallmarks of the homosexual ultra-right-wing subculture that Dmitri continued to infiltrate.

The man he shared his twenty-tatami apartment with, Sergei Alegeev, had no sexual interest in men, but was not bothered by anything Dmitri got up to. Perhaps it was Sergei's navy background that kept him broad-minded.

I haven't given in to all my needs.

Before starting this mission, Dmitri had thrown his collection of human fingers into the Moscow River; since then, he had made no attempt to replace them. Personal safety, more than mission security, motivated him. Torture was fine, but not with him as the subject.

'Another evening' – Dmitri raised his third cup of saké – 'spent rolling around on the floor with brawny men. You must have enjoyed yourself.'

He was sitting on the straw mat opposite Sergei.

'I did, Chief.' Sergei spoke German, as they both did in the apartment, though they had checked yet again today for microphones or human eavesdroppers. His fluency came from his mother, for he was far from the image of a studious linguist: never pretty, he had developed true cauliflower ears during their sojourn here, and broken his nose twice. Tonight, his left cheek was raw, reddened with the ongoing condition he called mat-burn. 'I strangled one of the bastards unconscious,' he added, reaching for his own saké. 'So yes, a good evening.'

'Next you're going to tell me how you once got choked out by what's-his-face himself.'

'Oshchenkov.' Sergei lowered his voice. This was not a name he would want overheard, by their current hosts or by their masters. 'Well, I did. A cross-collar choke, and I'm proud I fought him. So long as you don't tell those bastards back home.'

He refilled his cup from the porcelain flask.

'I won't.'

Dmitri meant it. For all that he knew was wrong with him, betraying the closest he had to a friend was unthinkable. Sergei was able to train with the local judo men because of his background in grappling, in civilian clubs in Moscow and in the navy. The man Sergei admired, Oshchenkov, had been a judo great: practising at Tokyo's Kodokan where Sergei trained now, then transforming the discipline back in Mother Russia. Under official orders, Oshchenkov had taken the various indigenous wrestling styles of the Soviet republics, and aggregated them around a skeleton of judo.

But Stalin was paranoid and foreign contact was suspect, so five years ago, the NKVD had snatched and killed Oshchenkov. The term *judo* was now illegal; the transformed discipline was called *sambo*, and Sergei – as much as Dmitri could judge – was pretty good at it.

'Anyway' – Sergei tossed back the saké and went for the flask again – 'I lined up a treat for you tomorrow. A young Lieutenant Kanazawa wants to show us, that's you with me tagging along, something special.'

Sergei's features became sharp and full of depth in Dmitri's vision, as saké-induced vagueness vanished. 'What kind of special thing?'

'*Todé*.' Sergei beamed. 'You'll love it. Also called China Hand, or Empty Hand since the buggers here got as paranoid as Uncle Joe himself.'

Dmitri, translating in his head, realized that China Hand and Empty Hand would sound the same in Japanese.

'This *kara-té*,' he said. 'It's not another kind of wrestling, is it?'

'Not wrestling, but it is fighting.'

'Oh.' Dmitri took the saké flask from Sergei. 'And I'm going to be interested why, exactly?'

'Because Lieutenant Kanazawa is on Admiral Yamashita's staff, and he's unhappy about something.'

'Ah.'

'Perhaps you can console the poor man. And perhaps' – Sergei leaned over to peer into the flask – 'you could get more saké, Chief, since I've been doing my patriotic duty while you've been polishing off the booze.'

'I'll get right on it.' Dmitri rolled onto his knees, then made himself stand. 'Since we're all equals in the great workers' paradise.'

'Chance would be a fine thing.'

'Yes, wouldn't it just?'

But he fetched the saké anyway, because it was precious, this concept of having a friend; and besides, they both knew who was in charge.

And we both despise our masters.

Except that in Dmitri's case, it was not just Stalin and the political apparatus he served: there was a darker force that he believed existed in the world – not just inside his head – with goals he could never know; and his feelings for that force were ambiguous and always had been.

I hate you.

But he also loved it, the darkness; and that was the problem.

In the training hall, Dmitri sat with Kanazawa and Sergei on actual chairs – pretty much hidden by tall paper screens – while the pyjama-clad fighters were in *seiza*: kneeling, sitting back on their heels. Beforehand, Kanazawa had said something about the instructors' being special, and you could sort of see it: healthiness, alertness and posture combining to give the two senior men an apparent aura.

There was a concept that Dmitri wanted to admire but could not: *shugyō*, meaning ascetic discipline. It applied to more than combat; but it was obvious here in the dojo as the fighting drills commenced. Moving in straight lines, throwing first hundreds then thousands of techniques against imaginary opponents, was militaristic if not realistic, until the mad fire in their eyes made it obvious that the goal was to induce combat insanity. Here, they succeeded.

When they sparred, they did not hold their hands up high like boxers, but they hit hard. Soon blood was brightening on the yellowish-white jackets. One man in particular was taking a battering. Dmitri heard Kanazawa suck in a breath; but they were supposed to watch silently, so this was not the time for a question.

Soon it became apparent that everyone was fighting this poor bastard in turn – except that they would not all get their chance, for a large flat-faced man leaped forward, arm thrusting like a battering-ram into a cheekbone, and his victim was down, showing zero sign of getting back up. The others responded by carrying the limp body off to one corner and dumping it there, then resuming their training.

Once the session was over and formal bows were in progress, Kanazawa stood up fast. It took a second for Dmitri to do like-wise; Kanazawa was already striding for the side exit. Dmitri and Sergei caught up with him outside, where he was putting on his boots. They retrieved their own shoes, and tugged them on, then followed Kanazawa to his borrowed staff car.

He's upset about the one they beat up.

The man lying in the corner had been very still.

'Is he dead?' Dmitri asked in Japanese. 'Is that it?'

'Yes.' Kanazawa trembled. 'Come.'

Once they were in the car, Kanazawa started it up, making metal grind as he put it into gear. The car rolled off, Kanazawa's steering unsteady.

'But why did they kill him?' asked Dmitri. 'Was it something political?'

'Because he wanted to leave the dojo,' said Kanazawa. 'He wanted to concentrate on his studies at the academy, because he was falling behind.'

That would be the Naval Academy.

'It happens,' said Sergei. 'If someone wants to leave a dojo, they get ordered to come back for one last lesson. A memorable lesson, except sometimes—'

He did not need to finish.

Sometimes it really is their final lesson.

Dmitri had done worse, so he was surprised to recognize his own disgust, though not as strong as Sergei's or Kanazawa's. Or perhaps Dmitri's subconscious was causing him to mimic the lieutenant's reaction, broadcasting sympathy, sensing an opportunity to get the man to open up.

'Saké,' Dmitri said. 'We need a drink after that. Our apartment is fully stocked.'

Kanazawa must have duties to attend to, but this was a moment of weakness.

'Please come,' added Dmitri, wording it as a polite request, inflecting it as a command.

'All right,' said Kanazawa, pushing down on the accelerator.

They were in fits of laughter. Each cup of saké had intensified the redness of Kanazawa's face while eroding his balance: the prim, controlled, ivory-featured man from the morning replaced by this jerky comic marionette. And now it was Dmitri's turn again for singing.

He lurched to his feet.

I am a loyal Nazi.

Dmitri followed nothing without question, neither the darkness in his head nor the tenets of dialectical materialism, and even in this most intimate of moments when he hoped Kanazawa would let his guard down, Dmitri's own cover must remain intact. Blurting secrets to allies was one thing – and

Kanazawa was not quite there, not yet – but for him to betray his god-Emperor to an enemy would be different.

And so Dmitri danced; and even worse, sang:

'Raise high the flags!

'Stand rank on rank together.

'Storm troopers march

'With steady, quiet tread . . .'

His left arm was raised in exaggerated salute, his right forefinger held horizontal above his upper lip to suggest a dictatorial moustache; and his hand did not move from his face even when he tumbled sideways to the mat and continued the Horst Wessel song to the end.

Kanazawa was crying, the laughter allowing him to weep.

'Are you all right, sir?' Sergei thumped Dmitri. 'Did you hurt yourself?'

In German, Kanazawa roared: 'He no sir! Not now!'

All three of them laughed: deep, belly-straining laughter because everyone lived under tension and any form of release could hurt.

'We should do this every week,' said Dmitri.

'*Aloha*,' said Kanazawa. 'If only we could. Goodbye and hello again.'

Squinting, Dmitri searched in his mind for the word.

'*A-lo-ha*,' Kanazawa repeated. 'Useful . . . word. But. One strike, one kill.'

Sergei was frowning, perhaps because the old samurai principle of *ikken hisatsu* had applied this morning in the dojo where long, all-out single strikes were the order of the day.

'Like a woman's treasure.' Kanazawa giggled as he raised a porcelain cup. 'The pearl in her harbour.'

As Kanazawa drank, he missed Sergei's reaction; but Dmitri caught it: facial tension then relaxation, falling back into role.

What did he notice?

But in the end Dmitri did not need to ask, because sometime before they drank themselves into oblivion, he remembered naval charts and Hawaii marked with the red circle that designated a major US base; and when he awoke the memory was bound to remain because it was so preposterous, so admirably insane, just the kind of thing these marvellous, misguided warriors would do.

Sen sen no sen, the most audacious of the three timings: to strike while the enemy was unprepared.

THREE

Grey and black, the pulsing complexity of walls and space; purple, the lightning that flickered without sound throughout the cell. Max had not even tried for a fastpath rotation, knowing the geometric turbulence would tear him into twisting, bloodied strips. From the outside, though, an insertion was possible – hence the growing silver light, and the thin man who stepped from it and smiled at Max, like a vulture sighting dead flesh.

Tendrils from the floor formed helical bonds, holding Max in place.

'You're here to debrief me?' he said.

'No, I'm here to torture you.'

And so it commenced.

In Roger's apartment – granted by the authorities, whoever they might be, for a duration that he had not been able to determine – all of Labyrinth's public service offerings were his, provided he had the talent to make use of them. For a second he tried to initiate a fastpath, succeeding to the point where the air began to waver with a hint of geodesic turbulence, very dangerous; then he backed off and blanked his thoughts, letting go of the summoning induction.

I'm still like a child here.

Only *her* presence in Ascension Annexe gave meaning to his life in Labyrinth. Perhaps he should call Med Centre and talk to that counsellor he had brushed off before. In the meantime, he had to get to Poincaré Promenade, where he was supposed to meet Jed for breakfast. At his command, a section of wall became a blizzard of Koch snowflakes which dissolved, leaving an opening. He had at least mastered the art of opening doors.

'Stop whinging,' he said aloud.

From his silver balcony he descended into a maze of Labyrinthine architecture, passed through halls and galleries – here, a helical colonnade where 'up' pointed to the horizontal axis, and walking figures formed changing radii – out onto Fourier Flyway where the path flowed, carrying him high over a wealth of buildings and structures, to deposit him on a golden concourse. From there, he jogged to an exit he recognized, came out on Poincaré Promenade, then walked fast to the Café d'Alembert, where Jed was already sitting at a table, juice and daistral in front of him.

'Do you feel as bad as you look?' said Jed.

'Probably.'

'Breakfast is what you need.'

Not so long ago, living at home with his parents, breakfast for Roger had been an occasion for smart remarks and shared jokes, a time of bonding before each of them began their separate work-day. It had been sacred and fragile and ritualistic, in ways he had never appreciated before his world shrivelled into death.

'Here,' said Jed. 'Let me show you something gruesome.'

Roger sat down. 'I'm afraid to ask.'

'No, see' – Jed pointed – 'follow my finger with your gaze, then relax all your muscles and just let— There, you've got it.'

Something twisting, shards of transparency and blood; and a sound: a modulated screech that matched the awful rotation.

'Ugh.' Roger pulled back in his seat, snapping his senses back into mean-geodesic reality. 'What the hell is that?'

'Sort of a public monument, in a nasty way. Every now and then,' said Jed, 'someone raises a petition to get it removed, but nothing happens. Exactly as Dirk intended, I guess.'

'You mean Dirk McNamara?' Roger tapped the tabletop, placing his order, while trying to remember something of Pilot history. Dirk and Kian had been the twin sons of the first true

Pilot, Ro McNamara; that was all he knew. 'That's Dirk in there?'

'No, that's Admiral Schenck at the moment of his death which will last literally for ever, provided no one intervenes. The moral of the story is, don't pick a duel with Dirk, unless you've got a really unpleasant death wish.'

'Dirk killed him? Really?' Roger's food rose through the tabletop, but he ignored it. 'I'm still trying to get to grips with this place, but wasn't Admiral Schenck opening some official building yesterday?'

'That's the grandfather in there.' Jed nodded toward the distortion. 'The current Admiral Schenck is also supposed to be a nasty piece of work, but what would I know?'

Roger chewed a hotbean sandwich.

'I don't really understand what the Admiralty Council does,' he said. 'I mean, sometimes I think it's the high command of a military-style fleet, but at other times it seems to be the government, and sometimes . . . I don't know. A different thing entirely.'

'That's because,' said Jed, 'our culture and protocols are Byzantine.'

'You mean Labyrinthine.'

'There, you're getting the hang of it.'

For a while they both ate – Jed had ordered some kind of omelette – then Jed answered more seriously. 'People rotate in and out of different styles of service. Most of the time, the majority of us are free traders. Then there are the Shipless of course – not everyone in the Admiralty has their own vessel. The Council is all of those things you said, and none of them. They say that the regulations had to be written in Aeternum, because no other language supports the temporal and philosophical concepts that underlie the entire system.'

'Bloody hell,' said Roger.

'Yeah, pretentious, isn't it? But it's still true. It also allows for things like Pilots raised in realspace who don't yet know their way around Labyrinth.'

Roger stopped eating. 'What do you mean?'

'Like, if someone has to attend a hearing, an enquiry, then they have the right to take a friend with them. Someone with a bit more experience.'

'I thought we were here for breakfast.'

'We are,' said Jed. 'And over breakfast, right now, I'm telling you about the hearing.'

'What hearing?'

'The one I'm accompanying you to, old mate.'

'Is this one of those regulations you were talking about? Like, I have to attend a hearing and you're the one who finds out about it?'

'Pretty much. I asked proactively at the Admiralty, they confirmed the meeting, and I took responsibility for telling you.'

'Shit.'

Roger turned away, his eyes acidic with confusion, feeling light-headed with shame. He was a child here, unable to travel by fastpath rotation, unaware of the institutions and laws surrounding him, needing a grown-up like Jed to look after him.

'We have to get you in training,' said Jed. 'So you can get a handle on how things work.'

'I'll manage.'

'There are programmes, and the reason no one's suggested it yet is that you're in mourning. Think of the word *bureaucrat*, and you'll understand what I mean.' In Aeternum, it held none of the emotionless or parasitical overtones the words conveyed in three out of the four other languages that Roger knew. The Aeternal term resonated with warmth and selflessness. 'So come on. If you're done, we'll walk to the Admiralty.'

'All right.' Roger stared at the dishes sinking back inside the table. 'We don't pay for this, right?'

'Of course n— No.'

Some meals were free; others were not.

'On Fulgor,' said Roger, 'every financial transaction involved a vector in a two-hundred-dimensional phase-space. After twenty years of living there, my parents still had to concentrate when buying anything. For me it was natural.'

The concept of currency was simpler here; but it applied in fewer contexts than he was used to. The complexity lay in figuring out when payment was relevant.

'I've operated on Durston IV,' said Jed. 'Four continents, two where bribery is everywhere, and you can't do business without knowing how to offer payment to an official but not spelling it out, because *that* would be illegal.'

They stood and walked onto the Promenade.

'I should grow up,' said Roger, 'because everyone learns to adapt. Is that what you're saying?'

'Seems to me,' said Jed, 'you'd grown up already when I met you.'

That was after Roger had rescued Alisha from the brothel, having first committed violence on a large, thuggish bartender, forcing the man to tell what he knew. Perhaps that was the moment when the hesitant schoolboy Roger dissolved, replaced by whoever he was now. Or perhaps it happened when he turned away from his parents, letting them flee Fulgor while he stayed behind, imagining that he was the one at risk, not them.

'So which way do we go?'

Jed indicated a spiralling route.

'We follow Heisenberg Helix, take the Bessel Boulevard exit, follow it as far as Archimedes Avenue—'

'Or we could just fastpath.'

'Right.' Jed grinned. 'If you don't mind me doing the business.'

'Summon it slowly, if you can.'

Jed let out a breath, then raised his hands. Tiny sparks glittered inside his eyes of jet: fluorescent overspill from the satanase/satanin reaction inside the inductive neurons. Roger felt the air grow chill and prickling. Then reality flowed, pulled into a vortex, and a pane of nothingness rotated, just beyond the edge of what Roger could grasp.

'Come on.' Jed's voice was tight, for this was hard work, slowing the rotation. 'Step in.'

So Roger did, with Jed beside him, and the universe whirled.

I still can't—

They stepped out into a reception chamber, vast as a cathedral, cemetery-cold.

When Max had finished screaming, the interrogator introduced himself as Fleming, his voice as pleasant as if they were meeting at a picnic. Then he added:

'We *are* on the same side, you know.'

Sagging against the tendrils that held him, Max coughed, the nearest to laughter he could manage. Tears were chilling his face, while pain was washing everywhere, an ebb after furious surges.

'Bastard. I did *not* kill her.'

Something in Max's words, some rhythm, matched Fleming's style of speech. So here was the danger: to be seduced by the torturer, to believe they cared because the entire world was here, defined by their words, their facial expression, and the pain they induced: magnificently skilled, the architecture of agony, the pulling-apart of personality.

Schenck, you bastard.

It had to be him, but there was no point in laying accusations. Stick to what he had seen and heard.

'Admiral ... Kaltberg.' Max licked salt and blood from his mashed lip. 'She was under ... compulsion. I told you ... She had a graser, set to auto-destruct.'

'Hardly the suicidal type. A prominent admiral on the verge of well-deserved retirement?'

'Not suicide. Murder. It was compulsion.'

'But you escaped through your bolthole. Very slick.'

As a senior officer in the intelligence service, Max had years ago established a fast covert exit route. What else did Fleming expect?

'She short-circuited … Neural induction. Burned out her corpus callosum.'

'Lobotomized herself?'

'Not that. Femtoviral patterning in her … her right cerebral hemisphere. The compulsion … She divided her brain. In two. Fought against … herself.'

'That's one hell of a story.'

'Truth. She warned me. Get clear.'

Fleming popped some kind of sweet into his mouth and began to suck.

'I'd like to believe you, Max.'

Max's rank was commodore, but there was no point in insisting on etiquette, because in this place Commodore Gould did not exist: there was only a prisoner responding to whatever name Fleming chose to use.

'Just as soon,' Fleming added, 'as you tell me the truth.'

A tsunami of pain burst open.

NO!

Max yelled for oblivion to take him.

They sat behind a table like a panel of examiners, while Roger faced them like a doctoral candidate preparing to defend his dissertation – except that he had Jed beside him. Among the panel of questioners was a familiar face, the man who had introduced himself as Dak Stilwell, a counsellor.

'We can use real names,' said the thin man in the centre. 'I'm Pavel Karelin, this' – indicating 'Stilwell' – 'is Zeke Clayton, and that's Clara James.'

The woman looked like a competitive runner, poised for the start.

'Are they really real names?' asked Jed.

'For all official purposes, yes,' said the woman. 'Call me Clara. First names are appropriate, don't you think?'

'On the basis that Roger has done nothing wrong?' said Jed. 'I'll agree with that.'

Roger swallowed.

'Ask me anything,' he said. 'Er, except . . .'

Pavel said, 'What is it?'

'I don't understand security clearance or any of those things. Including *your* clearance.'

'We can assume, I think, that they've authorization.' Jed touched a fist against Roger's shoulder. 'We're in the centre of the Admiralty.'

Clara's mouth twitched. 'If there's anything *you're* not authorized to hear, Pilot Goran, we'll let you know.'

Jed looked about to blush; then he grinned.

'Good point,' he said.

'My father was an agent-in-place on Fulgor,' said Roger, 'for over twenty years.'

The trio nodded.

'Look, *I* came into this,' said Jed, 'because I was at Sanctuary in Lucis City. Carl Blackstone's ship appeared overhead, and he identified himself as an intelligence officer breaking cover, then warned us about the Anomaly. Not the word he used, of course.'

'What did he say?' asked Pavel.

'We were already tracking the gestalt-mind's growth in Skein,' said Jed. 'Al Morgan and Angus Cho were with me. What Carl Blackstone told us was the gestalt would be able to absorb everyone, not just Luculenti linked to the virtual environment they called deep Skein.'

'And what else?'

'Then he said he was going to fly here. It was pretty clear what he meant by that.'

'Hellflight?'

'Exactly.' Jed looked at Roger. 'I never saw him face to face, but he was a good man.'

Dad had killed himself to raise the warning, to get an evacuation fleet under way. But that was after Mum had died. Roger had no way of knowing how Dad had felt in the hours before death.

There was something missing from Jed's story: the secret

legacy from Dad, safe in her Ascension Annexe hangar, growing by the day.

=It's all right.=

Roger tightened his abdomen, then relaxed. In hiding his own reaction, he almost missed it: near-subliminal twitches from both Clara James and Zeke Clayton. Sensing that Labyrinth had spoken?

Pavel said: 'Clayton, you have a question?'

So much for first-name informality.

'For Roger, yes.' In that roundish, bearish face, the eyes were hard. 'How did your father know what the Anomaly was capable of? That it would be able to absorb minds without the medium of Skein?'

'I . . . There was the Zajinet Research Institute. That was my fault.'

'Did your father often share operational details with you or your mother?'

'Never. I mean—' Roger had to think about this. 'They tried to raise me as a Pilot without taking me here, away from Fulgor. Occasionally they talked about Zajinets. Not much, only that they're the other realspace species to function in mu-space.'

'And the Institute?'

'Mentioned by chance,' said Roger, 'and I didn't know it was part of Dad's work. I knew it existed. It just didn't advertise itself. You wouldn't find it unless you knew of it.'

Unsure whether the answer made sense, he was relieved in any case to tell the truth.

'You're implying' – this was Clara – 'that the Anomaly reached through realspace hyperdimensions to link with human nervous systems. How do you know that?'

'I don't,' said Roger. 'I know Zajinets teleport along the hyperdimensions. As for the Anomaly, I thought that's what people have agreed it must use. The only sensible explanation.'

Jed said: 'Reports of blue glows, especially the eyes, suggest Witten radiation from transitions of—'

'We know the rumours.' Pavel nodded to Roger. 'I'm still curious as to why you raised the subject of Zajinets.'

'That's ...' Roger took time to exhale, then breathe in. 'I'll have to backtrack for context, but the immediate reason is that I told my ... friend ... Alisha about the Institute, and we went there. I think we were under surveillance by Rafaella Stargonier, the Luculenta who started the whole thing. The seed that became the Anomaly.'

Neither Pavel, Clara nor Clayton altered posture; no micro-expressions delineated their thoughts; yet the atmosphere had shifted. Call it pheromones.

Call it fear.

'What was the relationship between you and the Stargonier woman?' said Clayton.

'I only ever saw her from a distance.' Roger felt as if he had drunk too much daistral. 'I saw some odd things, but it was Alisha who met her directly. And that was because of our tutor, Petra Helsen. She was the one behind everything.'

All eyes, including Jed's, focused on him.

Pavel said, 'Behind everything? Behind the Anomaly?'

'She manoeuvred people. She ...'

Roger was out of his depth, here in a city-world where he could barely open a door; but when it came to Fulgor, he was talking about his home. He knew it in a way no other Pilot could.

Right now, I'm the expert.

Once more exhaling to regain control, he felt his throat relax.

'She, Helsen ... manifested *darkness*. I can't tell you what the phenomenon was, but it was real, even if I was the only one who could—'

Pavel raised both hands, palms forward. 'Let's stop there for now.' And to Jed: 'Pilot Goran, we appreciate your help, but this would be a good time to talk to Roger alone.'

'Excuse me?' Jed did not look about to budge. 'According to regulations, Roger has a right to—'

'This is no longer a public hearing. I'm invoking security protocols.'

'You can't—'

But a fastpath rotation came out of nowhere, descended upon Jed, and whirled him away to leave an empty flowmetal chair. Roger stared at the chair until it liquefied, flowing back into the floor.

'We're assuming you want to help us,' said Clara.

'I do.'

Put it this way: without the Anomaly, his parents would be alive.

'The more we understand, the more effective we'll be.'

'I'll tell you everything.'

So with the exception of his secret in Ascension Annexe, that was what he did.

FOUR

EARTH, 777 AD

Ulfr woke with Heithrún's naked body against him, their legs entwined, her breathing soft and satisfied, his bladder fist-tight with the need to piss. He tried to shift and slip free, but her eyes came open and her hand went down, and then he was spear-hard and thrusting inside her – '*Pierce me, warrior,*' her whisper – and they rode to white explosion and the shuddering, conjoined aftermath.

Then he *really* had to piss.

'Sorry.'

'Ow.'

'Sorry.'

He clambered out butt-first from beneath the heavy cloak.

'I'll see you shortly.'

'Mm.' Heithrún turned onto her side, eyes closing. 'Mm.'

Norns help me.

But those three sisters – Fate, Being and Necessity – were implacable now and in the past, and always would be. He had killed Eira's brother out of mercy, not considering how his spear – his real spear – might sever the love that Eira had held for him, or seemed to. And now this, with Heithrún: unplanned but natural after the violence: lust as the giver of life.

And another *volva*. Did he have a thing for seeresses?

At the camp's edge, he was not the only one to piss against the scrubby heather, hot steam rising to join the receding cloak of mist around them. Dawn light, pale-rose and smooth, draped magic across heathland and the hills beyond. Brandr, faithful war-hound, pissed like his master.

Afterwards, Ulfr grinned, and patted his head.

'Come, brave friend. Let's get clean like true warriors.'

The lake was like steel, reflecting clear sky, and part of the discipline was not to cry out as you waded naked into coldness, pressed your nostrils in, and ducked under. Then Ulfr launched himself up, shaking arms and head, every sinew alive, the water foaming. Now it was time to yell, in lustful triumph and challenge to Norns and gods alike: may they damn themselves as they played games with human lives.

Brandr churned water, swimming with mad joy.

Ulfr dried himself and Brandr with the cloak-fragment he carried for that purpose. Then he dressed, and stood watching the lake as he cleaned his teeth with a fresh willow twig, spat out, then dragged his bronze comb through his hair. Last-minute work with his tiny nose- and ear-spoon, and he was clean, warrior-presentable.

Heithrún was gone from their sleeping-place. As one of Chief Gulbrandr's *volva*s, she would have work to do: healing or scrying, or leading a traumatized warrior into dreamworld to mend his spirit.

'She's a mistake,' he said to Brandr, who was at his side.

The war-hound gave a gruff, abbreviated bark.

He knows it, too.

From the ground, he picked up the weapon that Heithrún had given him: her own staff, refashioned as a spear.

Me, the troll-slayer.

He went to find the rest of his own party.

When he reached them, Chief Folkvar was staring after a white-haired woman who was walking away: Eydís, senior *volva* and Heithrún's teacher. Then Folkvar noticed Ulfr, stared, looked away, shook his head, and turned back, finally with a beard-spreading grin.

'Piss on all mystics.' He clutched the Thórr's hammer amulet at his throat. 'I need some Kvasir's Blood.'

Was she saying something about me?

Big Vermundr filled a horn from the deerskin bladder slung over his shoulder, and held it out.

'Here we are. Get that down you, Chief.'

'Ah.' Folkvar swigged half of the mead. 'Sweet. What I needed.'

'Ulfr?' asked Vermundr. 'You want some?'

'Not if there's anything else going.'

'Goat's milk.' Hallsteinn offered a cup. 'Nice and warm.'

'Brilliant.' Ulfr drank it down, feeling better. 'So what's up with old Eydís? Is she casting spells on you?'

'More like, she's spitting mad because some young warrior's been entrancing her student.' Folkvar held up two fingers in a V. 'Doing some log-splitting with his axe-head.'

'A very small axe-head, from what I hear,' said Hallsteinn. 'Nothing to be ashamed of though, eh, Ulfr?'

'It's not the weapon,' said Ulfr, 'it's how you wield it.'

'Must be all that solo practice,' said Vermundr.

'Oh, for Thórr's sake.'

'Actually, *he* has a massive hammer. No comparison.'

Ulfr shook his head, but he was not blushing; nor was he blind to Chief Folkvar's frown, or deaf to his silence.

What did Eydís say to him?

At least Ulfr's judgement was confirmed: bedding Heithrún had been a mistake. Yet he would do it again, given the chance, which seemed unlikely. For the Thing was breaking apart, each tribe and clan returning home, with nothing resolved.

Twin ravens arced and spiralled overhead, warning Stígr of something but not danger. A strange mist boiled: silver pin-points whirling in sunlight, invisible when he turned his back to the sun, beautiful when he faced the light. But the more his eye beheld wonder, the more his scar-filled eyeless socket itched and crawled. He was close to the village of that bastard Ulfr: a dangerous retracing of paths.

Stígr's hat was shapeless, keeping cold sunlight from his face, allowing him to make out the dun-brown form at the base of a pine-tree. Someone wounded, dead, sleeping or pretending weakness for the purposes of ambush.

The ravens would have warned me.

He twisted his shoulders to loosen them, hefted his staff, and walked towards the human form.

'Help me, sir.'

It was a young voice, that of a youth fewer in years even than Ulfr, the fresh-faced bastard who had bested Stígr. Damn them all, these young ones: bodies in one piece, minds fresh, untainted by self-hate. This one lay splayed beneath a high, slab-like outcrop.

'Sir—?'

'I'm here.'

Stígr pushed his cloak back over one shoulder and knelt, still holding his staff.

'Did someone attack you, boy?'

'No, I . . . fell.'

'All right. Shh.'

Both legs were twisted, one with an extra angle where the shin had sheared through. The best thing Stígr could do now was summon help, if people were near.

'Are you with Chief Folkvar's clan, boy?'

'No, Chief . . . Snorri.'

So. Not with Stígr's enemies. One of their neighbours.

'You need help,' said Stígr. 'What's your name?'

'Sigurthr, sir.'

'A hero's name.'

With the staff, Stígr pushed himself to his feet.

'Close your eyes, brave Sigurthr. Close your eyes and rest now.'

He raised the staff as the boy's eyes closed.

'Rest, because everything will be all—'

It came down fast, the iron-shod end. The wet crunch seemed distant.

'—right.'

Like stepping on a snail.

Eira stood at the edge of a mist-cloaked lake, at the border between two worlds. She had slipped in and out of trance dozens of times since pre-dawn glimmered; now, as a vast prow rose shadow-like in mist, she moved entirely into dream-world. It was hard to look at, this immense, other-worldly ship, for it belonged to the realm of ghosts, and its hull was formed of dead men's fingernails: so many dead to create a vessel one hundred times the size of anything the living might build.

And *he* was on board: her brother Jarl, slain by Ulfr out of mercy but still dead.

—*Oh, my brother.*

His shade moved from ship-deck to lakewater in some fashion she could not see. Then he waded closer and stopped, ankle-deep but not wet. He was grey, and if Eira squinted she could see through him.

—*Sweet sister, it is not your time to sail on dread* Naglfar, *not yet.*

She nodded.

—*Are you ... well, good Jarl?*

It was a strange thing for a trained *volva* to ask. The dead could not be well; nor could they answer such questions. But Jarl was her brother, and she loved him.

—*You will be with me soon enough, dear Eira. But that is not what you wish to ask.*

The time of her death was in the Norns' hands: her death and everyone else's.

—*I don't know what to ask.*

—*Yes, you do.*

Old Nessa had trained Eira well, with love and harshness; but the discipline was slipping from her now.

—*I miss you, by the gods.*

A shake of a spectral head.

—*My own feelings are a memory.*

Eira shivered. She placed her palms on the bronze ovals that cupped her breasts, worn outside her robes. The narrow supporting chain made a chinking sound, muted by corpse-mist.

—*I don't know what I seek.*

—*Things will happen, my sister. No need to search for them.*

To be a seeress was to live with ambiguity; but this was Jarl, for whom her feelings were certain.

—*Tell me, please, what I . . .*

A distant sound filtered through fog: a muted whimper, or something more.

—*The answer is yes.*

Jarl was aboard the vast, dread vessel again.

—*What do you mean? Why are you—?*

—*Forgive him, sweet Eira.*

Something was happening beyond the mist. Something behind her.

—*I don't know what you—*

—*He did right by me. He honoured me.*

Then it sounded clear: a woman's scream.

—*Jarl?*

But the vessel known as *Naglfar* was slipping back as the mist roiled and thickened. The dead were gone. The world was cold. Now, from beyond the mists, there was more to hear: the roar of men; a crescendo of hooves; the clash and thud of weapons; the crackle of buildings set alight. And the screams of children dying.

FIVE

LABYRINTH 2603 AD (REALSPACE-EQUIVALENT)

Roger would have liked to return to Ascension Annexe on leaving the Admiralty complex; but he had company – Clayton and Clara – and *her* existence was the one thing he had kept secret. Dad's legacy: the one wonderful thing that survived, beyond memories of a loving upbringing.

It was Clayton who summoned the fastpath rotation that took the three of them into a palatial apartment suite. The first surprising thing was the ease of the rotation; the second was Clayton's saying: 'This is your new home, and we hope you like it.'

Clara looked at Roger – her expression saying, *you're not as surprised as I am* – then her face blanked.

'It's what we call a safehouse,' added Clayton. 'But then you'd know the term.'

'I'm a big fan of *Fighting Shadows*.' But this was Labyrinth, not Fulgor. 'Er, it's a holodrama series. Was.'

One more fragment of a global culture lost. For Roger, the present had been severed from the past. His future was a landscape seen through the thickest of lenses: distorted, unknowable.

'Why would you need a safehouse,' he added, 'right here in Labyrinth?'

'Good question,' said Clara.

Was that an edge to her voice?

Clayton, looking at Roger, said: 'I'm asking for trust here. This needs to be secret, so you'll have to stay inside.'

But it was not Roger's trust he was asking for – it was Clara's. At least that was how Roger read the subtleties of communication: the tonal emphasis, the implied semantics of words unsaid.

'You think I'm in danger,' he said. 'From someone with access to classified information?'

Clayton blinked – perhaps because he had not expected Roger to work that out – and the corners of Clara's mouth twitched.

'That's a good assessment,' she said.

After nodding, Clayton gestured to the sofa and chairs, which moved closer.

'Did you ever think of following your father's career choice?' Clayton sat down and leaned back, the upholstery morphing around him. 'I'm sure you've got the aptitude.'

'Commodore Gould wanted to recruit me,' said Roger. 'My one time here, besides when I was a baby, he showed me around—'

Micro-expressions from both their faces told him that he had forgotten to mention this earlier.

'I'm sorry,' he added. 'I thought I'd told you everything. There was a Pilot, a prisoner, in a cell somewhere in Labyrinth, and the darkness manifested around him. It was weird and huge, the way it appeared, though I don't think the prisoner was as dangerous as Helsen. If that makes sense.'

He definitely had told them everything he knew and suspected about Dr Petra Helsen, intellectual bully and probable causative agent behind the whole Fulgor Catastrophe; and he had drawn a holosketch of the bearded man who might be her accomplice. He had even mentioned the nine discordant notes that accompanied the sightings – *da, da-dum, da-da-da-dum, da-da* – sounding only in his head, not the external world.

'That knowledge should not leave this room,' said Clayton. 'No word to anyone about this prisoner.'

Once more, it seemed that he spoke to Clara while addressing Roger.

=I agree.=

All three of them looked up.

After a moment, Clara said: 'So we've something in common, then.'

Roger had learned that few people heard Labyrinth directly.

'Looks like it,' said Clayton. 'So let me be more open. When you report to Colonel Garber, not everything needs to be mentioned.'

Clara looked like an endurance athlete, her body-fat minimal. For a second, her face showed every muscle tensing below the skin. Then: 'I'll not endanger Roger.'

'Thank you,' said Clayton.

'And thanks from me.' Roger heard the relaxed tone of his own voice, and noted it as interesting, nothing more. 'Since I'm the one you're keeping safe.'

The idea that he might be in danger was simply a fact: one more datum to process.

Everything changed when Fulgor died.

His world or his parents: pick either disaster, or both.

'Before the murder,' said Clayton, 'I believe Commodore Gould told the Admiralty Council that you failed the test, Roger. It's in the report files, with the actual test details unspecified. Your father took several minutes to be able to see the darkness. Gould said that you stayed there for longer, and noticed nothing.'

'Er . . .'

That description made no sense.

'What is it?' asked Clara.

She had glanced at Clayton first. It seemed Clayton was more informed than she was, when it came to the darkness.

'It doesn't take minutes,' said Roger. 'It doesn't take any time at all. It's right there in your face, whenever the darkness is present.'

Clara sucked in air, then blew it out at length.

'I begin to see why you're so valuable, Roger.'

'Oh.'

'And maybe,' she continued, 'this safehouse is not as off the books as you think.'

That last was to Clayton.

'You're kidding,' he said.

'Sure I am. See me laughing.'

'Fuck.'

Internal politics – or worse – inside the intelligence service. This was so far beyond Roger's experience that he might as well have been a months-old baby: dependent on the adults around him for everything, even basic safety.

'Maybe there's a better place to hide me,' he said. 'Like, not in this universe.'

They looked at him.

'Realspace?' said Clayton. 'Where would you go?'

Given that his homeworld was gone.

'They're starting to ship the refugees out,' said Roger. 'Jed volunteered to be one of the Pilots involved.'

'We can work with that,' said Clara. 'Without alerting anyone.'

'Even our own people.' This was Clayton. 'Right?'

'Shit. Right.' Clara turned back to Roger. 'Listen, why don't we chill out over daistral and run through everything once more. I mean, relaxed this time.'

'Er, sure.'

'What for?' asked Clayton.

'In case there's anything else I've missed out,' said Roger. 'Like the darkness. Because I forgot, or didn't realize the significance.'

'No wonder Gould wanted to recruit you.' Clayton's smile tightened then attenuated. 'Damn it.'

'What is it about Gould?' asked Roger. 'His name provokes strange reactions, but no one's actually—'

'He's under suspicion of murder,' said Clara. 'The victim being Admiral Kaltberg, which is hard to believe, because he admired her. I'm sure of it.'

This was too strange to grasp.

'Let me add something here,' said Clayton. 'Just among ourselves, to get some perspective. Roger, your father's ship, when it arrived here the first time – I mean, with your mother on board.'

With Mum aboard and near death, before Dad flew back to Fulgor alone and grieving.

'I understand.'

'Well, then. Your father's ship had been attacked. Her hull showed all the signs of battle.'

'I didn't know that,' said Clara.

'No, we buried the information.' Clayton gestured a holo into existence. 'See the scoring, here and here?'

It was a still image of a black, dart-shaped ship, edged with scarlet. Dad's ship: fast, ultra-powerful, manoeuvrable. Made for evasion and fighting, with no space for cargo.

'That's not good.' Clara leaned forward. 'Crap.'

'Who fired on him?' said Roger. 'I don't get it. The Anomaly?'

'It happened in mu-space.' Clayton pointed at the holo. 'And it wasn't from Zajinet weaponry.'

'But that—'

'Pilots,' said Clara. 'Firing on their own kind.'

'Exactly,' said Clayton.

'And that's why you want me to keep this from Colonel Garber.'

'Yes.'

'Holy fuck.'

Earlier, Roger had thought she looked capable; now, he could not tell whether she was worried or scared witless. Either way, things were bad.

I don't want to leave.

Not least because *she* was in Ascension Annexe. But if something happened to him, what would be the effect on her? He had to keep himself safe.

'Get me on a ship to Molsin,' he said.

Golden space, and flying fast.

Someday, it will be me and her, alone.

But for now, Roger rode as Jed's passenger, sitting diagonally behind him in the near-featureless control cabin. The glow and gentle distortions of fractal space told him which universe this was. A widespread holorama replicated an outside view suitable for Pilot eyes; while in front of Roger, a smaller display listed the cargo hold's contents along with status updates for their comatose inhabitants: three hundred stacked med-drones, Alisha's among them.

I was falling in love with her.

There was no getting around that. And she, the Luculenta-to-be, had feelings for him, or so it seemed. But with her mind shattered from Rafaella Stargonier's attack and the depredations of the brothel—

Maybe it's not just her who's traumatized.

Fat wobbling belly, dripping penis, and the panicked voice of the middle-aged punter backing away from Alisha's naked body . . .

Stop it.

'Transition soon,' said Jed.

'Got it.'

Their voices rippled in pale-amber air.

Concentrate.

Roger waved the status holo out of existence. The forward holorama was more interesting, as a flaring virtual ribbon denoted the geodesic they were following. Some day, he would be doing this himself: plotting the insertion angle just right to avoid disaster during—

Transition.

Black space shivering into existence in every direction: stars and pinpoint galaxies appearing silver-white at first, before the eyes could adjust to the true richness of colour.

Realspace.

'There's the place.' Jed nodded towards the gas giant filling the holorama. 'Big old bastard, isn't it?'

'Molsin.'

'One of the top worlds,' said Jed. 'Influential.'

Just as Fulgor had been.

Stop it.

Her skies were yellowish from here, but once inside the atmosphere, all would be orange, swirling in endless turbulent patterns. There, among the layers and currents, drifted the quickglass sky-cities that Molsin was famed for: peculiar and spectacular, different from Roger's home, wherever that was. While deep below, under killing pressure, oceans of hydro-fluoric acid waited to eat flesh and bones alike, to devour any morsels that might fall to the lower realm.

SIX

EARTH, 1941 AD

Booming explosions and the deck tipping beneath his feet:
Dmitri might have been back on board the ship that took him
from Vladivostok across the Sea of Japan; but there had been
no gunfire then, and the transfer to the Panamanian-registered
freighter had been without incident, he and Sergei smuggled
aboard to a private cabin where they assumed German iden-
tities. Sergei was convincing because his mother had been from
Sudetenland; Dmitri because he had a gift for languages, and
a compulsion to prove himself.

But this was his kitchen, in his Tokyo flat; and any thunder
came from inside his head, born of last night's vodka mara-
thon – no, saké, much the same thing – which meant he knew
how to cope: drink water and get on with it.

Pearl Harbor, then.

If Lieutenant Kanazawa had not been delusional, then it
would be something to find out about. Outside, it was a muggy
June day, two months since Japan had signed a pact with
the Soviet Union (going undercover and resurfacing as the
Russians they really were formed one of his and Sergei's back-
up plans) while Roosevelt had, two days later, announced that
the US would supply materials, under the Lease-Lend Act, to
Japan's major enemy, main target of their plans for aggressive
expansion: China.

Think it out.

It was hard, with Kremlin bells ringing in his head, but this
was what he thought: that China's 'magnetic warfare' strategy
seemed like frustrating magic to the Japanese. The Chinese
simply withdrew from the area surrounding every city that fell

to the invaders. They had never even declared war: not ten years ago during the Mukden Incident in Manchuria, nine years ago when the Nihon Imperial Army moved on Shanghai, or eight years ago when they took Chengteh's capital Jehol, so close to the Great Wall.

The Chinese did not fight the invasion: they absorbed it.

So what will America do if Admiral Yamashita attacks?

The United States were something of a mystery to Dmitri. Their Great Depression had failed to convince the proletariat of the madness of free-market thinking; that, or they were too cowed by their imperialist masters to rise up in revolt. But those were explanations that anyone might trot out in a Moscow bar after some vodkas, whereas when it came to Western Europe – especially Germany – Dmitri could always see through simple explanations and ideology.

Pose the question in a different way, and different answers rise up.

No, what will China *do?*

If attacking Pearl Harbor caused China to declare open war on Japan – in accord with its treaties, now it depended on American supplies – then Japan would take the gloves off and attack any ships delivering aid to China, even if the flag they flew was the Stars and Stripes.

So maybe Kanazawa was right: this insane plan was real.

'Morning, boss.' Sergei looked fresh. 'Have you started on breakfast?'

'Have you seen Torginov recently?'

Torginov, a long-term Kyoto resident and naval intelligence specialist, was only nominally a part of their network.

'I would have told you if I had.'

'He'll have picked up word of this Pearl Harbor thing,' said Dmitri. 'If it's real, I mean.'

'Ah.' Sergei's smile was cynical. 'You don't want him getting the credit.'

The man had access to a separate courier route, distinct from the one Dmitri and Sergei used, his affiliation looser than that of other agents. He could report to Moscow via the well-placed Sorge, another agent working under German cover. Had Dmitri been less senior, he would not have known of Torginov's existence.

'I've no idea what you mean. I was thinking of cold rice and fish.'

'For breakfast?' said Sergei. 'So long as there's plenty of tea, I can handle it. And I'll keep quiet about the other thing.'

Meaning Torginov, but Dmitri's concerns were not what Sergei thought.

I am my own man.

Right now, to the best of his informed knowledge, Wehrmacht tanks were beginning a three-pronged westward invasion: von Leeb's force to the Baltic states, Rundstedt's further south, while in between was Bolk's army that included both Guderian's and Hoth's panzer divisions.

There were intelligence officers like Sergei who operated best with a small-field detailed picture, while others like Dmitri made decisions based on strategic background concerns. The Nazi forces were superbly equipped in comparison to Mother Russia, for all Stalin's rhetoric; but if manpower could hold them back throughout the summer – or at least slow them down – then the secret Soviet weapon could be brought to bear.

Winter-time in Russia.

I do not belong to the darkness.

In his dreams, he thought that the occurrence of warfare mattered more to that pseudo-imaginary power than any particular victory; still, he felt that it preferred the Union of Soviet Socialist Republics to suffer defeat, meaning he had a choice: which of his masters to betray.

'I tell you what,' said Sergei. 'Since you're busy with that thinking stuff, I'll make breakfast for both of us. All right?'

'Huh.'

Because this piece of intelligence was crucial: he was sure of it. So he had three choices: take credit with Moscow, as Sergei suggested; allow Torginov and his contacts to investigate further and perhaps make their own report; or shut the whole thing down, killing Torginov and burying the news of Japanese plans to strike eastward.

He felt the expression grow on his face: the Trickster smile, the harsh-humoured grin of Loki, both a god and betrayer of Asgarth. Ever since Dmitri learned the meaning of the word 'Russia' and associated it with the natural redness of his hair, he had felt kinship with those Old Norse beings, a resonance that spanned the centuries, and never mind that the Nazis did the same.

A choice between evils.

What could be better?

Hideo Kanazawa had wept in his sleep: something that should not be possible, surely; yet it brought back his first days at Naval School, and the bullying he had received as a sissy-boy who missed his parents. Now, he stood in his thin yukata kimono, cold despite the sunlight outside, and stared at the smart, serviceable kanji he had inked in what had been a blank, virgin book.

The written words spoke of pincer attacks and the importance of intelligence; and they mocked him just as the bullies had, because they were not his thoughts: they were words strained from thickened idea-stuff forced through him like grains from cooked rice. It was turgid, the language of von Clausewitz, but not enough to hide the psychotic brilliance of that military mind. Kanazawa picked up the volume he was trying to translate, and pictured himself hurling it across the room to rip through a *shoji* screen; then he replaced the book with exquisite gentleness, and let out a silent breath.

What did I say last night?

Drunkenness was necessary and even encouraged, from time to time; but with fellow officers, not gaijin. Shame filled him like tea inside a cup. Yet what should embarrass him? Letting down his guard with the wrong people . . . or immersing himself in the group insanity that swelled all around?

I befriended the gaijin because of Kano-san.

One of the two foreigners trained at the dojo of Dr Kano, the brilliant educationalist who – as a spare-time activity – created judo from the brutality of old jujitsu schools, forming moral fighters who defeated the best that the thuggish older styles could throw at them. His creation was modern, western-influenced (which few understood), yet a recreation of purity from ancient times, one that deserved to spread worldwide.

Dr Kano was a friend of Kanazawa's uncle, hence the visit which resulted in meeting the gaijin. He and the great man had spent long hours decrying the militarism which was rising tsunami-like to engulf Japan – all that, despite the uniform that Kanazawa wore. On one occasion with his new western friends, he took down Sun Tzu's *Art of War* – required reading at all military schools – and related what he knew of the author.

'One day the Chinese emperor commanded Sun Tzu to appear,' Kanazawa said, 'knowing the man's reputation, and needing someone to lead the imperial army. Sun Tzu had declared he could instil discipline in any group – even the emperor's wives.'

At that, the foreigners had made ribald jokes – like last night, much saké had passed through their lips – before Kanazawa finished his story.

'After extracting an imperial promise that he, Sun Tzu, was to have total command, he ordered the women to line up and march. The result was giggling – at which he ordered the imperial guard to behead one of the wives.

'The emperor tried to intervene, but Sun Tzu reminded him of the promise. Then the wife was beheaded, and the remaining wives marched in perfect, coordinated silence.'

The gaijin had asked what happened afterwards. When Kanazawa told them that the emperor gave Sun Tzu command of all his armies, both foreigners had laughed.

Perhaps it was national pride or shame that prevented

Kanazawa from discussing Miyamoto Musashi, the heroic *kensei* – sword saint – that his countrymen revered in preference to the Chinese Sun Tzu. But Musashi, that most solitary of men, had suffered from scrofulous skin, stinking since he never bathed – after assassins ambushed him in a bath-house once – and had the temerity to write of a lifetime committing homicide as if he were the greatest of artisans or artists.

Kanazawa touched the tiny shinto shrine in the corner of the room.

My country is wrong.

From the two-sword stand, he took a sheathed *katana*: the warrior's primary sword, his a century old. Then he put it back, and picked up its smaller companion for close-work, the *wakizashi*.

My emperor is wrong.

He knelt, placed the sword on the tatami mat, then sat back on his heels. Time slowed as millimetre by millimetre he pulled open his light robe, shucked it from his shoulders, and bared himself to the waist.

The Japanese spirit is wrong.

It whispered from its sheath, the killing blade. Forged in the ancient way, incandescent metal folded on itself over and over in ritual, the *wakizashi* could part falling silk, or split iron-hard bamboo without sustaining damage. Or slice through a man's body with ease.

It hurt.

He hardly felt it. Just the beginning: the parting of the skin.

So beautiful.

Pantheistic, his view of the world: everything imbued with its own spirit; everything beautiful; the universe demanding worship.

Even the dust.

White-gold dust in sunlight. Straw scent from mats. Softness of cotton on skin.

All to be extinguished, because of the . . .

Now is the time.

Because of the . . .
Time to do it.
The darkness, the twisting evil.
End it.
Amid beauty, the loathsome *other*, the enemy.
End it all.
Blade, ready to be pulled in, elbows close to his body for one tug inwards, then the sideways drag through stomach and intestines, to feel hot slickness spilling out.
Golden, the light.
So exquisite, the pain.
Sweet, the dreaming.

When he woke, sprawled on the mat, he knew the world had saved him. Sunlight had spoken, told him he was better than the darkness, and directed him to live for himself, not wrong-headed others who confused bullying with courage, sadism with strength.

There was a monastery, and he knew the way.
I will find the path.
Not just the physical way.
I swear it.
His body moved slowly but his spirit danced as he prepared to leave possessions and his world behind.

SEVEN

Orange clouds pulled away from the front of their ship; and there, across a kilometres-wide gap, hung the floating city of Barbour: elongated and convex, gleaming orange encrusted with sweeping, ice-like external promenades, spars and buttresses: beetle-like from their first perspective, changing as they flew beneath, nearing the pendulous stalactite-form that depended from the asymmetric underside.

Jed slowed their flight, docking against a questing quickglass tendril, as gently as if his ship were kissing a long-time lover. At Jed's command, an oval melted open in the control cabin wall. The city's hollow tendril, to which the hull was conjoined, formed a tunnel into the city, wide enough for Jed and Roger to walk in side by side.

They wore black – in Jed's case, edged with narrow gold – and their eyes were natural obsidian. Pilots, openly so.

'They'll want to talk to us first,' said Jed. 'Before off-loading the cargo. Er ...'

'It's all right. I know what you mean.'

Roger had been feeling sick, imagining Alisha cocooned in delta-coma; but for Jed this was just another mission. Thinking of med-drones as cargo was part of getting the job done.

The air smelled different – a hint of honey, overlaid with something Roger could not name – and the gravity was odd. He could not tell whether it was greater or less than the mass-force of Labyrinth, designed to induce one-g acceleration. Instead, his sense of balance seemed to be searching for missing directions, axes of reality that were not there.

Because I've been in mu-space too long?

It was a question for later, when they were back in the ship and preferably in mu-space. When you grew up with a spy for a father, privacy became a habit.

In a greeting-hall – as near as Roger could decipher the holo-kanji – a pale-faced man bowed, his two fists pushed together. Jed returned the gesture; Roger copied it in haste.

'Greetings, sirs. I am Bodkin Travers by name, and I hereby grant you all best—'

'Knock off the bullshit,' said Jed. 'I'm a working man, and I've been here before. No need to treat me like one of the toffs.'

'Thank Cosmos for that. You can call me Bod, if you like.'

'Fair enough. I'm Jed and this is Roger.'

Grinning, Bod held out his right fist. Roger bumped it with his own – smiling: it was like being home on Fulgor – then Jed followed suit.

They were speaking Spanalian, one of Roger's languages since the age of three. This might not be Lucis City, but face it: Barbour was closer to the place he grew up in than Labyrinth could ever be.

'The commercial formalities' – Bod grinned at Jed – 'are waived in any case. It's not exactly a trade mission today.' More seriously: 'The first lot, two hundred or so, are being released from the med-halls today. Poor bastards.'

'One of Roger's friends,' said Jed, 'is among this consignment.'

'Oh. I am sorry.'

'She got clear,' said Roger. 'At least it means that much.'

With treatment, she might recover. It was a splinter of hope amid the reality of so many dead or Anomaly-absorbed.

Maybe I need treatment too.

But that was soft thinking, and there was work to do.

'What happens to the refugees after the medics have released them?' he asked.

'There are support groups,' said Bod. 'Cabin suites are arranged, so they've somewhere to live. Plus employment, based on capabilities, part-time at first.'

'It's good of you take them.' Jed almost growled: 'Unlike other worlds.'

'An attitude that's hard to understand, at least among the rich ones.'

Some colonies could scarcely support the scrabbling inhabitants they already had: that *was* understandable. But Roger thought that perhaps if Bod had seen Fulgor's final hours, he would be less keen on refugees coming here, no matter how minuscule the risk of another Anomaly might be.

'What can I do to help?' asked Roger. 'With getting the refugees in from the ship, I mean.'

Bod said, 'The ship's Pilot is supposed to start the process from on board, then come out into the reception space to oversee things. If you, Roger, could do the overseeing – not that you really have to do anything, you understand – then Jed won't have to pause things while he returns from the ship.'

'Good plan,' said Jed. 'Can you send me to my ship the quick way?'

'Ah.' Bod smiled. 'You really *have* been here before. So, brace yourself.'

'I'm braced.'

'In that case—'

Bod's chin dipped and his eyes narrowed, triangulating on some mental image; then Jed was ankle-deep in quickglass, and filaments were coiling around his legs and torso.

'—go!'

Jed whisked down the tunnel and was gone.

'Bloody hell,' said Roger.

'Trivial,' said Bod. 'Are you up for the same?'

'Crap. I suppose so.'

'I tell you what. I'll slow it down, since it's your first time.'

Roger was used to quickglass architecture, but he should not say so – at least, not to reveal the extent to which he had lived his life incognito, along with Mum and Dad, hiding what he was. In any case, he thought, as a thick band wrapped around his waist, this place seemed different.

'With me.' Bod's hand clamped Roger's upper arm. 'Ready.'
'Shit. OK.'
'Now.'
They flew, without leaving contact with the floor.

It was grand and huge, the great reception hall, though not in comparison to Labyrinth's spaces. Roger stood on a balcony with Bod, now almost bored with the slow-floating shoal of med-drones manoeuvring into twin corridors that led apparently to the med-halls. There was no telling which drone contained Alisha; she might have already been carried out, or remain in the ship's hold, the last of Jed's cargo to be discharged.

Some twenty watchers stood scattered around the hall. Official observers, it seemed to Roger: no casual passers-by. When the last of the med-drones had slipped past, the watchers drifted together into clumps, conferred, then made their way out in twos and threes.

'I'll take you to the med-halls,' said Bod. 'Jed can obviously find his own way.'

'Thank you.'

Bod must have other duties; it was good of him to take the time to help.

What if I weren't a Pilot?

Too cynical. The matter-of-fact manner suggested Bod's behaviour was natural and professional both, ready to assist anyone, not caring who they were.

'We'll take our time,' said Bod. 'You're OK just walking?'

'Of course.'

Roger did not really process the peripheral sights – cross-corridors, convex-ceilinged halls edged with colonnades, something that appeared to be a market-place filled with a swirling crowd – as he walked with Bod along a thoroughfare whose shining blue floor curved up to form the walls, while white decorative panelling ran horizontally some four metres up, beneath a concave white ceiling with the visual texture of icing. The city must be richer in colours and style than the outside suggested.

Trying not to think of Alisha.

Will they wake her straight away?

Trying very hard not to think of her.

One trick was to imagine something else entirely, but sod that because Alisha had been through evil and did not deserve to—

He stopped, shuddering.

... da-da.

No.

He could *not* have heard what he thought. Not possible.

'Roger? Are you—?'

'Fine. Let's ... carry on.'

It had to be stress and the ongoing shock of the new.

There's no way it can be here.

Really, it just had to be.

No. Absolutely, no.

All in his mind.

Alisha's face looked blue as the upper carapace grew transparent. Purple-garbed medics tended holodisplays. All around, the med-hall was a vast space of mint-green and icing-white quickglass, the floor shining, reflecting the dozens of med-drones laid out in rows. Peripheral archways led to similar halls. Here and there, green hemispheric quickglass bubbles grew from the floor to enclose a med-drone, cutting off the patient from view as human medics and the city's inbuilt systems got to work.

'—your friend?' someone was saying.

'Sorry?' said Roger. 'I missed that.'

The medic had short white hair and green eyes, matching the surroundings.

'Alisha Spalding is your friend,' she said. 'Have I got that right?'

'Yes. Yes, she is.'

Jed was off somewhere with Bod, sorting out the overall disposition of the comatose refugees. Roger could have done with Jed's support.

'We're going to try to wake Alisha now.' The medic nodded towards three younger-looking colleagues whose hands were flickering through control gestures. 'Taking it carefully.'

Many of the other drones appeared to be cycling to slow wakefulness without human oversight.

'She was . . . traumatized,' said Roger. 'I guess the annotation data shows that, right?'

'It does. Seeing the city come apart around her must have been frightening, so it's understandable that—'

'Alisha is – was – pre-upraise, about to become a Luculenta.'

Two of the medics stiffened.

'She doesn't have plexnodes implanted,' Roger added to forestall their panic. 'She's not vulnerable in the way true Luculenti were. But she did get attacked through her interfaces, and she was, er, almost catatonic when I found her. Before everything went insane.'

At some point the Anomaly had gained the ability to link to ordinary minds; but at first it had been Luculenti who formed its components, linked through the virtual Skein: formerly their paradise and playground, finally the enabling mechanism of extinction. That was why Pilots had killed every Luculentus or Luculenta among the refugees, dumping the corpses before they dared fly to Labyrinth.

Medics would understand the need to squash a nascent epidemic.

'We're blocking cortisol and noradrenaline production,' said one of them. 'Dr Keele? We can bring her to full consciousness now.'

'One moment.' The white-haired medic turned back to Roger. 'Alisha's going to be spaced out, somewhat. She may not be able to focus on you.'

'You need her to wake up feeling good.'

'That's the idea. All right, everyone. Let's bring her out of it.'

Alisha blinked three times, then opened her eyes fully.

'Good,' murmured Dr Keele. 'Very—'

The veins on Alisha's forehead stood out as she saw Roger. And screamed.

'Shit.'

A medic gestured. Alisha's eyelids fluttered. She dropped back into coma.

'Pilot Blackthorne.' Dr Keele's voice was silken as brushed steel. 'Pilot?'

'Er, yes?'

'Are you married to Alisha Spalding, or occupying any legal capacity allowing you to make medical decisions on her behalf?'

'No.'

Why would she ask such a thing?

'Then I have to ask you to leave. I'm very sorry.'

'But can't I—? I beg your pardon.' Roger had no idea what to say. 'Will she be all right?'

Meaning, can you fix her?

'Leave her with us,' said Dr Keele. 'Will you be OK finding your friends?'

Jed and Bod, presumably.

'Sure.'

'Then . . .'

Roger was blinking – as Alisha had been, moments before – and he seemed to have swallowed warm salt water.

'Take care of . . . Just . . .'

He turned away.

Get out of here.

Striding, he moved fast, fleeing like an electron tipped from a local maximum: filled with momentum, inherently uncertain in direction.

I don't have anyone.

His last connection to home, severed by a scream.

EIGHT

The aftermath of attack lay before them: smoke-stink of extinguished fires, exposed beams black as charcoal sticks even from this distance; children corralling animals into makeshift pens; whimpers and yells from unseen wounded; the torn clothes and plodding motion of survivors clearing wreckage.

'Ride!' yelled Chief Folkvar.

It was rage, not urgency, for no raiders remained around the village. Ulfr, from his saddle on black Kolr, whistled down to Brandr. The warhound leaped up and Ulfr caught him. Off to one side, Hallstein did likewise with brave Griggr, who barked when she was steady in Hallstein's arms. Then they kicked their horses into a gallop, following the rest of the party.

Folkvar's mount thundered in the lead, the grey stallion's legs a blur: there might have been eight legs, like Sleipnir of the sagas, ridden by the Gallows-Lord. It pulled ahead, faster than the others, while Folkvar's cloak billowed in chill wind.

They all rode horses, everyone in the party, because Chief Gulbrandr had exhorted the other clans to generosity. Ulfr's actions had saved the Thing from ensorcelment through *seithr*, the unclean magic of shapeshifters and gender-changers.

From the poet Stígr, most unholy.

They thundered into the village, wheeled the horses to a standstill, and slipped down. Each man used reins to hobble his horse, knotting the leather fast, then strode off, some following Folkvar, others heading towards someone precious they saw or sought.

Eira. You'd better be all right.

Ulfr wheeled, staring, searching for signs of her.

There.

The shriek of a wounded man in sudden pain came from beyond the ruins of the men's hall. Brandr gave a small yip. Perhaps Eira's scent floated through the stench. They ran around the hall, and saw her: kneeling by a wounded man whose shoulder was wrapped in stained cloth, while his face glistened with poultice.

Eira's robe was streaked with brown, glistening here and there with battle-sea red.

No, by Thórr.

But the gods did not exist to prevent disaster.

'Eira.'

From the whiteness of her face, much of the blood was hers.

'Eira, talk to—'

Her voice was a song, rising and falling, and along with her gestures was leading the wounded man – the wounded *stranger* – along the path to dreamworld.

One of the raiders?

'And tell me, good Arrnthórr,' Eira was saying, 'what led Chief Snorri to call a vengeance strike?'

Ulfr nearly shouted, but held it in. Snorri, their neighbour, behind all this?

And why *vengeance*?

The wounded Arrnthórr's tone was slurred, detached.

'Killed . . . Sigurthr. Folkvar, by his own . . . hand.'

Ulfr's knife was in his fist, though he had no memory of drawing it.

'How do you know?' asked Eira. 'Tell me how Chief Snorri learned that.'

'Told . . . us. Wanderer. Found poor . . . Snorri.'

Arrnthórr's eyelids fluttered.

'Describe this wanderer,' said Eira.

Even before the words came out, Ulfr knew what the description would be: a one-eyed man in a wide-brimmed shapeless hat, perhaps accompanied by ravens, as if the most dreadful of the Aesir chose to walk the Middle World: the one who was both All-Father and Gallows-Lord, Spear-God and God of the Hanged.

To worship Óthinn for true meant human sacrifice. While the clan would normally avoid dark ceremony, perhaps this Arnthórr and others of Snorri's war-band might deliver pleasing screams to the All-Father's ears before their souls went to Niflheim. Except that Stígr had clearly ensorcelled them, much as he had done to others here – Vermundr, Steinn and Halsteinn among them, even Chief Folkvar – when they put poor Jarl to torture.

Eira's brother, dead at Ulfr's hand.

Another survivor, Arnljótr by name, had just finished confessing a similar story when Ulfr found him, trussed on the ground at Chief Folkvar's feet. At the prisoner's head stood two boys: Davith and Leifr, watched from a distance by the crone Ingrith. Both boys held spears pointed at Arnljótr.

'You should not have listened to lies,' said Chief Folkvar. 'But then, we ourselves—'

Davith stabbed downwards, spear-point crunching into the throat. Leifr's spear, a second behind, went through to the heart: a quick death.

'Ah, boys.' Chief Folkvar glanced at Ulfr, then placed a hand on each boy's shoulder. 'It was well done, Leifr Oddsson, Davith Oddsson. May your father feast amid the Einherjar in Valhöll tonight.'

If Folkvar wished Oddr among the warriors picked by Óthinn's Death-Choosers, then Oddr was dead and the boys were orphans. Hence Folkvar's forgiving them for killing without command.

'We need to prepare ourselves.' Folkvar addressed Ulfr. 'Get the able-bodied and make sure they're armed. Strip wound-fires of the slain if you need to.'

He meant, take dead men's swords.

'We shouldn't attack,' said Ulfr. 'Stígr won't stay to goad

Snorri's people on. If he's not gone already, he'll fade away when we turn up.'

Making his escape through dark magic.

'Yes, and we'll go in under truce,' said Folkvar. 'But we'll keep a war-band close.'

'Chief Snorri's not known as a betrayer.'

'Nor a reaver, but look what he's done.'

Ulfr nodded.

'I'll tell the men to gather,' he said.

By the time they rode downslope towards Chief Snorri's village, it was sunset. Folkvar rode in with Vermundr on his right, Ulfr on his left: a prominence that Ulfr was not used to.

I'm no chieftain.

But he remembered a conversation with Folkvar on Heimdall's Rock some time before they departed for the Thing. Folkvar had wanted Ulfr's assessment on the qualities of various men at fighting practice, and how they might fare as leaders of warriors. The sort of conversation a chief might have with a young man who showed potential talent for leadership.

Blades, axe-heads and helms gleamed with reflected torch-flames and the eerie steel-and-pink of dusk. On all sides, eyes were trained on the interlopers. Women stood here and there among the men, blades ready, vibrating with hatred.

'Hold now.'

A tall, narrow-shouldered man with a long-handled war-hammer stood in front of them. His hair was wild and tangled – not combed or braided as a warrior's pride demanded – but the air seemed to thrum with ferocity held fast, under tightened control.

'I am Arne,' he said. 'Chieftain here, now that Snorri is slain.'

Folkvar, having drawn rein, performed a controlled slide to the ground, then stepped away from his mount, hands held wide.

'That is a grievous sorrow,' he said. 'I did not know. It happened in our village?'

Arne turned to one side and spat downwards.

'Snorri was never one to stay behind in battle.'

'Nor is Chief Folkvar,' called Vermundr from his saddle. 'For we have only just returned from the Thing, many days ride from here.'

'You are ly—'

Arne stopped, for to accuse a leader of falsehood before his men was a serious matter.

A chieftain cannot speak as the spirit dictates.

Ulfr had not thought of this before. Not in such plain terms.

He must plan his words, however quickly, before he utters them.

Like going into battle: you needed strategy and a true object- ive, or failure was certain.

'They tell the truth.' It was a youthful voice, from behind Ulfr. 'I saw them arrive at their village.'

Arrnthórr, his forearms and wrists bound but his legs free, walked into view.

'Folkvar killed Sigurthr,' said someone among the sur- rounding warriors. 'The poet told us that he—'

'Stígr is an unclean shaman,' said Folkvar, 'a soul-changer and gender-shifter. He caused us to kill one of our own, poor Jarl. And he nearly roused the Thing to some dark purpose, but our Ulfr here' – he gestured – 'stopped him. Dark elves took Stígr to safety.'

Arne sneered at the mention of supernatural beings.

'The gathered chieftains,' said Vermundr, still mounted, 'gave us these gifts in thanks for Ulfr's courage.'

He gestured at the horses they rode, at a polished band on Folkvar's upper arm.

'We demand neither vengeance-gold nor blood,' said Folkvar. 'We offer only sympathy, because you have been caused ill by dark sorcery, just as we have.'

'It is we who seek vengeance.' Arne glared at the men and

women in the circle, the clan he now had to lead. 'But perhaps we've been searching in the wrong place.'

'Stígr is long gone,' said one of his warriors. 'Disappeared as soon as we rode out to attack Chief Folkvar's holding. The women told me Stígr slipped away, but they don't know how.'

'He is an adept of *seithr*,' said Folkvar. 'Slippery beyond ordinary cunning.'

Arne wore a Thórr's hammer amulet; he clutched it now.

'The chieftains gave you horses,' he said to Folkvar. 'Let us give the poet Stígr a horse of his own.'

It was wordplay without humour: *horse* meaning gallows-tree. Skaldic language for a poet who deserved to hang.

'We'll find an ash for him to ride,' said Folkvar. 'Once we've found the bastard.'

'Yes.' Arne held out his hand. 'Together, we'll give him the long ride into night.'

'Together, by Thórr.'

They clasped forearms, two chieftains forming alliance, discarding bad blood. For Ulfr, this was a masterclass in chiefly conduct; but in literal terms he considered their oath ill-wrought.

Because Stígr is mine to kill.

All around, the watching warriors shifted, taking some moments to catch up with the changed mood of Arne, still new as their chief. But Arne was resolved, that was clear; and several men growled, thumping blade against shield in agreement. It began a clamour of weapons clashing, and the conjoined cheer of men whose purpose was obvious once more, confusion tumbling away.

Vermundr caused his horse to step sideways, coming daintily alongside Ulfr.

'Courage and wisdom,' he said. 'A good way for chieftains to behave.'

'Yes.'

'When *you* are chief, remember this.'

'What?'

But Vermundr was already moving away, jumping down from his horse, leaving his hammer hanging from the saddle.

'By Freyja's creamy tits!' he shouted. 'Is there no mead to drink in this whole village?'

'If your horn's big enough for the job,' called one of the women. 'I've all the sweetness *you'll* ever need, big man.'

The men roared, called out insults, laughed and gave cheers as they sheathed and slung their weapons. After tension and battle-fear – and despite the wounded – they needed release.

As the feasting began, Folkvar looked in Ulfr's direction and winked.

I understand.

Ulfr grinned back.

This is how to lead.

Whether he himself would ever command warriors, that was a different question. While Eira hated him and Stígr still lived, there was only one clear purpose to Ulfr's life. For all Arne's and Folkvar's words, their villages depended on people staying close to home, tending animals and crops, hunting as required. Deserting their land for vengeance on a single man was out of the question.

While hunting the poet alone was exactly what Ulfr planned to do.

Until you die screaming, Stígr, just like Jarl.

Then the world would be right again.

Life would be fine.

NINE

It occurred to Roger that he was being selfish. Watching the crowds passing through a concourse, gleaming quickglass everywhere, he allowed the world to slip from focus, and re-examined his reaction to Alisha's scream. He had thought of it as severing his last link to home, but she was the one who was suffering.

Mum. Dad. At least you were never taken.

His parents might be dead; but Alisha's family were as likely to have become part of the Anomaly gestalt as to have perished.

Acid bubbles gurgled: his stomach, calling him back to mundane reality.

'Can I help you, Pilot?'

The man's scarlet outfit looked like a uniform, but a cheery one, suggesting customer assistance more than emergency services.

'I, um, could do with a bite to eat.'

'Of course, and there'll be no charge to your good self,' said the man. 'We like Pilots to feel at home in Barbour. So, let's see.'

A quickglass pillar twisted up from the floor, formed a loop, and displayed a hanging sheaf of menus. It was a showy way to project a holo display. Like Bodkin Travers earlier, this man had commanded the quickglass surroundings with no visible word or gesture.

'These are eateries?' asked Roger.

'Indeed. If you hold up your tu-ring, Pilot, I can transfer standard public-service interfaces.'

Roger's tu-ring glinted.

'Done,' he said.

'That was fast.' The man's eyebrows were raised. 'Er, I can recommend the Orange Blossom, one deck up' – he pointed – 'at the top of that ramp. If you're truly famished, you'll find there's an Eat Now service on offer anywhere at all inside the city.'

He looked at the nearest wall. An orifice opened, tiny cilia-like protrusions inside – ready to offer nutrients, Roger assumed – then melted shut.

'That's very nice,' said Roger. 'And I'll take your recommendation. Thank you for your help.'

'Any time, Pilot.'

Roger walked to the ramp which flowed upward, carrying him to the next level. There, orange and white blossoms – fine-structured quickglass extrusions, he thought – arched around an eatery entrance. Inside, small nodules in the floor indicated potential table positions; only three tables were currently formed, each with a solitary diner.

Near the rear wall, he chose a nodule, cranked up the sub-menu in his tu-ring, and commanded a table and seat to form.

No wonder the guy thought it loaded quickly.

His tu-ring was already configured to access local services, including city-admin functions not available to the general public. Timestamps showed his ringware making adjustments since his arrival – updating out-of-date configurations, coming back into synch with Barbour.

Dad? You were here?

So many secrets when you worked in the covert world. Dad had never mentioned spending time on Molsin; yet the ringware he had transmitted in those last seconds on Fulgor showed all the signs of an earlier visit. From the number of seconds spent on re-synching today, Dad's visit had been years or even decades ago.

Perhaps before Roger was born.

Ah, Dad.

Now the time of his parents' existence was gone, and it was

his turn. The best he could do was make a fraction of the difference that they had. To be half the man his father was: that would be good enough.

'Trust your instincts,' Dad had told him. 'Uneasiness comes from deep neural processing of atavistic senses – like smelling danger – which even with modern psych techniques are hard to bring to conscious awareness. Bad vibes are your primitive brain's way of warning your civilized self of danger. For example, don't ever step into an enclosed space with someone who makes you feel uncertain, never mind whether it might seem impolite. The point is to remain alive.'

Roger ordered a citrola from the table, broke off the quick-glass goblet when it formed, and took a sip. The sweetness gave him a flashback to Lucis Multiversity and the day he met Alisha – and Dr Helsen.

He put the goblet down.

Helsen, and the day he first heard those nine strange notes: *da, da-dum, da-da-da-dum, da-da*. Perhaps it was not just the taste of citrola flinging him back into the past. Earlier, with Bod in the reception hall, he had – for a moment – caught the end of that sequence, and told himself it was imagination.

. . . da-da.

It was not sound, no more than the darkness twisting around Helsen had been an optical phenomenon. Instead, his perception came from synaesthetic processing in his brain – like people sensing auras or vibes – delivering exotic data translated to a mode he could recognize, much as his tu-ring used adapters and façades to link to Barbour's local services.

If Dad were here, he would tell Roger to trust himself.

'Shit.'

He tapped his tu-ring.

'Jed? Listen to me.'

Roger knew that, to make his report, Jed would have to re-enter mu-space, and establish signals contact with a group of seven ships due to arrive in several hours. Before that, he would have to complete the formalities here in Barbour. Or he could try talking to local law-enforcement authorities, but he would need more than Roger's fleeting auditory hallucination to convince them of danger.

Roger understood that.

'I'll wait in the city,' he told Jed. 'Just in case.'

Catching a glimpse or echo of a single darkness-controlled individual in a teeming sky-city was unlikely; but if he left, the chances dropped to zero. Plus Alisha was here.

Still sitting in the Orange Blossom, he ordered a pair of smartlenses – his tu-ring indicating that he had a substantial cash reserve: monies deposited by Dad and earning interest – and when they rose through the tabletop, he unwrapped them and popped them onto his eyes.

There. No longer a Pilot standing out from everybody else.

Conjuring a holospace, he created a virtual sketch – for his eyes only, invisible to other diners – and outlined Dr Petra Helsen's features. Once he had approximated the colour of her eyes and hair, he collapsed the image in cache; then he set about ordering food.

He believed someone in Barbour was infected by the darkness, hence the auditory phenomenon. Perhaps it was not Helsen, but someone local, a stranger. He did not know which to hope for: a profusion of darkness-controlled individuals, or Helsen's escaping the catastrophe she had caused.

I'll find you, bitch. If it is you.

He forced himself to eat, his thoughts still of Helsen. It took a while to realize that a woman with silver- and violet-striped hair was staring at him from another table.

'Oh, hello,' she said. 'I beg your pardon, Pilot. Don't let me distract you.'

Her voice was wonderful. She was older than he was, though by how many years, he could not guess.

'How did you know I'm a Pilot?'

'I saw you' – smiling, her chin dipping – 'put the lenses in.

I assume you want to blend in, so I shouldn't call you Pilot, should I?'

'Er . . .'

'I'm Leeja,' she said. 'Leeja Rigelle. Would you like me to join you? I can tell you about places to go and all.'

Everything was serious and confusing. He had no time for making friends with anyone, no matter how charming, or how intelligent the dance of light in their eyes might be.

'Yes, please,' he added.

A second chair morphed into place as she came over.

'I'm Roger Blackstone,' he found himself saying.

Her hand – man-meeting-woman implied a handshake rather than touching fists – felt soft when he took it. Her eyes widened; perhaps his did likewise.

'Um . . . Shall I order food?' he asked.

'I've pretty much finished,' said Leeja. 'I'll have a drink with you, though. Is that the remains of a citrola?'

'Er, yes.'

Two fresh citrolas rose through the tabletop.

'You want to take a walk afterwards along the main thoroughfares?' said Leeja. 'I'll show you how to read the morphplan annotations.'

'Annotations on what exactly?'

'On holomaps. If you live on board a quickglass sky-city, you're amid architecture that's always morphing. Main routes change slowly, but even the overall city-shape changes over time. There are fifty-three levels of authorization to determine who's allowed to cause what alterations.'

'That's . . . different,' said Roger.

'For you.' Leeja gave a sort of mature simper (for even her facial expressions were new to Roger). 'We live with, well, fluidity. Static surroundings make me feel edgy. Have you ever been to Earth?'

'Er, no.'

'It was interesting – I went there on holiday – but I was very glad to get back home.'

'So . . .' Roger tried for an intelligent question. 'Does that mean you can alter your own dwelling's layout, but not this place, for instance?'

'Actually, I've a one-hundredth share in the Orange Blossom's ownership. But the main hall outside' – Leeja gestured – 'requires city council oversight for every amendment. There's a core principle of keeping the centre of mass well-defined and sensibly located.'

'So you can't shift all the quickglass mass to one end of the city?'

'Exactly. Have you finished your citrola?'

'Er, almost.' He swigged down the last of it. 'All done.'

'Then I'll show you my city,' she said.

At some point as they walked, Roger smothered a laugh at the sight of orange pennants outside a confectionery shop: on Fulgor, such pennants had signified porn stores offering off-Skein perversions. He felt no need to share that information. But Leeja, her arm tucked in his, said: 'I don't like it when I don't know what you're thinking.'

It was a strange thing to say to a virtual stranger rather than someone known intimately for years; but then, he was not sure exactly when she had slipped her arm in his, or when they had begun to walk in step, their bodies close.

'I'm just responding to the exotic feel of the place,' he said.

'Does an exotic feel sound good to you?'

'Bad boy.' She pulled her elbow in to squeeze his arm. 'Very bad boy.'

In slow synchrony, they walked on. Pace by pace, Roger felt ever closer to her. Eventually, at the high intersection of seven main halls, she stopped and took his hand.

'That one,' she said, 'is Vertebral Longway, which runs along most of Barbour's longitudinal axis. The smaller one, over there, leads to where I live.'

Roger swallowed warm saliva.

'The smaller one, then,' he said.

Her smile promised softness and abandon.

'Good,' she said.

Once inside her apartment, she cupped his face in her hands, then pressed herself against him as they kissed in an explosion of warmth. Then she was clasping his groin, and his excitement leapt, strong and furious.

Incredible.

They kissed and ran their hands over each other. He unfastened her clothing, revealed a sweet breast – she moaned at his light touch – then took her cherry nipple in his mouth.

'Oh. Oh.'

Finally, she stepped back from him.

'We don't ...' she stopped. 'We've only just ... It's fast. I don't want to rush you.'

'Whew.' His exhalation was shaky. 'Yes. Fast.'

They stared at each other, she with her beautiful breast still exposed.

He had no words.

So beautiful.

He undid his clothing to the waist. Leeja said nothing.

Then they were tangled in each other, pulling clothes, licking and caressing, using their whole bodies as instruments of pleasure, lost together in the maelstrom of warmth and lust, of freedom and love, enjoying each other in a way that seemed as new to her as to him.

The crescendo of orgasm was merely a beginning.

TEN

EARTH, 1941 AD

The Victorian manor house at Bletchley Park was everything it should be. Around the extended grounds, huts were being painted. Gavriela understood, from her briefing with Rupert, that there were eight thousand people stationed on site, and more arriving by the day; yet the place had the air of an underpopulated school for the privileged élite, however plain the huts, however great the contrast with the lustrous panelling inside the house.

Not that she expected to be working in here. Codebreakers kept to the huts. What surprised Gavriela was the number of women: fully half the figures in civilian clothing, along with the majority of the uniformed staff: WRENs fighting the war to as much effect (if less danger) than their husbands and lovers overseas.

On the other side of the ornamental pond, a serious-faced man ran past, dressed in vest and shorts, his eyes intent.

'That's AMT,' said a young WREN beside Gavriela. 'Turing, right? Last week, he ran from here to London for a meeting.'

'But that's' – Gavriela did the conversion from kilometres – 'forty miles, isn't it?'

'What I mean, he's nuts.' She grinned. 'One of the real geniuses, I reckon. I'm Rosie.'

'Gabby.' She was still using the cover name that Rupert had given her. 'Gabby Woods.'

Rosie's handshake was straightforward and strong.

'I guess you're one of the boffins, then,' she said. 'Nice that it's not only blokes, don't you reckon?'

'Just what I was thinking,' said Gavriela.

'It's mostly us girls. But they're nearly all posh, like. Cheltenham Ladies' College kind of people.'

'Oh.'

The Received English of the educated classes was something like Hochdeutsch in its crispness; but there was a whole dimension of the language orthogonal to locality that Gavriela was still getting to grips with.

'Anyway, Frank will see you now. He's nice.'

'Oh,' said Gavriela again. 'I hadn't realized you were here to fetch me.'

'This way.'

Rosie's heels clacked Morse code-like along parquet flooring – *dot-dash, dot-dash* – as she led the way to an unlabelled door, knocked, opened, stood aside. She winked.

As Gavriela went in, a long figure unfolded from a chair, and held out his bony hand to shake.

'Frank Longfield-Jones,' he said. 'Pleased to meet you, and do call me Frank.'

'I'm Gabby Woods.'

'Of course you are, dear girl. Now sit down, please, and when Rosie brings the tea and biscuits – ah, there we are.'

He took a small tray off Rosie, who closed the door. Then he handed a cup to Gavriela, took one for himself, and sat back. It was a ritual designed to settle her nerves. With surprise, Gavriela realized it was working.

'Welcome to Station X.' Frank's grin spread his moustache. 'Lovely name, but we're the Government Codes and Ciphers School, if you want to know the organization you're working for. Well done on the crossword, by the way.'

'Sir? Oh. When I can do the same for *The Times*, then I'll be happy.'

Her initial interview included attempting a crossword taken, she assumed, from one of the better German newspapers before the war. It had taken her eight minutes and twenty-seven seconds to complete.

'Right now,' said Frank, 'it's your facility with technical

German, particularly with respect to physics, that's useful. You'll find we're mostly linguists and mathematicians, and some who are both, along with some rather eccentric polymaths.'

If an Englishman was calling his colleagues eccentric, they must be odd.

'Gabby Woods is a cover name,' he said. 'Have I got that right?'

He crossed his narrow legs, in what Gavriela had come to recognize as the languid pose of the public schoolboy.

'Yes,' she said. 'My real name is—'

'No, no, old thing. I don't need to know that. My point is, most of us are using our real names as worknames, but not everybody. Part of the subterfuge is to pretend that *all* names used here are real. Do you get my point?'

'It's secret work. I understand that. I'm here to learn about codes?'

'Our organization name, GC & CS, is rather, what, disingenuous. You'll find we're not exactly a school, and the work we're doing is the most important in the war. That's not just my opinion – it's his.'

Frank gestured to a photograph of Winston Churchill on the wall.

'Incidentally,' Frank went on, 'our name is due to change by the year's end. We will then be known as GCHQ, that's Government Communications Headquarters. Rather more of a give-away, but never mind.'

The point of secret war work was that everything was covert. Throughout her recruitment, which had started with Rupert Forrester chatting to her over sherry in an Oxford pub, she had gained no clues as to the nature of the job they wanted her to do.

'I'm still not sure of my role,' she said.

'That's rather a good thing, don't you think?' Frank's smile showed longish, tobacco-stained teeth. 'Our victories are private, you see. Everything we do, it's just among ourselves.'

'I don't feel the need to share things with people.'

'No, we gathered as much. That makes you ideal. There aren't many actual Germans here, by the way, though some of German parentage, and rather too many Frenchmen.'

'The Nazis took my parents and killed them. At least' – this was hard to say – 'I hope they're dead.'

'I'm very sorry.'

'My brother moved to Amsterdam to get away from the regime. I don't know what happened to him.'

It went without saying that Erik had not travelled far enough. The Wehrmacht had rolled over the Netherlands like an avalanche, a vicious cascade, burying resistance.

'Your loyalty to England, or at least hatred of that fidget Herr Hitler,' said Frank, 'is beyond question, or you wouldn't be here. Now, what I'm about to tell you must sink in, do you understand?'

Despite the cosy room, she understood that this was both a briefing and a test: if she failed now, she would go no further.

'I understand.'

'GCHQ is the largest and most professional secret organization in the world, and consists of this: layer upon layer of subterfuge. All right?'

'Yes, sir.'

'Our first layer of defence is that we don't exist. Our second layer is compartmentalisation. Many of the people here on site – it's eighty per cent women, by the way – know little of what happens outside their immediate function. For example, the strategic meaning of decrypted intercepts passing through their hands.'

Gavriela nodded. This was why she was here: to wage a secret war. Also, she had underestimated the percentage of female staff, which was interesting.

'Our third layer,' Frank went on, 'is the illusion of ephemerality, something knocked together in the usual haphazard English way in response to the Nazis.'

He smiled, drank tea, then looked at Gavriela.

'The truth is,' he said, 'GCHQ is in its fourth decade of operation. You could say its raison d'être was confirmed in its fifth year, when the first captured German naval codebooks were handed over by Frenchmen to the Royal Navy, enabling thorough decryption of the most vital signals. The rendezvous took place in 1914, and the receiving British officer' – he pointed to the photograph – 'was a gentleman called Winston Churchill.'

Her spine tingled.

'If enemy agents penetrate that far into our secret layers' – Frank's voice hardened, all languor gone – 'then the next subterfuge is that we work solely on something called the Enigma code, which you will be briefed on later. There are four other main areas of ciphers and intercepts that we work on. At least two of them outweigh Enigma by a considerable margin, in their importance to the war effort.'

Frank rubbed his moustache.

'One of those areas is subdivided into three sub-projects, one of which you'll be working on. What they have in common, the sub-projects, is their concern with German teletype codes. Recent intercepts include,' he added, 'signals to and from the Führer himself. So far we've not been able to break anything at the time of sending. Nevertheless, three-week-old news is rather better than none at all.'

Gavriela swallowed. Already she was party to privileged information she could never hint at.

'You don't need to know what the other areas are,' Frank finished. 'At least for now.'

'Do you issue cyanide capsules?' she asked, not knowing if she meant it.

'We'd rather you don't get exposed to the possibility of capture,' said Frank. 'Parachute drops into occupied territory are for the SIS boys – and they *are* based here at BP, alongside ourselves – plus SOE. But not us.'

That was just as well, because Gavriela could be more effective with pencil and paper than with physical action.

'But that brings me,' Frank continued, 'to the last layer of subterfuge.'

'What's that?'

'Given our somewhat academic background, anyone who learns of GCHQ's existence is likely to think of us as boffins and nothing more. Naive and dithering, the stereotype of the English academic. It provides useful cover. But the truth is, everyone needs to learn a little tradecraft.'

'What does that mean?' asked Gavriela.

'We're going to train you to notice everything. Any hint of enemy surveillance beyond these grounds, we expect you to pick up on instantly. The slightest thing out of kilter when you're travelling, you'll learn to escape and evade and go to ground.'

Gavriela nodded, her throat tight.

'You won't be a commando, but you'll have go through the course that includes learning how to kill' – Frank held up a fountain-pen – 'with this into someone's throat, for example. If that's what's required to get clear. Frankly, we don't train long enough for it to become reflex, and we're certainly not silent-killing types. But you never know.'

'I . . . all right.'

'The main thing is spotting if someone is following you. If you suspect someone is a fifth columnist or simply too nosey about your work, no matter where you are, you'll have a telephone number to call. The result is the party in question will disappear.'

A privilege with consequences.

'We're serious here,' Frank added. 'The question is, are you on board?'

'I am.'

Frank held out his hand.

This is commitment.

A solemn oath, their handshake.

'Civilization,' Frank said, 'is fragile, requiring protection.'

'I'll give my life if I have to,' said Gavriela.

After eight weeks of training and helping out in Hut 6, she began the new year by moving to the virtual Hut 27 – of no fixed physical location, but temporarily in Section F – where the new team introduced themselves.

Clive was a mathematician, a musician, and something of a wet drip according to Harry and Fred. A perpetual underlying odour of chilblain ointment emanated from his desk, and he always found something to moan about while they toiled in a safe hut warmed by endless cups of tea, while around the world thousands were dying by the day.

'We're an offshoot of Bill Tutte's team,' he told Gavriela. 'Young Bill worked out how the Tunny machines operate purely on the basis of intercepts. It's at least as impressive as anything AMT has done' – he meant Turing – 'and the Tunny signals are orders of magnitude more important than Enigma, whatever they might have told you in Hut 6.'

Perhaps Clive knew what he was talking about. He had worked first on breaking the Enigma codes: hence, perhaps, his habit of humming out intercepts in Morse while he worked on them, even though the teletype codes were a 5-bit encoding and transmitted as such.

Then there was Harry, with his narrow Errol Flynn moustache and over-use of Brylcreem – he kept a tube in his desk drawer – always the self-styled charmer of the group. Having spent time in the Foreign Office before returning to teach modern languages at Durham, he considered himself wise in matters of strategy in a way that annoyed the others. But he was bright, and had taught Clive to correct his mangled pronunciation of German words in quite a creative way: he encouraged Clive, as a pitch-perfect musician, to sing the syllables.

Fred and Olivia were similar opposites: a large Cantabrigian and a thin Oxonian, mathematicians who viewed languages as logic systems – they sometimes argued in dry-sounding classical Greek – and both incessant pipe-smokers. (Olivia would sometimes stare at Gavriela in ways that made her uncomfortable for several weeks; then she accepted it and nothing happened.)

Silvester was the elder statesman of the group: a professional intelligence officer who had carried out similar work in the Great War (and was responsible for recruiting Clive and Harry), he could occasionally be persuaded to reminisce about the cracking of German naval codes and the difficulties then of persuading the military to act on signals intelligence.

'Can't blame them, really,' he said. 'Partly because they had no idea what Room 40 was, and partly because we had the same problem as SIS with human intelligence: had we revealed our sources to show our credibility, we would have compromised those sources. Revealing an agent's name or which cipher one has cracked are equally damaging.'

Room 40 in the Admiralty had been one of the roots of the fledgling GCHQ, with at least as much codebreaking success then – a quarter of a century ago – as now.

The remaining four codebreakers were Brian – handsome, one-armed, who had been staying in the same Oxford digs as Gavriela when they met – plus Harriet, June, and Sophie, all with cut-glass accents, impeccable manners and ferocious focus once they had a problem in their grip. The three women belonged to the social class Rosie had described on Gavriela's first day; and they were nice enough.

They broke codes by hand – or rather by brain – not with mechanical calculating machines; and they took pride in their work. Once, Olivia fell asleep at her desk, faced with an intractable cipher she had worked on for nearly a week. No one said anything, and even Clive dropped his incessant humming to near inaudibility. When she finally woke up, Olivia yawned, took her pencil in hand and wrote out the intercept contents in clear, from beginning to end.

Several days later, Clive was working on a batch of intercepts from some newly established outstation when his Morse-code humming made Gavriela's stomach clench, interrupting her work.

'Mm, mm-hmm, mm-mm-mm-hmm, mm-mm . . .'

The solidity of the room seemed to twist apart around her.

That night in her digs, after the long walk through the village in night-time gloom, she sat atop her bed, eyes open but with nothing to see: the lights were off and the blackout curtains kept any stray moonlight from entering. She thought of the classical Greeks and their Italian renaissance counterparts (natural imaginings for someone working alongside Fred and Olivia), and a discussion she had once had with Florian Horst in her days at the ETH.

'Memory palaces,' she aloud in the dark, remembering how she had argued that the psychological technique was a waste of vivid imagination that could be put to better creative use than memorizing a list of words you could just as well write down.

Then she lay back to sleep.

In the morning, because of the blackout curtains, it was still pitch black. She sat up, barely conscious, saying: 'Thank you, Roger.'

As she pulled open the curtains, the tag-end of her dream and her waking words were like frozen CO_2: solidity evaporating straight to invisible gas, lost from sight.

I can't tell the others what I think.

Talk of darkness twisting in odd geometric ways – a darkness visible only to her, her brother, and a Soviet agent called Dmitri Shtemenko who was haunted by it – would surely result in her removal to a quiet ward somewhere. The nine-note auditory analogue, the nine notes hummed yesterday by Clive, might easily be her hallucination, nothing real.

I need to break that code.

Because Clive had been humming while he worked at his desk on the enciphered enemy message.

Which means I need to steal the intercept.

And that was treason, wasn't it? But she checked that she had blank notepaper and a sharp pencil, before she went down to breakfast.

*

Gavriela plodded through her day, finally breaking off to go the ladies room at the shift's end. There, Rosie was powdering her face, her headscarf draped across her shoulders.

'Hi, Gabby,' she said. 'Are you coming along on the bus tonight?'

'I'm not, er, feeling all that good.' Gavriela put a hand on her stomach. 'You know. Anyway, I'm all right walking home later, when the cramp goes.'

'You want me to stay?'

'Oh, no. Thank you.'

'Well, you take care. I'll let people know not to hang around waiting for you.'

Gavriela slipped back into Hut 27 just as Harry was locking up.

'Sorry,' she said. 'Um . . . Can I carry on working for a while? I don't really feel like going home just yet.'

'Are you all right?'

'A bit under the weather, if you know what I mean.'

'Are you—? Oh. Right. I'll, er, see you in the morning. Toodle-oo.'

She gave a smile that probably looked as ill as she felt – though not from the woman's trouble she was hinting at. For ten minutes, by the light of the overhead bulb above her desk, she stared at her own intercept decrypt-in-progress, scarcely seeing the letters, never mind thinking about the code.

The hut was very quiet with only her inside. The thing was, no one kept regular hours, and any one of the team could return at any minute. She waited, until she no longer could.

Clive had not been in all day. Fred claimed he was going to be with some Admiralty types for the rest of the week, along with Brian; Gavriela thought he did not really know. In the meantime, everyone had their own intercepts to work on; no one would be attempting to complete Clive's unfinished tasks.

The truth was, the content that Clive had deciphered so far in this batch had been of little interest, its triviality a contrast to some of the other intercepts, including several direct from the Kaiser Wilhelm Institute regarding the atomic bomb programme.

Was this a remotely sensible thing to be doing?

Remember the music.

Those nine discordant notes that Clive had hummed.

You know it's the darkness.

She went to Clive's desk, pulled open the drawer, and extracted the intercept. It seemed to have been several messages in one, after a single 12-character prefix: at least, there was one section that remained enciphered while the rest was now in plain text. The prefix, when broken, assigned the ten-wheel settings (two for each bit of each character) on the sending machine. No British officer had ever seen a German Tunny device, yet the mathematical analysis was certain. A peculiarity of this encryption was that 'adding' the key to the plaintext (actually performing a bit-wise transformation) produced the enciphered signal, yet performing the same operation again reproduced the original message *en clair*.

But not in this case, it seemed. The explanation was probably a misread portion of the signal.

What if it's been enciphered twice?

More precisely, what if part of the signal was so sensitive it could not even be read by the security-cleared teletype operator? So what if someone had encoded once according to their own scheme – starting with the prefix that sounded like the darkness, the horrible rhythm of EAVI as hummed by Clive – and given *that* message to the operator, as part of a longer signal, for further enciphering and transmission?

The still-enciphered portion read:

EAVI5 N1BF 961Y0 1N2B6 WRRQY 5N172 B5QUB
UN1BU N40BF RBLGB F07B5 N19U2 QTBN9 B27QV
QYTQ7 DYQ2H BRN2B 519BQ 5Y17B 271VV 19BRF
1UU19

Gavriela concentrated, stringing the random characters like

party streamers among the decorations of her childhood bedroom, in the image constructed in her mind: as vivid, almost, as being there once more. She was feeling odd by the time she had finished; but whenever she closed her eyes, she could see the message in full once more: exactly as on the intercept sheet when she checked in reality. Finally, she slipped the sheet back inside the pile, the pile inside the drawer, and closed up the desk.

A message from the darkness lay enciphered in in her mind.

Back in her own chair, she sat for some time with her eyes closed, walking around the imagined room again and again, until she was sure she could reconstruct it at will. Then she opened her eyes, and got ready to leave.

As she was walking past the courtyard, she looked back and saw Silvester heading for Hut 27. Perhaps he would be carrying out an audit – he was that conscientious – but what she had stolen was only inside her head.

I must be insane.

Yet she knew she was right.

At home, she wrote out the message as memorized, without the first four characters she believed to be an identifying prefix.

5N1B5F961Y01N2B6WRRQ95N172B5QUBUN1BUN40BFRB
LGBF07B5N19U2QTBN9B27QVQYTQ7DYQ2HBRN2B519BQ
5Y17B271VV19BRF1UU19

The simplest form of cipher is a monoalphabetic sub-stitution – replacing each letter of the clear message with a different letter. But if this were, say, an Enigma message contained inside a Tunny signal, then the cipher would be far less trivial, most likely polyalphabetic: after each character was encoded, the machine would shift to a new letter-replacement scheme. That type of cipher was nearly impossible to break without a crib: a section of message whose plaintext was known or could be guessed. But this message was a cipher-within-a-cipher, and with luck the enemy had relied on the sophistication of the outer algorithm for the main protection, while the inner cipher was simply to prevent a casual glimpse from German signallers.

She looked for a character that might be a word delimiter. Alphabetically, the first likely candidate was B, occurring at reasonable intervals in the message, giving a three-character initial word. So what might a message begin with?

Der. Die. Das. Wer.

They were likely candidates. Setting the first word to *der* was unpromising, so she tried again:

DIE DF96E*Y0*E**I**2 *6WRRQ9***DIE***72* **D***QU UIE UI40 FR LG F07*
DIE*9U2QT I9 27QVQYTQ7DYQ2H RI2* **DE***9 QDYE7 27EVVE9 RFEUUE9*

It was about the darkness. Her skin crawled as *Dunkelheit* floated and billowed like a spectre in her mind's eye. And if the fifth word were *Sie*, she now had nine entries – her lucky number – in her decrypt table; so this was progress.

0→H 1→E 2→T 5→D 9→N F→U N→I U→S Y→L

The next stage was fast, since d-something-s gave *das*, then she had *sich* and *um*. Two more words popped out: *Dienstag* and *muessen*.

DIE DUNKELHEIT *6W***MMANDIE***7***T DAS SIE SICH UM** *LG* **UH***7* **DIENSTAG IN T***7***AVALGA***7***D**LAT*H* **MIT DEN ADLE***7***T***7***E***VV***EN MUESSEN**

Now *Adler* – meaning eagle – was inevitable, along with *Trafalgarplatz* and *treffen*.

THE DARKNESS COMMMANDS THAT YOU MEET

THE EAGLE AT ?? O'CLOCK THURSDAY IN TRAFALGAR SQUARE

She stared at it for a long time. Most of the intercepts were weeks old, but this had been sent last Friday.

I'm scared.

Because the pictures in her mind no longer featured code but two dangerous figures in shadow, meeting in secret while unknowable darkness watched from wherever it manifested; and if she had learned anything in Bletchley Park it was that a handful of people could change the world.

The rendezvous must not happen.

ELEVEN

MOLSIN, 2603 AD

Roger opened his eyes, still tangled in Leeja's nakedness, warm and satisfied and drowsy. So much tension was gone that his muscles felt too soft to allow him to stand. He had no desire to shift, save for the bladder-pressure that forced the matter.

'Sorry, Hei— Leeja.'

'Mm?'

'I've got to get up.'

He had been going to call her Heithrún, which made no sense: the name belonged to no one he knew. Pulling on his trousers, he looked around for the bathroom facilities, saw nothing obvious, and called up his tu-ring menu with its quickglass commands.

'You want the bathroom?' said Leeja. 'Look.'

She pointed and the wall puckered and opened back. Smiling, Roger went inside, and waited for her to command it shut. When he came back out, his skin was tingling and smelling of pine – he had used full cleansing facilities – but some of his warmth was gone.

'My tu-ring can't ping external services,' he said.

'That's the privacy shield.' Leeja smiled as she pulled back the covers. 'We don't want to shock the neighbours, do we?'

Her entire body was an invitation, soft and glorious.

'Yeah, but ... Sorry. My ... friend's in the med-hall and I was waiting for news.'

Leeja blinked, then pulled the cover up around herself.

'If you need me to drop the shield, then— There you are.'

The message cache glowed scarlet: a single message, priority-one urgent.

Alisha?

But the sender ID was Jed Goran, and the message playing out in Roger's smartlenses, accompanied by collimated audio, said nothing about the fate of one traumatized refugee among so many.

'*We're holding off in mu-space,*' Jed said. '*Me and the seven ships that have turned up, none of which have offloaded their refugees. Investigations are ongoing, so I've been told. At twenty-seven hundred your local, I'll perform a realspace insertion. Meaning, I'll be available to take your call, my friend.*'

Not promising to come back to Molsin and take him away.

'Shit.'

'What is it, lover?'

There were no addenda to the message, no smart-query facilities to allow follow-up questions with best-heuristic generated answers. Two-and-a-bit standard hours before he could talk to Jed again.

'I've got stuff . . . happening.'

What ongoing investigations could Jed have meant? If the ships were waiting in mu-space, then who was doing the investigating? On Fulgor, a dispersed army of roving in-Skein netAgents would have been ideal; but Molsin was clearly a different world.

'Privacy is important here, isn't it?' he added.

'I'll share everything about my life with you,' said Leeja. 'Any detail at all you want to ask about, I'll tell you.'

There was a wondering note in her voice, as if surprised by her own offer. Older than he was, with years of additional experience, still she seemed lost in something new, just as he was.

'Thank you,' he said.

It was a unilateral response – implying no obligation on his part to divulge his innermost thoughts, for example about Alisha – but Leeja smiled, accepting his answer.

He kissed her bare shoulder.

'I . . . I get lost in you,' he said. 'You know?'

'My world has been simplifying,' said Leeja, 'since I met you.'

This was not helping him do what he needed to do.

'I'm going to have to go back to the med-hall,' he said. 'To check on my friend. All right?'

'Girlfriend?'

'Girl and friend, who might have become my girlfriend. But it didn't happen, and now everything has changed.'

Leeja smiled, though she was not the only change he had been thinking of.

'You'll come right back to me, then?'

Roger pulled back the cover, leaned over and kissed one cherry nipple, then the other.

'Of course I will.'

Her stomach was smooth-skinned, so kissable; and so he did. Then his lips were murmuring and kissing and travelling lower. Her inner thighs were ultimately soft; and her core was sensitive and wonderful.

Some time later, entangled and spent, they smiled and kissed each other.

'You're really going now?' said Leeja.

'Only if you'll wait for me to return.'

'Do you have any doubts?'

'Not about that.'

He dressed, then blew her a kiss as she commanded an opening in the wall. She made it a double affair, with inner and outer doors. He stepped into the airlock-like passage, blew her another kiss, then waited for the inner door to flow back into place and the outer to melt.

Then he was out in a main corridor and the wall was sealing up. Complex patterns whirled inside the quickglass: art-forms he did not know how to read, not yet.

A new world.

Despite all previous trauma, he was smiling as he queried his tu-ring for directions to the med-hall and Alisha Spalding.

Roger and Dr Keele sat in a small consulting-room. One wall was either a one-way transparent window or a full-function holo displaying a private ward. Beyond, Alisha was sitting up in a green quickglass chair next to her bed, while a male physician talked to her.

'Your eyes are different.' Dr Keele placed a fingertip on her own cheekbone. 'It changes your appearance rather a lot.'

'I'll take the lenses out, if you like.'

'Not at all. I wouldn't dream of violating your privacy by suggesting it.'

'Oh.' Roger glanced out at Alisha. 'But we're spying on her, aren't we?'

Dr Keele smiled and nodded. 'Very good.'

As if he had passed a test.

'Because medical ethics change behavioural standards,' he said. 'For her own good, sort of thing.'

'Something like that.' Her voice was neutral. 'And I think that's enough.'

The wall blanked to opacity.

That was a test.

His emotional reaction to seeing Alisha – that was what Dr Keele had wanted to observe.

And I've failed it.

The faint rose-hip fragrance of Leeja was on his skin.

'So what's going on?' he asked.

'One moment.' Dr Keele glanced into the air – a her-eyes-only display lased on to her retinas from the walls – then her lips moved, mouthing: '*Go ahead. Protocol confirmed.*'

Anti-sound prevented him hearing, but she had not bothered with optical distortion to prevent lip-reading.

'You haven't treated her?' he asked.

'The final phase just started. Can I assume that Meta Ed was part of your schooling?'

'Er . . .'

'I mean learning about learning.'

'Of course.'

He could speak of Fulgidus education – as was – rather than what happened in Labyrinth; but that was good enough.

'I thought so,' said Dr Keele. 'I understand you grew up on Fulgor.'

How could she know that?

From Alisha's memories.

That was disturbing.

'So,' added Dr Keele. 'you'll know about potentiation, including long-term memory formation.'

'Yes, I— Why?'

But after discussions about Dad's induced amnesia, he had a premonition before Dr Keele confirmed the nature of Alisha's treatment.

'We're using full cognitive rollback,' she said. 'The process was largely complete, which was why she looked so calm just now. I wanted confirmation that we could proceed to the optimum potentiation boundary. Taking out entire waking days is always best.'

He should not have gone with Leeja. He should not even have talked to her.

'Could you explain that, please?' he said.

'The boundary is before her first meeting with someone called Helsen. From her neuroassociative mapping results, this Helsen was tied up causally with the Stargonier woman who carried out the neural assault.'

Dr Keele swallowed, no longer professionally calm.

'Law enforcement officials have already scanned everything,' she went on. 'I'm sure you can appreciate why.'

Given what had happened on Fulgor, Roger would have been surprised if they had done anything else, regardless of privacy laws.

'Wait a minute,' he said. 'The day Alisha met Helsen was my first day on—'

He remembered sitting on the circular balcony that overlooked the campus. Seeing Alisha for the first time – and, across the plaza, Helsen and the bearded man with her: both darkness-haunted.

Helsen, the bitch who had killed his world.

'Exactly why I needed to gauge your degree of emotional attachment,' said Dr Keele. 'If you wish to get to know Alisha Spalding again, you will have to begin all over as a stranger.'

He forced his attention back to the moment. 'You don't sound like someone who's negotiating, Doctor.'

'The treatment is already complete, save for final integrity checks.'

Like a finishing glaze or varnish on archaic craftwork, the main creation complete.

'So if I walk in now' – he gestured to the blank wall – 'she'll not recognize me.'

Dr Keele just looked at him.

I get it. You already told me that much.

On holodramas, medics were good-looking and empathic. But this, now, was not the severest lesson in reality to have hit him lately.

'You think I let her down,' he added. 'Is that it?'

Her nostrils flared, as if picking up the scent of recent sex.

'Your moral standards are up to you.'

'But I don't know if she had any feelings for me at all. All I really know—'

Dr Keele's head-shake was tiny, a micro-expression.

Shit.

But coming from someone adept at reading the stuff of thought from scans, it formed a clear and authoritative signal.

Alisha was in love with me.

Past tense, and now something further removed: Alisha's emotions belonged to an alternate subjective reality cut off and discarded, just as old-time surgeons might have snipped out an appendix and tossed the organ aside.

And if he walked in to see Alisha now, what would he say?

Hi, I'm the guy who pulled you out of the brothel where you'd been servicing that fat old guy with the dripping dick. Remember him? No, I guess you don't.

Arcs of tension bracketed his mouth.

'I'm sure you think you've done the right thing,' he said. 'Why don't we leave it at—'

Scarlet holo icons streamed at eye-level between them.

'That's a security alarm,' said Dr Keele.

'You get security emergencies in the med-halls? How often does—?'

Her face was stony.

'I've never known it to happen.'

Dr Keele rushed out, Roger striding after. She ran to a large therapy room and stopped, breathing hard in the doorway. Inside, the room was largely empty. As a group of junior medics trotted up, Dr Keele turned on them.

'Where the hell is my autodoc? My new autodoc!'

'I can't—' The nearest medic had paled. 'No one came past us.'

But scarlet alarm-icons continued to flare.

'Look.' Dr Keele opened a holovolume. 'See?'

In the holo, a narrow-bodied woman with dirty-blond hair came into this room, tu-rings blazing on her fists, and commanded the autodoc to open. She stopped, stared into whatever area of wall had recorded this, and pulled a rictus expression, a corpse's smile.

Bitch.

Her eyes were colder than a reptile's. Or perhaps it was simply this: he knew what she had done, what she had caused with her manipulation.

You fucking bitch.

Inside the image, Helsen climbed into the autodoc, and crouched as it sealed up. Roger could not help his grasping gesture; but it was too late to catch her, at least like that.

I will kill you.

Beneath the autodoc, the quickglass floor began to spiral, creating a viscous vortex into which, seconds later, the autodoc sank. Then it was completely under. Movement showed as a rippling shadow, then nothing, as if a pond-fish had flicked its muscles to swim from sight.

'She walked right in,' said Dr Keele.

'That's not possible.' Another medic was shaking his head. 'Not without light-bending tech to create invisibility ... but even so, we were right outside.'

'Not light-bending,' said Roger.

It was the darkness that was the enemy, not just a single, manipulative, psychotic woman.

'Not—?'

'Mind-bending,' said Roger. 'She's very good at it.'

'You *know* her?' Dr Keele, unsympathetic before, used her voice like a flail. 'What is this about, Pilot Blackstone?'

The other medics looked surprised. Roger was still wearing smartlenses.

Just as well.

Because energies were building inside his eyes: energies he wanted to let loose, coruscating and deadly; but there was no point because the bitch from hell was gone.

'That was Dr Petra Helsen, formerly of Lucis Multiversity on Fulgor,' he said. 'And I've reason to believe she engineered the coming of the Anomaly.'

The medics stared.

You think I care about a piece of stolen med-kit?

Movement caused his attention to flick to a new location: a doorway where a scar-faced man was entering. His shoulders were thick, his limbs stocky and muscular; but that was not why the medics moved back. Authority came from his gait and gaze.

Law enforcement.

'Pilot Blackstone,' he said. 'I think you and I might have a useful chat. My name's Tannier.'

'All right,' said Roger.

But less than an hour and a half remained before Jed's reinsertion into realspace, and Roger's only chance of getting away from this place.

Helsen is here.

Dr Keele's harsh face was a reminder that doing the right

thing was a matter of seeing straight and planning: something Roger needed to do more of. He could start by clarifying what he wanted.

'Catch Helsen,' he said. 'Just catch her.'

'If we can,' said Tannier. 'She's disappeared, and that's quite a trick for an offworlder.'

'Disappeared with an autodoc?' Dr Keele sounded scathing. 'How can that be?'

'About as easy,' said Tannier, 'as stealing it from under your noses, Doctor.'

Roger felt his mouth twitch.

'Take me in to headquarters, or whatever you do,' he said. 'And I'll talk to you gladly.'

He looked at Helsen's image as the video log replayed.

My enemy.

And Tannier's reply was lost in the surf-sound of auditory exclusion, a facet of the adrenal stress response that Roger was becoming used to: his neuromuscular system reacting to the threat of lethal danger, the atavistic recognition of a non-human predator, because that was what Helsen had become: a conduit for the darkness, a vessel for a power that had created a mind-consuming planetary entity for unknowable purpose. Helsen was a thing that needed to be stamped out, crushed into particles that could never form a threat.

While the Anomaly and greater darkness remained hostile and aggressive, their magnitude and potential vast, their goals impossible to perceive, even in outline, their weaknesses boiled down to this: precisely none.

Was all of humanity at risk?

TWELVE

EARTH, 2147 AD

They met up at a travelling diner in New Phoenix, one of two hundred or so establishments slowly circling the city along Annular Beltway, some thirty kilometres away from DistribOne where they all theoretically worked. Rekka performed some hatha yoga breathing, needing the calmness. Beside her, Simon grinned, clearly anticipating a friendly meal and good conversation.

You've not been getting much from me, have you?

But Simon could not understand her grief over Sharp's self sacrifice. A xeno behaved according to its species' evolved behaviour patterns; that Sharp was her friend who had given up everything – in a slow, awful death – seemed not to register.

'The girls are here already,' said Simon. 'Hiya!'

Rekka slid in to sit facing Amber – whose steel eye-sockets glittered with reflected faux candle-light – while Simon gave Mary a peck on the cheek before sitting opposite her.

'I was going to wear shades,' said Amber. 'But Mary reckoned that would make me more conspicuous, not less.'

'Probably right,' said Simon. 'People are used to seeing Pilots around here, after all.'

Amber was supposed to be far from DistribOne, on sabbatical in Australia.

'Anyway, food.' Simon growled at Mary: 'Need. Food.'

'Poor Rekka.' Amber reached out to find Rekka's hand, then patted it. 'I don't question your being straight, because I know you can't help it. But your choice of men—'

Mary laughed.

'Excuse me?' Simon said to her. Then, to Amber: 'Isn't motherhood supposed to make you mellow?'

'Exhausted, more to the point.'

Rekka said, 'So how is the most beautiful baby boy in the universe?'

'Two universes.' Lines disappeared from Amber's face as she smiled. 'And Jared's wonderful. This is the first time I've been out without him, and it's actually tough.'

'He's with Jenna,' said Mary. 'Who's being the adoring aunt, and loving it.'

They ordered the first course, took their time eating, their conversation lightly seasoned with friendly insults, then finished up. An actual human waitress took their plates away, while menus displayed on the tabletop, Amber's with fast-audio enabled: she ran her fingertips along the icons, a high-speed gabble sounding.

Gabble to Rekka; comprehensible to Amber.

'So the rumour mill is one hundred per cent operational,' said Simon. 'And looks to be correct. DistribOne's capacity is being reduced by seventy per cent over the next two years. I'm not supposed to know, even in my exalted position, which is why I can't possibly be telling you this right now.'

'And the workload's going where, exactly?' asked Mary.

Rekka was blinking.

He didn't say anything earlier.

Or maybe she had broadcast leave-me-alone signals by pure body language. Sharp had been on her mind – again – all afternoon.

'Shaanxi Province, mainly. And some other centres in the region, like Singapore.'

'They can't do that,' said Amber. 'I mean, they're UNSA and they can do what they like, but Pilots have personal lives too. And for most other personnel, it's an even bigger change.'

Mary was staring at Simon.

'It's the Higashionna cousins, isn't it? They seem to be behind every weird change at the moment.'

'Good guess, sweetheart,' said Simon. 'Our charismatic senators are poking around everywhere. Especially at Pilot welfare.'

'Welfare,' said Amber. 'Right.'

But Rekka remembered Sharp's reaction at DistribOne on seeing the two Higashionnas – good-looking Japanese-Brazilians, appearing like brother and sister but actually cousins, both UN senators – and the questions he asked in private: *Do you not taste their evil?* and *Can you not smell dark nothing?*

Even the visiting Zajinets had acted perturbed at the Higashionnas' presence.

The entrées arrived – 'Shouldn't it be the starters that you enter with?' Simon asked – and Rekka, Amber and Mary tucked in. But Simon had not finished talking.

'China's the place to be, isn't it? Vibrant, go-ahead. Good schooling.'

Amber paused.

'We're still talking about that,' she said.

Rekka looked at Mary, who was frowning.

Is there an argument there?

'Karyn McNamara's school in Zürich is still supposed to be the best,' said Rekka. 'But sending your child away like that can't compete with a good home life.'

What none of them was saying aloud was that Jared's birth – although registered as a home birth in New Phoenix – had taken place aboard Luís Delgado's ship in mu-space, an illicit act that had required Rekka's and Simon's complicity.

Which meant baby Jared, already nanovirally treated as an embryo, was a natural-born Pilot of the kind that Karyn McNamara specialized in rearing. Karyn's daughter Ro, who had come as an adult to DistribOne six years earlier but was rarely seen these days, had been the first of the new kind of Pilot, with black-on-black eyes instead of the silver sockets that both Karyn and Amber wore, their natural (and newly useless) eyes removed during the nanoviral alterations they had undergone as Pilot Candidates.

'UNSA has no right,' said Mary, 'to determine how a child is raised.'

Amber put down her cutlery.

'You can't drive me to tears,' she said, 'because they took out my tear ducts along with my eyes, remember?'

'Shit, sweetheart,' said Mary. 'I know that, but—'

'Which is why I'm a fucking invalid in this world, while you *literally* cannot imagine the beauty of mu-space, the entire universe that is Jared's birthright. OK?'

Mary's face clenched.

'I'm sorry, everyone. Shouldn't have brought up a touchy subject, right?'

'If you can't talk about it in front of your friends,' said Rekka, 'then where?'

Mary glanced at Simon, then looked down at her plate.

'I am enjoying this, really. Why don't we just eat?'

The meal lumbered on.

Rekka went to a meeting the next afternoon. Her infostrand had given her directions – McStuart's office, 14:00 – but the meeting's purpose was listed as *Project composition*, which could mean anything. Which project did it even refer to?

Simon was so much better at this stuff than she was. His forward planning was meticulous always; he could visualize and rattle off the minutest details of last year's work as easily as the next quarter's plans; and he never entered a meeting without a clear objective in mind, and at least three possible strategies for achieving it. She, on the other hand, met deadlines only because she had to, while her idea of fun was to deeply immerse herself in the moment, and that applied to coding autofact software or modelling biospaces as much as to yoga or sex.

'Sit down.' McStuart smiled. 'As you can see, Matt is helping us out today.'

Rekka nodded to Matt Kilborn, who as Chief Flight Controller had the final say on mission assignments. She was glad to see him, because McStuart was not as friendly as he was pretending to be.

'I'm not in trouble, I hope,' she said.

Kilborn smiled; McStuart's façade slipped back to his normal serious expression.

'You're in our good books, Rekka,' said Kilborn. 'Otherwise we wouldn't have a choice new assignment for you.'

Adrenaline washed through her arteries.

'An offworld mission?'

'Er, no.' McStuart shifted. 'Naturally, you're shortlisted for the choicest of new pre- and first-contact missions' – with a glance at Kilborn – 'since your success with the Haxigoji.'

That was a change in sentiment since the shouting match that followed her arrival at DistribOne with Sharp aboard a Pilot's vessel.

Kilborn said, 'You have my deepest sympathy regarding Sharp. He was a remarkable individual.'

The words were standard but sounded genuine.

That's more than Simon's managed to say to me.

'Thank you,' she said. 'He was brave for sure.'

'Which is why,' said Kilborn, 'I believe you're the best possible person we could send to Singapore to work with the Haxigoji.'

Singapore?

She used the yoga breathing as a pause for taking stock.

The Haxigoji?

So Sharp's people had sent a replacement; but UNSA had chosen not to receive him here, in Arizona.

'There are seven in the party,' added Kilborn. 'Exceptionally bright, all of them.'

McStuart eased back in his chair. If he thought that letting Kilborn take charge was the way to get Rekka to listen, then he was right – for once.

Asshole.

She focused on Kilborn once more.

'—xenopsych and primary linguistic mapping,' he was

saying. 'Poliakov and his people did a terrific job, following on from you, and Peter Chong's group have everything we need to take it to this next stage.'

Rekka swallowed. Simon would have a game plan all mapped out, but she was winging it, still trying to work out the background.

'It sounds substantial,' she said. 'So what kind of duration are we talking about?'

'Ah,' said Kilborn. 'Well, seven months is our initial estimate.'

McStuart nodded.

'And when the project is complete,' she said. 'What then? Am I to come back here?'

Kilborn started to smile, while McStuart coughed.

'Well,' said McStuart. 'That's the thing.'

'Don't tell me,' said Rekka. 'Organizational restructuring, right?'

'There's some long-term redistribution of responsibilities coming up.' Kilborn looked at McStuart, then back at Rekka. 'That's corporate bullshit-ese for winding things down in some places, and cranking things up elsewhere. Being posted to Singapore for the foreseeable future will do your career a lot of good.'

'But offworld missions will still be part of that career?'

'Of course. Flying out of, say, ShaanxiThree is no different than here.'

Rekka pushed out a breath, deciding in that moment what she needed to get out of this meeting.

Simon would do it better.

But that was sort of the point: she was the one who temporarily had some kind of power.

'If Simon were based in Singapore,' she said, 'or in the nearest Chinese station, that would make my decision much easier.'

There was no need to say which Simon she referred to.

Kilborn said: 'He's a good man. I'll recommend him for any posting he wants.'

She believed him; and she knew his recommendation would be enough to swing any transfer.

'A good meeting, then,' said McStuart. 'Very good.'

Considerably different to their last conversation.

'Yes,' said Rekka. 'Good.'

But as she left the room, acid sourness swirled in her stomach. Because she was not used to corporate politics played that way? Or was it the thought of mixing with Haxigoji, the touch of their fur and the air filled with complex scents of communication?

And Sharp, dying slice by slice as the blades came down.

THIRTEEN

MOLSIN, 2603 AD

Tannier commandeered a room adjacent to the furthest med-hall. Chairs morphed at his command, and he waved at Roger to sit. At the same time, one wall trembled and pulled apart, and a grizzle-headed man stepped in.

'I'm Bendelhamer,' was all he said to Roger, before nodding to Tannier. 'Carry on.'

'Sir. Pilot Blackstone believes he knows the woman who stole the autodoc. What's more, he says she's implicated in the Fulgor Catastrophe.'

Bendelhamer nodded.

'Tell me your story, Pilot.'

Roger told as much as he could without detailing Labyrinth or Admiralty conspiracies; but he did confess that his father had been an agent-in-place on Fulgor for decades. Neither Bendelhamer nor Tannier showed any reaction to the notion of spying: clearly they were, if not spies themselves, then senior police officers whose work bordered on the secret world.

'This darkness,' said Tannier finally. 'It's not something real, is that what you're saying?'

'Right,' said Roger. 'The visual aspect is a, what, artefact of perception, sort of thing. I'm detecting something but it's not really light. Not an optical phenomenon.'

Bendelhamer leaned his head forward.

'And any Pilot would be able to detect this? Am I right?'

Roger wanted to lie, because if they believed all Pilots saw what he did, it would lend weight to all he had told them.

'No, sir,' he said. 'I've had independent verification that

some other Pilots can perceive the phenomenon, though not as easily.'

Tannier waved one roughened, scarred hand.

'This Helsen woman definitely stole an autodoc,' he said. 'If she set up this Luculenta Stargonier, entrapped her into becoming the start of this Anomaly, then she's a criminal, possibly a war criminal.'

'Meaning we don't care about psychological phenomena as far as her legal status is concerned.' Bendelhamer nodded. 'That is clearly correct.'

'I know you don't have SatScan as such,' said Roger. 'But shouldn't you have tracked her down via internal surveillance by now? That's not an accusation. I just don't understand.'

Tannier's face, battered by the years, somehow made his smile look genuine.

'"A surveilled society is a safe society." Isn't that what they used to say on Fulgor?'

The past tense was a judgement.

'Used to,' said Roger. 'I suppose they're sort of safe now, as components of a global organism. Just not human.'

'All right,' said Tannier. 'But here we have a concept called privacy, as you might have noticed.'

'Er ... Surely not for you people. Not for official business.'

'We have far fewer restrictions.' This was Bendelhamer. 'But a less unified surveillance architecture which is marginally easier to slip through, though it requires enormous expertise, even so.'

'Helsen's a bitch,' said Roger, 'but she isn't stupid.'

Then he stopped, looked around the room – it retained the look and feel of the med-halls outside – and added: 'Why would she steal an autodoc? Wouldn't it have been easier to go to ground quietly?'

Bendelhamer and Tannier glanced at each other, perhaps because of the jargon – *go to ground* – or perhaps due to other factors.

'That particular model,' said Tannier, 'allows reworking of DNA all the way through.'

'Why would she want that?'

'Possibly to avoid surveillance,' said Bendelhamer. 'But we're not as unsophisticated as you might think, Pilot.'

'Call me Roger. Your quickglass tech is far beyond anything Fulgor ever produced, and I'm aware of that.'

The two men nodded.

'What will you do now?' asked Tannier. 'Go back to Leeja Rigelle's apartment?'

So much for privacy laws.

'I guess so,' he said.

Roger was halfway along a crowded gallery when his tu-ring flared, and a private holo unfurled in his smartlenses, the narrow-collimation audio surrounded by anti-sound. He backed up against a quickglass buttress, out of the flow of people.

'I tried pinging you,' said Jed, 'but you were still hiding away somewhere shielded. That was against instructions, mate – trying to contact you, I mean – but I'd have got you offworld if I could.'

It was a recorded, non-interactive message, as before.

Against instructions?

In the holo, Jed looked frustrated, and his voice was tight.

'They've declared quarantine. Molsin's powers-that-be are receiving notification that no Pilot ships will be visiting the planet. They're not giving a reason, not in actual clear speech, but there's something about "recent events concerning a new arrival" that points at what's-her-name, Helsen.'

Had Tannier and Bendelhamer known of this? Or were they only just learning of the quarantine themselves?

'Check the auth-codes, appended,' Jed added. 'We're leaving you funds to live on.'

The message had been sent while Roger was in the med-halls, not Leeja's place. He was going to have to change his tu-ring to warn of loss of contact, a condition that on Fulgor had been inconceivable.

'I'm really sorry, mate. I'll be back for you as soon as I can, right? Shit. Take it easy.'

The holo winked out.

'*Shit* is right,' said Roger.

He went to the great reception hall where they had offloaded the med-drones from Jed's ship. No one was there, apart from him: tiny in the huge, echoing space. Insignificant and lost.

Cut off from Pilotkind.

From *her*, growing so fast in Ascension Annexe.

What am I supposed to do?

But the notion of caring, benevolent authority was no longer relevant. He did not need anyone to tell him what to do, to give him a purpose.

Not while Helsen was free.

Leeja smiled at him, her chin dipped, her eyes alight.

'Come in, lover.'

The door flowed shut behind him.

At some point in the night, they were awake together. Leeja touched his lower lip.

'You said her name, darling. In your sleep. Your girl from Fulgor.'

'I'm sorry.'

Earlier, he had told Leeja that his friend from Fulgor no longer knew him, thanks to medical science.

'I'm not going to see her,' he added. 'I can't do that.'

'Mm.' Leeja wriggled, put her hand on his stomach. 'And is she beautiful?'

'She's in the past.'

Leeja kissed his earlobe.

'But is she beautiful, this Gavi?'

'She— What?'

'What do I have to do so it's *my* name you moan when you're asleep?'

He rolled on top of her.

So warm, soft and exciting.

'I'm not sleepy,' he said.

They rode to the stars once more.

FOURTEEN

EARTH, 1941 AD

Gavriela rode in a train compartment whose other occupants – two men in uniform, two in heavy tweed overcoats and three-piece suits – nodded as politeness dictated, but conversed only in small, meaningless bursts during the entire journey. At Paddington, she felt nervous as she walked along the platform while the blackness of the engine loomed, steam banked overhead, and pigeons swooped amid metallic echoes bouncing from the steel-arched ceiling.

The ticket-inspector, old and efficient, stood at the black-rubber barrier, one thumb tucked in his waistcoat pocket as he checked each traveller in turn. He nodded at Gavriela's travel warrant, and gave her a kind smile.

'Thank you,' she managed to say.

Her body wanted to collapse concertina-like, folding at hips and knees; but she used force of will to walk on, and a train-whistle sounded as her head began to clear.

Checking tickets, that's all.

The Gestapo had no power in England, at least not yet.

Frank had arranged the warrant, at her inveigling. Her excuse was a desire to talk to the code-makers at SOE, to get another perspective on the more intractable signals passing through Hut 27. What's more, she had managed to obtain a day's leave, so that she did not have to report to Baker Street until Friday, while tomorrow she had free rein.

THE DARKNESS COMMMANDS THAT YOU MEET THE EAGLE AT ?? O'CLOCK THURSDAY IN TRAFALGAR SQUARE

Yesterday, she had peeked at every intercept she could, trying to find another signal with the EAVI prefix, or anything else that might suggest a message from the same source. There had been nothing, no extra data: therefore no chance of deciphering the two-digit time.

I can't do this.

But she had to, because the clunky German content of the message implied an English agent composing it. If she were sure that it was Germans meeting in Trafalgar, she could have bluffed her way into decrypting the message in full view, showing it to the team, and getting Frank to make a phone call. As it was, the people at the rendezvous could be anybody, possibly part of the British establishment and above suspicion.

This was a machination of the darkness, not the German war machine. Even with all she had seen years before, it would have been delusional to believe a strange power was intimately directing the actions of key Nazis. The reality was subtler, the shared visions of a glorious, blood-soaked future arising more from known insanity and the contagion of mob psychology than from unknown forces. But a tiny deflection, applied in a timely manner, can bring about a massive change in trajectory over an extended duration. Poincaré had pointed that out, several years before Gavriela's birth, in his papers on dynamical systems.

And a bullet is such a small object.

That was what scared her: not the travel arrangements, which were all in order – *alles in Ordnung*, such a Teutonic concept, more than the sum of its words – but the possibility that someone might notice the weight of her handbag, and ask her to open it. She had tried to fabricate cover stories to justify carrying a loaded Webley; but all of them sounded in her mind like the desperate, lightweight lies of a guilty child.

A revolver has only one purpose, after all.

The boarding-house room in Swiss Cottage was comfortable enough, but sleep came in short, incomplete bursts. No one knocked on the front door, no constables demanding she accompany them to the station; but someone must have noticed the gap in the display case at Bletchley. She would have preferred to raid the armoury proper, but it was guarded always. She had settled for Frank Longfield-Jones' firearms-and-fishing-rod collection, on display in the snooker room at the mansion house.

At dawn she left, bundled up in coat, headscarf and gloves, the Webley in her handbag. From the Tube station she caught a southbound train, heading for the West End. Two of the stations she passed through bore the chaotic signs of use during the night: lost blankets and general detritus. The people who had sheltered from the bombs were gone, back above ground. She wondered how many had found their homes destroyed, their pets killed or lost, or their neighbours dead.

At Trafalgar Square, she worked out where to watch from: the area between Charing Cross Station and St Martin-in-the-Fields. The square itself, with the neo-classical National Gallery to the north, had the same imperial sensibility as the Brandenburger Tor in Berlin, even the Reichstag: not a comparison to win her favour, should she ever share it.

And so her long day of watching began.

The station's proximity was useful, along with the subterranean lavatories; but every time she gave in and took a break, she came back wondering if she had missed everything. On three occasions, she fell in with small groups of wives and girlfriends waiting for men to arrive home on leave, and joined in the chat with her fictitious tale of a husband due home today, but not knowing the time of his train. Once, she made sure a policeman overheard the story. It helped that her gloves hid the absence of a wedding-ring.

When darkness – the ordinary absence of daylight – settled over the open square, she was worried as her presence became more likely to attract police attention. But a night-time meeting made sense, so she forced herself to remain in place, watching.

Finally, shivers of that other darkness manifested across the road, somewhere close to one of the black lion statues.

I have to do this.

She wanted to pee, but that was impossible. She wanted her hands to stop shaking, and that was not happening either. Still she walked across the road, reached the steps – slowly, slowly in the blackout with only a hint of moon – down to the level of the square proper. The handbag clasp opened with an unexpected snap.

A palsy took over her entire body.

'—that?' a voice muttered.

A vague sense of two men searching the darkened square.

Over there.

The revolver felt so massive. She crouched down, placed her handbag on the flagstones, and rose with both hands trying to keep the Webley aimed.

A faint hint of nine awful notes on the air.

I've got you both.

But the barrel was shaking – small deflections, big trajectory changes, so forth – which meant she had to get closer. Trying to be soundless, she advanced.

'There!' yelled one of her targets.

'I see—'

Then metallic whistles sounded on all sides, torch beams swung through the air, and a leather-gloved hand reached over Gavriela's shoulder and fastened on the revolver, while her insides dissolved in the acid of fear, reality swirling around her.

'I'll take that, old girl. You must be freezing.'

Rupert Forrester smiled at her, his breath steaming white by torchlight. Twenty policemen or more were converging on the enemy: two strangers, who dropped their guns and put up their hands even before the command.

'Bloody risky night to be a brass monkey,' Rupert added. 'So a nice hot cup of tea would be in order, don't you think?'

FIFTEEN

The concept of a single amateur outguessing the authorities to apprehend a criminal, so facile, ground away at Roger's confidence. What he had going for him was his ability to perceive some resonance – *something* – from Helsen; but it was nothing he could replicate for others to use, or use himself at long distance. Barbour was an entire sky-city, and he could wander it for years and still not lay eyes on any given inhabitant.

Especially if she was avoiding him.

From the authorities' viewpoint, their target's appearance was unknown, likewise all the markers – such as DNA traces or neural clique configurations – normally used for suspect identification. At least, if Roger had understood Tannier and Bendelhamer correctly, that was why Helsen had stolen the autodoc: to give herself a new identity, all the way down to her molecules.

Bitch.

And the man who had been with her on Fulgor – were there two of them here, looking to replicate the Fulgor Catastrophe on Molsin? Roger walked through the halls and galleries of Barbour at random, trying to notice everything while despairing of the probabilities, with not even a halfway decent strategy for searching.

What is she after?

Assume Helsen's objective was to create a second Anomaly, or an extension of the first. (And that *was* an assumption: perhaps she planned to live out her days in hiding, her life's goal accomplished.) On Fulgor, the genesis had been a rogue

Luculenta attacking her peers in Skein. On Molsin, neither concept – Luculenti or Skein – applied. Perhaps Tannier's people had some notion of a local equivalent, some route by which a nascent Anomaly might attack. They must be smart enough, and have resources whose strength he could not gauge; but they would have no reason to share their thoughts with him.

Hence the amateur, all alone.

At an eatery, while he drank daistral, he observed a teacher accompanying fifteen pupils, all young, as they worked a holodisplay above the table they had been eating at.

'There's our forecast,' she said, 'and Jacqui, can you see the numbers?'

'Yes, miss.'

'So if you play with them, just a little, what happens?'

The forecast views changed in real time with the girl's manipulations.

'If we change the numbers by a small amount,' said the teacher, 'does the forecast change very much?'

Shakes of young heads all around the table.

They look really bright.

Clearly the teacher was going to show them another region where altering parameters by a tiny amount shifted the prediction enormously. In a sky-city in Molsin's streaming, complex atmospheric system, its flows made visible by predominant orange clouds, this was an everyday example to introduce chaos, the first step in learning about non-linearity and complexity.

In the holo, an image of what might have been Barbour floated amid cloud-banks, while a pulse of tiny dots streamed out from its aft end.

'Excuse me,' he said to the teacher. 'Are those things just markers in the display? Or are they real?'

'Quickbug flyers,' the teacher said. 'Children, I think we have an offworld visitor. What do we say?'

'Welcome to Barbour, mister,' they chanted.

'Would you like to talk to us,' asked the teacher, 'about where you—?'

'I'm sorry. I'm really, really sorry.' Roger waved at the children. 'You guys are terrific.'

He jogged out of the eatery, flushed with the probability of behaving like an idiot, but trusting himself deep down. On this level, he had been the length of the city, from the bow-end of Vertebral Longway to the rear. He had not liked the atmosphere in the aft sections.

Bad vibes.

Subliminal hints that he had failed to process consciously? Perhaps the people really had been less friendly there, the decor and underlying architecture less pleasing; or perhaps some other perceptual trace had been attenuated beyond his capacity to detect.

Tannier's people would know about the flyers. But if Helsen could avoid security checks, she might reach another sky-city, and maybe another after that. If this privacy culture was global, the further she went, the deeper she could hide.

Two median strips offered fast-flow transport. Using the public service interfaces displayed above his tu-ring, Roger caused a vortex to form around his feet; then the vortex whirled around his ankles, and twisted him into the main laminar flow.

He sped along Vertebral Longway, sure he had missed another opportunity.

If there was security, Roger could not see it, unless it was the two scarlet-uniformed helpers who chatted with people, younger folk in particular, as they prepared to fly outside. That preparation consisted of sitting on an extruded block of orange quickglass – here in this chamber, everything bore the hue of old marmalade – while a thin bubble formed then thickened; and finally the bubble slid across the deck and into the solid hull.

Through yellow-tinted view windows, you could see the

bubbles pop out into the sky, now as teardrop-shapes with stubby wings, all of orange quickglass.

'Are they gliders?' asked Roger.

One of the assistants frowned – clearly a blunt question was impolite – but the other answered: 'Mostly gliders, with arterial fuel for a full-burst emergency return if the winds increase.'

Even more than on Fulgor, quickglass was filled with intricate structures and systems, threaded through the malleable substrate.

She's out there.

There were dozens of these quickbug flyers, maybe hundreds dipping in and out of cloud banks: an entire flock trailing the city. At some point, Helsen had slipped out in a flyer to join them, perhaps from some lower level where no one would expect a quickbug to form.

He could not hear the music, not even a fragment; nor could he see darkness twisting through impossible geometric transformations; yet certainty was crystallizing.

'I'd like to take a flight, please.'

'Certainly, sir. The orientation and flightware tutorial takes several—'

'I really need to get out there now.'

'It's not just the matter of queue-jumping, sir. Your safety is important to us.'

'I . . . Forgive me. Sorry.'

'That's quite all right, sir.'

He shrugged at the waiting people as he left. Once outside, he projected the public interfaces from his tu-ring as before; then he released his burrowers and introspectors, code-forms evolved to infiltrate and unravel, passed into the unsuspecting service operations disguised as innocuous parameters. Besides his secret in Ascension Annexe, this was the other thing he had not mentioned to anyone in Labyrinth, or anywhere else: Dad had bequeathed a copy of all his subversion ware, every covert utility he owned, dumped in a zipblip from tu-ring to tu-ring, father to son.

It was a simple hack of a public service to descend through the deck to the level below, and pass through the wall into a storage bay half-filled with stacks of penrose containers. Creating the quickbug took another two minutes, due to the amount of security-breaking computation required.

Then he was sitting inside a hollow sphere sliding towards the metres-thick hull.

Let's hope I got this bit right.

The hollow passed inside solid quickglass. Then the front cleared. Vertigo startled Roger: there was only thin quickglass between him and the long drop to the cloud-banks below. Being a passenger in a mu-space ship had not prepared him for this.

Behind him, the rear of his quickbug looked darker and more solid: the tail of the teardrop. As the wings extruded on either side, he forced himself to reinterpret his fear as fight preparation, to be grateful for adrenaline that would power him through the hunt.

The quickbug flyer launched.

And fell away from the city.

By the second hour, he was enjoying himself. Dipping in and out of clouds, floating past other flyers – waggling his wings to say hello, all other comms disabled – and the simple process of controlling the glide-configuration with occasional pulses from the drive arteries: it absorbed all his concentration, yet his feeling of freedom bordered on elation. Still with no sign of Helsen, though occasionally he had felt something close by, like sensing thunder before it occurred.

There.

And she was on him.

The other flyer was huge in comparison, shearing overhead, tendrils smashing into his quickglass bubble – *tendrils!* – because it was configured for attack. There were two figures inside, he was almost sure of it, as the big flyer banked left and down, and he twisted his own quickbug's wings to follow.

Diving now.

They were inside intermittent cloud, all the other flyers lost from sight, and not by accident: that bitch Helsen had set an ambush, and attacked but failed to kill him. He let loose the drive power, accelerating downwards, everything beginning to shake, vision blurring as his eyeballs vibrated.

I'll take you down with me if I have to.

There was someone waiting for him in Ascension Annexe but Helsen was here and now and she had killed everyone on Fulgor including his parents and there was no way she could be allowed to live. The sound inside the quickbug was rising and he wondered if the flyer could shake itself apart but that did not matter because his target was – *there, left* – and then he was diving even faster: full power, designed for emergency climb, driving him down.

She pulled aside at the last moment, once more whipping her flyer's tendrils against his hull.

Shit shit shit.

His quickbug flyer was finding it hard to respond, shaking as he tried to pull it level, sudden loss of vision all around as cloud swallowed his quickbug; and then a high, splintering sound cut through the roar, a second before he saw the cause.

The quickglass was cracking.

It's not supposed to do that.

He spread the wings further, wondering what he had done wrong.

Venom in the tendrils.

Helsen was smarter than he was, that was all.

'Bitch bitch bitch.'

The cockpit was opaque, webbed with cracks, about to fail.

Shit. No.

But the rear of the teardrop remained intact, or seemed to, and there were seconds left before the cockpit bubble exploded but Dad's subversion ware had been the best and he trusted to it now.

'I'm not going to die, you bitch.'

A hollow opening appeared inside the teardrop tail.

'Not before you.'

He crawled inside.

Close up.

The command was executing, the gap closing to a hand's width, when the world disappeared in a massive percussive bang.

Drifting, his sleep so peaceful. Mum and Dad were with him, and all was warm with the soft wind so distant. Wonderful to curl up in here for ever.

A bump.

Go away.

Voices, and then the hands upon him.

'—deprivation, and acid in the lungs.'

Shaking. Tipping him.

'—bubble aloft so long, he's lucky.'

Falling once more.

SIXTEEN

EARTH, 777 AD

The solitary hunt.

This is where I belong.

Ulfr hid with Brandr alongside him, man and war-hound sharing body warmth. The landscape was crinkled ice under snow, patches of tough heather and grasses showing through, and the lakes like steel. The deer-herd moved as a compact unit, their deep wordless wisdom protecting them against lone hunters, for they were vulnerable only when split from their fellows.

Not like me.

For all Vermundr's nonsense about Ulfr's being chieftain one day, this was the best life: just himself and Brandr below the sky, and the immediacy of the Middle World without men: dark-smelling soil, cold purity of air and the skin-toughening breeze, tiny thumps and crunches caused by moving deer, fine detail of their hides, and the lustrous, knowing eyes.

Ravens, in the distance.

If you catch a dark poet on his own, can you run him down as you would a deer?

Not all ravens are Stígr's.

But these, but these . . .

You are, though. Aren't you?

Brandr's growl was a deep vibration. Two hundred paces away, a stag raised his head to look.

'We hunt.' Ulfr placed his hand on Brandr's back, feeling the quiver of muscles lusting to explode with movement. 'But not the prey we thought.'

He rose, spear held horizontally at his thigh, and the tableau broke, deer-herd galloping away to the right, maintaining the group formation.

Live free, until we meet again.

Then he began to jog along the icy ground, Brandr at his side as always.

But something attacked Stígr before Ulfr could get there.

It reared up from the soil, spilling roots and clay and ice. Worms wriggled, exposed to the air. It was the earth moving: swinging a disintegrating limb to hit Stígr's shoulder as he scrambled back, shouting. The noise of the torn earth drowned out the words. From inside the moving mass came a glimpse of glowing scarlet.

Stígr pointed his staff at the creature – he moved easily despite earlier wounds and the troll's impact just now: more dark *seithr* magic – but the staff's tip flared with crimson fire, not his doing. He flung it from him as if burned. Ravens whipped down from the sky, attacking the mass; but the mud caught them, enveloped them, then flipped their struggling, mud-soaked forms aside.

Their intervention was enough: darkness folded around Stígr, then sapphire fire blazed, and as the mud-form lunged, Stígr twisted away – turned impossibly – and was gone: the moving soil passed through air and thumped onto solid ground.

Thórr's blood.

Eira and other *volva*s could work with men's spirits and heal broken bodies; but this was the true, dark sorcery of legend. For the second time, Stígr had been rescued by demons, carried away in a manner no man could see or understand. And now the massive, moving soil-creature was turning towards Ulfr.

'Hold, Brandr.'

The war-hound wanted to attack, but Ulfr would not sacrifice him as Stígr had sacrificed his ravens.

Soil continued to spill from the thing.

Is it attacking?

Roots and stones fell aside, the last dark soil spattered on the earth, and what remained was a tangle of glowing scarlet lines, a complex tracery of light. Before the Thing, when Ulfr had fought the troll, it had been like this: scarlet fire animating a mass of moving stones.

'What are you?' he said.

It blazed more strongly.

<<Far-sighted man.>>

<<Darkness you see.>>

<<Blind, the rest.>>

<<You know the enemy.>>

Hanging in place, it neither attacked nor withdrew.

'If you mean the poet Stígr, then yes, he is my enemy.'

<<Good, is good.>>

<<Trust, alliance.>>

<<Next time, ally.>>

<<Slay comrade.>>

Ulfr lowered his spear.

'I do not understand, troll-spirit. We fight together against Stígr, yes?'

But the blazing scarlet twisted, blueness flared around it, then its presence was extinguished: gone, like a snuffed-out flame. Only the spilled earth, and the churned pit from which it came, remained as evidence: this was no dreamworld visitation, but a tangible power in the Middle World.

In the sagas, when humans tangled with greater powers, it rarely ended well.

Back in the village, he left Brandr in Steinn's care. Brandr and Griggr, Steinn's hound, had played together since they were pups. Now, Steinn clapped Ulfr on the shoulder, grinning and nodding, as if he knew what Ulfr was about and did not wish to say it, but wished him luck.

Maybe this is madness.

Outside Eira's hut, a sheep was hobbled. He wondered why she had it: for wool, some kind of sacrifice, or simply for food.

'If you're eyeing up my sheep' – Eira's voice, from inside the hut – 'you might as well know, you're not her type.'

'I'm not *that* lonely.'

'No, I dare say you're not. Come in.'

The interior stank of poultice and potions. Eira was sitting on her low cot, on deerskin stretched across a frame of slender branches. Rune-engraved pots were arrayed before her.

Her eyes were bright, her neck tense, her smile wide: a tangle of contradictions.

'If you're mixing concoctions,' Ulfr said, 'then I can help with the ingredients. You know, gather water, pick herbs, harvest Vermundr's testicles. Whatever you want.'

'I'm mixing healing potions, not poisons.'

'Good point.'

But the poultice-smell came from her, not the pots.

'Ulfr . . .'

'You're wounded.' He crouched down in front of her. 'Do you want to show me?'

'Mind my pots.'

'Sorry. Can I move them?'

'Yes, if you don't spill anything.'

He made room, then knelt on one knee, and dared to take hold of her hand.

'Show me,' he said.

Eira stared at him. Her eyes were passages to dreamworld. He wanted to fall inside for ever.

'I'll have to take my gown off for that.'

'Oh. I'm, er . . .'

'Give me a hand, then.'

He helped her remove jewellery and then the robe. Her body was beautiful. Either the poultice or the wound it covered was damp, and he tried to look; but her fingers were at his belt, tugging it open. Pulling off his clothes took an instant, then he was lying alongside her on the cot, pressed against her.

'I had a vision,' she said, 'of a great warrior's spear. And . . . I think I've found it.'

'Eira. Gods.'

'It's just you and me, my warrior.'

Then he was plunging like salmon in a mountain stream, lost in cascades of sensation, everything he wanted now granted to him, because this was Eira, his seeress, his love, and she was all and all was her, while thoughts of scarlet fire and the spirits of trolls, of one-eyed poets and murderous ravens, were banished to Hel's grey realm.

For as long as he could keep them there.

SEVENTEEN

LABYRINTH, 2603 AD (REALSPACE-EQUIVALENT)

Clayton was an athlete of the old school, using his battered electromag-banded suit to work his strength in all directions, after a sparring session with combat mannequins set for random bursts of anaerobic violence. Session over, cleansed and refreshed with dodecapear-flavoured carb-ion fluid, he travelled to the Admiralty on foot, taking his time, trying to keep calm, to think of anything other than Darius.

Shit.

That was Darius Boyle, his former partner, now home on indefinite leave – his career surely over – from the side-effects induced by that careless cow Sapherson. Working for the intelligence service was far from a sedentary occupation; but you did not expect to be sidelined by your own medics.

Stupid, moronic cow.

Except that Sapherson had clearly been under orders to burrow deep. Orders emanating, as far as Clayton could tell, from the desk of Admiral Boris Schenck, chairman of the Admiralty Council, ferociously intelligent, aggressively conservative and proto-isolationist: the biggest asshole in Labyrinth.

This afternoon's meeting was with Pavel, the venue a conference chamber deep within the hypergeometric core of HQ complex. After passing through the security levels, Clayton stepped out into the chamber to find Pavel waiting, his face calm. It looked like the calmness of someone exerting conscious neuromuscular control, slowed-down breathing and visualizing kittens, or whatever it took to stave off images of failure.

'What's your assessment,' said Pavel, 'of Clara James?'

'I like her. Fast-thinking, decisive.'

'Despite her place in the command structure.'

'You mean' – Clayton felt his mouth pull up to one side – 'on account of her reporting to Colonel Garber, whose nose is permanently docked up Admiral Schenck's rectum. Tell me this is not on the record, boss.'

Pavel did not respond to the humour.

'We're off the books down here. I need someone clear-sighted and professional, not irrational, revenge-oriented thinking.'

'Sorry. Forget I said anything.'

'Good. There *are* some questions to be asked about Admiral Schenck's decisions.' Pavel gestured, and a four-dimensional tree-structure rotated in a holoview. 'Game-theoretic analysis of his objectives leads to some dubious results.'

Running operations off the books was neither new nor safe. Running them against stated policy could be considered treason.

'Are we opposing Schenck in some way?' said Clayton. 'Forget emotion, but if that's what you're after, I'm in.'

They had worked together for years. Professional trust had always linked them.

'I have – sources – within Internal Investigations,' said Pavel. 'There are certain enquiries I've been keeping track of.'

Espionage thrives on psychological paradoxes. Subverting the internal watchers, though: that was a covert *pièce de résistance*, the kind of victory every operative held dear: sublime, unshareable. Except that Pavel was revealing it now, exposing himself. If it were true, the revelation was a sign of trust; if false, a test for a potential traitor.

'What enquiries?' Clayton was not committing yet. 'What's going on?'

'The response to Admiral Kaltberg's death,' said Pavel.

Clayton focused on everything he knew – and still remembered, despite Sapherson – about the case.

'She was a good officer,' he said. 'Gould deserves all he gets.'

'A little while ago, I would have rated Max Gould about as highly as I rated Adrienne Kaltberg.' Pavel banished the holo diagram. 'I'm not sure my opinion has changed.'

That was only a little indirect.

'You think he didn't do it?' said Clayton. 'Are you sure?'

'No, I'm not sure at all. Not about that.'

There was an implied offering there, and Clayton took it.

'What are you sure of, boss?'

Pavel turned. Off to Clayton's right, the air shivered, wavered, and rotated.

Fastpath inside *the core shield?*

A small, thin, black-uniformed man stepped out, only a tiny golden collar-stud betraying his rank.

'Admiral,' said Clayton.

This was Admiral Asai, a man with a reputation for agile strategic thinking, and the ability to pull off astounding tricks of expertise, both as an individual Pilot and at the head of a fleet. Clayton had never met the man. Beyond the technical realm, Asai was an enigma, his political philosophy unknown.

'I'm told you're considered reliable, Mr Clayton.'

'Sir.' Clayton smiled. 'That's two layers of indirection removed from whether I actually *am* reliable.'

Asai raised an eyebrow, turning to Pavel.

'It's not his fault,' Clayton went on. 'I know a conspiracy when I see one. Likewise a deniable operation. It makes me nervous.'

'So.' Asai bowed his head, just a little. 'If Boris Schenck is not a traitor, then what we propose will not affect him adversely. We are not moving against him personally, or those who support his ambitions.'

Clayton began to assess the implied information: that Schenck had an extended set of supporters, call it a political network; and there was another, possibly separate network with the potential for action.

'And if he is a traitor?'

He threw the word back at Asai. *Traitor* could mean many things; it was specific charges that made the difference. Pavel started to speak; but Asai raised his hand.

'If Schenck is a traitor and we do nothing, either Max Gould will disappear, or the personality inhabiting his body, when he comes to trial, will bear little relation to the Gould that some of us know and highly respect. Those who've served with him.'

This was manipulation on Asai's part. The mindwipe that Sapherson had subjected Clayton and Boyle to, after they had learned ultra-classified secrets while interviewing Carl Blackstone, had caused more than the specific planned amnesia. Besides forgetting what he had learned from Blackstone, Darius had also lost all memory of his own sister – consistently, throughout his whole remembered life – and developed an ongoing inability to recognize her face. He had also suffered a form of aphasia that medics were working to cure, and believed they could reverse. But his sister would be a stranger always.

So Clayton could be expected to have sympathy for someone facing neurological re-engineering.

'What is it you want me to—? Oh, no.'

Pavel was smiling now.

'That's why you're the man we need. You see it straight away.'

'You don't even know where they're holding him.' Clayton shook his head. 'No, of course you do. You've probably got a source right inside Schenck's personal staff.'

Of course Pavel was not going to respond to that.

'You think a solo operator can do the job?' Clayton realized he was arguing practicalities, a signal he had decided to accept the task. 'I'm assuming we're talking about breaking a prisoner out of one of our own establishments.'

'We think a second experienced case officer would do the trick,' said Pavel.

'And that's why you're asking about Clara James?'

Asai tipped his head forward. Clayton read the gesture as approval.

'She has the expertise,' said Pavel. 'I think she's feeling restricted by Garber's management style.'

'Has she tried to jump the chain of command?'

In the service culture, such acts had a flavour of disloyalty.

'No, she's too smart for that,' said Pavel. 'Smart or principled.'

Clayton nodded, acknowledging the problem: principled was good, while smart-but-self-serving could be utilized; but they required different recruitment strategies.

'Let's make it my initiative test,' he said. 'If I can recruit her for the op, then I'm the right person to carry it out.'

Asai and Pavel smiled.

'Good man,' said Pavel.

Clara watched the footage three times, rotating the angles and adjusting playback speed, reading Jed Goran's body language as much as his voice. The images originated several hours earlier in Far Reach Centre, a fractal warren of commerce and bureaucracy responsible for all Pilot logistics: a major Labyrinthine institution, therefore monitored by the intelligence service always. In the holo, everything about Jed Goran indicated a controlled, muscular anger. He was angry because he believed the authorities had deserted Roger Blackstone when they declared the quarantine around Molsin.

A good man.

She placed her fingertip against the insubstantial image of Jed's face. It would be nice to make a new friend outside the service, the problem – and opportunity – being that he had seen her on the interview panel, debriefing himself and Roger on the Fulgor escape. But she already had a backstopped cover identity as an ordinary Admiralty employee.

Or Jed Goran might be a useful asset: someone strong and used to acting in a crisis. That was the problem, because you could not consider someone as a potential boyfriend and later manipulate him for the good of an operation. At least, she could not work that way.

Her immediate superior, Garber, would not betray someone he cared for, either. But that was because the icy bastard had no emotions beyond his own self-absorbed career.

Shit.

With regret, she closed the holo down.

An hour later, she was watching another holo, this one rendered real time as a room-sized image, while Colonel Garber stood alongside her, and two specialists, Arlene and Michio, observed with the aid of subsidiary biometric displays. Reading micro-expressions and gesture-clusters formed part of every officer's training; the specialists were expert even by service standards.

'This is the third person to have seen Helsen at the relay station,' said Michio. 'Her name is Susannah Blaydon. The interrogator is one of ours, Tol Karden, under cover as a Far Reach distribution controller.'

'All right,' said Garber.

Unknown to the Molsin authorities, every ship with the exception of Jed Goran's had made a stopover at a realspace relay station manned only by Pilots. There, the staff roused each med-drone occupant who was deemed safe to awaken, questioned and scanned them, then blanked their short-term memory before dropping them back into delta-trance, ready for their onward mu-space journey.

The difference in Jed Goran's case had been that all of his comatose passengers were designated as high-probability severe trauma cases, who should be woken only in full-care medical facilities, and not returned to coma until their recovery was well under way, if not complete. The decision had been a balance of humanitarian versus security concerns; Garber had wanted everyone woken and examined regardless.

In the holo, the questioner, Tol Karden, gestured at an image of Petra Helsen – a holo within a holo – that had been created on the basis of Roger Blackstone's debriefing session.

'This was the main person,' he said, 'that you were tasked with looking out for.'

'That's correct,' said Susannah Blaydon.

She looked tense but not overly so. Clara read it as innocent concern, faced with official questioning but harbouring no guilt. Arlene and Michio looked intent, too busy observing to give a verdict.

'And you saw no sign of her on the day in question?' Tol Karden leaned forward. 'That would have been the third shipload you processed, is that correct?'

'Absolutely.' Susannah Blaydon rubbed her face. 'We were tired, maybe. But none of the women looked much like this one.'

They had been instructed to watch out for a certain male also; but his bearded image was less reliable – Roger Blackstone had scarcely seen the man on Fulgor – so a negative result had been expected in that case.

Tol Karden gestured. 'I'd like to show you this.'

Beside him, a moving holo-within-the-holo opened. Squinting, Clara could see Susannah's image inside the new holo-volume, next to an opened med-drone, talking to the female occupant who was sitting up. Two other personnel stood off to one side, observing Susannah Blaydon.

As she talked to Petra Helsen.

'No.' Susannah Blaydon shook her head. 'That's not me.'

'What do you mean?' Tol Karden's voice held just the right tone: questioning without accusation. 'Not you?'

'That' – pointing with a shaking finger – 'is the woman we were told to look out for. But I never saw her. That ... That's not me in the image.'

'It looks like you.'

'But it *can't* be me. I'd have remembered, wouldn't I?'

Arlene turned round to Garber.

'Immediate assessment, Colonel. She's telling the truth, same as the others.'

Michio nodded, still watching the interrogation.

'That's not good,' said Garber.

In the holo-within-the-holo, Helsen finished talking to Susannah Blaydon, then lay back down, delta-band across her forehead. The med-drone closed up as Blaydon stepped away, ready to process the next refugee.

'Sophisticated mindbending,' said Clara.

'And now she's loose on Molsin,' said Garber. 'Shit.'

Was that concern for a vulnerable planet or his own career? He had been instrumental in setting up the vetting procedure.

'All right.' Garber was summoning a fastpath. 'I've seen enough. You stay here, on the off chance something interesting develops.'

'Yes, sir,' said Clara.

As Garber disappeared, Arlene dropped Clara a wink.

'Lovely man,' she said.

EIGHTEEN

THE WORLD, 5563 AD

Harij stood in the doorway of the special classroom, teal-green patches of sadness shifting across his otherwise silver skin. All eight of the special pupils, shiny with concentration, rocked back and forth in time to the count, Ilara among them.

Whorl one whorl three whorl five whorl seven whorl eleven whorl thirteen.

The flux of their ritualistic counting formed a headache-inducing beat. They could go on like this from nightbreak to sunrise if the teacher allowed them to. Why his sister had been born like this while he was what people called normal, he had no idea. He believed Ilara cared for him in her own way, while he loved her more than their parents could manage.

This was midnight break and he was allowed out of school. He should eat – his desk contained a woven basket of fresh sweetfungus bread – but instead he went out through the side exit, and headed for the grey scree slope at the far end of the cavern, beyond the shell houses of their little town. Always, the outside drew him.

Vortices from deep within the rock tugged at his senses, but he climbed on and came out onto the familiar wide ledge. No one else was around. He had the landscape to himself: the mesa beyond the canyon, the distant aurora, and the silver-black filigree globe of Magnus high in the sky.

A trio of mating triblades hurtled past, swooping into the canyon. Motes of no-thought drifted peaceably. Harij sat down, his back against the rockface, opening himself up the sights and flux of midnight, everything peaceful and—

There.

He had to check twice, but he was right: far across the mesa, a lone robed figure was walking. Strong gait, upright and – even from here it seemed so – both courageous and open to all that was around, sensitive and determined. The second such figure he had seen within nine nights.

I want to be like that.

It was a private thought, and he kept the flux inside him, not allowing it to escape and drift away.

Just like that.

The distant Seeker passed behind a tooth-shaped outcrop, and beyond Harij's perception.

Rather differently to the way he felt about Ilara, he was more than half in love with Mistress Ahn, his teacher. Occasionally he wondered if the rest of the class had similar thoughts; if so, they kept them tightly curled inside their heads.

They spent the next session resonating one of his favourite story crystals, [[The Strongest Dreamlode]], though it was not the lonely Seeker that the other children identified with, but the girl he saved. After the short break that followed, several of the bolder boys came up to Mistress Ahn before she called the class to order.

Lintral saw tri-blades mating, miss!

This was the kind of cheek that could cause Mother Zil-Grania, the head of school, to bring out her nastiest cane: the thin one with the heavy polarization that left weals for nights afterwards, and memories of pain that lasted longer still. But Mistress Ahn was different, which was why the boys dared so much. Still, Harij held his breath until she answered.

But when you grow up, you'll mate with only one other sex. Isn't that right?

The boys turned away, embarrassed orange patches showing on their foreheads. Mistress Ahn grinned, highlights shifting like liquid on her flawless silver skin.

Harij had no name for the desire inside him.

*

Later, he would fail to work out why this was the night, the point when his decision crystallized. Over a hundred nights had passed since the time the class discovered his dream of becoming a Seeker, after Vitril (so aloof, the swot) had led them in imagining [[My Family]] and Harij's emotions had diverged and unravelled, picked up by even the least sensitive of his classmates.

Then, they had mocked him, their flux bouncing back and forth around the room, and he had run into the corridor. But Mistress Ahn's rage had frightened everyone; and when he crept back to his desk, no one had even dared to glance at him.

Tonight, as he paused beside the spin-coils that kept the fungal farms productive, he looked back at the school where Ilara and her special classmates remained, and decided that everything had to change.

I'll get you out of there.

He would save his sister from the town that failed to love her.

I promise you.

However dangerous the journey might be.

NINETEEN

The medic's perfume was wonderful. Roger inhaled his way to wakefulness.

'Welcome back,' she said. 'We've scrubbed your lungs out, and you're going to be fine.'

'Ugh.'

'Try not to run too hard for a couple of days. And you might want to lay off the adventure sports, but that's just my personal prejudice.'

Roger could not sit up. As he tried, the bed morphed, sinking and giving way to absorb the motion, leaving him nothing to press against.

'Sorry,' added the medic. 'I hadn't thought of that. You being an offworlder without control of– But look, your tu-ring appears to have access. You can use it to alter the bed.'

'I just want to sit up.'

'Here. This is all you need.'

She looked at the bed and it reconfigured, gently pushing up behind his back.

'Thank you,' said Roger.

The bed stopped shifting. He was in a private room, coloured lustrous green and icing-white.

'Someone wants to chat with you, Pilot. A police officer.' Again she smiled. 'Just stay sitting as you are. I'll come back later to check you out of here, OK?'

'Er, OK.'

The wall melted open, allowing her to step out and Tannier to enter.

'You're back on Barbour.' Tannier waited as the doorway

flowed shut. 'She looks nice, your medic. What's her name?'

'I don't . . . If she told me, it was when I was only half awake.' Roger thought back. 'It seems as if I've been in and out of sleep.'

'More than likely.'

'I was drifting in the sky. Did someone spot me?'

It was a redundant question, but his mind was still coming online.

'Someone from Deltaville,' said Tannier. 'They found a big flotation bubble – good thinking on your part – and pulled you in. You were lucky that you hit the right current and that we're visiting, what with the birth being due and all.'

'I was chasing Helsen. She was on board a flyer, and I went after her. But she attacked my quickbug, and I—'

'Nearly died, but never mind.' Tannier's tough, ugly-handsome face creased up in a smile. 'Officially I should reprimand you. Off the record, well done for trying.'

'She got away. I should've called you.'

'Next time, please do.' Tannier gestured, causing Roger's turing to beep. 'Now you've got my ident, you might want to set it as the emergency services port ID.'

Roger tipped his head, closed his eyes to inhale – it felt only a little unnatural, smartgel coating his lungs like mild phlegm – then breathed out and looked at Tannier.

'Why aren't you more annoyed? And what was all that about currents and births? Or did I hear it wrong?'

'All the cities are on converging trajectories,' said Tannier. 'Because of Conjunction coming up – which is what it sounds like – but that's still several tendays away. We're still far removed from each other, on the whole.'

'Er, right.'

'But Deltaville's close to giving birth, so Barbour's planning to be nearby when it happens. In fact, if it hadn't been for Conjunction, there would have been several more cities clustering alongside for the occasion.'

Roger tried to parse the implications from Tannier's words,

then put it aside for later. He preferred to read online rather than ask questions that would sound childlike.

'So is that where you think Helsen went?' he said. 'Delta-ville?'

Tannier said, 'That's the most likely destination, though not definite. She might have configured her flyer for a long haul to Popper or Dalton, maybe further.'

About to ask about the various authorities tracking incoming flyers, Roger stopped, not needing another lecture on privacy. A Pilot was supposed to be sensitive to cultural variations, not keep tripping over them.

'What can I do to help you?' he asked.

Tannier stared at him.

Then: 'For now, rest up with your lady friend, and keep out of sight and trouble. We'll need you to identify Helsen.'

Her theft of the autodoc and flight from Barbour were making Tannier, and by extension the Barbour authorities, take the matter seriously.

'Helsen's made her first tactical mistake,' said Roger. 'Hasn't she?'

'What do you mean? For an offworlder to make such good use of our systems and get clean away ... I call that pretty slick.'

Roger finally smiled.

'Yeah, but if she'd just kept her head down here in Barbour, the most you'd have had is a strange report from a youngish Pilot who sees things that others don't, not even other Pilots. Right?'

'Good point.' Tannier grinned back. 'Except we take all reports from the public with equal seriousness.'

'Sure you do.'

How would Dad have analysed this situation? Imagining yourself in the opponent's position was the usual first strata-gem.

'If Helsen just wanted to hide,' he added, 'she would have kept more low-key, don't you reckon?'

'Go on,' said Tannier.

'So if she's trying for another Anomaly, what resources does she need to gather?' He remembered something Dad had said about categorising problems. 'What people does she need? What technology? And what processes does she have to organize to make it happen?'

'Hmm.' Tannier was nodding. 'Good questions. I'll ask the people with the big brains what they think. So far, Helsen has only one specific objective that a simple copper can deduce.'

Roger said, 'What's that?'

Tannier's voice went mild.

'She seems to want you dead, don't you think?'

Time slowed, in a non-relativistic sense. Three tendays passed while Roger lived with Leeja, enjoying more uninhibited sex than he had thought possible; going for ever-increasing long slow distance runs along Barbour's upper galleries (where yellow-tinted view-windows looked out onto orange clouds and more recently the growing bulk of Deltaville); and regaining his strength and coordination with the combat-dance-acrobatics routines he had used for years, but had stopped more recently since the reality of violence became clear. Now he used the routines to elongate his muscles and keep his movements whippy, without the illusion that they made him a fighter. That, if he was serious about it – and he still had doubts – was something that would surely have to wait until he returned to Labyrinth.

Sometimes he daydreamed of wolves and axes in ways that afterwards were unclear.

In keeping with Pilot practice, he said little to Leeja about life in mu-space, never mentioning Labyrinth's name. Perhaps because of Conjunction, when Molsin's sky-cities came together once every four standard years, Leeja seemed to assume that Pilots lived with their ships clustered together. Roger hinted she was right, without ever telling a literal lie. For the first time, despite having had to hide his own nature as he grew up, he appreciated what Dad (and to some extent Mum) had gone through as they lived a life of subterfuge, interacting with their friends and colleagues on Fulgor through interfaces of deceit, layers of indirection hiding the complexity beneath, much as his tu-ring accessed local city services not knowing how they were implemented.

Once, out walking with Leeja, he spotted Alisha looking into a shop window, a peculiarity of Barbour: back home on Fulgor, shops had existed, but with no need to display their wares to anyone outside – that was what Skein was for. Alisha did not turn; but if she had, she would have seen just another stranger in the crowd.

After they had walked past, Leeja said, 'So that was her, was it?'

Roger stopped, then kissed her. As always, even the lightest contact with her softness felt like absorption, turning into a composite organism in the only manner humans should.

'And that's you,' he said. 'The only woman in my life.'

'I know. But she's young, isn't she? Like you, although you appear older.'

'Maybe because you've worn me out.' Smiling: 'In the nicest possible way.'

'Bad Roger.' She kissed him back. 'Come along.'

But he could feel her sadness as they walked on.

TWENTY

In Labyrinth, time could flow in any way one liked. Max Gould had been awash in pain for so long he perceived it as a single, ongoing instance of agony, the one surprise being the strength that remained in his screams. He was an instrument; suffering was the music; Fleming was the master musician. And now, amid the normal purple lightning, silver light was brightening, which meant that Fleming was coming back.

I still hurt.

How many layers was it now?

Three. No ... seven.

Not good.

Try to remember.

Or perhaps he had already given everything away. The layers upon layers of lies – entire world-views of falsehood laid on top of each other, a sequence of cover stories – were beginning to shift in his mind. But he could not have broken yet, not completely.

Because Fleming continued to bring the pain.

'Commodore.'

Changing his voice now, the bastard.

'Commodore Gould, look at us.'

Us?

Dried blood cracked and wet blood trickled as he moved his head and squinted. A man and a woman, right enough. Fleming's reinforcements.

Bastard.

Everything already hurt. What more was there?

'My name is Clayton. My friend here, we'll keep her name out of it for now.'

Secrets. Everyone had them.

Everyone wanted them.

'Come on.' Hands upon him. 'We're moving you now.'

Flares of agony.

'What have they done to you?' That was the woman. 'Evil *fuckers*.'

He liked her, despite the tidal wash of pain, and that was dangerous.

Silver light, growing.

What are they doing?

Grey and black rotating.

Where—?

The torture cell was gone.

TWENTY-ONE

EARTH, 1941 AD

From the pavement of Baker Street, the building was a massive bone-grey cube lined with blacked-out windows. Inside, it was a hive of orthogonality: square-cross-sectioned corridors and cubic interior rooms: windowless, functional and bleak. This was the headquarters of the Special Overseas Executive, home of code-makers rather than breakers, where even the air felt pressurized; and the stay-at-home executives looked even more strained than the agents getting ready to parachute in to some darkened field to be met by resistance fighters or Wehrmacht bullets; because you never knew, sitting at a radio set in London and listening to enciphered dots and dashes, whether the operator over there in Holland or France had been turned – was sending the signal with a Luger against their temple – or was even German, while the person they had replaced now whimpered in a Gestapo cell or rotted with a hundred other corpses in a pit.

But SOE had cells of their own, and that was where the two enemy agents went: down to the basement, under military guard. Gavriela remained somewhere in the core of the building – every floor and corridor looked the same – standing next to two soldiers, while Rupert Forrester went off to chat to a short civilian, or rather someone not in uniform; for everyone here was some kind of soldier, even her.

They're not going to do anything.

Not to her.

She had no logical grounds for optimism, beyond standing here instead of in a cell like the prisoners; but Rupert had looked at her as a subordinate in need of discipline, not an enemy. Still, she was better at reading codes and ciphers than human beings.

A one-armed man came around the corner and winked at her.

'Brian!' She could not understand why he was here rather than Bletchley. 'What's going on?'

'Well, darling Gabby, I'm feeling relieved' – with a grin – 'that you're on our side after all.'

He had never called her darling before. Tonight he looked like a man who had just tilted a massive rucksack off his back, thought that was it, then been given a heavy box to carry, and was trying to make the best of it.

'The message-within-the-message had a prefix *en clair*,' she said, 'which I happened to recognize. And the rest was a simple monoalphabetic substitution.'

They must have found the decrypt, because of the twenty policemen descending on Trafalgar Square. If they had simply been suspicious of her, there would have been a team of plainclothes watchers, no more. And clearly, from Brian's words, he had been working with Rupert on this.

'Really.'

'You're going to think I'm insane, Brian. Once I've told you how I recognized the prefix, I mean.'

'That's a possibility, I guess. But I think you're sane enough.'

He looked back along the corridor. At the far end, Rupert turned, and for a moment it was like a resonance cavity: some imperative signal bounced back and forth between them, growing stronger. Then Rupert nodded, touched the shoulder of the man beside him, and walked out of sight.

Gavriela wanted to ask about that, and why an SIS officer like Rupert chose to use SOE headquarters, and how long Brian had been watching her; but tonight she had better respond to questions rather than pose them. Curiosity about secret war work, beyond her own remit, could drop her into the kind of trouble she was trying to evade.

He was a friendly interrogator, it turned out.

They used one of the anonymous offices, and she told him quickly what the message said and how she worked through it. He nodded when she mentioned Trafalgar Square and the unknown time, then backtracked.

'So what are these cryptonyms?' he said. 'Eagle and darkness?'

'I'm guessing that one of the two men in the basement, or wherever you've got them, is the eagle. Maybe that's a tattoo on his forearm, or a design on his tie-clip, or something. For identification. Or maybe that's too easy, I don't know. But the darkness . . . that's different.'

She was vibrating inside, sick and scared and elated, on the brink of spilling her personal madness.

'It started when I moved to Zürich,' she said. 'Fourteen years ago, on my first day as a student, although it perhaps reinforced the occasional odd perception from childhood. Or maybe you'll call it hallucination.'

'Hallucination?'

'Yes—'

An endless hour later, a knock sounded and the door swung in. Rupert's face was corpse-white.

'What is it?' said Brian.

'A moment.' Rupert turned, nodded to someone in the corridor outside, and came in. 'I'd like to catch up, if that's OK with you.'

He used his heel to close the door.

'Gabby can, er, see things other people can't,' said Brian. 'Certain individuals are surrounded by a sort of dark aura—'

'Not an optical phenomenon.' Gavriela wanted Rupert to understand. 'It's a psychological artefact, like one of those Benham Tops.'

'Like a what?'

'Sorry. A spinning-top.' So much of her knowledge of people came from textbooks. 'If you spin a certain black-and-white design at the right speed, people see it in vivid colours: red, green, violet. There's no diffraction or refraction involved. It's a neurological effect.'

Brian closed his eyes, smiled as he pushed out a breath, then looked at Rupert.

'See?' he said. 'She comes out with nutty stuff and you have to believe her.'

Rupert frowned at *nutty*, one of those Americanisms he despised.

'And they're good at hypnosis,' Brian went on. 'Or something like that.'

'Who is?' said Rupert.

'The people with the auras. Possessed of demons, or whatever. The darkness.'

'And the two men at the rendezvous?'

Gavriela said, 'They're both tainted with it. I don't know whether "possessed" is the right word, but it might be. The intercept I decrypted used the word, so that much is not delusion.'

'What word?' asked Rupert.

Brian said, '*Dunkelheit.*'

Then he got up from his chair.

'Are you all right, Rupe?'

'Not entirely. Can I–?' Rupert sat down on what had been Brian's chair. 'Look, Gavriela—'

Brian raised his eyebrows. He knew her as Gabby Woods.

'—are you sure about this hypnosis? In fact, didn't you have a book on the subject' – his eyes focused on a remembered image – 'the night we first met in Oxford?'

'Someone had left the book in the pub,' said Gavriela. 'I took it with the barmaid's approval. It made partial sense of the things I'd seen . . . but only partial.'

Rupert rubbed his face, which remained bloodless: white, with the ghost of blue veins.

'That might explain how thirty minutes ago our German guest got away.'

Time seemed to jump: scratched record, gramophone needle; something like that.

'Got *away?*' said Brian. 'From this place?'

Perhaps it was the dungeons that had brought Rupert here rather than Broadway Buildings. But Broadway these days was only nominally SIS HQ, so close to Whitehall, that prime Luftwaffe target. The real headquarters was Bletchley Park, SIS squeezed in with GCHQ, plus the Whaddon Hall outstation down the road.

Such knowledge in her head. They would have to be sure about her, to allow her to leave.

'All right, Gavriela.' Rupert glanced at Brian, then focused on her again. 'Gabby. These hypnotists with the auras – or whatever – *are* Nazis, have I got that right?'

'I . . .' Gavriela stopped. 'It sounds like one of those serials on the wireless, doesn't it? But I really don't know.'

'So are they Nazis?'

'I don't think . . . I think the darkness is something real, and the thousand-year Reich would suit its purpose, but it's not the goal. It . . . I just don't know.'

Rupert said, 'You do make it sound like demonic possession.'

'The only real demons are people in uniform with sick dreams.'

'Fair enough. Bri?'

'She believes it,' said Brian. 'I'm not sure I do, but *Gabby* isn't lying.'

For the first time it occurred to her that the encrypted message might have been left for her to find, that Clive had decrypted it already – hardly difficult, once you realized it was not a misread transmission – and someone had known about the darkness, and the sound associated with it.

'You said the German guest got away.' The analysis could wait, because she was concerned about the remaining prisoner. 'Therefore the other man isn't German – I'm guessing English – and you've still got him.'

'And we have him in a chair, blindfolded and gagged.' Rupert made a half-fist, then flicked his fingernails against the desktop. 'Let's see him use hypnosis like that.'

It felt like hands around her throat, the panic.

'You've got to knock him out,' she said. 'It's the only way.'

'There's no way he—'

Now to find out what they really thought of her.

'Trust me,' she said. 'I'll come down with you.'

'To see the prisoner?' said Rupert.

Brian shook his head.

'In the circumstances—'

'Then go down there yourself, make sure you've got dull, level-headed, suspicious men surrounding him. A lot of them, preferably deaf.' She needed Rupert to be clear. 'You like bright people, I know that, but the more intelligent and imaginative someone is, the *easier* it is for them to go into trance. Only cretins and morons, in the absolute technical sense of the terms, can't be hypnotized.'

Rupert thrust himself up from the chair.

'Time to prove yourself, Dr Wolf.'

A blindfolded man sat in a chair in shirtsleeves, his upper arms bound to the chair's back, his wrists tied to the rear legs. In each corner of the blank room a soldier stood, rifle at port arms.

Gavriela stopped in the doorway, Rupert and Brian behind her. Then the prisoner turned to face her, and smiled a sightless smile.

No!

Four rifle barrels swivelled towards the doorway, aiming at her and Rupert and Brian—

'Ulfr!'

—but Gavriela flung herself low and spinning, hands on the nearest rifle, twisting, leverage and rage her weapons as she hugged the rifle close—

'Ver nær mér, berserkrinn!'

—with maximum torque continuing the spin, whipping out

through the target, hardwood and steel against nothing much, a distant crunch as rotation carried her past—

He's down.

—and the chair had toppled, while bound to it was a thing with a smashed egg attached to a crooked neck: an egg spilling copious yolk, pure red.

'My God,' said Rupert: whether appalled at her violence, or because he realized how close he had come to dying, there was no way to tell.

Three soldiers lowered their weapons; the fourth stared at his empty hands. Did he even remember the dream that had caused him to aim a rifle at his own superior officers? Did any of them?

'Go to your darkness,' Gavriela told the corpse.

She was holding the rifle like a hockey-stick. Slick fluid glistened on the butt.

TWENTY-TWO

Piet Gunnarsson did not deserve realspace sentry duty, not because it was beneath him, but because he was unworthy. Nine subjective day-cycles earlier, he-and-ship had been gliding in the direction of distant Labyrinth, just as the tail end of a massive fleet passed out of sight behind a blood-coloured nebula. He had flown on, ignoring the fleet because of his own travails – including wounds sustained on Sivlix III when a flash riot started around a group of Zajinet traders, during what should have been a simple commercial mission. Allegedly the Zajinets had flared up with strange energies in what someone had thought presaged an attack; in retrospect, the Zajinets fired on no one, evincing panic if anything.

With comms off, Piet had taken a long-duration geodesic, giving himself time to heal from injuries he now considered trivial, in light of the Fulgor Catastrophe. Had he been more alert, more of a true Pilot, he would have flung his ship into a hard curve, thrown all sensors open on maximum gain, and hailed the departing fleet to find out what was going on.

Saving one Fulgidus life would have been worth it. But he might have been able to evacuate hundreds, and he could not forgive himself for missing that.

If there's war, I'll be here.

Fulgor floated before him, no different to the archive holos in *her* memory – his beautiful ship, surrounding him and holding him, trying to comfort him now.

We are *here, doing our part.*

Yes.

Her sensors were fully trained on that hellworld, because

145

however unchanged the planetary chemistry might appear from this distance, the global Anomaly would surely be continuing to grow in strength. Theorists, working from sparse data, speculated on the gestalt mind linking to the nervous systems of other species, perhaps even those native to Fulgor: though ZNA-based, there had been ZNA-DNA hybrids created by human scientists in attempts to blend ecosystems. Subverting the hybrids would enable a transition to full absorption, combining the global web of life into some dark, perverted distortion of what others might call Gaia, but which Piet thought of as Jorth, both planetary goddess and mother of Thórr, himself a duality: war-god yet protector of freemen.

Forget the old myths. Concentrate on the science.

At some point, the new global organism would begin altering the atmospheric composition, so that even archaic spectroscopy might reveal the transformed nature of this once-beautiful world.

You awake, Piet, sweetheart?

That would be Alice, her own ship some three hundred kilometres further out than he was. He smiled as he sent his reply:

All OK. Pass it on.

Will do. Kiss, kiss. Keep alert.

You too, gorgeous.

So there was another reason to forget about boredom and just keep watch, however unchanging the planet before him might appear. If it reached out and got him, then Alice was next in line, and she deserved to live. So he would observe with all his senses – like Heimdall, Watcher of the Gods, from the legends of his ancestors – and report the slightest activity. Even if he-and-ship did not manage to escape, the others might live.

By now, Alice would have passed the still-OK message back along the chain of observing ships. Piet, as the closest, was outside the theoretical range of Calabi-Yau resonance transmitted by the Anomaly; but he had learned early on that the difference between theory and practice is that in theory there is no difference; and everyone knew how that went.

An hour later, nothing had happened, except that Piet had thought of something.

No one's talking about attacking the thing.

All efforts were focused on watching the enemy whose intentions and thoughts – if such concepts were even valid – could not be foretold, arising as emergent properties of a massively complex system unlike any other in existence, at least among the worlds known to humanity.

We're afraid of it.

He had known it all along, but codifying the thought made a difference.

It's the unknown.

Except that there was one aspect everyone knew exactly: from the Anomaly's point of view, humans were less than food, simply microscopic components; while from humanity's position, it was effectively mindless – paradoxically, since its nature was unbelievably transcendent compared to any individual – and therefore a dangerous force of nature, with one added feature.

Total malevolence.

TWENTY-THREE

MOLSIN, 2603 AD

In the midst of the street party, there was Tannier. If Roger had been a spy, then Tannier would have been his handler; at least that was how it seemed to be playing out. Barbour's police force numbered a thousand personnel, according to the public info services: a small number considering the size of the city; but this was a peaceful place with educated citizens. So if Tannier kept cropping up, it was because someone had assigned him to the role.

A group of older men and women, dressed in primary-coloured tunics, were dancing in a sprightly, coordinated way, the choreography intricate, the music too low-pitched for Roger to enjoy. The clothing hurt his eyes. Tannier circled them, a tankard in his hand, heading this way.

'Leeja.' Roger squeezed her hand with care. 'Here's the policeman I told you about.'

'Where?' Streamers flickered past overhead, distracting her. 'Oh. The hard-faced man with the smokebeer?'

'I guess.' There *was* a pale cloud rising from Tannier's tankard. 'Scar below his left eye.'

'Mm.' Leeja squeezed his wrist. 'I don't like him.'

'Er ...' Dad had always insisted on trusting intuition. 'I do, actually.'

'No, I mean ... He looks at home with danger. I don't want you hanging around with him.'

Who are you, my mother? But that was the one thing Roger could never say, not with the age difference. Then Tannier was in front of them, smiling, fumes rising from his tankard.

'Smells pretty bad,' said Roger. 'The drink, I mean. This is

Leeja. And this is ... I don't know your first name.'

'I'm just Tannier. Ma'am. Pleased to meet you.'

'Likewise, Officer. I admire the work you people do.'

'Thank you.' Tannier raised the tankard as though her words had been warm. 'It's always good to hear someone say that and mean it.'

Leeja leaned into Roger's side.

'Honestly? I'm scared of what you do,' she said. 'You're brave to do it, but please leave Roger out of your world.'

Tannier pointed to a deserted balcony, high up, close to the concave, over-decorated ceiling. 'Private talk? The three of us?'

'All right,' said Roger.

Leeja's two arms encircled his right, like twin serpents wrapped in a helix.

What am I doing to her?

The floor cupped beneath them, twisted, and carried them up on a curving stalk. The balcony folded back to receive its three new occupants. When they alighted, the long stalk sucked back down to the main thoroughfare and disappeared. Soon the street party had spread to cover that area of floor.

'Not long till the birth.' Tannier looked down at the crowd. 'The party will really kick into life then.'

How many of Fulgor's refugees were going to feel like celebrating anything?

'That's nice.' Roger looked at the lines in Leeja's face. 'We mostly wanted to spend time by ourselves. Quietly.'

Instead of answering, Tannier turned to stare along the broadway below. After seven seconds, by Roger's infallible time sense, a series of giant holovolumes sprang into life above the crowd, each showing the same scene from varying angles, all centring on the long, complex shape of Deltaville. Across her dorsal surface, waves of streamers fluttered, while tiny attendant vessels floated in clouds around her, particularly towards the aft end, where even in the holos, the city's quickglass showed waves of vibration, the ripples of impending birth.

'The thing is' – Tannier had turned back to face them – 'there's a city lottery in progress which you might have heard about. Two lucky winners get ferried across to Deltaville, to the posh celebrations. In the company of two of Barbour's finest and richest political types.'

This meant nothing to Roger; but Leeja's hand, holding his, began to vibrate.

'Posh dinners, all very formal,' Tannier went on. 'And, like, watched by everyone. Broadcast here and Deltaville especially.'

He nodded towards the giant holos.

'We haven't entered a lottery,' said Roger.

'Well' – Tannier's scar twisted when he smiled – 'that's funny, because you and I are about to win it.'

Roger did what Dad would have wanted. He drew his somatic awareness inside, concentrating on proprioception and balance, centring himself. He exercised minute control, conscious of the curved horizontal sheet of muscle that was his diaphragm, the complex chained interplay of intercostals expanding his ribs.

Calm.

Breathing happens under conscious deliberation or while asleep, to equal effect; hence the importance of those neural pathways for mental control: the bridge from conscious to subconscious thought, to the myriad nuanced perceptions normally lost to the civilized mind.

What's going on here?

Someone's complex game of strategy was touching his life – except that where it impinged on him, it was really quite simple, wasn't it?

'A Judas goat,' said Roger. 'That would be me, wouldn't it? Tied up and bleating, far too tempting for a hunter to ignore.'

'You can't go along with this,' said Leeja. 'Roger, you can't.'

The voice in his throat felt alien. 'Without Helsen, my parents and billions of people would be alive.'

Tannier's eyes were hardened by whatever mental images they saw.

'If she plans to do the same thing here, stopping her will save lives. Including yours, ma'am.'

'Then give Roger an implant.' Leeja gestured, and the quick-glass balcony floor sprouted tiny stalks, rippling in a virtual breeze. 'Something to make him less out of his depth.'

Was that how she saw him?

'He's not a citizen,' said Tannier. 'Naturalized or otherwise. Under the circumstances, implantation would be ... irregular. Actually, illegal.'

'Not like running a lottery whose result is fixed, then?'

Tannier's face clenched in a muscular grin.

'I'll be back in an hour,' he said. 'Or better ... Roger, I'll meet you at Mass Centre.'

'OK.'

The one place anyone could find was the city's centre of mass.

'See you.'

Tannier backed away and the balustrade melted. As he toppled, his body held straight, a quickglass tendril took hold and swung him down.

The balcony reformed.

'It may not be for ever' – party lights, reflected, were sparkling in her tears – 'but we have a choice in how we say goodbye.'

'What ... do you mean?'

'We can do it here and now, a clean break. Or back home and ... gradual. Like weaning off each other, or something.'

Roger stood close, put his hands on her lower back, pulling in.

'Home,' he said.

'Yes, my love.'

It was to be the longest, tenderest climb to weeping orgasm.

Mass Centre was a ten-metre hollow sphere, a complex con-cavity lined with baroque mathematical terracotta, while in the centre hung a three-way cruciform sculpture delineating vertical, vertebral and transverse axes. Compared to the immense bulk of the ever-morphing city, the sphere was the tiniest of bubbles, kept in position at the centre of gravity, the origin for every location reference. Outside the sphere, connecting corridors formed short arcs between linear thoroughfares: often used as meeting points, deserted today save for a few furtive couples.

Roger circumnavigated the place at several levels – you had to keep making switchbacks and cross-overs: there were no circular routes, only short linking corridors – with no sign of Tannier and no response to his tu-ring signal. Finally, he entered a corridor arc that was otherwise unoccupied, determined to make one more circular pass before giving up; then he stopped as both ends of the corridor sealed up, forming an isolated chamber.

It was the interior wall that melted open, revealing Tannier in the spherical central space, with the cruciform shape hanging behind him.

'Come inside,' he said. 'Not many people get a chance to see it.'

If Roger lived here, perhaps this would be a major deal, a highpoint of his life. When he stepped into the spherical chamber, he was impressed but not stunned; or perhaps he was simply worried, wondering what would happen next.

They were standing, he and Tannier, on part of the terracotta-like pattern of the curved wall. Tannier found a convenient protrusion to sit down on, and gestured for Roger to do the same nearby.

'All right,' said Roger. 'Does this mean we're waiting for something?'

'Your lady friend made a request, and I'm carrying it out. I like her, by the way.'

'Request? Oh, shit. What was that about an implant?'

The block he sat on had already absorbed his legs, wrapping them in solid quickglass.

'There's no need to hold still,' said Tannier. 'Or rather, there is, but *it'* – he slapped the block he sat on – 'will handle everything.'

Quickglass encircled Roger's torso, banded tight around upper chest and hips, but allowed him to breathe. Then it reached his neck, cupped his chin, and hardened around his jawbone, holding his head in place.

The insertion was a pinprick in the back of his neck.

Cold, the slithering quickglass.

As it reached up into his cerebellum, he closed his eyes, going deep inside himself, beyond the neurosomatic discipline open to every human being, to a mode only a Pilot could experience: the thrum of inductive neurons, resonating now with the quickglass nerve-analogues.

There was a point he would not go beyond.

Complete neural integration requires two-way flows. Visual information propagates forward in the skull, from the parietal lobes at the rear to the cerebrum at the front; yet most of the neural flow points *backwards*, in tight reverse loops. Adding a new control-system modality opened up Roger's brain to potential manipulation – but only if he allowed it.

Got you.

He burned out portions of the major two-way bridge as it formed between the sensor-lobes (newly created in his brain) and the control circuits of his cerebellum. Only someone who was both a Pilot and a product of Fulgor's intensive, neuroware-dominated education system – where so many had aspired to upraise, to become Luculenti – could have reconfigured such an implant as it occurred. As the quickglass restraints flowed away, he opened his eyes and nodded to Tannier.

'Very kind of you,' he said.

The big holoviews above the arcade showed Roger and Tannier taking in the applause, touching fists with the lottery hosts and then hugging them, before waving to the crowds and pointing to the golden starburst trophies they held as symbols of their prize: the trip to Deltaville's official celebrations, to take place as soon as the birth happened.

None of this had occurred in reality.

Maybe they could have faked everything.

As Roger and Tannier, amid the partying crowd, watched their pseudo-selves overhead, Roger wondered whether he could have stayed with Leeja while the authorities created a virtual bait for Helsen, rather than risking him for real. But Helsen might not rely on public info feeds if she were hunting him. The more succulent the bait, the more effective the trap.

'There they are,' said Tannier. 'The rest of our party.'

'Oh, please.'

Roger had thought his own formal clothing ridiculous, but on the golden dais by the view-window, a woman was dressed in a sweeping confection of dark-blue and gold, her massive coiffure wound through with gold thread and winking holo stars. The man beside her, in his diamond-encrusted surcoat and silver-dominated trews, would have stood out anywhere else. He looked relaxed, not caring that the woman had eclipsed him.

'She's Rhianna Chiang,' said Tannier. 'Socialite and artist. Well, mostly socialite. And that's Faubourg, no other name. Everyone knows who he is.'

'Like Tannier, then,' said Roger.

'Apart from me being unknown and not a fop, yeah.'

Roger looked from Tannier's callused knuckles to his facial scar.

'La-di-dah,' he said. 'You think Helsen's not going to notice you?'

'What are the chances,' said Tannier, 'that you'd win this lottery fair and square?'

She would know he was a Judas goat. Of course she would.

'So if she comes after me, it'll be all-out, with some devastating attack.'

'Probably. Right now, it's show-time.'

Tannier led the way to the dais, where they climbed up, and

someone in scarlet uniform made the introductions – Roger, Tannier, and of course this is Rhianna, and you'll know who Faubourg is, naturally – while the quickglass surroundings recorded everything for the public's viewing pleasure.

'Look.' Rhianna pointed to the great view-window. 'Did you see?'

A massive tidal ripple swept along the length of Deltaville, floating a kilometre away. Then another. The crowd's voice became a sort of hum, low but strong, then raised in pitch as quickglass split from quickglass, and the complex-but-roughly-spherical rearmost mass changed colour, reddening, beginning to pull from the mother city.

Outside the view-window, a promenade extended, a finger pointing into the void. A thin yellowish film covered it, transforming the extrusion into an elongated pavilion. Rhianna slipped her arm through Roger's, while Faubourg did the same with Tannier – Roger forced himself not to laugh – and they walked through the liquefying window and into the promenade, just the four of them. They walked right to the end – which later, presumably, would form a docking-point with Deltaville – to watch the birth unfold.

Glancing back at Barbour's upper hull, Roger saw streamers and pennants and tendrils flicking their teardrop-ends through an intricate choreography. It took a moment to realize that each teardrop contained a dancer or an acrobat, pinpoints of humanity against the city's vastness.

'Sky Dance,' murmured Rhianna. 'Very nice.'

All around Deltaville, a profusion of towers clenched, the great mass rippling and convulsing, pushing hard.

'Isn't it beautiful?' said Faubourg.

The corner of Rhianna's mouth twitched. Perhaps her true thoughts were like Roger's: that Deltaville's giving birth looked painful, an extended agony of effort, the sort of process that felt wonderful only in the aftermath, when everything was over. When everyone was partying, letting down their hair.

Letting down their guard.

TWENTY-FOUR

While Gavriela remained asleep, she awoke to that other reality, the one that would slip from consciousness in that long-past morning to follow, imprinted only in her subconscious mind, in the molecular depths of her mortal brain.

As always, the hall was airless, and she adapted to vacuum without thought as she swung her living-crystal legs down from the bier and stood. She checked the axes, spears and shields on the walls, and the pinpoints of light glowing below the ceiling. All was unchanged.

There were sounds as she walked through to the greater hall, but only the natural sounds from within her. She stopped at the entrance to the corridor leading to the external balcony, where she might stand and stare at the moonscape. But Ulfr and Kenna were seated at the conference table in their high-backed chairs, and they were looking at her, their crystalline faces glittering.

Kenna tilted her head.

—*You are most welcome, Gavi, though unsummoned.*

—*Unsummoned?*

—*Not summoned by me. Brave Ulfr and I are exploring the concept of contingent battle plans. Perhaps you are drawn to it.*

Spectra shifted inside Ulfr's shaking head.

—*Or maybe you've come to say thank you.*

—*I . . .*

—*But I enjoyed it, however brief, sweet Gavi.*

She held herself in stasis, trying to bring forward those memories of a half-million years ago; and then she smiled.

—*You were with me when I called, berserker. You have all my thanks, in truth.*

—*Any time.*

All three smiled rainbow smiles.

Then Gavriela walked to the table where complex phase spaces hung in dozens of orthogonal projected realities. A part of her – the part that had absorbed hundreds of millennia of strategy training – understood the problem they were trying to solve: given that no plan survives contact with the enemy, how do you plan for *that*?

With sheaves of alternatives that can be chosen in an instant, was one answer.

She examined the attacking forces.

—*A thousand billion of them, striking at once?*

Ulfr made a fist; but Kenna put her hand on it, and looked up at Gavriela.

—*We need the small-scale simulation first, before planning for the real thing.*

In apology, Gavriela put her own fist against her collar-bone.

—*I beg your pardon. Of course you do.*

For they had half a million years, still, before the end.

TWENTY-FIVE

EARTH, 1941 AD

It was a sound once associated with the limbo of factory work, empty and impersonal; now it signified the imminence of incandescent hell. Moaning strongly, then low, then strong again, the siren's sound resonated along the buildings. Gavriela held still, Brian's one arm around her back, as they stopped opposite Madame Tussaud's and looked to see where people were headed. The flow towards Baker Street Tube was already starting.

She could not hear them yet, the killers above the clouds; but then, was she so different? Gavriela Wolf with blood on her hands once more. Debriefing, she had said nothing about the Gestapo men she murdered in Berlin; but in the SOE cellar, Rupert and Brian had seen her every action. For her the moment had been confusion, a swirling of stroboscopic vision and physical motion, glimpses of the riflemen interspersed with blood-red nothingness; and then the corpse below her, and the wet slickness on the rifle butt. It was lucky that Rupert, sharp despite the danger, had interpreted the situation exactly: the prisoner having mesmerised his guards, causing them to turn on their own superiors; Gavriela entering *berserkrgangr* to save the day.

I did what?

But Brian was shaking her arm.

'Come on.'

'What?'

'Down the Tube, come *on.*'

Past banked sandbags, down metal-edged stairs, spherical lights a soft glow atop bronze stands, the glazed-tile walls wet with cold, condensed sweat, and down on the sooty platforms, the blanket-wrapped crowd sitting and lying, frail humans huddling and waiting for destruction to fall overhead. As always, every space near the exits was full, so they pushed and slipped among their fellow beings, eventually to reach a shadow-wrapped alcove, shared with a water-filled extinguisher. Somewhere around the corner, a child and an older person were weeping.

Why can't it ever stop?

She pressed against Brian, and he against her, his arm tight.

'It's all right,' he said. 'You did the right thing, and we're proud of you.'

Closing her eyes did not shut out the redness; neither weeping nor sirens could obliterate the thud of wood through skull.

I'm not a killer.

Except that in science she believed in operational definitions, and if someone who killed was not a killer, then what were they? But now, despite her insulating coat, here was an interruption to her guilt: Brian's manhood pressing against her, as her crotch grew warm.

No. Oh, no.

She had had so little to do with men, but she was scared and so was he – poor Brian, with demons of his own to fight, the loss of his arm among them – and then they were kissing, tongue against tongue, and it was urgent: the unbuttoning of heavy coats, wrapped around each other as they stood; fingers against skin, rough against nipples, the ripping of her knickers, the fumbling of her fingers unbuttoning his fly; and then he was in her, hard, thrusting, harder, and her fingers were like claws, nails like talons in his skin, pushing and hauling and wanting the hurt, needing the pain, forcing it, needing it to—

Oh. Oh.

—explode inside her, and she could not hold down the whimper and neither could he; but no one remonstrated or even showed they noticed; because this was wartime and life was ephemeral and things could change in an instant; and now they had.

She felt him slip out of her.

Brian.

Wet and slick against her thigh.

Morio was Dmitri's seventh male lover among the High Command, or rather the ultra-nationalists who held such strong positions there. Today's half-brutal intercourse had followed a bout of archery – shooting live dogs in snow-covered Shibiya Park, one of Morio's favoured methods for hardening his warrior spirit. Then he announced he was being sent to China.

'This time, we will crush Changsha,' he said.

'I'm sure you will,' said Dmitri.

The Chinese had held out against the previous two onslaughts; but in the wake of Pearl Harbor, Japanese determination was renewed.

'They declared war!' Morio's face was red with booze and outrage. 'War!'

'How dare they,' said Dmitri.

How dare they honour their international treaties, as they've always done? How dare they declare war on Germany and on Japan, which has been striking inside their borders for a decade, treating the population, women especially, with all the regard Morio showed Shibiya's dogs?

'When I come back, we will have much celebration.'

'Why wait?' said Dmitri.

But Morio lay back on the cushions, breath whistling in his nostrils, until his mouth dropped open and his snoring became an impression of a pig snuffling in mud.

So Changsha is under threat again.

It would be the last piece of news to be passed on via his existing courier network, before he boarded the ship for Germany. His cover had been deepened by Soviet agents in Berlin, so that he now had an opportunity to penetrate further;

or perhaps his masters were being kinder than usual, removing him from a zone made increasingly dangerous for westerners since General Tojo had replaced the civilian Konoye government with his own military cabinet.

Morio thought the world had changed last month, on the 7th of December; but for Dmitri, the turning point had occurred the day before, when General Georgi Zhukov flung 100 fresh divisions – infantry, the near-indestructible T-34 tanks, cavalry and artillery: seven army corps and two cavalry corps – against a shocked Wehrmacht army already worn down by mud then snow. No one, not the Abwehr or Hitler himself, had suspected the existence of such a force.

I may be a country boy at heart, but Moscow is my city.

They were élite divisions, Zhukov's forces, and they had been stationed on the border with Japanese-occupied Manchuria, guarding against the threat from Imperial Nihon ... until Dmitri's report informed Moscow that the Japanese were directing all of their attention against an American naval base, and the Pacific arena was about to explode into warfare.

So Mother Russia had vented her wrath at last, breaking the myth of the Wehrmacht's invincibility.

Are you shocked by my treachery?

But the darkness in his mind did not respond.

From her room in Swiss Cottage, as Gavriela peeked out from between the blackout curtains, only a small, broken garden and the back of another house were visible. But snowflakes were drifting, some curling back up, and snow lay like bunched loaves atop the garden wall, luminescent in the grey dawn light, while a thin layer obscured the soil, save for circles like bullet holes where clumps of defiant grass broke through.

She looked back at the one-armed man sleeping in her bed. When the landlady found out, she would no doubt throw them out; but she, Gavriela, was supposed to return to Bletchley today, while Brian had his own lodgings near Cambridge Circus.

How do I feel?

The world had turned cold and strange, and something else had changed: some new purpose forming inside her, whose nature she did not know, not yet.

Outside, the snowfall clenched, thickening and uncaring.

TWENTY-SIX

THE WORLD, 5563 AD

After a ninenight of planning, Harij was ready to break her out. When everyone in the town was asleep – even old Farkil, the daywatchman who guarded the fungal farms – he passed the shell-dome homes of those who lived close to the school, then stopped at the entrance.

Far above, on the cavern ceiling, glowfungus glimmered.

He teased apart the laminae of the locks, his flux control better than he managed in class; then he was inside, at the shielded door that led to the special dormitory, where Ilara and the others like her slept. This door locked from the outside, and opened the same way.

Ilara. Wake up. We're going for a walk.

Not time not time not time not time not—

Shh. Hold it in. Hold it in.

**HOLD IN. IN. In. In . . . **

She damped her flux emissions, curled them inside herself. He touched the polished silver of her face.

Good girl. With me, now.

Ilara trusted him, that was the thing.

This way.

Hand in hand, they passed out of the school, skirted the glimberry patches, and left the town proper, climbing the long scree slope that led to the outside. In an alcove at the top, where natural minerals twisted ambient flux into painful, intense knots, Harij reached inside – silver lips pulling back from his teeth: it had not hurt this much before – then dragged out three large sacks.

He covered himself and Ilara with hooded robes, slung the

foodsacks over his shoulder, and took Ilara's hand once more.

We can't go far in daylight, but we can make a little distance.

In. In. In.

So trust me, sister. Trust me.

They went out into the burning.

This was the beginning of the long trek, travelling when daylight was least searing, only switching to normal habits on the third night, when they were far enough away that no one would spot them. When Harij told her to, Ilara ate an algal wafer or drank from a sweetmilk sac. The only trouble he had was when she would stop, her attention taken by an oddly shaped stone or a scuttling tripion, and rock herself back and forth a thousand times before continuing.

At those times, he reminded himself of the old story, [[The Strongest Dreamlode]], and told himself he was doing the right thing.

Once, after they had stopped only when the sun was white-hot, he slept deeply and did not wake up until the night was far gone. He found Ilara bumping her head against a rock, over and over – insistent though not hard – while the silver-and-black glory of Magnus hung directly overhead like an omen. He placed his hand between her forehead and the rock, and kept it there until she stopped.

Seven thousand nine hundred and thirteen, tastes like a glimberry.

Very good, Ilara. That's nice. Shall we go on now?

Yes.

Across the mesa, they walked.

They journeyed until the sweetmilk and myobread were gone, and only a few algal wafers remained at the bottom of one flapping, near-empty sack. Harij cast everywhere as he walked and as he slept, without the faintest taste of the resonance he sought.

He had killed Ilara, along with himself.

I'm sorry, sister. I'm sorry.

She squeezed his hand, but her eyes were burned shut, and she could barely stumble on. Her skin was cracked and flaky, shiny no more.

He had been so sure the resonance lay in this direction.

Through here. The gap.

A broken outcrop stood before them, showing a fang-shaped opening they might be able to crawl inside. The night was ending, and soon the scorching would begin.

Their last day, surely.

He pulled her in with him, held her close, and slipped too easily into sleep.

When the night was at its coolest, something blasted in his mind.

IT'S ALL RIGHT, HARIJ!

He winced, trying to focus.

What?

YOU FOUND THE DREAMLODE. IT'S RIGHT BENEATH US, SWEET BROTHER. WAKE UP! WAKE UP!

Her words pulled him into the waking world.

Ilara? Ilara!

Was this her real voice, the flux contained inside her for so long, the thoughts imprisoned in her damaged mind? The potential Ilara made real?

Where are you?

EVERYWHERE, BROTHER.

He could not see her, though her words pounded through him.

WHAT YOU SEEK IS FURTHER BACK. SEE?

Crawling, hurting everywhere but not caring, he hauled himself deeper inside the crack; and finally he found her. Found *it*, the thing that once had housed her.

IT WAS ONLY FLESH.

Her body, blackened and cracked, desiccated to oblivion. But if that was Ilara, who was this?

Dreamlode. This is a dreamlode?

But he could sense it now, as he revived: deep thrumming resonance, a vast hidden seam of crystal below.

WE'RE FINE NOW, ALL OF US.

All?

WE UNDERSTAND BEING TRAPPED. BUT IDENTITY IS SUCH A FRAGILE CONCEPT.

Some of the flux was redolent of Ilara – of the stunted, unable-to-express-herself Ilara – but some of it tasted ancient; and some it was mere Ideas, snagged by chance, captured from the winds of flux.

Need to go . . . Home.

YES. YOU MUST, HARIJ. GO HOME.

But he could not carry her body all that way.

LEAVE THE FLESH-THING. SAVE YOURSELF.

There were algal wafers he had saved for her.

BEAR LEFT DOWN THE RAVINE AS YOU LEAVE, AND YOU WILL FIND A SPIKER BUSH. IT WILL SUSTAIN YOU FOR A TIME.

Leave . . .

YOU MUST LEAVE, HARIJ. YOU MUST.

I need to . . .

YOUR THOUGHTS ARE TOO TEMPTING, SO FRAGILE AND DELICIOUS. DO NOT TORTURE US MORE, OR WE WILL NO LONGER HOLD BACK.

I don't . . .

But he did understand, even in this pain-wracked state.

I love you, Ilara.

WE LOVE YOU ALSO, BUT GO.

He dragged himself out of the gap.

Harij found the purple spiker bush where the dreamlode mind had told him to look. He sucked on creamy nectar, and broke off leaves to carry with him. Then he worked out which direction to walk in, which way to begin his journey home.

To the punishment he needed the town to give him.

TWENTY-SEVEN

LABYRINTH, 2603 AD (REALSPACE-EQUIVALENT)

Silvermead swirled in Max's throat, luxurious and sweet, while the feel of clean clothes against bathed skin was an equal pleasure, along with the lack of pain in his healing body. His chair enveloped him like a soft throne, and the chamber was configured to cosy dimensions, lacking only a fireplace to turn it into a Victorian sitting-room.

Smartfluids threaded the hypodermic layers, giving him the appearance of scarlet veins; while seams and capillaries of the stuff enwrapped his organs, webbed the connective tissues of permysium, enomysium and epimysium, and threaded his muscle fibres: healing, building, repairing. He was under no illusion about the lack of pain: his rehab was just beginning.

'I regret we've never worked together.' Pavel Karelin's chair had morphed into a formal, minimalist design. 'Your reputation is the highest.'

'Still,' said Max, 'I know who you are.'

Clayton and Clara stood by the wall, clearly the junior members here.

'Likewise,' Max went on, 'I know who Ms James reports to.'

'Then you'll know the risk I'm running,' said Clara.

'I'm grateful for the rescue, if that's what this is.'

No one asked: what else could it be? The truth was, their operational lives existed in a medium of interpretation, of facts-as-tools, illusions within illusions; and this could so easily be an interrogation taken to a new phase, rendering the subsequent torture devastating.

'Give us something to justify our trouble,' said Pavel. 'That's all I'm asking for.'

'I told your two officers how Admiral Kaltberg behaved that day. She came to my office under compulsion, with a graser pistol that part of her brain tried to turn on me.'

To see a Pilot burn out half her own cerebral cortex was a landmark in a life of disturbing events beyond the norm.

'But you said the pistol was set to explode anyway,' said Pavel. 'So why bother?'

'Insurance, in case I had a bolt-hole. Which of course I did. I regret I couldn't drag her through with me.'

Whether these people believed him or not, Admiral Adrienne Kaltberg had been the finest Pilot he had ever served with.

'Accepting this as truth, provisionally,' said Pavel, 'who might have implanted such a compulsion in her mind?'

It was time to let them have some point of information, or clam up entirely and wait for the next stage.

'Admiral Kaltberg was due to retire shortly.' Max could not tell if this was news to Pavel, but the other two blinked. 'I believe she had been to see Dr Sapherson.'

'Mother*fucker*,' said Clayton.

Everyone looked at him.

'Sorry,' he added. 'Is my bias showing?'

Pavel said, 'Sapherson will have been acting under orders. That should be clear.'

Clara crossed her arms.

'So why don't we ask her nicely about that?'

'Yeah,' said Clayton. 'Very fucking nicely.'

'Enough,' said Pavel. 'So, Commodore. Assume we find that an amnesia-induction session turned into something different. That's a single datum. What else can you give us?'

Max shook his head.

'All right,' Pavel went on. 'How about this? Clayton went through one of Dr Sapherson's sessions because of something he learned talking to Carl Blackstone. Later, both he and Clara were part of the group who debriefed young Roger Blackstone, your dead officer's son.'

'My *what?*'

But this referred to events that took place while Max was in his bolt-hole, a hidden layer of reality. He had finally come out in the midst of unexpected crowds on Borges Boulevard, showing all the trappings of a state occasion, but with no time to absorb details before officers descended, whirling him through a fastpath rotation into imprisonment.

'Let me explain,' said Pavel. 'And afterwards, you might reciprocate by explaining what you know about this darkness that only a father and son could see. A darkness related to a prisoner locked up for what appears to be years.'

Meaning it was hard for Max, held and interrogated in secret, to claim the moral high ground. He had done the same to others.

Because I had to.

The traditional excuse for evil.

'Tell me about Carl,' he said.

TWENTY-EIGHT

Amid the burning clouds of Molsin, Deltaville was giving birth. The emerging sky-city was called D-2, but only for now. When she had gained inhabitants and developed a culture of her own, a process that might take three standard years or thirty, she would receive a new name by consensus, gaining true identity.

Now, she popped free.

'D-2 is born!'

Cheers resounded through Deltaville. An anxious team of urban-birth scientists would be aboard D-2 – the public holocasts were not privy to that process – but the focus of holoviews and partying people was the crescendo of celebration overtaking the mother city. In every hall and gallery, every corridor and colonnade, arcade and promenade, abstract holos burst in chaotic colours, while people jumped on the spot, waving their arms, and the quickglass beneath their feet and all around them hummed like a thousand choirs and orchestras, in a heart-rending composition created in the moment. Deltaville was singing of joy and proud fulfilment.

While Roger could not wait for it to end.

TWENTY-NINE

LABYRINTH, 2603 AD (REALSPACE-EQUIVALENT)

Max stared at the trio – Pavel, Clayton and Clara – still not knowing who they were: rescuers and allies, or creatures of the darkness ready to torture him once more.

Time to trust someone.

He put down his empty goblet and, sustained by the silvermead, considered all he had been told and all he had deduced.

'If there were a single person behind this,' he said to Pavel, 'then who would it be?'

'Whatever's going on, it's too complex to be an individual's doing.'

'Agreed,' said Max. 'But hypothetically ... If there's a network with a single person ultimately in charge, who are we talking about here?'

Pavel looked at Clara and Clayton.

'You brought them into this,' added Max. 'They need to know as much as I do.'

'I don't think anyone knows as much you do,' said Pavel, attacking the ambiguity.

'Wordplay aside,' said Max, 'if you were to turn Mr Clayton here on Dr Sapherson, and then she spills what she knows about clandestine orders, so you follow the trail back, all the way ... where does it end?'

For all the warm decor, the room seemed hard-edged and cold.

Clara said: 'We're talking about Admiral Schenck, aren't we?'

Clayton looked surprised – Max interpreted this as ignorance of Admiralty Council affairs – while Pavel was giving nothing away.

'That's one interpretation,' he said.

Max looked at him.

Time to change your perspective.

Because it was now an issue of trust; and it was Clayton and Clara who were questioning Pavel's unstated thinking, while implicitly accepting Max. That was what happened when you played mind games with someone who had lived in the secret world for so long. Then Pavel smiled.

'I heard you were brilliant, Commodore. Even so, I think people underestimate you.'

'And the name you were thinking of is—?'

Pavel nodded to Clara.

'Admiral Boris Schenck, then,' he said. 'Clara is right.'

'Good,' said Max. 'I agree.'

All four of them stared at each other. They had just declared the most powerful person on the Admiralty Council to be an enemy of Labyrinth.

'We can't move against someone like Schenck,' said Clayton. 'For one thing, it's treason.'

'You know the counter-argument to that,' said Max. 'It's an old one.'

'Not if we win?' Clara smiled.

'Exactly.'

THIRTY

EARTH, 1941 AD

They met in the cellar, Erik and Ilse and the group they had
joined, seven strong including them. Tonight, for the first time,
Gérard had brought in the new recruit they had been discussing
for weeks: André Wahlberg, originally Belgian, an employee
of a pancake house here in Utrecht since two months before
the Wehrmacht tanks rolled in.

'Hello, Erik,' said Wahlberg, holding out his hand. 'Good to
meet everyone, finally.'

Erik forced his expression to remain businesslike even as
he shook hands, despite the flickers of darkness that moved
impossibly around Wahlberg's head like some satanic halo.

'We could do with some drinks to celebrate.' Erik made his
way over to Ilse. 'Could you go up to the kitchen and get that
schnapps I hid?'

'I . . . yes. If you want me to.'

Damn it, she was going to give the game away. But then
Ilse's face blanked out, and he kissed her.

Run now, my darling.

She nodded, and made her way up the steps. Once out of
sight, she would have to move fast.

Gérard said, 'We've made up a new batch of leaflets. We
need to think about whether to place them around the Old
Town again, or go further afield.'

Wahlberg was smiling in a way that Erik did not like.

You're a creature of the darkness. Are you a Nazi too?

The one other man he had met like this, Dmitri Shtemenko,
had been a Bolshevik agent who had saved Gavriela's life – his
sister, who might be alive or dead and he would never know.

'Leaflets.' Wahlberg's expression was half-smile, half-sneer. 'I thought this group did more than leave seditious bits of paper lying around.'

'It's a bullet in the head regardless,' said Gérard.

Wahlberg was holding Erik's stare.

'Kill him,' said Erik, addressing Gérard.

'What?'

But a crash from upstairs meant the opportunity had passed. Boots clattered, louder as they neared the cellar stairs.

Knowing exactly which way to come.

They had breakfast in a Lyons Tea House in Kilburn where noise bounced off the ceiling in the steamy atmosphere, filled with the cheerful clatter of cutlery and the chatting of the clientele; and if it were not for the tape criss-crossing the windows and the number of people in uniform, you might have thought it was peacetime.

Rupert sat with his legs crossed. Brian had pushed his chair a little way back from the table. Gavriela tried to read the unspoken context of their conversation before her arrival, and failed. From the questions they had asked in debriefing, Brian had not known about the message that she had decrypted, but Rupert possibly had. Did that mean it had been planted for her to act on?

Alone with Brian, there had been no discussion of her actions, beyond his comforting her in the aftermath of shock. And the lovemaking, rough and urgent and a surprise to them both.

'Last night's shenanigans,' said Rupert now, 'weren't what anyone expects, not here.'

Their language had to remain oblique, because of eaves-droppers; but they were far enough from Baker Street that no SOE personnel were likely to be here, and Gavriela thought that was deliberate.

'Am I in trouble?' What she wanted to ask was, were they were going to arrest her? 'Because of what happened?'

Brian's face tightened. She hoped it meant he would fight her cause.

'Considering what you prevented,' said Rupert, 'you're a heroine, and that's exactly how you'll be described in our reports.'

She did not feel like a heroine. Nor did she imagine his report mentioned hypnosis of a kind that no psychologist would recognize. But so long as the four guards were not blamed, she did not see how twisting the truth could matter, not in a file that few people would ever read.

'Too bad we got nothing from the blighter.' Rupert shrugged his elegant shoulders. 'But *nostra culpa*, not yours, don't you see?'

'Gabby did a good job.' Brian's pale face began to colour. 'More than anyone could expect.'

'Indeed.' Now the raised eyebrow. 'I believe that's what I just said.'

Rupert's manner was beginning to annoy Gavriela, but she quelled the feeling. If this was provocation, it was likely to be deliberate. Bletchley Park had its share of chess grandmasters, but Rupert played all of life as if it were a game.

'And this is not the first such person' – Rupert's searchlight gaze swung to her – 'you've come across, is that right?'

'There was a man called Dmitri in Berlin, as I told Brian. Plus a Nazi rabble-rouser, once.'

She did not want to say anything about the man's identity, partly because she needed Rupert to believe her sane, partly because she did not want to give the appearance of an excuse to a murderous psychotic whose power derived from a conscious understanding of mass psychology and practised oratory as much as inductive hallucination. Or so she believed.

'So they're not all Nazis, then.' Rupert pronounced it in the Churchillian manner: *nah-zees*. 'Are you saying they've an agenda of their own? Or are they separate individuals who just happen to manifest similar odd attributes?'

Gavriela blinked. So did Brian.

He's taking it seriously.

You would think Rupert had considered this over an extended period of time. Then again, he would have studied Nazi mysticism, to the extent that it drove the regime's plans for conquest.

'I don't know,' she said. 'Separate, I think ... But it's a feeling, no more.'

'Well, regardless.' Rupert lowered his voice. 'I'm driving to BP this morning. I'll give you a lift.'

Brian said, 'There's no way I can get back, with this thing I'm seconded to.' He looked at Gavriela. 'I'll see you next week, most likely.'

'I'll ... see you then.'

Did she want to kiss him? In public, without Rupert's presence, she thought the answer might have been yes. As it was, her movements felt shut down, her body tight.

As they left the tea-house, both men donned their hats and nodded to each other. Then Rupert took Gavriela's arm, and they walked off in one direction, while Brian went the other way.

I don't know how I'm supposed to feel.

Something that happened far too often in her life.

No one said anything the next day in Hut 27: nothing about signals regarding some darkness, nothing about Gavriela's trip to London. Clive had returned, and was working on new intercepts with no mention of half-finished work from days before. During a break when Gavriela happened – by apparent chance – to find herself alone in the room, she hovered by Clive's desk but did not open the drawer.

They had given her a second chance. She needed to take it.

That night she walked back into Bletchley village with Rosie, who chatted about the trivia of her day. Gavriela, in the back of her mind, was ruminating on maths the way physicists often do: wondering at the way the right mathematical tools so often existed in advance of science finding a reason for using them, meaning mathematicians had explored such lofty abstract thought-spaces with no original connection to reality. Here in BP she had witnessed feats of mathematical reasoning – counter-intuitive statistics, rigorous Boolean logic, the depths of group theory – that she would find hard to explain to an outsider, even if she were allowed. But Rosie kept her grounded in reality.

'I had a letter from Jack yesterday! It was there when I got home last night.'

'That's great, Rosie. Is he all right?'

'He's fine, and getting a tan, he says.' Rosie took out a small, lace-edged handkerchief, waving it in the gloom. 'Got my initials, see?'

There might have been a curlicued *RD*, but the night was too dark to be sure.

'Jack bought the hankie on leave, and sent it—'

Rosie dabbed at one eye.

'He says we'll get married when he's home.'

'Oh, Rosie.'

They both stopped. Gavriela hugged her.

'He'll be OK,' she said. 'He'll be OK.'

But they both knew, in the sudden randomness of wartime, that letters from servicemen took time to arrive, and sometimes the sender was already dead or maimed when their sweetheart read those cheery words.

Rosie stepped back, sniffing.

'Now all we need,' she said, 'is to get *you* a nice young gentleman, and we'll be sorted.'

'Maybe,' said Gavriela.

They walked on, while she remembered the overwhelming lust for coupling that overtook her in the Tube station and the night that followed, all of it dislocated from her normal world; and she wondered whether it was romance or something more primal, and whether that made a difference.

'How about a nice cup of acorn tea?' Rosie's place was close, not quite on Gavriela's way home, but near enough. 'I've got a book you can borrow. I didn't finish it myself, but you might like it.'

'Love to.'

That night, Gavriela sat up in bed, reading her borrowed copy of *The White Company*, the slipcover worn grey and disintegrating at the edges. Whenever she paused, her thoughts would shift to Professor Challenger, then to the real Professor Möller whose leonine mane and clear gaze had been the personification of that fictitious scientist-hero; and she hoped that he remained safe in Zürich, though in the long term, in the face of the thousand-year Reich, neutrality had to be an ephemeral dream.

A photograph slipped out. Its edges were wave-like in the way special mementoes often were. Gavriela had occasionally wondered whether they were cut with sinusoidally edged scissors or something else, but never pursued it. The man in the picture wore dark naval uniform, aiming a long-jawed grin at the camera.

On the back, inscribed in careful copperplate, were these part-faded words:

From your Jaunty Jack,
Love always.
14th Sept. 1940

She stared at it for a long time, then put book and photo aside, switched off the light, and lay back, wondering if it had always been like this: years of peaceful idyll that no one appreciated at the time, interwoven with periods of desperation when violence and contingency ruled life and death, and certainty was vanished from the world.

THIRTY-ONE

Gavriela woke in her pliable, crystalline body, stretched in a way her older organic self could not have imagined, and rolled off the bier, onto her feet. The familiar vacuum was a comfort. The wall-mounted weapons tempted her, but she walked past them into the main hall.

Roger and Kenna were manipulating a many-dimensioned maze of silver lines that floated above the conference table. Trick perspectives and something more granted it an exotic, impossible architecture. Here and there, points radiated five, six . . . up to nine straight lines that shimmered like this: each pair of lines appeared to form a right angle, no matter which pair she focused on, so that after a time, the mutual orthogonality appeared to spread, to be a natural feature of all the lines simultaneously.

A refracted spectrum slid across Kenna's smile.

—*You can see why we need Roger.*

Gavriela put her hand on Roger's shoulder.

—*I knew there had to be a reason.*

—*Thanks, Gavi. I love you too.*

The complex image, had it been topological and not geometric – graph rather than shape – would have matched some long-gone memory, some resonance from Gavriela's past. It resembled . . .

—*What's the importance of computation, Kenna?*

—*In what we do? Nothing and everything.*

—*It seems I knew . . . Was I at some kind of nexus? The people I met were key, weren't they? Not just pioneers, but important in the course of human—*

Kenna held up a glimmering hand.

—*You were in a closed profession where everyone knew everyone else. Don't speculate beyond that.*

—*But I was at the beginning of*—

—*Yes, and that is why speculation is so dangerous. The wrong information surfacing to your conscious mind back then would be disastrous.*

Gavriela waved at the surrounding hall.

—*To all of this?*

—*No, to you. The universe is more robust.*

Roger, with a series of control gestures, collapsed the silvery graph into a fist-sized ball, then to a bright point which he twisted out of existence.

—*So what now?*

Kenna touched them both on the upper arm.

—*Why don't you take a walk out on the surface, both of you?*

A walk with Roger on the surface of the moon. There was nothing that Gavriela wanted more; but Roger gave a crystalline frown.

—*Are you trying to get rid of us, Kenna?*

She could as easily have banished them back to unconsciousness, but Roger was right: Kenna had some purpose in mind.

—*Our newest member is about to arrive. You two can come back and meet him, but it would be best if I greet him alone on waking.*

Gavriela looked at Roger, at the minute interplay of light behind his transparent face.

—*Let's take that walk.*

The pain of a thousand blades coming down, the intricate agony of slivers cut from him, reducing him, with no way to deaden the torture because sharing his full, untainted self was all, the reason for putting himself in death's way. It ached, it hurt, it burned across millennia—

Sharp pulled himself awake.

—*Greetings, good Sharp.*

Oceans of agony ebbed, pulling back until he could function

once more, though his memory of pain was permanent. Rolling his eyes, he saw his antlers had become like glass, sculpted transparency, while the rest of him ... He held up his clear hands, bending all four thumbs, wondering why he was not afraid.

When he sat up, the crystalline being in front of him had her mouth curved in the first expression he had learned from Rekka: smiling, the human counterpart of sweetbloom-scented humour.

—*You're not a human.*

—*No, good Sharp. But I am friend and ally to them, as I am to you.*

—*Truth.*

There was no air in this place, but the resonance of scent still operated, and there was no tinge of falsehood in Kenna's communication.

—*I died.*

—*You did, and most courageously, my friend.*

She held out one hand. Little taller than the humans Sharp had known, she barely came up to his chest. He took her hand in his, and allowed her to lead him out of the chamber, along a corridor where he had to bow his head to pass beneath each archway, taking care not to scrape his antlers, finally to come out on a balcony that overlooked a sere, grey landscape beneath a black, star-decorated sky.

Two small figures walked there, hand in hand.

—*Humans?*

—*And friends. They spend periods of time here. For now, they sleep for long periods also, while they live their ordinary lives.*

Stars refracted in his antlers as he shook his head.

—*And will I sleep as well?*

—*No, Sharp. You and I remain awake.*

He stared at the distant human pair.

—*For ever?*

—*At least until the final days.*

The landscape looked timeless, static for eternity.

But that was illusion.

THIRTY-TWO

Celebration exploded throughout Deltaville: streamers and holobursts in the halls and thoroughfares, fountains flowing with goldenmead shandy and indigoberry beer, exotic jantrasta confections free for the taking from extruded quickglass tables; and everywhere the pounding music, spontaneous dancing, and couples in corners engaged in snogging.

Beside Roger, Rhianna Chiang said: 'It's a madhouse full of fun, don't you think?'

'Sure.'

Tannier looked no happier than Roger: hard-faced, checking the crowd and surroundings, mapping the geometry of ambush.

'Plush clothes do not a partygoer make,' said Rhianna. 'Lighten up, why don't you? I'm going to chat to Faubourg.'

As she made her way over to the famous fop, Roger stretched up to ask Tannier, 'You think she knows?'

'That we're here on business? It doesn't matter. Once we're on camera, she'll make sure it all goes the way it should. That's what professional socialites do.'

'You don't like her, then.'

'I've met her kind, put it that way.'

It seemed to Roger, from the manner in which officials and others had acted on their arrival in Deltaville, that being a celebrity meant everybody wanted something, if only to be seen with you. Why anyone would seek such a parasite-ridden existence, he had no idea.

'Come on.' Rhianna returned with Faubourg alongside her. 'Big smiles, because we're about to visit the baby.'

'It's a big deal,' Tannier told Roger.

'To somebody, at least.'

'My dear chaps.' Faubourg waved a limp wrist. 'How delightfully rough-edged you both are.'

'Er . . .'

An amber saucer-shape formed beneath the four of them; then slender quickglass tethers, splaying out to the surrounding walls, began to rise, carrying them upwards. Once they were above the partying crowd, the tethers moved along the walls, bearing them horizontally. That was when the public holoviews became filled with their image: Rhianna and Faubourg waving naturally, Tannier and Roger looking like powered-off mannequins.

Just wave at them.

He stopped looking at the images, knowing he must be the least photogenic in the quartet and not caring. In fact, the more he stood out as awkward, the more likely Helsen would be to spot him – if she were watching, if she had not escaped to a more distant city.

The damned thing moved slowly, but finally they reached an outer wall. It was no surprise when the saucer merged into the rearing quickglass. A moving bubble enclosing the four of them, becoming the interior of a complex, baroque sky-barge as they floated free, heading at stately speed for the newer, smaller mass of D-2. She remained darker and much smaller than her mother city, but already she was changing: spreading out, with less redness than before showing in her hull.

'It's so exciting, and such a privilege.' Rhianna turned to him. 'Don't you think, Roger?'

'Er, absolutely. She looks . . . nice.'

'Well said, sir.' Faubourg's voice slid into their exchange. 'She has a nascent beauty, ready to flower, and you can see it in the lines of her . . .'

Roger tuned out, grateful for the conversational rescue. He wondered if Tannier was analysing their situation as he was, in term of angles of approach and fire-vectors, of system robustness against subversion in the quickglass that formed the sky-barge, in the walls of D-2 herself.

Did the goat know, as it was being tethered, that the tiger was out there, hunting?

Finally, as they flowed into D-2's outer hull and stepped out into a hemispherical chamber, Rhianna said: 'Relax now, you two. We're off camera until we eat.'

'You did perfectly fine,' said Faubourg.

'Cheers.' One corner of Tannier's mouth twitched. 'We didn't, but thanks for pretending.'

'Any time.'

A party of four was here to greet them: Professors Dalywn Kort and Eda Langfeld, lead scientists on the urban-birth team, along with Friss Reejan, Lady Mayor of Deltaville, and Ward Kalshin, who seemed to be famous mostly for being rich, unless Roger read the situation wrongly. As everyone touched fists or shook hands, appropriate to gender, it was Ward Kalshin who stopped, looked at Roger's cocked fist, and said: 'You're Fulgidus. My word.'

How can you tell?

Tannier stared at them.

'I am, sir,' said Roger. 'Pleased to meet you.'

'Likewise, and my condolences. I hope we do everything possible to make you feel at home here.'

The words seemed pompous but well meant. Compared to the behaviour of other worlds, every sky-city in Molsin had been exemplary in its willingness to accept refugees. Still, anyone looking at the newscasts surely felt fear.

To avoid being haunted by trauma, Roger had pushed away the memories using every psych technique he possessed. When the quickglass towers walked ... But that was behind him.

Except that this occurred to him: in dealing with the memories that way, he had perhaps underestimated the continuing threat of the Anomaly. Or perhaps it was simply that the darkness was a vaster danger in its own right, so that even the

Anomaly had to relinquish centre stage in the part of Roger's mind that dwelled on fear.

To Kalshin, he said: 'Everyone's been good to us, sir. It means a great deal.'

'Not at all. And I think first names would be appropriate, don't you, Rhianna?'

'Absolutely, Ward. And it's good to see you again.'

The two scientists, Dalwyn and Eda if they were using first names, drew close.

'Were you there when the Anomaly manifested?' asked Dalwyn.

'I was, yes.' Roger made himself exhale, forming the mental image that was his trigger for calmness. 'I was on a rooftop in Lucis City when the towers went wild.'

'The city walked,' said Eda. 'Is that right?'

The thrashing, writhing cityscape became vivid in Roger's mind.

'Luculenti were absorbed in the thing,' he said. 'You have no idea what they're – what they *were* capable of.'

'Ah.'

Advanced though Fulgor had been, its quickglass tech had never matched Molsin's. But whatever the city's inbuilt systems had lacked, the nature of the gestalt organism controlling it outweighed the limitations.

'That *is* what puzzled us, the speed and power of the urban mass.' Dalwyn looked at Eda. 'The phenomenon must have begun in The Marrows, all the same.'

Eda nodded, then looked at the dignitaries.

'Sorry,' she said. 'Would you like the short tour before we eat?'

'Marvellous idea.' Faubourg checked his cuffs and ruffles. 'Absolutely marvellous.'

There was a softness to the walls of the chamber where they dined – on camera apparently, though no holoviews showed in here – but the banquet table was ornate and solid enough, the food delivered through quickglass capillaries; and as far as Roger was concerned it was genuine *haute cuisine*. Faubourg and the others agreed, though in their case every word was a performance, the truth irrelevant.

Friss led a toast, goblets of goldenmead raised all round, to the newborn city's health and longevity.

'Health and longevity,' the group echoed, then sipped.

Or in Tannier's case, quaffed a goblet's entire contents.

'You know your body contains none of the atoms it consisted of seven standard years ago.' Dalwyn pointed at the food. 'Since you're going to rebuild yourself anyway, the finest of ingredients are definitely in order.'

'Very good, Professor. Perhaps our companion here' – Faubourg gave a languid gesture in Tannier's direction – 'can rebuild his brain with little goldenmead atoms.'

Stillness held the table ... then Tannier fell back in his seat, laughing uproariously, and a heartbeat later, everyone else joined in.

Perhaps Faubourg wasn't so bad after all.

After four courses which tasted wonderful – Roger had to make sure to leave food each time, leaving room for what was to follow – Friss announced a special treat. Unlike the other dishes, composed inside D-2, dessert – she called it *first* dessert – was to be something brought over from Deltaville for the occasion.

'Oh, goody.' Faubourg clapped his hands. 'Delightful.'

Tannier winked at Roger.

Then a silver case was melting open, and the party passed around the prepared bowls, chill to the touch. Roger put his fingertip into his dessert, then licked it. Explosions of ecstasy rushed from his tongue, and his toes curled as his back arched.

'Bloody hell,' he said.

There was laughter all round.

'That,' said Friss, 'is pulseberry orgasmousse. Enjoy, everyone.'

But whether the cameras were on him or not, Roger pushed the bowl away.

Rhianna looked at him.

'One burst of taste is enough,' he said. 'You can't improve on that.'

'Interesting philosophy.' Faubourg dipped his spoon, then tipped his head back for the first mouthful. 'Oh, my word. Mm.'

Only Tannier, among the others, had the self discipline to resist clearing the bowl. But it was not distrust of overwhelming sensation that held Roger back from enjoying the orgasmousse further – it was knowledge of its origins.

Is Friss playing some game here?

Or was it just what it seemed: a celebration with one of the most expensive delicacies available? But the received conceit – if not the literal truth – was that only the world of Pickover IX supported the correct growth environment for flavourful pulseberries, and the gravitational and atmospheric conditions for forming the delicate foam-filled structure of the finished dessert.

A dessert that, according to connoisseurs, degraded in taste after some twenty standard hours in realspace.

That's so stupid.

What kind of idiot strategy were the authorities pursuing?

From her hidden room at the far end of Deltaville, Petra Helsen watched the holocast. Young Blackstone, clearly bait, was looking uncomfortable among the urbane, cosmopolitan dignitaries; but his reaction to what seemed a simple dessert caught her attention.

The wall sucked open, and a clean-shaven Greg Ranulph came through. His own chamber, smaller than hers, was equally hidden.

'Do you know what that dish is?' she said, pointing at the holo.

Keeping systems access to a minimum was part of her

strategy for remaining undetected. She did not want to simply ask for data on a whim, especially not if there was a chance Greg might know.

'The pudding? It has to be orgasmousse.' His gaze seemed ambivalent. 'It's supposed to be intensely pleasurable.'

She had turned down his requests for sex. Perhaps he thought this was some kind of teasing game.

'Just tell me,' she said.

Without the beard, he did look better, but so what?

'That's all I know.'

'Blackstone thinks otherwise.'

'Who? Not that young Pilot from the multiversity?'

They had known what Roger Blackstone was, just as he had recognized their nature.

'That's the one.'

'I don't really— No, that's it. You can only cook the dish, make it, whatever . . . on one planet. Don't ask me which one, but the point is, it doesn't stay fresh.'

'So they vacuum-froze . . . You're saying they can't do that.'

'Not when it's served the posh way.'

From her seat, Helsen reached up, took hold of his big, square-fingered hand, then drew it down between her thighs, and commenced rubbing.

'You're a genius, Greg.'

'I . . .'

'Come here.' She tugged open his clothes. 'Lie down.'

'I . . .'

Pulling her own garments apart, she straddled him, sliding down onto his hugeness, settling and tightening up.

Yes. I can use you.

Beginning the ride, hard and rhythmic.

'Oh, yes,' he said. 'But . . . why now?'

'Because' – her pelvis was thrusting as he began to buck – 'someone's broken the blockade.'

'Pilots . . .?'

'Oh, no.' Grinning, she rode him, squeezing intensely. 'Zaji-nets for sure.'

'Ah!'

'Yes, exactly.'

Riding harder now.

Galloping toward crescendo.

THIRTY-THREE

EARTH, 2147 AD

Singapore felt like the sauna of the gods. After years in Arizona, Rekka was acclimatized to air-conditioning more than the dry outdoors, and certainly not this sweltering humidity where hot moistness seemed to drip in the air itself. She walked along Orchard Road, where single-storey buildings with curled-up Chinese rooftops nestled amid bioluminescent towers. Everything was bright, while she felt dislocated, alien and out of synch.

It's only another part of Earth.

One far from Simon, who had not been talkative during their last days and nights together. She had stuck her neck out to get him transferred here or to mainland China during the coming UNSA re-org. He had avoided saying anything about it until the final night.

'Damn it, Rekka. Couldn't you have fucking *asked*?'

Simon never swore. Nearly never.

A question in what sounded like Urdu pulled her back to reality. The woman wore a sari, her head moving in a lateral nod.

'I'm sorry?' said Rekka.

'Oh, I am speaking English. I thought—' She pointed at Rekka's skin, then her own, their colouring identical; then she frowned. 'But you were touched by *vritra* and *dasu*.'

'So were a lot of people, if you mean the Changeling Plague.'

'I am so sorry.'

The woman walked on, shaking her head. Rekka watched until she disappeared among a crowd of shoppers, many of them women with headscarves, Chinese Muslims rather than Indian.

A great start.

She wanted to sleep, but tomorrow she would have to be in synch with local time. Past the tall glass UNSA tower she walked, as far as Duby Ghaut. At the station she turned back, taking smaller roads parallel to Orchard, finally to reach Stanley Hill, where she entered the park.

For a while, she sat on a low stone wall in the old fort, a preserved relic of British imperialism from a nearly forgotten time. Finally, with no one to see her, she performed repetitions of Salute to the Sun, the heat working out her muscle kinks, then went through her *asana*s, holding each pose to a mental countdown, shallow breaths sucking in humidity.

Afterwards, feeling weak-limbed, she went back to her hotel, a hollow cylinder of a building with an open court where tropical trees grew. A tiny gekko, perched on the outside wall, scuttled away from her.

Sharp, my friend. I wish I could have shown you this city.

She went in to the icy air-conditioned reception, took a glass-walled lift up to her floor, entered her room, lay down on the soft bed, and dropped into deep, exhausted sleep.

Breakfast was hot spicy noodles and jasmine tea. Afterwards, with time to spare, she bought a light silk scarf in a mall on Orchard Road. Her gestures had been no different than if she had been in Arizona; but then she watched a local woman paying for a new blouse, noted the way goods were passed from seller to buyer using two hands, their bodies facing each other squarely.

Rekka had been rude through carelessness.

In a different shop, she bought some eau de parfum, this time with the correct body language and a small bow; and the cashier's smile was clearly genuine as well as polite. It made Rekka feel good, and at least halfway competent to interact with an alien species whose anthropological history bore no relation to anything seen on Earth, except for occasional chance parallels. Later, in a coffee house across the road from the UNSA tower, she drank an espresso, fastened the new scarf around her neck, took controlled breaths, and deliberately relaxed her shoulder muscles, raised her chin, and smiled at nothing whatsoever.

I can face this.

She crossed the street, entered the glass-dominated reception lounge, and announced herself to the AI, which told her to take a seat and wait. Instead, she stood looking out at the city until someone approached.

'Ms Chandri?' The young woman looked Chinese. 'I'm Google Li.'

It was an old-fashioned forename, the kind that ought to belong to someone's grandmother.

'Call me Rekka.'

As they shook hands, Google asked, 'Would you like to meet the team straight away?'

'I'd love to.'

They rode a lift to the seventeenth floor, while Google enumerated the available facilities.

'We've category C and F xenoatmospheric facilities on this level, and category B on the next floor up.'

'I needed minimal meds on their world,' said Rekka. 'And ... Sharp got around on Earth just fine.'

'They're not contained. Strangers are always safe here.'

'Um, of course.'

The Haxigoji were standing in a group, waiting for her. At the front was a female, strong-looking but lacking antlers, her tabard and skirt of white and gold; while behind her ranged half a dozen huge males, deep amber eyes unreadable, dressed in dark, mossy colours. Only the female wore a translator unit, fastened at her throat.

'We honour you, Rekka, good friend.' It was a feminine voice, with subtleties of modulation matching the received scent. 'My name is Bittersweet.'

Then Bittersweet clasped her double-thumbed hands together and bowed.

'I know you to be brave and honourable people.' Rekka bowed back. 'I'm glad to be working with you here.'

Off to one side, Google Li and other staff were staring, eyes wide, as if this behaviour was unexpected.

'As are we, knowing that all humans' – Bittersweet performed a swiping gesture – 'are our friends.'

They had not noticed, the other UNSA personnel.

Shit?

It was a faint smell but unmistakable, gone in a second. She remembered her and Sharp's amusement when they realized the one word that translated directly between their languages. But in his scent-speech, that odour when compounded with others denoted degrees of negation, all the way up to outright falsehood.

'I understand,' said Rekka.

Tiredness split off from her, like a shearing iceberg falling away.

Not all humans are friends. That's what she meant.

Bittersweet had covered the sensor for less than a second, just long enough to prevent it from catching that momentary scent. The message was therefore secret, for Rekka's . . . nostrils . . . only.

'I hope,' Rekka added, 'we grow closer in mutual understanding.'

'Yes.'

Bittersweet bowed again. Then she turned as the males drew apart, allowing her to walk through. They fell in behind her, and the group continued in to their private quarters. Doors slid shut.

'That was promising,' said one of the researchers.

'I hope so,' said Rekka.

As she went forward to introduce herself to her new colleagues, what replayed in her mind's eye was the subtle swiping gesture that Bittersweet had made. It was a surprise, yet Sharp would have known to do that, wouldn't he?

Oh, my brave, brave friend.

He had sacrificed himself so others could taste and absorb his knowledge. Rekka did not want to think how Bittersweet knew such details from the past.

'I'm Rekka.' She held out her hand to the nearest researcher. 'Good to meet you.'

'Randolf. And this is . . .'

But it was the memory of Sharp that dominated her attention, while her co-workers seemed insubstantial, figments that scarcely existed in her world.

Google absented herself from the technical discussions – she was management, not research – so Rekka was able to lose herself in details of xenolinguistics for the rest of the day. The others seemed awed by her rapport with Bittersweet. By the end of the afternoon, however, Rekka had made sure to introduce the researchers individually to the Haxigoji, allowing them each to have a short conversation with Bittersweet. It went down well. At the end of the working day, she was afraid that they would ask her to socialize; but either that was not the custom or they remained awed by her, or they could see that she felt wrecked, in need of food and sleep.

Travelling down in the lift, she was joined by Google, who got on at the sixteenth floor.

'Good first day?' asked Google.

'Yes, for sure.'

It was just the two of them. Was it psychological, or was the lift really descending more slowly than expected?

'Your mission to the Haxigoji world was very successful,' said Google. 'Everyone recognizes that.'

'Thank you.'

'The team leader was Mary Stelanko, is that right?'

'You know Mary?' said Rekka.

'Not as such. I heard her partner's on sabbatical. Amber, isn't it?'

The lift was definitely going slow.

'I've not been in touch with either of them.' Rekka did not like this. 'Not for a while.'

Google's shrug looked almost unrehearsed.

'It's just that I heard about the new utilization criteria. Ships that have been idle for too long are being decommissioned or reconfigured for another Pilot. Getting with the programme is the best thing Amber could do.'

The lift stopped and the doors opened. They had only descended as far as the thirteenth floor.

'Have a good evening.' Google stepped out. 'See you in the morning.'

'And you.'

As the descent resumed, Rekka reflected that it was not only Bittersweet sending private messages; but in Google's case it was neither friendly nor subtle. Needing comfort, Rekka tapped her infostrand, trying to call Simon; but a red icon indicated he was offline: whether to the world or to her specifically, there was no way to tell.

Sharp. No one knows how much I miss you.

The world outside was bright, hot and alien.

Shoulders drooping, chest concave with fatigue, she headed for her hotel.

THIRTY-FOUR

Dr Imelda Sapherson was working in a slowtime bubble, sealed off from the rest of the room. Her experimental data was promising: a neural deepscan showing activity of the spatio-temporal grid in the subject's entorhinal cortex, correlated with eye-muscle motor signals, precuneus activation and other distributed neural resonance. In realspace humans, mental images appear to have a real location in space, sometimes with a geometric representation of time – as in the front-to-back timeline denoting verb tenses in sign languages: formerly for the deaf, more latterly for kineme-based system-control gestures – while giving rise to spoken linguistic idioms like 'putting the past behind me', meaningful even to the extent that people act more charitably when standing higher than the surrounding ground level, as they take the literal moral high ground.

In Pilots, the entorhinal cortex was connected differently. What interested Sapherson was the extent to which that was driven by neural growth in mu-space, and how much was due to immersion in Aeternum. The language's effect on brain architecture extended far beyond the neural centres called Bernicke's and Broca's areas. Recently, she had been reading a paper written by a Luculentus noting the correlation between alphabets and neurology – in particular, the way that old-fashioned 2-dimensional alphabets without written vowels were read right-to-left, allowing for greater right-hemisphere processing to distinguish context, while ideographic scripts ran vertically – and wished she could have talked to the man, before his world was destroyed.

It's why I do what I do.

She pushed the words away – behind her, if she decon-structed her subjective experience deeply enough to tell – because the truth was, doubts had been with her for a long time. But the appearance of the Anomaly in realspace told her she had been right to work with the intelligence service and the Admiralty in the way she did. Civilization was clearly fragile, therefore extraordinary measures were sometimes necessary to safeguard the common good.

Sapherson was aware that outsiders, not understanding the hard necessities of her discipline, would consider her a psy-chopath. At least history provided her with a centuries-long chain of antecedents, all of them as cruel as she had to be.

Perhaps training Fleming and his small corps of torturers was the most questionable thing she had done. Or maybe it was the increasingly vicious – because deep – mindwipe procedures carried out on innocent witnesses and on officers of the intelligence service itself.

What would they ask her to do next?

And why do I always agree?

But her subjective analysis could not be so deeply rigorous without self-honesty to a degree few people were capable of. Lying to others was an art; lying to herself was impossible. That was why she knew about the hidden reason, the one she would never admit to.

Twisting other minds was a rush, a power trip.

When she came out of slowtime, her chief assistant, Alfredo, was waiting to talk.

'Hey, boss,' he said. 'I did the check-up you asked for on Darius Boyle.'

'Using Med-Centre cover?'

'Well, yeah. I wouldn't want him to associate me with his condition. He's a bit too ... physical for me to handle.'

'And what *is* his condition?' said Sapherson. 'The same as before?'

'The aphasia's stopped increasing for sure, and the remedial therapy is probably pushing it back. Visits from his sister – from his viewpoint, a stranger claiming to be his sister, and with what appears to be fake evidence to prove it – remain upsetting. I observed that firsthand.'

It proved the strength of her technique for following associative potentiation. Say that much for it.

'I saw Colonel Garber on the way in,' Alfredo added. 'He said he has another assignment for us. Same kind of thing as Boyle, in fact.'

'Another one?' Sapherson had performed the amnesia treatment because Boyle had learned classified information beyond his authorization level. The necessity arose from the way the field officers worked, from other people's imperatives, not her own. 'Maybe they should manage their officers more carefully.'

'But we'll do the job?'

'Of course we'll do it,' she said. 'Where is this person?'

Alfredo gestured.

'I've got the rotation set up.'

'Let's go see, then.'

She stepped inside, with Alfredo following, and allowed him to control the fastpath. They stepped into a chamber containing three people, one of them seated. He was a shaven-headed, bulky man, familiar enough.

'You captured Gould?' she said to the others, while staring at Gould himself.

'Not exactly.' He stood up, and gestured at the seat. 'Why don't you relax, Doctor? A little chat, and there'll be no harm to anyone.'

Sapherson jerked back, hoping the fastpath was still in place. *No.*

But Alfredo was standing off to one side, shaking his head. Her exit route had disappeared at his command, it seemed. It took a moment to process his betrayal.

'We've been asked to do questionable things,' he said. 'Except *you* didn't question them.'

'Not in front of my subordinates, no.'

Max Gould gestured again.

'Pretend you're a warm, reasonable person,' he said. 'And sit down before we make you.'

She looked at the others standing behind him. One man, one woman, both hard-faced.

'Very well, since I'm under coercion.' Once on the seat, she felt flowmetal encasing her forearms and lower legs; but she stared at Gould rather than look down at her bonds. 'Murder and treason,' she added. 'Now you're bringing collaborators into your game. Bringing them down with you.'

The woman walked from behind the chair and stared at Sapherson.

'One person in this room is working with Labyrinth's enemies.' Her voice was pitiless. 'Only one.'

'I work for the Admiralty—'

'We *all* work for the Admiralty, but only one of us is erasing memories of threats to Labyrinth.'

Threats?

'You need to be more precise.'

'Boyle and his colleague,' said the woman, then smiled as Sapherson flinched. 'So you recognize him.'

The other man walked into full view.

'Nice to see you again, Dr Sapherson. On behalf of Darius Boyle, I really, *really* want to hurt you. That's something you might bear in mind.' With a nasty smile: 'Don't go forgetting it now.'

'The necessity for fullest depotentiation,' she said, 'was impressed upon me by Admiral Schenck himself. I was acting on a wholly legal order, isn't that obvious?'

'And Admiral Kaltberg,' asked the woman. 'How legal was what you did to her?'

What is this?

'I gave her the normal treatment for someone in her position. She was looking forward to enjoying full retirement,' said

Sapherson, 'unburdened by classified secrets from her time in—'

Gould's fists were clenching.

He's the danger here.

But from the corner of the room, Alfredo looked up from a pulsing holodisplay.

'She's telling the truth,' he said. 'She administered the normal amnesia regimen.'

'In which case' – Gould leaned close, almost spitting in her face as he spoke – 'who induced the suicide compulsion and forced the graser pistol on her?'

'On Admiral Kaltberg?' Sapherson swallowed. 'Someone conditioned her?'

Again, Alfredo backed her up.

'Everything indicates real surprise,' he said. 'Someone used black psych techniques, but it wasn't her. It's not like there's a shortage of people with those skills.'

'Not exactly a glut on the market, though.' Gould was leaning close again. 'And the real bastards are the ones you've trained, aren't they, Sapherson?'

There was only one answer possible.

'Yes,' she whispered.

'In which case,' said Gould, 'there's one question left that'll determine whether you survive this little chat.'

Her limbs began to shake, despite the restraints. These were the symptoms both of hypothermia and hyperthermia in the final stages, and of simple hyperventilation, the last of which she ought to be able to control.

They're willing to kill me.

She did not need instruments to know that Gould meant his threat.

'When you wiped the memories of Boyle and his colleague here—'

'Clayton,' she said. 'I remember his name.'

'—right, when you did that, did you isolate the memories from a location and timestamp, or did you know the content and theme of the memories to erase? Was it a *themed* amnesia?'

For all Sapherson's efforts to stare hard, Gould's face seemed blurred, yet filling her visual field.

Stress symptoms.

She needed to answer him.

'Time and place,' she said. 'That's all I needed.'

Gould looked over at Alfredo.

'Say the word.'

'It's the truth,' said Alfredo. 'She doesn't know about the darkness.'

None of this was coherent. Darkness?

'Confirmed by her ongoing reaction,' added Alfredo. 'She's clean.'

Her restraints melted into the chair.

'Only in a manner of speaking,' said Gould.

They gave her three choices: death, mindwipe at Alfredo's hands, or helping them. She made no smart remarks about the illusion of freedom, because Clayton's desire to avenge Boyle was unfeigned, and because however much Alfredo's analysis had exonerated her, clearly she was unconsciously associated with Admiral Kaltberg's murder in Max Gould's mind at least, and probably in the nameless woman's.

'What do you want me to do?'

'Trample through someone's brain,' said Clayton. 'That's your talent, isn't it?'

'Perhaps with a bit more finesse than that,' said Gould.

'I'll do it, of course.'

A variety of facial expressions formed silent responses to her words; but a mid-air ripple drew her attention from her captors. A fastpath rotation was forming—

Rescue?

—from which two men stepped, both of them familiar.

'What is this?' The first was Admiral Turnbull. 'I thought we were going to—'

His eyes rolled up as his body lost muscular tensegrity, and collapsed.

'Got you.' Clayton caught hold of a sleeve and shoulder. 'Someone get support under him, will you?'

'Doing it.' Alfredo gestured. 'There you go.'

Flowmetal rose up, forming an inclined seat beneath Turnbull, then straightening out as it took his weight, turning into a horizontal table or bed.

Turnbull's companion was Pavel Karelin.

'How many of you people are there?' asked Sapherson.

'I'd tell you,' said Karelin, 'but I'd have to mindwipe you.'

Only the woman barked a laugh.

'Here's how it goes.' Gould was taking charge. 'We're going to ask the admiral here some questions under trance. He's backed some bad decisions in the Council, but we believe that's more due to his being fed misinformation—'

'And being a total arsehole,' said the woman.

'—plus his own personal ambition, let's say, rather than actually plotting against Labyrinth.'

Sapherson rubbed a knuckle under her eye. Were these people prey to a group delusion? One charismatic leader and partial isolation from peers could produce a situation where every group decision reinforced the leader's conviction and fed on his approval. It was a basic form of cognitive bias liable to surface in group situations.

'You'll be able to judge for yourself,' Gould told her, as if she had delivered her analysis aloud. 'There are two outcomes possible. One is, Turnbull is essentially innocent but manipulated. In that case, you will wipe his memory of our interrogation and that's it. Nothing more. No implanted suggestions. We let him go as he is.'

'All right.'

'Option two is, he's one of the bastards we're up against, and you'll hear from his own mouth why Labyrinth is in danger.'

'And then I mindwipe him.'

'No.' Gould looked at the others. 'In that case, amnesia will be unnecessary.'

Sapherson wanted to say, so the ends justify the means for you as well as for me. But she was not that stupid.

'If it's option one,' she said instead, 'then I guess I'll never know what this conspiracy is about, will I?'

'Yeah, you will,' said Karelin. 'Because once we're done with Turnbull, I'll bring the next one in, and then the next. We're going to find one of the bad guys for sure.'

She did not smile at *bad guys*.

'How many people?'

'Enough to be certain.'

So they were serious; but then, that was obvious.

'And what happens after that?' she said.

'Then things will move very fast,' said Gould.

That was when the fear-for-self left her, because there were greater things happening here than the life of one neuroscientist, things of moment; and for all her failings, when it came to the city-world that nurtured them all in this ur-continuum, there was one thing she knew, deep inside, deeper even than the needs that drove her in her work.

She would sooner die than allow Labyrinth to fall.

THIRTY-FIVE

Ulfr woke up thinking of wisdom personified as a woman – *Kenna?* – but that was too abstract because he was holding *her*, his sweet Eira; and they fitted together in every way, as he had always known they would. Two halves of a single shape, now complete.

'Hey, warrior.'

Her eyes were clear. He ignored the scent coming from her poultice, inhaled the breath she had exhaled, and kissed her. That one kiss contained more sensuality than every experience with every other young woman in his life.

'Ulfr, my wolf.'

'Yes.'

'Love me.'

And so he did, and it was marvellous once more.

The sheep hobbled outside Eira's hut was a present from Chief Folkvar, she said, supposed to cheer her up. Then she tucked her arm inside Ulfr's, and her smile was a reflection of the sun, bright enough to blind.

'Take me for a walk, warrior.'

'I'll take you anywhere.'

'Hmm. Heimdall's Point, then.'

'Are you up to it?'

Her gait was slow and off-kilter, limping to favour the torso wound; and she was already breathless, just a little.

'Perhaps a strong warrior will carry me if I get tired.'

'Perhaps he will.'

Smiles were everywhere as the clan members saw them

walking as a couple. In the aftermath of violence, good things might happen; and when they did, they should be celebrated. Even Vermundr grinned, without a sarcastic witticism, not even a whistle.

Eira. At last.

All of the Middle World seemed to brighten as they walked.

From the promontory, they could see the lake, sparkling now, the blueness of far mountains, and the village down below. Close to the edge, the potential of that cliff-like drop exhilarated like the life-giving air, pure and washing through them.

'It's a perfect place,' said Ulfr.

Every patch of lichen glowed with inner life, every narrow blade of grass, the richness of existence pressing in on him, creating a sharp intensity of awareness.

'And I thank you for it, my handsome wolf.'

There had been some carrying involved, and it had been a joy to use his strength in a way far removed from violence, bearing his most precious love to this impressive site. While he stared out across the view, she stepped in front of him, facing him, and touched his lips with her fingertip.

'I've tried everything, my best potions and deepest trance. The Norns have made their will clear. My wound is worsening. The poison is spreading through me, promising a long, bad end. Which is why I've chosen this, after you've brought me happiness. And I thank you.'

'No, my love, don't say that. There are other *volva*s who can—'

'You're the best, my wolf.'

She took two steps back, and then a third—

No!

—and her smile remained but only in his mind as she dropped beyond the edge.

Was gone.

*

It was Hallsteinn who discovered the broken body, but he waited for Ulfr to make his sobbing, heart-pounding descent from Heimdall's Point, because Eira deserved to be carried by the one she had loved. He laid her in the waiting-place at the edge of the village; and then he broke.

For a long time all was rage and howling, the world gone in blackness and madness, denying him prey, refusing him the satisfaction of bones to crunch and the spraying of blood, because the clan knew to stay away as he flailed and thrust in the depths of *berserkrgangr*.

Then finally he sat, far from everyone, only Brandr daring to be at his side, while in the village the pyre's flames leapt high, burning the last of goodness from the Middle World, and in Ulfr's heart, he cursed the Norns.

I hate.

He cursed everything.

THIRTY-SIX

THE WORLD, 5568 AD

Harij staggered down the familiar scree slope, back into the caverns of home, his silver skin blackened here and there, aware only of the void left by his sister, by sweet Ilara whose thoughts remained trapped in a distant dreamlode, brightened and sharpened but different, part of something that was more than her. His wonderful, damaged sister was gone.

Daywatchmen found him, and carried him to the emergency hospice where staff lathered healing cream upon his burns, and immersed him in calming flux to heal, or at least to rest. For some number of nights that he was long past counting, they kept him in this crepuscular state, taking him out of near-coma long enough to eat and exercise basic bodily functions. For the rest, they kept him under, to ravel thoughts and body together once more.

Finally, he was fit enough to face the tribunal.

Only Mistress Ahn made a plea on the basis of his character and the goodness of his intent. His parents were too distraught to approach, never mind address the tribunal.

When the three judges asked Harij, towards the end of his testimony, how he felt about his own actions, there was only one thing he could tell them.

I am guilty. Deeply guilty.

Tension attenuated in the room at that point. Afterwards, matters proceeded with unbroken momentum, rolling to a conclusion.

They tied him to a pinkstone pillar at the centre of the flux chamber: proctors and councillors wearing heavy, shielded robes, hurrying despite the protection, because it helped only a little. Soon they had scurried out, leaving him to face the wildness.

It tore at him, the raging flux.

Ilara!

Twisting torrents that pulled reality apart.

In the cool of the night, the youth looked down at his new robe, at the cleansed glistening of his silver skin. Beside him, on the wide exit ledge, lay two carry-sacks of his provisions.

A cavern lay behind and below, cradling a subterranean town, but it was nothing to him.

Wait.

It was a feminine cast. He turned and waited.

I'm Ahn. Mistress Ahn. Do you remember me?

He stared at the woman, liking her.

No, I do not.

She passed a polished hand across her face. Then she straightened her stance.

I came to wish you well, good Seeker.

Then I thank you, Mistress Ahn.

He looked out to the night sky, to the black-and-silver filigree disk of Magnus above the horizon, and the mesa stretching far away. Then he picked up his provisions, slung them over his shoulder, and walked out into the open.

The Seeker travelled until dawn, when he found shelter and rested up, his mind stilled but receptive to the faintest hints of Idea or Memory. At dusk, he set off once more, for that is what it means to Seek.

Above him, a single triblade soared, casting for the tiny flux-knots of its prey.

THIRTY-SEVEN

EARTH, 1942 AD

It was a returning Liberty Ship, plunging through North Atlantic waves at lesser risk on its way to New York than it had been travelling east, but only just. Wolf packs of U-boats would pick off whatever shipping they could, because every vessel contributed to the ongoing survival of a Great Britain unable to support itself while the Reich continued its expansion. Gavriela, puking over the rail, could not understand how Rupert had done this to her.

And Brian?

She had left Bletchley before his scheduled return from the London secondment. Their night of desperate lovemaking had awakened an itch in her, some long-repressed physicality that seemed to have little to do with Brian as a person. It was a conundrum she would hardly solve from thousands of miles away. It was hard enough to think at all, with the ship rising and plunging this way.

Sickness kept her shuttling between cabin and deck for the rest of the voyage. Down below was cramped, but she was the only occupant of her two-bunk cabin. Tiny streaks of rust underneath the porthole looked like tears. She tried to work – in her head, because a notebook would not be safe – reviewing everything she knew about atomic physics. The signal intercepts originating from the Kaiser Wilhelm Institute had already caused her to go back to her textbooks; but Rupert had set her a greater challenge.

What does he expect me to do?

Even a permanent relocation would make more sense than this short-term mission, except that Rupert had impressed this on her: gauging the Wehrmacht's progress in building an atomic bomb was vital to determining strategy. That was plausible: it was less about helping the Americans than about her learning enough to judge German progress. Rupert's objective was tactically sound; only his means, she thought as she threw up again, were questionable.

And so it continued, her voyage, until the Manhattan skyline was silhouetted magnificence against an eerie dawn sky, the New World reaching to take her in. Dislocated from her previous life, she hauled her small case down the gangplank, then stood on the solid dock, swaying.

'Rough journey?' The man wore a black overcoat and grey fedora. 'I'm Charles Payne.'

He took the case from her.

'Er, thank you. I'm Gabby Woods. My passport is, um . . .'

'I recognize you from your photograph, ma'am. We can go straight to the car. It's only a few minutes to Grand Central, where you'll be able to freshen up. And there's time for a New York breakfast before we catch the train.'

'I . . . thank you.'

She felt safe as he took her upper arm and guided her to a dark, bulbous automobile. He opened the back door for her and settled her in, before stowing her case in the boot, except it wasn't called that here, was it? Everything looked and smelled different; even the quality of sound seemed altered in this air. Behind the steering-wheel, the driver looked in the mirror and tipped his hat.

'Ma'am.'

'Oh. Hello.'

Then Payne was sitting beside her, and the driver was adjusting a stick poking out of the steering-column – it took a moment to realize it was a gear lever – and the car began to roll along the dock.

It might have been twenty minutes later when they stood in the marble space of the Grand Central terminus. The high hall was awash with echoing sound even at this early hour.

Neo-classical, the concourse might have been in London, Paris or Berlin. Soldiers in well-tailored uniforms were numerous. The familiarity relaxed Gavriela, just a little.

'We already have our tickets.' Payne held her case in one hand, his own in the other. 'Let's go downstairs and eat.'

She was not hungry, but the small café below ground offered enticing smells. For the first time in over two years, she drank real coffee and nibbled from a bagel.

Then she rushed to the ladies room and threw it all back up.

The New Mexico heat was beyond anything she had experienced. Minimal humidity and a Martian landscape, the desert colours and the clarity of the air razoring into her vision: all of it was unexpected. Wherever she looked, some subliminal aspect would throw her off balance.

'You'll like the people,' Payne told her.

But after a soldier accompanied them to the wooden house that was to be hers, while she laid out her spare clothes on the bed, she heard him say to Payne outside: 'Begging your pardon, sir, but Sergeant McGregor sends his compliments, and says he'll be available in Hut 17 at fifteen-thirty hours, if you're up for another ass-kickin'.'

'Tell the sergeant' – there was a pause – 'to save the last dance for me.'

'Yes, sir.'

She leaned out of the open window, and saw the two men continuing up the dirt street between the rows of wooden buildings. Her watch read five past three.

It's hardly my kind of thing.

As a woman and a scientist, she ought to consider what she had overheard to be working-men's banter – assuming she had understood correctly – and not the kind of matter that men in her circle would attend to. But something about the New World told her that the old strictures were arbitrary; while something minimally remembered inside her spoke of the joy of violence, the committed focus of combat.

I'm dizzy with the heat, that's all.

That did not explain her being out on the dirt street twenty minutes later, asking a jeep driver for directions to Hut 17 – in fact he drove her there, chewing gum as he whipped the jeep too fast around corners before screeching up outside the long hut – and walking up to the doorway, open because of the heat, then standing quietly to watch the men inside.

Perhaps she ought to go back. Earlier, the soldier who had seen her to the house had told her to knock on either of her neighbours' doors, where the wives would make her welcome.

'Ya gotta understand something.' Inside, the man had a gorilla's muscularity, running one huge hand across his buzz cut as he explained: 'Ya poke someone in the chest when he's just standing relaxed' – he demonstrated on one of the other men – 'he'll say ouch, right? Do the same in the middle of a fight when punches are swingin', he won't even know you've poked him.'

There were nods from the men, some twenty or so, all in sweat-stained T-shirts and combat trousers. In the far corner, Payne, now similarly dressed, was limbering up.

'Next time someone offers to show you his deadly nerve strike,' said the instructor, who had to be Sergeant McGregor, 'see if he can manage it while you're beating seven bells of shit outta him, all right?'

Then he got the men in pairs to practise ramming the heels of their palms into each other's chins, with control of sorts, following with knee-strikes to liver or spleen. Along one wall stood battered dummies formed of sandbags and wood; the men took it in turns to break off from partner practice to belt the dummies with full power.

Eyes attuning to the darker, sweltering interior, Gavriela made out the bold-scripted notice framed on one wall:

In war you cannot afford the luxury of squeamishness.
Either you kill or capture, or you will be captured or killed.
We've got to be tough to win, and we've got to be ruthless –

tougher and more ruthless than our enemies.'
—CAPTAIN W. E. FAIRBAIRN

Since her arrival in America, the war had seemed to draw away into some imaginary nightmare reality. Now, in this odd, baking-hot venue, the truth came pressing back to stifle her.

While part of her wanted to join in the combat training, however insane and inappropriate that might be.

'Right, everyone.' The sergeant, McGregor, was calling them to order. 'Injuring your buddy weakens the unit, should we deploy into combat. That's why we use control.'

Payne walked to the centre of the hut and faced the sergeant, eyes serious, mouth pulled back, not quite in a grin.

'On the other hand,' McGregor continued, 'my old buddy Charles is deployed behind a desk these days, so if I forget myself a little, ain't no big shakes to the war effort.'

'Still talking a good fight?' Charles raised both hands, palms forward. 'Words are cheap, my friend.'

'Hoo-*ah*,' someone said.

They all stepped back, grinning as they formed a ring.

McGregor and Payne circled, then tore into each other with open-hand blows – not so much slaps as punches with palm-heels – and thrusting knees, then Payne was behind McGregor, locking on a stranglehold. McGregor rolled over, taking Payne with him, twisting free as his shirt tore, but Payne came to his feet and jumped, heels coming down close to McGregor's head—

'Bronco, Sarge! Look out!'

—but he shifted and kicked from the ground, creating space to stand up, one hand outstretched as a guard. They closed again and then again, battering each other, hitting and grappling, until one of the soldiers called time. Then McGregor and Payne, sweat-slick and blood-covered, torsos heaving bellows-like, grinned at each other while the others whooped.

McGregor looked at Gavriela and winked.

You saw me watching.

She nodded back, then stepped away from the doorway, down to the dusty road, and headed for her temporary home, one hand on her stomach while her thoughts roiled, no longer understanding her place in the world or why she was here. From behind her sounded the diminishing yells of soldiers as they resumed their practice of hand-to-hand skills that with luck they would never have to use.

The party was pleasant, civilized and surreal. So many of the physicists were dispossessed Europeans that it might have been a celebration of peaceful escape, or even a conference back home before the bad days, with a sprinkling of American visitors in white shirts and broad ties, some of them loosened at the neck. Payne, in his dark suit, was once more the civilized being, with the beginnings of a facial bruise not yet turned obvious. He was talking to a tall man with flashing blue eyes who reminded Gavriela of Alan Turing, though his face and physique were longer, quite different.

A woman in a polka-dot sleeveless dress and white cotton gloves came to stand beside Gavriela. 'Is that a sarsaparilla you're drinking, dear?'

'Yes, that's all I wanted. I'm Gabby.'

'And I'm Mary. Nice to meet you. That's my husband over there.'

She indicated a thick-bodied man with heavy black glasses, unlit pipe in hand as he argued some point with colleagues.

'I presume,' added Mary, gesturing towards Payne, 'that he's your husband.'

'Not at all,' said Gavriela.

'Oh. Well, look, let me introduce you to the other girls.' Mary indicated a group of women sitting around a young, joker-faced man, the centre of their attention. 'If we can distract them from Dick for a second or two, that is.'

In the usual random manner of party sounds, a region of quietness developed around Mary's husband and the men he was arguing with, allowing words to carry.

'—properties like angular momentum defining the limit of the liquid-drop model,' he was saying. 'So you might want to keep that in mind when you assume nuclear incompressibility.'

A blond man said, 'You're saying Bohr and Wheeler give wrong values for the fission barrier?'

'I'm saying the absolute limit is too high compared to experimental—'

Gavriela walked away from Mary.

'Excuse me,' she said to the men. 'I understood that Z-squared over A is the critical ratio only for *symmetric* spontaneous fission. It's possible that asymmetric fission occurs for values under 50.'

'Huh? Thank God,' said the blond man, 'that somebody gets the point. Given the probability of barrier penetration, the model predicts a *gradual*, not sudden introduction of—'

And then they were into it, in a manner which – to a reflective part of Gavriela's mind – was not dissimilar to McGregor's fight with Payne, despite the vastly different arena; but this time she was a participant, immersed in the argument as much as any of them. The wives' frowns and wrinkled noses were a contrast to their husbands' reaction: the men ignoring everything but the physics. It was after glancing at the women again that Gavriela noticed the man across the room, and then her concentration derailed.

No. Not here.

A thin man with brilliantine-slicked hair was talking as part of a group, not standing out from the others ... except to one who could see the curls and twists of darkness surrounding him.

Then Payne was in front of her, blocking her view.

'I've got someone you ought to meet,' he told her. 'If that's all right.'

The others were already engaged in a new topic.

'Of course.'

Dampness had sprung out over her face, and she dabbed at it as she left with Payne. Outside it was still darkening, less hot than before, but still too much for her. There was no conversation as Payne led her to one of the working huts, its interior lit; and they went inside to a plain office where a blue-eyed man was waiting.

'Dr Oppenheimer,' said Gavriela. 'It's good to meet you.'

'Likewise, Dr Wolf.' Oppenheimer smiled. 'But I'll call you Dr Woods or Gabby in public, I promise.'

'They seem to think it's best,' she said.

'Understood. Niels Bohr was Nicholas Baker while he was here.' Oppenheimer seemed not to notice Payne's frowning. 'You know, he worked out that slow neutrons are the key to successful fission while he was sailing here from Europe.'

Gavriela had spent most of her voyage being sick, or perhaps that was an exaggerated memory.

'So.' Oppenheimer fiddled with his tie-clip, then stopped and focused his startling eyes on her. 'We saw you flinch when you caught sight of Laszlo. It was a clear observation.'

'Don't worry,' said Payne. 'I don't think he noticed you.'

The solid wooden furniture seemed to swirl.

'What *is* this?' she asked.

'A rather direct confirmation' – Oppenheimer sucked in a little air – 'that this darkness phenomenon exists.'

'I don't—'

'In the sense that I've never seen an atom directly, but everything from Brownian motion to X-ray crystallography tells me they're unequivocally real. Not to mention the likelihood that we'll be able to make a chain reaction soon.'

Payne was smiling a little.

'Is *this* why Rupert sent me here?' Gavriela said.

'I don't know any Rupert,' said Payne, 'and I sure as heck wouldn't christen any son of mine with a name like that, but yeah, that's why you're here.'

Oppenheimer unfolded his narrow body and walked across the room, then back.

'Actually, your other purpose is real enough.' He glanced at Payne. 'We're happy to share our progress with you, though

I'm rather sorry you have to go back to England. I think you'd be a fine addition to the project.'

It occurred to Gavriela that Turing, with his ferocious mind and his interest in fundamental physics, would be a boon to the work here; but she dared not suggest it, because he was needed where he was.

'Ever the recruiter, eh?' said Payne.

Oppenheimer grinned, and for the first time Gavriela realized what an egalitarian set-up he had managed to create at the heart of a wartime military establishment, even more so than Bletchley Park. But that was distracting her from the situation.

'You knew something about this Laszlo already,' she said.

'We had a suspicion—' Payne began.

'There are others with your perceptual abilities, if not as acute.' Oppenheimer's eyes twinkled. 'Perhaps even a mystic-minded introspective Dane had something to contribute on the matter.'

Payne was shaking his head.

'Security, Robert. Security.'

'And open exchanges of ideas, or we'll never get this project off the ground. Rather a nice paradox, don't you think?'

Gavriela tried to wipe more sweat from her face, using a handkerchief already moist from earlier attempts.

'And this Laszlo?'

'We believe' – Payne focused on her – 'he has a signals pipeline reaching all the way back to the Kaiser William Institute in Berlin.'

'Kaiser *Wilhelm*,' corrected Oppenheimer, with good Teutonic pronunciation.

Now they were in Gavriela's other, newer field of expertise: signals intelligence.

'You could turn him,' she said, 'and force him to send disinformation. But if he's like the others, he has psychological skills, including a form of hypnosis, that will make him impossible to control.'

When Payne's jaw muscles tightened, he looked as he had when fighting.

'Then we'll use the other option,' he said.

Oppenheimer rubbed his face and shook his head.

'This war is awful.'

And that was a paradoxical sentiment, coming from the man determined to bring a new and devastating power into the world.

THIRTY-EIGHT

Roger woke up, used the facilities in the alcove that melted open, then flowed shut when he was finished. He worked out with bodyweight exercises and, using his newfound implant-aided expertise, immersed himself *inside* the quickglass floor that flowed to form a swift current, while he swam hard to remain in place relative to the rest of the room.

For a baby city, D-2 was surpassing his expectations.

Afterwards, fragrant with pine-scent smartgel, he pulled on his self-cleansed clothes and used his tu-ring to place a covert call to Tannier. The reply was: *Gimme time to take a piss.*

Taking it as camaraderie more than insult, Roger grinned. After some four minutes – according to his time sense – the wall pulled apart: an opening to Tannier's room.

'We're not under surveillance in here,' said Tannier, stepping inside. 'So you can relax your paranoia. Except you'd be happier with SatScan everywhere, I expect. And how come you look so energetic?'

'I kept away from the goldenmead, and I worked out already. Is breakfast going to be another public show?'

'It better bloody not be. What's on your mind, Roger?'

Maybe this was when he found out who to trust.

'Deltaville is dealing with Zajinets.'

Tannier blinked at him, stared hard-faced for several moments, then said: 'That *bloody* dessert. I knew there was something odd about it, but I couldn't work it out. Has to be flown in fresh from offworld, right?'

'So you didn't know about them breaking the embargo. Quarantine. Whatever.'

'That only applies to Pilots, surely,' said Tannier. 'It's not as if it's our idea. But point taken. And before you ask, it's quite possible that the authorities on Barbour as well as Deltaville know about it. No one told me, that's all.'

If Barbour knew, maybe they were in collusion, dealing with Zajinets themselves.

'Do they *want* another Fulgor Catastrophe?' said Roger.

'Maybe their analysis of the situation is different from yours.'

'Yes, and maybe I'm wrong, but why would you risk it? Even if the probability of enabling another Fulgor Catastrophe is low, the consequences are so high you need to mitigate against it any way you can.'

It was as if Dad's words were flowing through Roger's mouth: how to calculate risk factors regardless of context.

'I'm convinced,' said Tannier. 'But I'm not speaking for the powers that be.'

'You're the closest thing there is to it round here. Unless I go talk to Friss when she appears. She's the Lady Mayor, so that has to give her some sort of power in law-enforcement circles.'

Tannier stared at him.

'Let's have breakfast,' he said.

'What?'

'Empty stomachs, low blood glucose, after exercise in your case. Bad conditions for making important decisions.'

Something else Dad used to say: sometimes doing it fast is better than doing it right; but usually it works the other way round.

'Plus I'm just a simple copper,' added Tannier. 'I need time to get going in the mornings. Monosyllables only till I have some daistral.'

But, 'I'm not sure there any decisions to be made,' said Roger. 'I've just got to confront Friss and try to persuade her that she's wrong.'

'Maybe.'

'What do you mean? That's all we can do.'

'Tell the chief local government official that she's wrong?

That's one way. Or we could just find these Zajinets ourselves if they're still here, then wait and see what happens.'

It took a few seconds.

'You mean, use them like bait just as you're using me?'

'That's a cynical way of putting it.' Tannier grinned. 'You're getting the hang of things.'

As they walked along a curving corridor that looked like the interior of an artery – much of D-2 retained this unformed, anatomical appearance – Tannier zipblipped a report to superiors in Barbour whom he trusted. Whatever scanware he possessed agreed with Roger's assessment, that they remained free from surveillance as they explored the newborn sky-city.

'To the limited extent that we monitor other cities' traffic' – Tannier checked a virtual his-eyes-only holo – 'there's no sign of a Zajinet vessel in the region. If they'd been docked at Deltaville, they'd have had to disappear before Barbour hauled alongside.'

'You mean they're long gone,' said Roger.

'Probably. Pilots tend to spend longer, even when they've not been stranded here because their mates have abandoned them—'

'Cheers for that.'

'—but we know, because of the dessert, that it's not that long since the Zajinets arrived.'

Roger stopped walking. The quickglass surroundings glistened here, already odd; but everything was beginning to distort, even Tannier: colours and depths ran together like some animated surrealist painting.

I've been poisoned.

Fear was a tidal wash of noradrenaline, flooding him.

—Breathe.

Everything was dim. Tannier's mouth moved but his voice seemed lost beyond an insulated barrier.

Can't see right.

When he swung his head, part of him felt a weight that was

not there, while part of him sensed loss, a disquieting lightness. Worse, his field of view was not wide enough: his world was disappearing at the edges.

—*Calm. Breathe. Explore.*

He blew out carbon dioxide, and sucked in . . .

What's this?

. . . a richness of textured sensation, redolent with time and distance as he tasted perspective and drank duration, the old world forgotten as this new, resonant reality replaced it.

—*That's right.*

Everything was remade: the world, his existence, the comfortable smell of his friend Tannier . . .

—*Continue.*

. . . and there, distant and deliberately hidden, the twisting tang of strangeness, electric and not unpleasant. He pulled it into him, that sense of the trail, and then he began to walk, eyelids narrowing to horizontal slits while air currents defined obstacles and the full geometry of his surroundings. Tannier smelled puzzled, keeping close as Roger drank in the increasing fragrance, finally to stop before a great bulkhead in some unfinished hall.

—*Yes, so strong here.*

Then he shuddered and dropped to one knee.

'. . . all right?' Tannier's voice growing louder as if approaching fast, though he was right alongside, holding Roger's arm. 'Talk to me, Pilot.'

'Ugh.'

So strange, the way it disappeared like mist, like a spore caught in the wind.

What's happening?

And such a sense of loss as the richness disappeared.

—*You did well, my friend.*

Reality was re-established, shivering into place.

'I'm OK.' Roger pushed with his legs, straightening up, centring himself. 'There.'

The bulkhead formed a static bulge, dense and unmoving.

'Say what?'

Roger put a fingertip against the solid quickglass.

'The Zajinets are hiding in there.'

Roger's tu-ring, with the espionageware inherited from Dad, had capabilities he remained a long way from knowing fully. Breaking the architectural authorization codes should not be that hard, however. And it was only the security features that prevented him from commanding the bulkhead to open up: once he had access, he could command the procedure using his implant, just as any Molsin native might.

But Tannier was taking his time, going through official procedures that presumably involved communications between Barbour and Deltaville authorities, with additional complexity due to this being the daughter city. Perhaps there had been subterfuge or cover-up, but if so, no one was going to the length of denying Tannier's very specific request.

The bulkhead was beginning to glisten as if sweating, about to change state. Then splits opened, and three glowing lattice-shapes floated out, one – a brilliant scarlet – in the lead.

<<Not welcome, unwelcome.>>

<<Kinds diverge, disjunction.>>

<<For humans, salvation perhaps.>>

<<To your kind, stay clear.>>

The simultaneous non-acoustic words formed in Roger's mind, seeming to be addressed to him. From Tannier's stare, shifting from Zajinet to Roger, he understood the message in the same way: a warning to Pilots.

'Is this because of our quarantine?' he said.

<<Yes.>>

<<Is no.>>

<<Neither-nor.>>

<<Yes.>>

Tannier rubbed his face, masking his reaction.

'But you must—'

Roger stopped. At the far end of the room, another section

of wall was liquefying. Then he picked up a resonance, and blinked.

'It's OK,' he said, as Tannier turned to look. 'Not a threat.'

All three Zajinets pulsed with luminescence.

'You have to know what happened on Fulgor' – he raised his hand to the nearest Zajinet – 'don't you?'

The wall was melting open.

<<Cognition equals resonance with the real.>>

<<Understanding flows throughout.>>

<<Blind humans, blind Pilots.>>

<<One or none to save from night.>>

The woman who stepped out had shed the most glittering, confection-like parts of her haute-couture robe, so the remaining gown was black and gold-trimmed, already reshaping itself into a practical (though stylish) jumpsuit.

'Rhianna Chiang,' said Tannier. 'May I ask what—?'

She dabbed at her eyes, removing smartlenses.

'Just to save time explaining,' she said. 'You'll inform your superiors, I'm sure, but it's mutually beneficial not to make things public.'

Rhianna's eyes were glittering obsidian; but Roger had already sensed the neural induction that she had kept quiescent before, fooling him as well as everyone else.

'She's an agent-in-place,' said Roger. 'Just as my father was on Fulgor.'

'Very well play-acted,' Tannier told him. 'You fooled me, pal.'

'He didn't know until this moment.' Rhianna's eyes remained devoid of golden sparks, but her nervous system thrummed with energy. 'If things are moving into the open, we need to be ready. D-2's defensive systems are largely unformed. You know that.'

Tannier's facial tension was a confirmation. Roger turned back to the scarlet Zajinet.

'Why do you call Pilots blind?'

Sparks moved along the shining lattice-form.

<<Ignorance and inability throughout.>>
<<Assessing risk along null channel.>>
<<Acuity is void from appearance.>>
<<Danger pervades without response.>>

Rhianna came close enough to cup one hand on Roger's shoulder.

'Let me do the—'

But Roger felt the words come sure and strong:

'You think that none of us can see the darkness, is that it?'

The Zajinets, normally shimmering and adjusting, became frozen 3-D images for a moment.

'What did you say?' whispered Rhianna.

All three Zajinets slammed into a conjoined configuration – in human terms, it might have been a huddle – and blazing patterns of light swirled around and around the new joint figure, white-gold and emerald green, sheets and webs of brilliance whirling and twisting and rippling through transformation after transformation. After a time, they separated, then drifted closer to Roger. Rhianna and Tannier both backed off, saying nothing but clearly alert, giving Roger his lead for now.

I have to get this right.

He had seen one world die; but the implications here might stretch even further than saving Molsin – assuming Molsin really was in danger – for these were Zajinets, at home in realspace and mu-space both, just as Pilots were: not tied to any one world.

And they know about the darkness.

Anthropomorphizing xeno behaviour was problematic – sometimes deluded – but this was one reaction he felt he could read.

<<Assess.>>
<<Assess.>>
<<Assess.>>
<<Assess.>>

Could he turn the Zajinets, at least these three, into allies?

If they're enemies of the darkness, why not?

He shook his head at Rhianna, then turned to the Zajinets.

'You *do* sense the darkness, don't you?'

The Zajinets flared, one after the other.

<<Yes.>>

<<Yes.>>

<<Yes.>>

<<Proximity.>>

Fear drew the blood from Roger's face and skin, into his muscles.

'It's close?'

The air rippled around Rhianna – she was deploying a smart-miasma – and tiny nozzles appeared on the nearby wall and ceiling, Tannier's eyelids flickering as he entered into a deep control-trance, interfacing as best he could with the newborn city's untried, part-formed weaponry.

Da, da-dum, da-da-da-dum, da-da.

Roger could hear it now.

THIRTY-NINE

EARTH, 778 AD

Chief Folkvar met the traders and looked over the contents of their first two carts – weaponry and worked goods – while ignoring the captives in the third, for the village had no need of thralls. Hallstein had his eye on a fine-toothed comb formed from antler bone, a slit handle enclosing the comb proper. Beyond the carts, Ulfr walked, Brandr at his heel as usual.

A trader looked about to call out, but Folkvar touched his arm.

'Wait,' he said.

When Ulfr was past the women's hall and out of earshot, he added: 'We lost our *volva*, who was Ulfr's lover, nine days ago. The *berserkr* inside remains close.'

'My sympathies,' said the trader. 'Ulfr, you say?'

He indicated a bronze buckle, shaped like a wolf's head, with small runes inscribed:

ᚢᛚᚠᚱ

'So,' said Folkvar. 'That is well thought of. He was rewarded for bravery at the Thing, but not by me. Show me that sword, would you?'

The trader offered the sheathed weapon hilt-first. Folkvar drew it, admired the gladius-like heft, and slid it back into place.

'Is your weapons master among you?' he added.

'Yes, Chief Folkvar.'

'Can an inscription be made here without damaging the blade?'

'The sword was made with that in mind.'

'Have him put the same runes there, and we have a deal, master trader.'

The man was still business-like, not yet smiling.

'Do you pay in silver shards or coins, good Folkvar? Mead and food in part payment is welcome, of course.'

Folkvar gestured around the village.

'Do you see any kings here?'

'No, Chief.'

'Then we pay in honest metal, not coinage.'

'Aye, Chief.'

There was feasting, but not for Ulfr. He had eaten a little, while one of the travellers declaimed an Eddic poem – about Týr sacrificing his hand so that the hell-wolf Fenrir, offspring of Loki, would be bound in chains – but with too much skaldic cleverness and not enough feeling. Or perhaps this was not the time to celebrate anything.

From the longhouse eaves, a cat stared down at him, not bothered by Brandr or anything much. By a trader's cart, two figures sat hunched and bound near the front, while a woman sat on the ground by the rear wheel. All three were thin. Their heads were bowed.

Thórr's blood.

Ulfr returned to the feasting, then came back with three bowls of stew and a skin of sourmilk. The thralls muttered thanks in something that was not the Tongue. Ulfr offered the drink to the woman first, and that was when he heard the scrape of blade from scabbard.

Roaring, he spun to his right and thrust low and long, left fist to liver, slammed the top of his head against nose and teeth, then hammered down. The attacker dropped, but he was still alive. Ulfr shifted, ready to stamp down.

'Hold, warrior!'

Two traders with spears were standing back. Their comrade on the ground was curled up, breathing fast and groaning, his sword forgotten. Brandr, next to him, growled at the new-comers.

I'll kill you all.

But then Folkvar was among them, and Vermundr was coming from Ulfr's left, Hallsteinn from his right.

'Peace, Ulfr. Eira would have wanted peace.'

'Agh.' He pushed out a breath. 'Agh.'

'Let it go past you.'

'No—'

But he forced another exhalation.

Hold.

The imminent *berserkrgangr* began to fade.

'He was feeding your thralls as a kindness,' Vermundr told the traders. 'He had no interest in the woman.'

Ulfr nodded, staring at the downed man.

I still want to kill you.

Then he shook his head, teeth clenched and shoulders moving, and turned away, then stalked away from the firelight and humanity, only his war-hound at his side as always.

The next morning, he readied Kolr for travelling. The black stallion stamped down, wanting to be on the move. Brandr kept clear of his hooves. The last thing to fasten in place was the crystal-headed spear that Heithrún had given him.

'Folkvar thought you'd be off on the hunt,' came a low voice.

'Hallsteinn?'

'The same.' Hallsteinn came out of the gloom, bearing a blanket-wrapped sword, his war-hound Griggr beside him. 'You've friends here, and a chief that appreciates you.'

'Even though I nearly killed a trader?'

'He drew first and he's still alive.' Hallsteinn grinned. 'I call that lucky.'

Usually the man with the unsheathed weapon was the man who won, but Ulfr understood what Hallsteinn meant. No one had died; no one need cry blood vengeance. If Folkvar could be diplomatic enough, the traders might even return some time.

'Best if I'm gone before they wake.'

The liver punch would have done damage, and be painful days in the healing.

'Not without this sword.' Hallsteinn unwrapped it. 'From the chief.'

'What?'

'He wanted to do it all ceremonial, like. Take this with you, but when you come back he'll present it to you himself in front of everybody. That's what he said.'

There was a belt threaded through the scabbard, and its buckle was a wolf's head, inscribed as Ulfr.

'Draw the blade,' said Hallsteinn.

Ulfr did, and its runes matched the buckle's inscription.

'Be the wolf,' added Hallsteinn.

Ulfr looked at him.

I already am.

He sheathed the sword, and tied the belt around his waist.

For the next day and the next, making distance was everything, solitude his goal. Part of the time he rode Kolr, other times he walked alongside the stallion. When riding, he upped the pace to a trot for measured periods, while Brandr rode Kolr, lengthwise across the saddle in front of Ulfr, war-hound and stallion taking to the arrangement as if they had been doing it for years.

But he would not rely on the stallion. Riding was not like sitting on a stool, but still, Ulfr needed to keep his legs in shape by running. Many a battle was preceded by a full day's run or more to reach the battleground. Besides, only in movement could he forget.

It was the beginning of the second evening when he came across the injured wolf.

'Hold, Brandr.'

He slipped down and used the reins to hobble Kolr. Then he

crossed to the dark-grey shape, and stared into those circular irises, pale as bone.

'Hush, my brother.'

The foreleg was broken, but dark blood, spilled from a raking gash, was the greater problem. Much had poured out, and the wolf was weak, too weak to

No!

—attack, but a shape was flying at Ulfr's throat and he fell back, smashing forearm into fangs and then Brandr was there, snarling and rending—

She-wolf.

—making room as Ulfr rolled, the sword coming free, chaos all around like the swirling Ginnungagap before the worlds began, and then he could see his target and the blade went in, hard and deep, stopping the heart.

'By Thórr.'

He pushed himself up from the she-wolf, and moved on hands and knees to the male.

Dead.

Even as his mate had fought, the male's spirit had slipped out, unable to hang on.

Norns be damned.

There had been no need for this, for the male's injury or the female's confusion as she fought for her mate. There was no need for any of the harsh tricks the three dread sisters played on humanity. Perhaps they existed, but no one would ever worship them.

If I could kill the three of you, I would.

He checked that Brandr was unwounded, save for scratches. Then he made a small fire and sat down cross-legged, his back to the flames, looking at the two dead wolves.

Ulfr stared down at the part-grave, part-cairn. His friends, like Hallsteinn and Vermundr, would not understand his honouring the wolves like this. Burial, though not without skinning them first.

Folkvar's wrong about me.

It would be nice to fit in among the others, but part of his spirit was solitary, and people recognized it. Chief Folkvar, perhaps because his own abilities set him apart, seemed to consider Ulfr as an heir, as someone capable of command. It was an over-estimation: aloofness was not the same as superiority.

> *Medium wise should a man be,*
> *Never too wise.*
> *No man should know his fate in advance;*
> *His heart will be the freer of care.*

There were catchier verses among the best-known poems. There were some that stirred a warrior's blood, and others shining with cleverness. But this call for ordinariness was something that Eira used to sing.

'I know my fate, so damn you, Norns.'

Blood and death and hatred.

And my heart is not free.

Bound to a rock, like Fenrir or Loki, was more like it.

Yet while he imagined a solid rock and a fell creature tied to it, what he saw in the distance was very different: a moving mass of soil and stones, misshapen, squat yet huge, far bigger than a man. Something rippled in the air in front of it, then twisted out of existence.

'You've let him escape again!'

It was the troll, and it was hunting Stígr.

'NO!'

In the distance, the troll stopped moving. Then it, too, began to rotate, pulling the air with it until it was gone from sight—

Bastard creature.

—before rearing from the earth two spears' lengths away.

'Shit and blood.' Ulfr leaped for the reins. 'Shh. Brandr, come. Shh now, Kolr.'

Blowing into the stallion's nostrils, he held the big head, wrestling against the strength of equine neck muscles.

Hobbled, Kolr could not run, but he might still rear and fall.

'Easy, that's it.'

The troll remained quiescent, only small amounts of soil spilling from its outer form, making no attempt to reveal the glowing spirit within. Perhaps it understood the effect it was having.

'All right, stay like that. Good boy.'

He rubbed Kolr's nose once more, then stopped. The spear – Heithrún's gift to him – was shining at its point. The embedded rune, normally invisible or close to it, was glowing scarlet, as it had once before.

Perhaps it's not just for killing trolls.

So he unslung the spear, walked close to the troll – 'Stay back, Brandr' – and planted the haft on the ground.

'Do we hunt Stígr?'

More soil spilled from the troll-form.

<<Distance we slay.>>
<<One-Eye is there.>>
<<Tunnel to death.>>
<<Brother must die.>>

Ulfr had no brother. Trolls had no ability to speak clearly. But that did not matter so long as it could help him kill Stígr.

'Which way do we go?'

And why were they wasting time instead of galloping after the bastard?

<<Come.>>
<<Come.>>
<<Come.>>
<<Come.>> ·

All of the Middle World began to rotate, in all directions at once.

Sorcery!

It curved, as the darkness surrounding Stígr curved, and yet this was different, as blueness sparked and hissed all around, and he knew he was not alone as reality revolved again and spilled him out onto ordinary ground.

Revealed in its true form, the troll-spirit hung beside him, a glowing tracery of scarlet lines, bright even in the sunshine.

Sunshine?

Ozone was in the air, and he was standing on a grassy promontory amid gleaming buttercups, while reflections like steel blades glinted off the crashing waves of the sea. In the distance, a stone building rose, taller than any man-made thing Ulfr had ever seen.

Neither Kolr nor Brandr were here.

Stígr?

From somewhere, he could hear the sound of nine dread notes.

Good.

The troll had carried him far from home, but his enemy was near; and that was all he needed.

FORTY

Tannier raised his hands like a witch-doctor calling down the thunder. He stared at Roger, focusing; and as he did so, a myriad tiny nozzles on the quickglass walls shifted to aim at Roger.

The three Zajinets, newly revealed in their hiding place, gleamed but did not move or communicate. Were they scared of the darkness they felt approaching?

'What are you?' Tannier's face was blanching. 'I don't know your species.'

But he was staring at Roger, not the Zajinets. And he was controlling the surrounding inbuilt weapon systems currently focused this way.

'It's me,' said Roger. 'I'm no alien.'

Tannier shook his head, as if trying to shut out noise.

He thinks I'm an enemy.

'Tannier, I'm your fr—'

Golden fire spat, coruscating across the quickglass walls. Then Rhianna flowed past Roger, whipping the heel of her palm against the side of Tannier's jaw – he had not seen her approach – and the knockout was immediate. He did not fall, but his brain had short-circuited – out on his feet – and that gave Rhianna the opportunity to take hold of his head between both hands and say: 'Relax.'

Already out of it, his mind dropped into a type of trance, as Rhianna continued, soft-voiced, to tell him to soften his muscles and let go.

'And when you awaken you'll see and hear everything that's around you so do it now!'

She snapped her fingers.

'What did you–?' Tannier turned fast, locking his gaze on Roger. 'Shit, you wouldn't believe what I just saw.'

'I bet I would,' said Roger. 'Keep sharp, because that bitch Helsen can mess with anybody's mind.'

But the walls were melting open at two points in the room, some sixty degrees apart, seen from his position near the centre.

Rhianna's gown had become jumpsuit and cloak. She whipped up the cloak as a white collimated beam of smartions tore at her, smashing apart on the shield her cloak had formed. Tannier gestured, causing a smartmiasma to propel itself from the walls and ripple through the air, heading for the man who had fired on them.

Which meant the other attacker had to be—

Helsen.

The nearest Zajinet was writhing and flaring, while the other two floated back, distancing themselves. Roger raised his fist, tu-ring pulsing.

Now.

Helsen's face was a snarling mask surrounded by twisting darkness, and she was clearly about to attack but he had no idea how. A pre-emptive strike was his only chance.

His ringware attacked on two fronts, launching subversive infiltration against every piece of smart-tech Helsen wore, carried on her person or held inside her body, while direct control of D-2's quickglass caused the walls to spit out a cloud of smartatomic needles. On a timescale of femtoseconds Helsen was fighting back; but the floor rose up around her, swirling, because Roger had intuitive, cerebellum-mediated control of the quickglass itself: he could move it as if it were his body.

Even that might not have been enough, were it not for the shrieks of public alarms, and Tannier's grin. Whatever comms interference Helsen and Ranulph had put in place, Tannier had bypassed it. Perhaps they had failed to realize he was senior law enforcement with appropriate authorization; or perhaps they had counted on the mind-altering trance to keep him out of the fight.

Darkness whirled around Helsen. And something more, involving sparks of sapphire blue.

No.

Roger glanced back at the Zajinet, now thrashing against invisible bonds.

'Stop her!' he shouted to the other two Zajinets. 'Don't let her leave!'

They might not emit sound, but they could either hear it or process the neural patterns involved in speech production. Blue light ran along their quivering forms.

You think you can teleport away?

'Fuck you, Helsen.'

He pulled away his smartlenses and let his inductive energies rip, tearing across the room. When his vision returned, smoke billowed from the place where Helsen had stood, but there was no stench of burning meat.

Shit.

She was gone but – he spun to check – the scarlet Zajinet remained, dimmed yet pulsing, free of whatever bonds had trapped it. Perhaps Helsen had tapped the Zajinet's ability to transport itself along the realspace hyperdimensions, using it to teleport herself away from here; but she had failed to kill it.

Or she didn't want it dead.

Rhianna and Tannier were fighting smartmiasmas that appeared to be closing in, both of them too busy to see Greg Ranulph stalking closer, ready to attack with primal violence while they focused on the high-tech battle. Ranulph's teeth showed, lips pulling back as he neared his targets.

'*Ek em Ulfr-inn,*' said Roger.

And felt the blood-rage upon him.

When he snapped out of it, the world pulsed away then back, regaining focus as his arms and shoulders shook. At his feet lay seven unconscious men in dark-blue body armour – where had they come from? – while behind him, bloodied meat streaked the floor. Ranulph's head was off to one side, tongue lolling and torn arteries leaking the last of its blood, its eyes swollen in death-fear, separated from the butchered torso and limbs.

Rhianna and Tannier looked ashen. Some two dozen armoured officers crouched near the walls, visors hiding their features, gauntlets raised to propel smartmiasmas at him.

'I'm . . . all right,' he said.

Quickglass and gore dripped from his hands. He did not remember security officers arriving. He did not remember death and blood.

That wasn't me.

All three Zajinets were pulsing in time, forcing their words into everyone's awareness.

<<Darkness so raw.>>

<<He saw it and fought.>>

<<Saved us, saved all.>>

<<Honour this Pilot.>>

Slowly, the officers straightened up. One of them dissolved her visor, stared at Roger, then turned to Tannier. 'You sounded the alert, Captain.'

'Yes, and *he*' – Tannier pointed at Roger – 'saved us, the Zajinets as well as Rhianna Chiang here. And me.'

Roger, still trembling, spoke as if freezing: 'H-Helsen is gone.'

The officer in charge, her face hardening, looked at him.

'She's the suspect responsible for this?'

'Yes,' said Tannier.

Opacity covered the officer's eyes, then her smartlenses cleared.

'City-wide lookout, here and Deltaville both,' she said.

'Good,' said Tannier. 'I hope your people are all right, Lieutenant.'

'They will be.'

The others were still focused on Roger, but the lieutenant in charge walked over to Rhianna, and stared at her now-revealed obsidian eyes.

'Pleased to meet you, Ms Chiang,' she said. 'You look a little different from your usual public appearance.'

'You know how it is,' said Rhianna. 'Can't stay in party best all day long.'

'Hmm.'

The lieutenant stopped in front of Roger. 'So. Pilot.'

'I'm sorry,' he told her.

Some of the supine officers were stirring.

'You saved your worst for the terrorist,' she said. 'Otherwise, you'd not be standing there.'

He nodded.

'Interesting lives you celebrities lead,' she added.

'I'm not famous,' said Roger.

'You are now. In certain circles, anyway.'

FORTY-ONE

EARTH, 778 AD

Waves smashed against rocks, down below to Ulfr's right. Wind rippled across the promontory's grasses. The salty ozone smell heightened his awareness as he turned, looking for his enemy, ignoring the troll-spirit that glimmered in the air beside him.

'Where is this place?'

He spoke but did not care about the words. Finding Stígr was the thing.

No ravens.

Those same dread notes sounded in sequence, their origin far off, yet he could not tell their direction. In the distance, the tall stone building stood but did not call to him. Stígr was somewhere else. Inside the crystal point of Ulfr's spear, the enclosed rune continued to shine red.

There.

Beyond a rolling hill, he had glimpsed what might have been a shapeless hat, and perhaps the top of a walking-staff. Instead of following, Roger walked off to one side, looking for a better perspective.

'There's a cottage, I think.'

Some kind of shelter anyhow, its inhabitants waiting to be betrayed and destroyed by this word-twisting, soul-knotting bastard of a poet.

<<Kill or save.>>

<<Save and kill.>>

<<Blue brother, there.>>

<<Kill, fight.>>

The troll had yet to speak clearly, but this seemed a call to action.

'Yes,' said Roger.

Spear horizontal at his thigh, he loped forward, reached the top of a low hill – Stígr was making for a round cottage, for sure – and ran downslope. He sped up at the lowest point of the dip and pounded up the next gradient, while the troll-spirit floated along, keeping pace. Could it not just appear in front of Stígr? Perhaps the journey carrying him, Ulfr, had exhausted the troll.

Then it stopped, hanging in place as if afraid to advance.

Thórr's balls, you coward.

Ulfr ran on.

Cresting the final rise, he saw Stígr pause, glance back from the cottage entrance, then duck inside. This was the time for Stígr to die, remembering Eira and Jarl and everybody else he had betrayed and killed with twisted words, causing others to deliver the blows.

In heartbeats, Ulfr was at the entrance, ready to plunge in.

Shit.

There was no sign of weaponry, but Stígr would be in a defensive position, so Ulfr threw himself inside, yelling, leaping deep into the darkened space – no, there was a source of light – and spinning to see Stígr drawn back against one wall, lit by the blue glow from the other side of the cottage, from a thing glowing like sapphire but stained here and there with blackness. Bound by the darkness, held in place.

Troll-spirit.

Not the one that had brought Ulfr here, but the one that – it was obvious now – had borne Stígr from place to place with its sorcery. Even now, Stígr grinned as darkness-within-shadow curled around him, and sapphire sparks twinkled as the air itself revolved.

'No!'

Twice before, Ulfr had launched an attack as Stígr was disappearing by sorcery, but this time the source of the magic was right here, and Ulfr yelled as he whirled and stabbed deep into the troll-spirit with his spear, the rune blazing scarlet as he struck, and a massive crash or perhaps Thórr's hammer flattened him, making the world go black.

It might have been a handful of heartbeats later when he pushed himself upright on the damp, mossy floor. Neither Stígr nor the captive troll-spirit were there. The cottage interior was in shadow. Though his spear lay intact, its point was quiescent, the rune invisible.

He crawled out of the cottage, every muscle sore.

'You.'

The scarlet troll-spirit hung there, darkened in places. Perhaps it had fought a battle of its own, holding off the darkness that was powerful enough to imprison a fellow troll-spirit and make use of it.

'I killed your . . . friend.'

<<Yes.>>

<<Yes.>>

<<Yes.>>

<<Yes.>>

Finally, a clear response. Whether it felt anger, he could not tell.

'I'm sorry.'

No further words came. Perhaps it mourned its dead comrade. Perhaps – Ulfr felt this insight come upon him – the troll-spirit's death had been a release from torture, as Jarl's death had been. Or perhaps that was a self-serving delusion with no meaning for the troll-spirit that survived.

'Did it – your friend – transport Stígr away from here?'

For a moment, it shone in silence, then:

<<Stopped it.>>

<<No.>>

<<One-eye is near.>>

<<Too late.>>

Ulfr snapped back to awareness, looking in every direction, all pain forgotten.

'He's here still?'

The troll-spirit bobbed, then rose to a level higher than the cottage roof before descending to hang level with Ulfr.

<<Come.>>

<<Wounded.>>

<<Come while possible.>>

<<Come.>>

So it meant to carry him to Stígr's side while it still could.

'Yes.' He transferred the spear to his left hand, and drew out his sword. 'Yes.'

His name in Runic adorned the blade, soon to be drenched with the poet's blood.

<<We go.>>

<<We go.>>

<<We go.>>

<<We go.>>

Halfway through the swirling, Ulfr knew that he had misunderstood the troll's words, or perhaps he felt the enormous distance that the sorcerous spell reached across; but though he tried to yell, no muscle could move until the magic's work was done.

Damn you!

Then he fell onto high ground once more, to the place he had enjoyed so much before Eira's decision to step into space, and death.

'Damn you.'

He was back on Heimdall's Point, and the wounded troll-spirit was rotating out of sight. Ulfr's home, his village, lay below.

Stígr leaned against his staff, sobbing. His cloak was torn, and damp shit caked his inner thighs. Even his ravens had deserted him.

'Ho, stranger!'

The words were not of the Tongue, yet close enough that he knew their meaning.

'Wounded, are ye?'

He tried to nod, but his head drooped, neck muscles softening, and he could not raise it again.

'Come, brethren. We carry him.'

Men in rough robes congregated around him, crouching to take hold. Then Stígr found himself being raised, his eye turned to the sky, glimpsing shaven tonsures on the heads of those who held him.

The other children, laughing.

It was a memory of childhood celebration, being tossed in the air before the feasting, long before the darkness came to rule him. Now, he saw the bobbing sky, caught an upside-down glimpse of a great stone building – his destination? – then old memories and new pain became too much and he let go, tears in his single eye, burning in the scarred socket as he fell into void.

FORTY-TWO

LABYRINTH, 2603 AD (REALSPACE-EQUIVALENT)

The reports said that Admiral Asai had passed away during his sleep, of natural (but unspecified) causes. Max, Pavel, Clayton and Clara, sitting around a flowmetal table in an off-the-grid safehouse, had a different view of the news.

'They're beginning to move openly,' said Pavel.

'Clearly.' Max reopened a 3-D graph, a globular web of arcs and nodes. 'That bastard Schenck has revealed himself. You think this is all of his inner circle?'

'You've been observing them for longer than we have.'

'Then I think we've got them identified, and most of the next layer out. Beyond that, we're still struggling.'

No one had tackled the most important question.

'Are they really secessionists?' Clara meant seceding from realspace. 'This darkness phenomenon seems a bit ... metaphysical, or something. But Schenck's not just after power, is he? It's his long-term vision that worries me, because I've no idea what it is.'

'I wouldn't overestimate him,' said Clayton. 'Just another sociopathic political type.'

'Who's already got as much power as you can achieve in the current system.' Pavel was staring at Max's graph. 'Clara's right. What direction would he take Labyrinth in if we let him take over?'

Max closed down the holo once more.

'I've got a suggestion.'

'What's that?' said Pavel.

'Let's not find out. Let's shut down Schenck while his plans are still inside his head, and nowhere else.'

'You've got my vote,' said Clayton.

No one pointed out that this was no democracy.

'All right,' said Clara. 'I'm going to bring it out into the open. We've all been worrying about it, I'm sure.'

Clayton said, 'Analysing, not worrying.'

'If they've taken out Admiral Asai, do they know about us? Do they know who we are?'

'We're still here,' said Pavel. 'That's a good sign.'

'Can we counterattack?' asked Clayton. 'Besides assassinating Schenck, which he'll be taking precautions against in any case, how do we stop them?'

Max was regarding Clara.

'Is Schenck associated with secessionist philosophy in most people's minds, would you say?'

'Er . . . Those who follow politics, yes.'

'Hmm. I'm pretty sure you're right.' Max looked at her, then Pavel. 'In which case, a little information campaign might be in order. If we leave realspace, it's not just that humanity will do business with the Zajinets. Scientists created us once, and they can do it again. A shortcut might include capturing some of us, perhaps with a bit of vivisection thrown in.'

Clayton's scowl signalled dislike of such an indirect response.

'I do have an additional idea,' Max went on. 'It involves using some skilled Pilots, preferably neutral in all of this, and preferably without their knowledge.'

'Recruiting innocents?' asked Clara.

'It's a tough game we're in,' said Pavel. 'I thought you realized.'

To save Clara some face, Max said: 'You're right, but there's some information we need to disseminate. Information I've been sitting on for way too long.'

Pavel shook his head.

'Any information known to come from you, Schenck's people will find a way to discredit.'

'That's why I need to churn things up,' said Max. 'And with luck, come back with eye witness testimony.'

Before they would agree to the plan, the others demanded to see Max's ship. His departures and arrivals had been covert for many years: few of his colleagues still living knew what she was like, his vessel. That felt poignant: thoughts of ageing might carry overtones of desolation for anyone, but more so for Pilots; for they were not always solitary beings: sometimes they were symbiotic partners.

The quartet stood in a place deep inside and orthogonal to the core of Ascension Annexe.

'Where is it?' Pavel looked around. 'I can't sense a—'

An opalescent wall dissolved.

'There,' said Max.

She hung at the centre of the hangar.

Hello, my love.

Max smiled, not allowing tears to form.

'Bloody hell,' said Clara.

The ship was huge.

At last.

Dark-blue and midnight black, thick delta wings webbed with startling white, throbbing with power and potential.

'I've heard old stories about you, Max.' Pavel stared at her, the ship. 'Rumours from the past. Now I know they might be true.'

Clayton was smiling.

'He can do it, can't he?'

Jed Goran stepped out of the fastpath rotation and onto a polished dark-green and silver platform overlooking Cantor Circus. Rowena James from Far Reach Logistics was there, along with a tousle-haired Pilot it took Jed a moment to recognize.

'You're Davey Golwyn,' he said. 'The man who got a huge number of folk off Fulgor.'

'Well, yeah.' Golwyn shrugged. 'Me and a couple of thousand others.'

From Fulgor, Jed had carried only Roger Blackstone and Roger's comatose girlfriend, Alisha ... plus Carl Blackstone's legacy, now growing by the day inside Ascension Annexe.

Perhaps I should have stayed to rescue more.

But the risk had been vast, and he had made a promise to Carl Blackstone, without whom no one would have escaped the Anomaly.

'So.' Jed turned to Rowena. 'Is this a big job you've got for us?'

'Pretty much. I'm waiting for a few more– Ah.'

Fastpath rotations were forming all around them. Over the next few seconds, eleven more Pilots stepped through onto the platform.

'OK, everyone.' Having greeted each Pilot by name, Rowena looked around the group, smiling. 'I've a nicely tricky schedule lined up, so I thought I'd use only the best Pilots I know for the job.'

'But they weren't available so you called us instead,' said Felipe Copeland, an old rival of Jed's. 'Right?'

Rowena laughed. 'Absolutely not. Follow me, children. Everybody hold hands.'

Jed held out his hand to Felipe, who gave a hooked-little-finger salute in return.

Skilfully, Rowena summoned a fastpath rotation to envelop them all, and they passed through to a promenade that ran along a vast cavernous area of docks. Jed's ship was already there as requested by Rowena, hanging among the fifty or so ships he could see. He presumed the others also had their vessels waiting.

Scarlet light blazed at the promenade's far end.

'Emergency?' said Golwyn.

A blocky, shaven-headed man came tumbling through a rotation. Two younger men in Admiralty uniforms came running after him, but he gestured and the air rippled, and his pursuers dropped.

'I've seen him before.' Jed remembered the state funeral, of

Carl Blackstone along with his wife, and the man who had appeared on Borges Boulevard only to be arrested. 'Who is he?'

Rowena had a holovolume open.

'Guy called Gould, chief suspect in Admiral Kaltberg's murder, according to this.'

From below, in the gleaming abyssal depths of the docking volume, a dark, powerful-looking ship with white-webbed wings was rising.

'Call security,' said Jed. 'Let's get him.'

Arms rising, he summoned a fastpath rotation to take him the short distance to where Gould was running. To curve around such a tiny spacetime interval was difficult, the geometric equivalent of minimal leverage; and the rotation did not begin to manifest until Davey Golwyn joined in, adding his manipulation to Jed's with energetic skill.

'Nice one,' said Jed. 'Come on.'

The two of them jumped through.

'Shit.'

'Nice try though, Pilot Golwyn.'

'Call me Davey.'

The air was twisting where Gould had performed a short-hop rotation of his own, coming out to stand on one of those powerful wings on the rising craft. Already, a man-sized oval was melting open on the fuselage, allowing him to enter.

'Where the hell is security?'

'There's no general alarm.' Davey looked around the docks. 'You think maybe there's some kind of sabotage involved?'

'I don't know,' said Jed. 'I think maybe I don't want to stand around and watch while a murderer escapes from Labyrinth.'

'Uh-huh.' Davey grinned at him. 'We *are* the best Pilots that Rowena knows, right?'

'Allegedly.'

In unison, each looked for his own ship; in response, each ship pulled back from her berth, bobbed up, then headed for the promenade where their Pilots stood.

'Good luck, man,' said Davey.

'Luck,' said Jed.

They jogged in opposite directions, making distance between them so their ships would have no problem in coming alongside. Up on the platform where Rowena stood, columns of twisting air told of fastpath rotations being summoned; while out in the dock space, other ships rose from their berths.

Looks like the hunt is on.

But the dark powerful ship with the white-webbed wings was heading for the exit portal; and with no sign of security alerts, there was every chance she would fly straight through, bearing Gould into open mu-space where the probability of capture diminished. Jed's silver-and-bronze ship settled level with the promenade, and he ran onto her delta wing as she opened to let him inside, while adrenalized joy washed tidally through every cell of his body.

Rowena and the last of her summoned Pilots, Justina McGowen, watched from the platform.

'Sorry,' said Justina. 'Not really my business, you know?'

Besides Jed and Davey, eight of the others had transported themselves close to their ships and were rushing to board, while two had created fastpath rotations to take them to the Admiralty where they could raise the full-on alert that should already have occurred.

'All right,' said Rowena.

She herself was one of the Shipless, though her skill in visualizing complex geodesics raised interesting questions in the minds of those who knew her.

Justina had recently paid off a massive fine for infringing Admiralty regulations, and her body language was more pulled-in than usual. Whatever the analysis, fast aggression was not on her agenda.

'The freight schedule is off, is it?' she asked.

'I think I'd better reschedule, Juss,' said Rowena. 'Don't you?'

'Right. Later, then.'

'Yeah.'

There was a dispirited fuzziness to the fastpath's rotation; then Justina slipped inside and it twisted from existence.

'Shit,' added Rowena.

Out in the docking volume, Jed's ship was following Davey's through the exit portal, both flying faster than allowed. Seven others followed. Another ship was tilted at an angle against the promenade, having collided in the haste of her manoeuvre, though Rowena had not heard the bang.

Because I'm too scared.

Beside her, the air shivered as another rotation manifested itself. Clara stepped out.

'Hey, sis,' she said.

Rowena could only swallow.

'You're doing the right thing,' Clara added. 'For Labyrinth.'

'Are you sure they're not in danger?'

At this, Clara's facial muscles tightened. For all her training, and the Admiralty role she did not discuss but which Rowena had long held suspicions about, they were sisters who could not, standing this close, sustain a lie to one another.

'Oh, no,' said Rowena.

The last of the ships slipped through the exit portal and out of sight.

As Max-and-ship tore through the portal, Labyrinth's farewell resonated in the control cabin.

=Good luck=

'Thank you.'

Then ship-and-Max were out in the golden void, taking a geodesic hard enough to challenge the pursuers without losing them. Ahead was a scarlet nebula that served as a destination for now, while black fractal stars lay sprinkled against the glowing stuff of mu-space.

The rear-view holorama showed nine ships following.

Good enough.

Max slipped out of conjunction-trance.

'They won't catch us before transition.'

I know.

He smiled as he dropped back into unification, and whether it was Max-and-ship or ship-and-Max who took a long, banking, geodesic-shifting turn was moot as the conjoined pair flew on, so very fast, as they were born to do.

Behind them, the pursuers accelerated.

FORTY-THREE

EARTH, 1942 AD

On the second day of the return journey to New York, when they were almost alone in the railway carriage – except Americans called it a car – Gavriela asked Payne about the hand-to-hand combat session she had witnessed, and the quotation fastened to the wall of the training hut.

> *'In war you cannot afford the luxury of squeamishness.*
> *Either you kill or capture, or you will be captured or killed.*
> *We've got to be tough to win, and we've got to be ruthless –*
> *tougher and more ruthless than our enemies.'*
> **— CAPTAIN W. E. FAIRBAIRN**

Payne said: 'Our own Colonel Applegate set up the training programme, but the start point was him watching a Limey, said Captain Fairbairn, demonstrating his stuff on attackers who ended up in the laps of the audience, all of them senior military officers.'

'It looked effective.'

Gavriela realized her analysis was likely to offend Payne – as in, how dare a woman offer an opinion on the matter? – but he nodded before adding an explanation that surprised her.

'The government are worried about *after* the war, when the soldiers are civilians again, but trained in silent killing and the rest. That's why G-men are being trained harder than anyone, though we're expecting to remain Stateside. It's for later.'

In Britain, planning was geared towards surviving the war or winning it, not beyond.

Payne delivered other tough-minded observations on the

political situation, but when he and Gavriela finally ended up in Grand Central where his wife was waiting on the concourse, he showed another side of himself: embracing his wife with no regard to anyone around, as though the rest of the world had disappeared. Gavriela thought of her night with Brian and shook her head.

'This is my wife, Sadie. Sadie, this is the Gabby I told you about.'

'Oh, nice to meet you, Gabby.'

'Er, yes . . .'

The station announcer recited a sing-song of poetic names – Poughkeepsie, New Haven – and Sadie said: 'They're going our way, except we're going by automobile.'

When they reached the car, Payne seemed content to sit in the passenger seat while Sadie drove. From the back seat, Gavriela watched the sureness of Sadie's movements, aware that this was another world in many ways. Outside the car window, much of the landscape was as alien as the Paynes' manners. From the desert around Los Alamos she had come back to Manhattan's skyscrapers, and soon enough the green of rural Connecticut as Sadie drove them through the countryside. Finally they pulled up before the perfect wooden-fronted house that was home to the couple. Payne got out first, rounded the car, and held open the door for his wife to exit, even though she had driven. Something about the gesture made Gavriela want to weep.

Two police officers came along the street, hats in hand, unbuttoning their tunics.

'Hey, good buddy.'

'You made it back on time.'

Gavriela got out, and suffered the introductions – the cops were Olly and Chet, and they were coming off duty – before Sadie led her through the house and into the kitchen. It was movie-perfect, down to the pleated curtains and the lawn beyond, with whitewashed fence.

'I'll get the boys their beers,' said Sadie, 'and then we'll talk.'

Once the men were settled in the front parlour, bottles in hand, Sadie came back, set coffee to making, and sat down at the table with Gavriela. She wiped a microscopic mark from the oiled tablecloth.

'Charles tells me you've been ill quite a lot.'

'I . . . yes.' Gavriela had noticed Sadie's gaze on her ringless left hand.

If I were Polish, the ring would be on the other hand. If I had a ring.

In England, it was better to be thought Polish than German, and she often was. The same probably applied here.

'Sick in the mornings particularly?' said Sadie.

'Maybe.'

Gavriela could hear the joylessness of her own voice.

'There are ways' – Sadie glanced towards the hallway – 'of making sure things don't go to term. You're not showing yet, so it's early days.'

'I don't—'

Gavriela turned her head, but none of the men had left the front parlour.

'This isn't legal, is it?' she added. 'What you're suggesting?'

'Oh, my dear.' Sadie took hold of Gavriela's hands. 'I'm not suggesting anything. I'm trying to find out what you want.'

'Oh.'

Charles Payne was clearly a good husband, adoring Sadie and adored by her. Could Brian occupy a place like that in Gavriela's life?

I should try, for the—

Even the thought was hard to complete.

For the baby's sake.

At least she had three choices: marriage, send the baby to an orphanage, or the whispered option that Sadie offered.

'I need to sleep on it,' she said.

'Of course.' Sadie patted the back of her hand. 'First thing in the morning, then. You're off to Washington in a couple of days, is that right?'

'That's the schedule.'

Sadie blinked, perhaps because Gavriela had pronounced *schedule* in the English rather than American fashion.

'Come on, and I'll show you your room. Dinner's in an hour.'

'You're so kind, and your house is so lovely, and your marriage and ... everything.'

Gavriela was crying.

I thought I'd forgotten how.

But now she had a link to the future growing inside her.

After breakfast, Payne – Gavriela had begun calling him Charles here in his house, but still thought of him as Payne – excused himself, saying he needed to read the paper alone in the front parlour, where he could concentrate on the funnies. Gavriela wanted to tell him he did not need to do that, not for her sake; but she did not have the words. She watched as he adjusted his braces – suspenders: American English was as bad as Schweizerdeutsch – and checked his tie and cuff-links, as though the *New York Times* demanded formal dress for reading. Then he went out with paper in hand.

Sadie said: 'He's being diplomatic.'

'I know. You love him very much.'

'Of course I do. Not everyone can be so lucky.'

It was an indirect way of asking, and Gavriela appreciated it.

'I don't know whether ...' She put her hand across her abdomen. 'I think he's a good man, the ... You know.'

The father. Sadie nodded.

'A child needs a stable family,' Gavriela added, 'and I don't know, but ... I want to try.'

Sadie's smile was beaming.

'Good choice,' she said.

Afterwards, Sadie went out to the front parlour while Gavriela freshened up upstairs. When Gavriela descended, Payne was waiting in the hallway, looking more relaxed than before.

'I've got a trip lined up for you,' he said. 'For your last day here.'

'Oh,' said Gavriela. 'All right. Thank you.'

Payne winked at Sadie, and she grinned.

They're so wonderful.

Later, as Payne drove, he taught Gavriela local pronunciation from *fahchrissake* to *wazitoyuh, huh?*, and expressions from 'doing a Brodie' to 'twenty-three skiddoo', the latter explained as they drove past the narrow-angled Flatiron Building. Gavriela smiled and occasionally laughed out loud as they left the city and headed for New Jersey – *Noo Joizey* – eventually to arrive in Princeton's clean, leafy avenues. Payne parked as close to Fine Hall as he could, went inside and came back with a blunt-faced older man and a student dressed in suit and bow tie.

'We're your escort,' said the older man. 'This way, Dr Woods.'

Could this be what she hoped? As they neared the building they were headed for, beautiful violin music drifted out to meet them.

'Brahms,' said Gavriela. 'Played perfectly.'

The rumour was that his playing was awful. Perhaps she had the wrong idea about what was to happen here; or perhaps she should not listen to gossip. Then the music stopped, and angry words followed.

'Uh-oh,' said the older man.

'Sometimes,' said Payne, 'you hurl abuse, you get a smack in the kisser in return.'

'It won't be like that.'

'It better not be.'

They went inside, and knocked on the study door. When the great man came out, his white hair formed a mane in disarray, while his creased bloodhound features were avuncular, as Gavriela had imagined. His baggy clothes were rumpled.

'This is Dr Gavriela Wolf,' said Payne, surprising her.

Her hand trembled as she reached out to shake.

'*Es freud mich sehr Sie kennenzulernen,*' she said.

'*Ah, Gott sei Dank.*' He smiled at Payne. 'Forgive me. English is a wonderful language, but not as alive for me.'

Their escort stayed outside, but Payne and Gavriela entered the study as bidden. Her attention was caught by the dusty blackboard, or rather the equations upon it. Written in *his* hand, that was the thing.

'*Was denkst du?*' From anyone else, the use of the familiar would have been unthinkable; here it seemed natural. '*Das Lambda hab' ich nicht gern.*'

He pointed at the Λ symbol, so necessary for an expanding, steady-state universe.

'*Ich weiss nicht–*' Gavriela began.

But he picked up the violin and plucked with his fingers, causing her throat to constrict as if one of Payne's soldiers had snapped on a chokehold.

Da, da-dum, da-da-da-dum, da-da.

The sickness that rose inside had little to do with her condition.

'*Es tut mir Leid, Gavriela.*'

Those twinkling eyes belonged to a man with human faults, but one who saw deeply into things, in more ways than she had suspected; while Payne was nodding, like a man checking off a point on a list.

FORTY-FOUR

EARTH, 2033 AD

Regent's Park, on this ninth day of September, remained green and splendid, a forest oasis in the centre of smoggy London. From the high window in his rented apartment – part of a townhouse built for a Georgian gentleman, or some such – Lucas stared at the treetops, and the parade of office workers beneath them, making the most of an end-of-summer lunchtime. Softness pressed against his back, Maria's breasts beneath his shoulder blades.

'Come to Rio with me,' she said. 'In the spring.'

'I don't know. Will there be sex?'

'There better had be, lover.'

Quantum resonance was one of Lucas's specialities, and for sure his innermost cellular self resonated with Maria's lusty energy. He laughed as she tweaked his nipple from behind. He twisted to face her, then followed as she pulled him back to the bed where she laughed as he entered her. At some point, during the rise to nova crescendo, a *ting* sounded from his holoterminal, but Maria Higashionna was everything, the universe he breathed in, the hot skin he melded with; and then it exploded for both of them, and they lay afterwards with only gentle adjustments and kisses, lost in each other, floating in the aftermath.

'My recital's at three,' said Maria.

'You'd better shower first.'

'Mm.'

She rolled out of bed and walked to the bathroom. Lucas watched her, wishing he had the equations to describe her nude beauty. Then she was out of sight and the shower was starting up.

'Oh, well.'

Bare-arse naked, he hauled himself to the holoterminal and tapped it into life. When he pointed, the floating-scroll icon unfurled to show a black-and-white photograph hanging in the air beside a vertical sheet of creamy writing-paper. The cursive script might have been written with a fountain-pen.

'Hey, lover.'

'Huh!' He had not heard the bathroom door open. 'You've left the shower running.'

'Just wondering if someone would wash my ... So what's that, anyhow? An old family photograph?'

Lucas leaned closer to the holo rather than magnify it.

'I think that *is* my grandmother, you know. Not that I ever knew her.'

'You're kidding. Turn the letter this way, would you?'

He gestured, and the image rotated a little. Slipping his arm around her soft, exciting waist, he made himself read.

Dearest Lucas,

How wonderful to have a grandson! My words will seem very strange, since we do not know each other and I speak from your past. Still, I must ask you a favour, and be assured it must be this way. Even banks can fail over time, although it is to be hoped that some familiar names survive, so I am forced to contact you in this indirect way, with the hope that you will feel curious enough to investigate as I tell you.

He gestured at the paragraph.

'Her first language wasn't English.'

'Neither is mine, *meu amor*. Read on.'

'Yes, but ... Never mind.'

Please, my grandson, look under the parquet flooring, in the right-hand outer corner as you look out the window at the park.

Love,

Gavi (your grandmother!)
XXX

Lucas pulled out a chair and sat down. Maria leaned against him; his hand cupped her buttock.

'Is this a little physics joke arranged with my friends?'

'Nothing to do with me, lover,' said Maria. 'Is there any actual nerdy science in the note?'

'A logical paradox, maybe.'

'Didn't you say maths is built on paradox-infested foundations? Russell and Gödel, right? When you got into that argument with Jim in the One Tun.'

'No.' He shut down the display. 'I mean, that's sort of what I said.'

Maria looked at the space where the letter had hung.

'What is parquet flooring?'

'Excuse me?'

'The letter said parquet flooring, in the corner.'

He squeezed her.

'That's parquet.' He pointed at the wooden floor. 'Blocks arranged in patterns. And you're going to be late for your recital.'

'Yes, but—'

'And you're wasting water, more to the point.'

'You're a monster.'

'Yes.' He kissed her nipple, and ran a finger down to her mons. 'Your monster, and I'll be here all night.'

'Bad monster.' Maria glanced at the floor in the far corner of the room. 'All right, I'm going to get clean by myself.'

Lucas grinned as she returned to the bathroom. Then he pulled on a pair of discarded shorts, and went in to the kitchen alcove to make coffee.

Silly buggers.

He went back to the terminal and checked the message's metadata.

'Thought so.'

These terminals were new and still scarce, each model with varying capabilities. The message had been directed to this physical device by address, not just to his cloud ID, with model-specific image optimization.

Sorry, grandma, but you died before I was born, so this is impossible.

He wasn't sure of the year, although it was related to an historical event, the year that . . . something happened. World-shaking at the time, no doubt.

You could not have known I'd be in this room, right now, today.

Not to mention arranging for a message to be sent via a technology no one dreamed of then. Although, to be fair, the message content was old school: an inked letter, a black-and-white two-dimensional photograph.

And you definitely wouldn't have known what I was up to. Did they have sex back in your century?

There was something weird about talking to one's grand-mother this way, even in imagination, so he closed off his thoughts. Coffee in hand, he wandered back to the window. Maria left the bathroom and opened the wardrobe, moving fast.

'Who owned the building' – she wriggled, pulling a dress down over her head – 'before they turned it into apartments?'

'I can't remember. Someone told me.'

'Some rich duke, or something, I'll bet.' She checked herself in the mirror, changed the tuning on her eyelid make-up – the liquid crystal layer grew pinker – then came over to kiss him. 'Meet in the bar at six, right?'

'You've got it.'

'And you'd better get going now yourself. No time to dawdle.'

'Yeah, you're right.'

He began to hurry now, because he really did have a meeting booked, followed by a get-together with two of his PhD students. They were ten years younger than he was, and far too polite regarding his shortcomings. He remembered how his own supervisor, Vadim, had been a nightmare to pin down for meetings; that was why he wanted the next generation to have a better experience.

Maria slammed the front door shut as she left.

'All right. Shower.'

Someone had once told him that soldiers could get showered and dressed and make their beds in under ten minutes. Military discipline was alien to his nature, but he liked this idea. Soon he was fresh-smelling and dressed, still damp-haired, collecting the things he needed for the rest of the afternoon. Then he stopped, stared at the window, and said:

'Secret Intelligence Service. Well.'

Maria had asked about the building's earlier owners. How could he have forgotten?

She doesn't want me to investigate.

More likely, she did not want him tearing up the old, expensive-to-repair floor. Some people are elegant experimentalists, hands-on as well as in design; Lucas was better with the thinking aspect: his circuits tended to drift with noise instead of settling, his plug-in components rarely plugged in, while apparatus in general tended to come apart in his hands.

'Plus it's a practical joke, right?'

But how practical?

'No. Stupid.'

There couldn't really be something buried under the floor, could there? And if there were, it surely would not be something secreted by his decades-dead grandmother.

Would it?

Like spilled, dirty milk, the majority of the floor appeared slick and greyish. Lucas had forgotten about the protective membrane, now in the aftermath of some chemical catastrophe caused by his digging around. Wooden blocks, dug up, lay around him. Several kitchen utensils were bent beyond recovery; a spatula and a carving-knife had snapped clean through.

All he had found was a square of old, folded canvas, stained but intact.

'Message from the grave. Jesus.'

He had dug a miniature grave-hole in the once-flawless floor. Maria had been right; the landlord was going to be bloody hacked off.

'So which of you buggers' – he imagined his colleagues' faces in a row – 'is going to be responsible for this?'

Unfolding the canvas revealed something small, a card or letter, wrapped in flimsy paper. Inside the paper was a black-and-white photograph – no surprise now – showing two young women in hats and skirt suits, in what he supposed was the 1940s, maybe 50s.

On the back, the ink had faded to a brownish colour splotched with black.

Frau Doktor Gavriela Wolf & Frau Ilse Wolf, Amsterdam, 9. September 1930

One of the women, dark-haired and with intense eyes, was the same woman as in the holoterminal message, but younger.

'Hello, Grandma.'

And there was a folded sheet of notepaper. Of course there had to be something more to the joke than an old photo. The cursive, copperplate writing was hard to make out, but the note was short.

You will see three. You will be wrong.
   G
P.S. Pass it on! $\kappa_\infty = 9.42$; $\lambda_\infty = 2.703 \times 10^{23}$; $\mu_\infty = .02289$

Lucas stared at nothing, imagining spies in double-breasted suits working in here, the air filled with pipe-smoke, their patrician accents alien to modern ears.

'The game's afoot,' he said. 'So three what, precisely?'

But none of this, really, felt like a joke.

He slowed walking past the Royal College of Music. Heavenly sounds floated from an open window – it might have been Maria's recital, but it could be any one of the students at practice. Opposite was the round, redbrick Victorian flying-saucer-like Royal Albert Hall where they dreamed of performing for real. Musical mastery and leading-edge science on the same street. A hundred and fifty years ago, things would have looked just like this.

Then he was at the corner, swiping his Imperial College ID ring to gain entrance to Huxley, where he nodded to a couple of technicians he knew, then rode up to the top floor, and strode past the biophysics rooms, heading for his office in Blackett.

You will see three.

Three buses? Sparrows dropping dead? Moments of random kindness? Maria was going to be pissed off when she saw the floor. The landlord was the least of Lucas's worries.

'Scientists,' his friend Arne had said over several pints of Stella, 'just do not get hot babes like Maria as girlfriends.'

In reply, Lucas had brought the big intellectual guns to bear, quoting Richard Feynman: 'If experiment disagrees with theory, then the theory is wrong. All of science is contained in that sentence.'

'Sod off,' Arne had answered. 'So whose round is it?'

Anyway, never mind Maria or the stupid messages. He was in Imperial where he belonged. Time to decipher the nature of the universe – or have some tea and biscuits while chatting with his friends. Whichever came first.

Arne, Jim and Fatima were waiting in the small seminar room. The chairs were battered and the walls need repainting, but the holoterminal was state of the art.

'Here.' Arne handed Lucas a cup of coffee. 'You'll need this to keep awake.'

'Excuse me?' Fatima was fiddling with her wristband, communicating with the holoterminal. 'You are a bad person, Arne. My talk will be riveting.'

A phase space blossomed.

'Solar flux resonance,' she added, 'is fascinating anyway, and we've got some solid work finished.'

'I've got hot acid reflux,' said Arne. 'Does that count?'

'Peace.' Jim raised his hands. 'Fatima, why don't you start.'

Arne grinned. He would not interrupt again until it was time for formal questions, and then his queries were likely to be pointed and serious.

'So, good afternoon, everyone,' said Fatima. 'Here are the latest results from the—'

A knock sounded, and a young-looking woman peeked in.

'Sorry, everyone,' she said. 'Er, Arne? Could you come look at something, please?'

Jim frowned. So did Fatima.

'We've just started here,' said Arne. 'Can it wait an hour?'

'There's a major anomaly on LongWatch, but Palo Alto's showing it too. It's just happened, like a minute ago, but the web's already alive with—'

'All right.' Fatima tapped her wristband. 'Arne, you want to take over?'

'What? Oh, yeah.' Arne worked his own wristband. 'Have I got it? Right, let's link in.'

The holo view was of deep space, bordered with subsidiary sheaves of data. Lucas dimmed the room lights all the way down.

'There.' The young woman was pointing. 'See?'

'Holy shite,' said Arne. 'Hang on.'

Jim was leaning forward, almost inside the holovolume.

'You say Palo Alto's seeing this too?'

'That's right.'

'But they're not using the LongWatch satellite array. Plus their sensor tech is totally different.'

In the middle of the display, amid the blazing points of both stars and galaxies, three identically brilliant spots were glowing. Laid out in a perfect equilateral triangle.

You will see three.

Lucas checked the tabular data.

'Gamma-ray bursters,' he said. 'But three of them.'

In seconds they might die down – this being a real time

display – but for now they were blazing with far greater energy than any supernova could muster.

'What's their origin? Where the hell are they?'

'Other side of a void, looks like,' said Arne. 'A hundred and fifty million lightyears across, and still we get to see events like this.'

'But the triangle's an artefact.' Jim stabbed his finger into the image. 'Has to be. Gravitational lensing wouldn't split the image that way. It's the software.'

'We're seeing it, but we're not the only ones.' Arne shrugged. 'If Palo Alto agree, it's not a sensor artefact, so it's an artefact of something out there.'

'Unless,' said Fatima, 'there really are three gamma-ray events that were not just simultaneous from our viewpoint, but lined up in a beautiful equal-sided triangle. I mean, how likely is that?'

Jim remained staring at the image.

'A single black hole wouldn't produce the triangle, and I'm pretty sure that two gravity sources in line wouldn't do it either. But some other arrangement, maybe.'

Lucas had a memory flake in his pocket, an accessory that came with his new holoterminal, useful for setup and working offline, given that holoterminals were still rare, therefore not fully supported. As a child, he remembered Dad taking backups of his work, but these days everyone relied on redundancy in the Cloud, with offline copies a rarity.

He worked the flake, unnoticed by the others, copying several seconds' worth of the LongWatch data. Then he thumbed it off and put it back in his pocket, alongside the old photograph.

Why did I do that?

A second later, the LongWatch image began to shiver and fall apart.

'What the fuck is that?' said Arne.

Fatima shook her head at the language, but she was already

bringing up a subsidiary image, while Jim was working on his wristpad.

'Worm attack,' he said. 'The whole LongWatch system is going down.'

'Bastard shitting—' Arne looked at Fatima. 'Sorry.'

'It's all right,' she said. 'Jim's right, it's a worm attack. I know how you feel.'

They stared at the visual noise in the holovolume, rippling colours signifying nothing. Then the student spoke up, the young woman who had interrupted the meeting with the news and had since remained silent.

'Er . . . I'm just talking to my friend in Palo Alto.' She waved her wrist. 'Their system's been hit by the same thing, looks like.'

Such worm attacks rarely got through these days, which was one of the reasons everyone relied on the Cloud. But hundreds of scientists at least would have seen the images before the data was corrupted to oblivion.

'Maybe the triangle was the start of the attack.' Jim had never sounded so glum. 'Corrupt a portion of data cleverly, get everyone worked up, then take down the lot. Bastards.'

Lucas put his hands in his pockets.

I could tell them I've a copy.

Perhaps he was not the only one in the world. What if anyone who might possess a copy was in danger?

It's a paranoid fantasy.

But the photograph and note were real. From the creators of the worm? That seemed far more likely than a message from his grandmother, long deceased.

'—OK there, Lucas?'

'Uh, yeah. Just hacked off at all that.' He nodded at the terminal. 'If this was April Fool's, you might just about understand it, you know?'

'Malicious fuckers,' said Arne. 'Begging your pardon, Fatima.'

'All right.'

Another memory of Dad surfaced – Dad, who had never (to Lucas's knowledge) been in a fight, telling him: 'Trust your instincts always, as my old Mum used to say. Four billion years of evolution are responsible for gut feelings, so go with them.'

Call it another message from Grandma.

So what do I do?

Think about it alone, was the best answer he had for now.

And Maria?

No. Alone meant alone.

'I know it's friggin' early,' said Arne, 'but … Union Bar, anyone?'

'Yeah,' said Jim.

Even Fatima nodded.

'Can't do it,' said Lucas. 'Sorry. Got my students to look after.'

He watched as they all left.

Scared scared scared.

Even alone, he did not dare take the memory flake out of his pocket to look at.

FORTY-FIVE

MOLSIN, 2603 AD

Jed-and-ship burst into realspace, then decelerated, beginning a spiral trajectory around the yellow-orange gas giant. As Jed disengaged from ship-rapport, he opened up comms. In a moment, he was linked to City Customs in the sky-city of Barbour; and the face that appeared in the holo was familiar.

'Bodkin Travers,' Jed said. 'Bod, it's Jed Goran here.'

'I remember you, of course, sir. But I'm a little surprised. There's been no notification of– Well, you know. Still' – with a nose-tapping gesture – 'there's no problem here if someone needs to slide in and out under the old QT.'

'The embargo's not revoked. Sorry. But I'm not breaking it, either. Special dispensation from the powers that be.'

'Er, right.'

The political powers that Bodkin Travers recognized had nothing to with an Admiralty or mu-space city-world that he had never heard of.

'Look,' said Jed. 'The embargo ... It's for your own good.' With a grin: 'I always hated it when my mum said that.'

'Mine, too,' said Bod. 'So look, have you got another shit-load – er, shipload – of refugees? I'll have to warn the—'

'Just me, coming to visit.'

'Right. I'll warm you up a daistral, shall I?'

'We'll drink one together. Give me an hour.'

'Looking forward to that, Pilot.'

'Me too, Bod.'

Roger woke up in Rhianna Chiang's bed. Alone, in a sump-tuous room that was part of an extended, luxurious suite, still on Deltaville. Guest quarters, not her home. And he had slept alone, he was sure of it.

So how do I know it's her place?

Maybe it was the scent, that exotic fragrance she wore. Lately, he had been so much more attuned to smells; whether that was due to Molsin's atmosphere or some chemical effect of the sky-city quickglass all around, he could not be sure. Yesterday he had, he had—

He looked at his hands, but there was no blood.

Shaking, he rolled naked from the bed, accustomed to the easy movement – complex physical exercise had always been part of his life: the whole-body yoga/dance/martial art routines that brought suppleness and coordination to the forefront – but today there was something more: the prowling of a fighter scanning his surroundings, alert and ready to kick off.

I don't remember killing him.

His memory was stroboscopic, gestalt flashes of struggle against a backdrop of chaotic movement; but in the aftermath, no longer berserk, he had looked down on the bloody, shattered corpse of Greg Ranulph, along with the Deltaville law officers he had knocked down, and that was clear in his mind's eye. Blood-rage had descended on him, and then it was gone.

'They won't be pressing charges.' Rhianna's voice, but he had sensed her a half-second before the quickglass melted open. 'If that's what was making you frown.'

'Right.'

He felt lean and predatory, and his nakedness was no worry.

Get a grip.

Ignoring Rhianna, he found his jumpsuit and pulled it on. As the clothing reconfigured, an all-over rippling sensation indicated it was cleaning him as well itself. A pine scent that he normally would not have noticed, rose from his collar.

'While you slept,' Rhianna said, 'I tried using hypnotic techniques to relax you more deeply, and work on the trauma and guilt.'

'I do feel OK about Ranulph.'

'But that's not my doing, that's the point. There was nothing much to work on.'

'Oh.'

The man's face had been a reddened mess.

'I'm a little surprised by the shift in your behaviour patterns, Roger. But it made for one hell of an adaptation to the circumstances.'

Roger blinked, then felt his eyes narrow, aggression beginning to rise.

'He killed millions by creating the Anomaly.'

'In which case,' said Rhianna, 'he got off lightly. I'd have gone for elongated torture. Preferably after interrogation, but that's not a criticism of you. He was trying to kill us, and you used deadly force in response. Totally appropriate, also legal.'

'Yes.'

He had become a killer but not a criminal. There was no joy in it, but nor was there guilt. Because he had a strong, integrated personality that accepted necessity? It would be nice to think so. He was still Roger Blackstone, but everything was different, and he felt strong enough to deal with it.

'On Fulgor,' he said, 'Rafaella Stargonier – look you know the details of what happened there, right?'

'I don't know about details, but I know she was the seed. Merged with other minds through the virtual environment there. Skein, is it? Formed a group mind, a gestalt, obviously inhuman.'

'Only Luculenti used Skein in full, so she attacked them first. But she had Zajinet tech in reserve. Eventually she – well, by now she was *it*, the Anomaly – it was able to start joining its global mind to the ordinary Fulgidi, by creating shortcut links through the Calabi-Yau dimensions. Creating neural connections as if all their brains were physically wired together.'

'Perhaps my briefing was a little more detailed,' said Rhianna. 'Our analysts looked at how Skein worked – we had agents in place on Fulgor since its beginning, and by the way

I knew your father – and did you know the story of Rafael de la Vega?'

'Er . . . You knew Dad?'

'Not well. He lectured a couple of times at Tangleknot when I was training.'

'Tangleknot?'

'The intelligence service academy in Labyrinth.' Rhianna gestured at the quickglass walls. 'We're surveillance-free in here, by the way. This de la Vega guy was a rogue Luculentus, a psychopath, and he attacked his fellow Luculenti through Skein, and also copied torn neural patterns from the buried plexcores of dead people.'

Roger knew enough neuroscience to understand that thought is holistic, mental state emerging from the interplay of neural-clique activation across the brain – or brain-and-plexcores as a single unit.

'So when did this happen? I grew up there and I never heard of it.'

'A hundred years ago, mean geodesic. It wasn't like the Anomaly, not quite. De la Vega's so-called vampire code performed copying based on destructive quantum measurement: he copied his victims' thoughts and memories into himself, while destroying the originals. It was fatal to the victims.'

Dad had never mentioned this, but why would he? He might not even have known the story. Clearly the intelligence analysts had gone back to their archives to make sense of the Fulgor Catastrophe. Perhaps they understood far more than he did; perhaps being caught up in events was not the best way to interpret what happened.

'How many victims?' he said.

'That I can't remember,' said Rhianna. 'It was definitely dozens at least. His mind must have started to shift into non-human cognition, but unlike the Anomaly, we're talking about a single human body, de la Vega's. A body linked to external plexcores – too much hardware to fit inside his body, you see. Pilots based in Sanctuary were involved in the peacekeeper operation that took de la Vega down, so the old reports are full of detail.'

Roger rubbed his face. His bladder was full, and he needed a cup of daistral: output and input to start the day. But he also needed to understand why Rhianna was telling him this. Dad would have called it a background briefing.

'Sanctuary.' Roger tightened his bladder muscles. 'That's where Jed Goran was when the whole thing began this time.'

'And all he could do was get clear, luckily with you on board. So the point is, a hundred years ago, the Luculenti had these plexcores inside themselves, each the size of a large daistral mug, you know?' She gestured. 'This big.'

Roger stopped himself groaning.

'Give me a moment.'

He gestured for an opening in the wall, the formation of a bathroom-facility alcove, and went inside, the quickglass sealing up as he was still stepping through. Peeing in his clothes would have been possible – smartfabric lived up to its name – but not without Rhianna noticing. Relieved, he used smartgel to cleanse face, hands and hair. Feeling human, he went back out into the bedchamber.

An extruded table was laden with daistral and pastries, and two chairs were in place, with Rhianna already seated.

'Breakfast.' She gestured. 'Eat.'

'You're a genius.'

'I wouldn't go that far.' She waited while he took his first sip of daistral and began to eat, then: 'Plexcores, we were talking about. Large things, bigger and heavier than the modern plexnodes. So de la Vega, the more he had in his array – outside his body, remember – the more he was affected by lightspeed delays fragmenting his holistic thoughts.'

Roger pushed in a half-eaten mouthful.

'You mean – sorry – he used Zajinet tech to get rid of the delays.'

'Well done, except that he actually used our tech. Mu-space

relays of the kind we don't let realspace folk have access to, not these days.'

'Ah.'

Perhaps this was not such an obscure story after all, not for educated Pilots, if it had caused a policy shift.

'But that is exactly why Rafaella Stargonier was after Zajinet technology. Realspace hyperdimensions or mu-space, either one will do to shorten lightpaths. Incidentally, our analysts think there's an eighty per cent probability that the Fulgor authorities had a captive Zajinet in the research institute you visited, and a ninety-seven per cent probability that there was such a captive somewhere on the planet.'

'A prisoner?'

'They believe that your benign Fulgidi government institutions were involved in torturing a Zajinet over a period of two decades to extract its knowledge and capabilities. That's based partly on intelligence supplied by your father. They also think the Stargonier woman succeeded where the Fulgidi failed.'

It occurred to Roger that Rhianna must be a senior officer to have access to so much classified information.

'And from your own report, Roger,' she continued, 'it was this Helsen woman who manoeuvred Stargonier into thinking about Calabi-Yau manifolds. Using a friend of yours to convey the suggestion.'

'Alisha, yes.' He put down the food. 'She ... You know what happened to her?'

'I'm sorry.'

'Right.'

'But the question now is' – Rhianna appeared to become more relaxed than ever – 'what use Zajinets would be here on Molsin, given that there's no Skein and no Luculenta Stargonier to subvert.'

'Maybe Helsen just wants to be able to teleport,' he said.

Not much of an answer. He had not thought about the bitch's intentions: he simply wanted to kill her.

Steady on.

Understanding an enemy was a prelude to destroying them. That made sense.

'You think Helsen and Ranulph were trying to capture the three Zajinets?' he added. 'It looked like they were trying to kill us all.'

'They did something to Tannier that made him want to kill you specifically. It's not hypnosis as such, more like the hypnosis of melodramas than real trancework. You *can* get someone to do things they normally wouldn't, but you do it by deep unconscious association, subliminal operant conditioning, that kind of stuff. More Pavlov than Mesmer, if you know your psych history.'

Roger wondered how she knew so much about mind-bending. Perhaps there were aspects to intelligence work that Dad had never chosen to mention.

'Tannier's going to be all right, by the way,' she added.

'Oh. I . . . Oh.'

'We won't tell him you forgot to ask. So, that Pavlov. He was a sick son of a bitch, did you know? Surgically operated on children, attached glass vials to their faces, so that when he stimulated the unconsciously installed saliva response, he could measure the volume of generated saliva.'

'Oh.'

'My doctoral thesis was called *Torture, Sadism and the Birth of Neuroscience*. And then' – she gestured at herself – 'I became a Barbour socialite and fashion icon. Isn't life strange?'

'Is this some psych manipulation thing you're doing on me now?'

Rhianna smiled.

'Always,' she said. 'Do you feel better for having had breakfast?'

He understood enough basic psych to be sensitive to her intonation, *feel better* having the emphasis of a covert command.

'I don't *feel awful*, anyhow.'

Rhianna's laugh sparkled, echoing from the quickglass surroundings.

'I think you'd make a fine intelligence officer, Roger.'

'I'm no longer sure that's a compliment.'

'Maybe it isn't. OK, last thing, almost: the Zajinets have gone. I talked to them after yesterday's events, and they summoned their ship – one vessel for all three of them – and disappeared. Before they went, they mentioned the darkness more than once, but not in any way that made much sense. You know what they're like.'

'Sort of.'

'Plus I have my own bias, given that my uncle died fighting those bastards.' She presumably meant in one of the occasional violent incidents that had broken out over the centuries without ever escalating into war. 'But the Zajinets also asked whether we were staying, you and me, meaning Pilots. When I said yes, they said we should flee as well. That part was clear.'

'They're afraid of Helsen.'

'And they see her the same way you do, Roger Blackstone. Infested with this darkness, and they even use the same word. So perhaps you're not delusional after all.'

'Thanks.'

'Not that thinking like a Zajinet is anything to be proud of. Are you done?'

'Sorry?'

'With breakfast. Are you finished?'

'Oh. Sure.'

She gestured and the table melted back into the floor, the crockery dissolving, organic leftovers digested by the quickglass.

'Final item you need to know,' she said. 'If Helsen's goal is to create another Anomaly, and if she has the means to do it, Zajinet-inspired or otherwise, then we have ten days to find her. You know about Conjunction, right? I mean, I gather you were shacked up with an older lover in Barbour. No better way to get to grips with local culture, is there?'

Roger looked at her, feeling not the slightest hint of blushing.

'There was quite a lot of conjoining going on,' he said. 'I was too busy to pick up trivia.'

Rhianna gave a slow nod.

'Noted. But you surely knew that sky-cities are always on the move, and that Deltaville's giving birth to D-2 would normally be attended by more than just Barbour.'

'Because all the cities are moving to this Conjunction, which is . . .?'

'Exactly what it sounds like.'

'Of course.' He clasped his hands, interweaving his fingers as he used to do when Dad was thrashing him at chess or go. 'Every city in Molsin's skies coming together in one spot. Cultural interchange. Very natural.'

'Happens every four standard years.'

'Shit,' he said.

'Right. I don't think the authorities quite appreciate what Helsen might do, or don't believe what we're telling them. The cities are far too independent of each other for effective action anyhow, despite Conjunction. At best we can hope they'll give us the nod if surveillance spots her, and then I'll set you loose.'

Roger stared at her.

'Interesting wording,' he said.

'But you're dying to kill Helsen, aren't you?'

So it was not an illusion: he had changed, and she saw it too.

'Yes.'

'Then I think you should.'

FORTY-SIX

EARTH, 1942 AD

Gavriela spent four days in Washington amid an absence of skyscrapers, talking to codebreakers working on Japanese naval ciphers. Then it was back to Princeton via train, thanks to Payne, where a student from the Institute of Advanced Studies met her at the station, rode with her in the taxi to Fine Hall where she left her bag, and walked with her to Nassau Street. They were in time to see two gentlemen perambulating towards them, one with the mane of white hair and farmer's moustache, looking as if he were strolling through his olive orchard.

'There they are, ma'am. You want I should introduce you?'

'No need, thank you. The professor and I are old friends.'

'You know Professor Einstein?'

Morning sickness and the train ride had kept her irritated, deprived of sleep.

'Why else would they have asked you to take me here?'

'I thought—'

'I'm not familiar with Princeton, that's all.'

'Then, um ... Do you want me to wait for you?'

He was gawky, the young man, embarrassed to have annoyed her, and uncomfortable in the proximity of the great men approaching. Gavriela realized she was behaving badly, and softened her voice.

'You've been kind,' she said, 'but there's no need.'

'Um ... OK.'

After the young man left, she waited, trying to force away the gritty, sleep-deprived feeling behind her eyes.

'Gavi.' Another familiarity, as if they had known each other for years. Einstein kissed her cheek, then continued in German: 'Kurt, allow me to make introductions. Herr Professor Gödel, meet Fräulein Doktor Wolf.'

Those eyes that saw so deeply were twinkling as he added: 'We're discussing the existence or otherwise of time.'

'In the context of entropy?' she asked.

Gödel's answer was in precise, logical German.

'A lifeline is a fixed geodesic in a four-dimensional continuum.'

And every moment exists for ever, outside time-flow. She understood the concept, and why it appealed to anyone considering their own mortality.

'There are six million murdered Jews,' she said, not knowing where that number came from, 'that you can't have a conversation with now.' She tried to soften her tone, but if anything her throat tightened even more: 'I beg your pardon. I feel so stuck in the past at times.'

Either Gödel forgave her or he had no idea how to respond to such emotionalism, for the three of them began to walk, continuing the journey to Einstein's office, while the two men brought her up to date on their discussion.

'Kurt distinguishes coordinate time from what he calls Kantian or pre-relativistic time, and his cosmological model allows closed time-like curves.'

Gavriela did not think relativity had supplanted thermodynamics in any way, therefore hardly invalidating its implied arrow of time; but she said nothing as Gödel responded:

'If you can return to the past then the moment has not truly passed. That is my point.'

'Or send back information?'

'Absolutely equivalent in the causative sense. Of course . . .'

The discussion grew ever more rarefied as they walked on to Fine Hall. After Gödel left to work by himself, Einstein led Gavriela into his office.

'Kurt is trying to prove that God exists,' he said. 'By rigorous logic, I mean. Perhaps I am glad not to be a mathematician.'

'You can see the darkness.' When it came down to it, Gavriela had no idea what lay behind her visit to the States. 'What is it, do you think? What does it want?'

The blackboard no longer showed the equation featuring the Λ constant that had caused him to pluck those disquieting notes on his violin.

'I see it less well than you, I think, dear Gavi. And as for what "it" wants ... ascribing goals to natural phenomena sits no better with me than trying to prove that if God is possible then He must exist in all realities.'

'The key word there is "if", isn't it? Anyway, the darkness is an observed phenomenon.'

'And acting in human affairs, or at least appearing to.' His eyes glowed with their own deep lustre. 'Does a phenomenon affecting human minds necessarily have a mind of its own?'

Gavriela was blinking, off-balanced.

'Military men,' he added, 'need a definite target to aim at, or so I believe. I think our counter-conspiracy, if we even have one, will die out in the absence of clarity.'

After a prisoner in the basement of SOE Headquarters broke out using abilities that seemed almost mystical ... perhaps Einstein was right. Whatever the SOE files said, the language would not reflect the reality. Unless people like Rupert back home, Oppenheimer in New Mexico and the great man here continued to talk about it and organize – what? resistance? – even the recognition that the darkness existed would eventually be forgotten.

Or perhaps that was a problem for future generations, while everyone currently alive needed to concentrate on the actual world around them.

Back home.

A part of her realized that she had been thinking of England as home.

'... may be a post available somewhere,' Einstein was saying. 'My word carries a little weight, you see, and I take advantage because it is necessary.'

She backtracked through his words.

'I have to sail back,' she said. 'I don't know ... I just have to.'

Now the dark eyes shone with sadness.

'I spent four good weeks there in Southampton, before I left for the United States. But I think ... I think I will never leave the New World, now I am here.'

'Perhaps you've gained more than you've lost.'

It was strange to be speaking to her idol in this way.

'I hope so, Gavi. I hope so.'

Sickness defined her voyage home. Six ships in the convoy sank, broken apart by U-Boat torpedoes; survivors, plucked from row-boats, were looked after in the infirmary and its makeshift extensions: a ward room, a group of cabins, and another room whose original purpose Gavriela never discovered. She knew little of medicine, but helped where she could, even when that consisted only of throwing blood-soaked bandages into the wide, crashing sea, or emptying bed-pans that carried the stink of infection as well as waste.

Docking was both anti-climactic and a life-changing relief.

Walking to her lodgings from Bletchley station felt surreal. But there, strolling ahead of her, was a familiar female figure, headscarf failing to hide the volume of her hair-perm.

'Rosie!'

'What? Gabby!'

They hugged.

'I thought you weren't due yet,' Rosie added.

For a moment, Gavriela misunderstood, and put a hand on her belly.

'Oh. Er ... The convoy made good time. Saved a whole day.'

Partly from weather, partly because the slowest ships perished.

'Well, come in and have a cuppa, won't you?'

'I haven't had a decent cup of tea in forever.'

'So come on, then.'

Rosie's landlady, Mrs Lockwood, bustled around them making tea, then left them alone to catch up. They sat at the kitchen table, happy to see each other.

'Oh, nearly forgot. If my head wasn't attached ...' Rosie searched in her handbag, then came up with an envelope. 'Special delivery. Hand delivered, don't you know.'

Gavriela took the envelope.

'Who's it from?'

'A certain gentleman called Brian, that's all I'm saying.' Rosie was smiling as she took a sip of tea, cup held in both hands. 'I got the impression that my best friend Gabby hasn't been keeping me up to date on gossip.'

'We didn't– It was very ...'

It seemed even a pregnant woman could blush like a school-girl.

'Well, I *thought* so. Seemed obvious enough from the way he shuffled his feet, even before I knew what was in the envelope.'

'What do you mean? Oh.' From the feel of it, it was obvious. 'It's a key.'

'A front door key, no less.'

Rosie was giggling now.

Gavriela said, 'And I suppose you know which door it fits?'

'Your boyfriend's gone and bought himself a cottage, hasn't he? Thatched roof and rose bushes, you should see it. Well, I guess you will, won't you?'

'A cottage.'

'Penworthy Lane, absolutely lovely.'

'Well.'

Gavriela sat back in her chair, feeling queasy. Then she realized Rosie was staring down at her belly.

'Er ...'

Someone less thin would not have been showing, not this early.

'A cottage.' Gavriela put her hands on the nascent convex bump. 'A nice place?'

'Oh, my God, yes. It's ... Does he know?'

Rosie was smart, doing the sums in her head.

'I only worked it out,' said Gavriela, 'when I was at sea. On the way over.'

Blinking tear-damp eyes, Rosie leaned over and hugged her.

'Oh, well done.' Then she held up the envelope that Gavriela had put down. 'With a bit of luck, he might be home already.'

Gavriela could only nod.

It's so fast.

She tore open the envelope. A label, tied to the key with rough twine, showed the address. There was no note.

Sniffing, Rosie wished her luck.

Everything consisted of minutiae: the rippled grain of greyish wood that formed the gatepost, the clink as she raised the latch, the smooth swing of the gate; the *pat-pat* of her shoes on concrete, the smell of roses and damp grass, and the gleam of new paint on the door; the shaking of her hand and the clean metallic sound as the key went in, and she twisted.

Stepped inside, silent and awestruck.

Oh, it's wonderful.

Low ceiling with exposed beams, old uneven flagstones forming the floor. She could see through to the kitchen, where Brian sat in his dressing-gown, bare legs revealed, holding a cup of tea in both hands as he—

Both hands?

The lean face was not Brian's, and for a moment she thought she must be in the wrong place – but the key, the key fitted – and then footsteps clumped as another figure emerged from what looked like the bedroom. He wore striped pyjama trousers and a white singlet that revealed the stump of his left arm, which looked natural to her.

'Rupe?' said Brian. 'I can't find—'

When Rupert looked up, he saw her; and then they were both staring.

I'm a day early.

It felt like her fault, but only for a second.

'Hello,' she said.

A milky stain on Brian's trousers, probably unnoticed by him, confirmed what every sense, including smell, was already telling her.

'We ...' Brian stopped, then: 'We can't help what we are, Gabby.'

'No.' She looked at Rupert, who had grown very pale. 'And you couldn't help sending me across the Atlantic and out of the way, could you?'

Because Rupert had realized, that day in Baker Street, what had happened the night before between her and Brian. She wondered if they had talked about her since, and what they had said.

'I'm sorry,' said Rupert. 'But Brian's right, we can't help—'

'You think it would've been all right if I found a *woman* here?'

Her voice was a roar, causing Brian to step back. But his hand was pointing, trembling.

'Is that ...? Are you ...?'

'I am. It is.' Suddenly she was grim, her rage pulled deep inside like the furnace at the heart of a destroyer. 'Yours, yes.'

Both men grew even paler.

'Which is why, when I return to work at BP tomorrow, you'll use all your influence to stop the whispering. Plus I'll continue to draw salary while I'm having it' – she patted herself – 'and you can make a contribution towards the nanny when I go back to work afterwards.'

Rupert said, 'That's impossible. In your condition ... and afterwards, unmarried ... out of the question. Unless ...'

He looked at Brian.

'Don't ask him,' said Gavriela. 'Ask me. And no, I'm not marrying him or anyone else, so you can forget that.'

It was very clear now.

'Look.' Rupert changed his tone. 'Even if you were married, you know that having a job would be out of the question. In these circumstances, it's quite impossible to—'

'What's impossible,' said Gavriela, 'is for you two to stay out of prison if I tell what I know. And don't tell me there won't be other evidence all over the place if the police start looking.'

Of course, there was the possibility of violence, the two of them against her, which she had not considered. But they had seen her in action in Baker Street, hadn't they?

'Very well,' said Rupert. 'We agree.'

Speaking for Brian as if they were a couple.

Well they are, aren't they?

For a moment she wondered if she were being unfair. But she had an unborn child to think about, and they had betrayed her, both of them in different ways.

'And I won't be needing this.'

She put the front-door key down on a small table, beside a single rose in a vase. The petals were edged with brown, and curling.

'See you at work.'

The front door clicked behind her as she left.

FORTY-SEVEN

LUNA, 502308 AD

Usually, when Gavriela awoke in the distant future – which became her dreamlike *now* – she felt clear and solid, without any of the contradictions or confusions that defined her earlier life. This time, as she sat up on the bier, she felt conflicted. Then, when her transparent hand cupped her abdomen, she had a sense of emptiness and disturbance.

—*Are you well, dear Gavi?*

Roger, her dependable Roger, was standing in the archway. From the points of light glowing overhead, strange reflections glinted in his living crystalline form, his existence here as much a mystery as her own.

—*I'm glad to see you.*

But things were different, and he must have sensed that. He walked close, and went down on one knee. Here, in this strange airless place, it seemed a very ordinary gesture.

—*What is it?*

—*I'm ... I was pregnant. Back in my old life.*

Save for these dreamed interludes – some lasting for subjective days, weeks, even months – their lives were centuries apart, her death (whenever that might be exactly – whenever it had been) preceding his birth by six centuries.

Roger was staring at her.

—*You're the woman of my dreams. You know that.*

—*Ha.*

A child. Would she have – had she had – further children? If so, they were dust, and so were generations of descendants, if any. She did not know, truly, whether *homo sapiens sapiens* survived; nor could she try to find out, because Kenna had impressed upon them all the dangers of paradox.

Then Kenna's words were in their heads.

—Life continues, or there would be no reason to fight for it.

Roger smiled a crystalline smile.

—I guess that's a summons.

—It is. Bring swords, unsheathed.

That was unusual, but there was always a reason for Kenna's commands. Roger slipped two swords from their wall-mounted scabbards, then held one by the cross-guard, blade down, and offered it to Gavriela. She took it left-handed: it happened to be the nearer hand.

Again Kenna's words came to them.

—Ulfr is about to awaken. Escort him, will you?

The overtones were serious, precluding questions. Gavriela led the way; in seconds, she was standing at one side of Ulfr's bier, Roger at the other. A slight twitch started in Ulfr's crystalline body, then another. Then his eyes opened and he sat up with legs straight, looking from Roger to Gavriela.

—You're guarding me?

—We don't know what's happening.

—So we ask Kenna for explanations, as we always do. And shut up if she tells us to.

Gavriela had resonated, in the distant past, with Ulfr's fierce berserker energy. Here, if he chose to unleash it, she thought Roger and herself might last two seconds, with luck.

She touched Ulfr's shoulder with her right hand.

—We are not enemies, brother.

Ulfr swung towards her and came to standing.

—To the main hall, then.

There, the conference table was missing, while their ornate chairs stood in a row, raised high. Kenna, in the centre, was seated highest, her hands upon the chair-arms, her attention fully upon Ulfr. But what startled Gavriela was the crystalline figure sitting next to Kenna: huge, broad-shouldered, with spreading transparent antlers. Other differences included double-thumbed hands and – though it was hard to tell with bodies of living crystal – what might have been horizontally slitted eyes.

—*This is Sharp.*

Kenna addressed them while focused on Ulfr. She continued:

—*He is one of us, my sister and brothers, as you can see.*

Ulfr's chest expanded as if inhaling, though they were in vacuum.

—*His smell is not new, yet we meet for the first time.*

Kenna's tone was calm and not defensive.

—*Our bonding and communication had to evolve differently. Yet we all reach the same place.*

Ulfr shrugged his shoulders as if readying to fight.

—*So we have demons on our council now?*

—*Sharp is no demon.*

Then Sharp broadcast his first words, and they were redolent with awareness and courage. Gavriela felt her spine straightening.

—*I fight alongside you, my human brother, against demonkind.*

Kenna stood up.

—*Sharp has proven himself in sacrifice, brave Ulfr, brave Wolf. He will not turn against us.*

Ulfr's lips pulled back, and his teeth were like fangs of ice, of diamond.

—*And you think I will?*

Kenna raised her arms.

—*I did not say that. Some things require testing, that is all.*

Tiny scarlet dots flickered across Ulfr's transparent skin.

—*What is this?*

Sharp, too, stood up, taller even than Kenna. He tilted his head back, chest expanding, much as Ulfr's had earlier.

—*He is not tainted.*

Ulfr took a step forward. Gavriela shifted, not sure what she should do.

—*What?*

—*Troubled, but yet untainted.*

Then Ulfr whirled, and two swords were in his hands.

Gavriela's left hand was holding nothing. Roger, off-balanced but only in Lunar gravity, had plenty of time to take a half step and not fall. Ulfr looked at them all, snarling, then threw the swords aside. They tumbled end over end before striking the floor without sound, bouncing before settling.

—*No. Damn you, Kenna. Damn you to Niflheim.*

His crystalline body underwent slow collapse, joint by joint and limb by limb, slumping to a mound upon the flagstones. Roger looked up at Kenna.

—*You did that?*

—*No, he severed his own connection.*

—*Severed . . .?*

Gavriela tried to read Kenna's face. Had she made her first mistake as leader? Emotion swirled inside those eyes, but when Kenna replied her words were definite and sure.

—*You're not slaves or conscripts. If this is a dream, it is one that does not trap you.*

Roger's answer was a surprise.

—*Good Sharp, you have helped me in my distant past, so thank you. But Ulfr, too, has saved both me and Gavi. I'm talking about resonance, and the way it . . .*

Kenna interrupted.

—*We understand. But in the Council, to be anything other than single-minded is to be a tool of the enemy. I cannot expect you to understand that at this time.*

Gavriela looked at Roger; he was looking at her. They were drawn to this place – this time – as much by what they felt for each other as whatever Kenna-driven technique enabled it to happen. What if they had been misled, mistaking teamwork for purity of purpose, camaraderie for enlightened conviction?

—*Roger, you know what I feel for you.*

—*Dear Gavi, of course, because it's mutual.*

They understood each other: perhaps the price they paid for being here was too high.

Kenna stepped down towards them.

—*No. You are required in the Council.*

Gavriela dared to face her.

—That was what we thought. But perhaps we cannot trust our intuitions, not in this environment that you control. How do these bodies even function, anyway?

She looked down at her crystalline body. Even on her first awakening, she had felt natural in this form. How could that have been? What manipulation had prevented a natural human hysteria?

—Do not ask for explanations.

—Why not, Kenna? Why not?

—Because the answers are dangerous. The act of forming an answer can itself be deadly.

—To whom? To you?

Gavriela felt Roger standing at her shoulder, supporting her. Meanwhile the newcomer, Sharp, remained where he was. In Gavriela's peripheral vision, Ulfr's form remained slumped on the floor.

Kenna turned away. For a moment, sapphire sparks coursed through her. Then she was clear once more, and turning back to them.

—This is not the first Ragnarok Council.

Even Sharp made a movement at this, perhaps an involuntary surprise reaction. Gavriela felt Roger take her hand as he asked:

—If we're the second, what happened to the others?

Kenna paused for the duration of an inhalation, though her torso did not move.

—They perished in paradox.

Her words were resonant with overtones of sorrow, undertones of emptiness, as she continued:

—I will not allow you to fall that way.

Then she gestured with both hands, and Roger's eyes turned up half a second before Gavriela felt reality pull away, dropping her back through hundreds of millennia to the nothingness of sleep.

FORTY-EIGHT

EARTH, 2147 AD

Six weeks into Rekka's new role in Singapore, she was still waiting for Simon to give her the date of his moving here, of his relocation from Arizona. Instead, the daily calls had become weekly, their manner increasingly tightened, even stilted. Perhaps it was just that Rekka suspected UN Intelligence might be eavesdropping.

Here, so long as she avoided Google Li, work remained compelling: the challenges of strengthening the mutual linguistic understanding with Bittersweet, working with colleagues like Randolf who proved to be very smart, and even conducting occasional short conversations with the six male Haxigoji who seemed to be here as Bittersweet's bodyguard more than anything.

But Google had dropped further hints that Rekka should pressure Mary Stelanko, back in DistribOne, to spill the beans regarding Amber Hawke's location. The threat of decommissioning Amber's ship had been repeated in various ways. To be a Pilot, blind in this world and without a chance of returning to mu-space, was surely not the life that Amber wanted. But neither, it seemed, did she want to hand over baby Jared, natural-born Pilot, or even tell UNSA of the boy's existence.

They're not spying on me. I'm being paranoid.

More precisely, maybe someone was eavesdropping on her communications, but if so, the operation would be amateurish, contrived perhaps by Google herself. If UN Intelligence really wanted to track down a missing Pilot, they surely had the resources to do so.

Halfway through a Wednesday morning's session in the xeno facility, cramps caught Rekka's mid-section, and her arms began to tremble. The disconnection was the strangest and most frightening thing: the vibration of her limbs had nothing to do with her, would not stop at her mental command.

'Rekka—?' called someone, probably Xin.

'It's OK.' Randolf, his pale bearded face a blur, was beside her. 'Here, sit down.'

The chair he guided her into was stiff with newness, smelling of new-grown upholstery straight from the vat. Her shaking grew worse.

'All right.' His hands helped her rise. 'Come on. You need to get out of here.'

He half-carried her from the xeno area to the lifts, held her as they descended, then let her lean on his arm as they walked out through reception. Outside, in the hot sauna-damp air, he led her to a European-style coffee shop. Inside, coolness shivered across her skin, and she felt better as he sat her down in a corner booth.

'I'll get you something calming to drink,' he said.

'H-how did you know?'

That this was doing her good, she meant. That she needed to calm down.

'I've seen hypertension before. Besides, my wife' – his voice softened – 'gets migraines from time to time.'

Did Simon's voice change that way when he talked about her, Rekka?

Does he talk about me at all?

It was not a question she would have asked herself six weeks earlier.

'Thank you,' she said, taking the tea that Randolf brought back. 'Thank you so much.'

She sipped, and it helped a little more. Jasmine, camomile, with a maybe a touch of something synthetic underlying the added honey.

'And I got this.' Randolf held out a small, soft silver ovoid. 'It's the brand my wife uses.'

She took it from him and ran it across her forehead.

'Better. Yes.'

Closing her eyes, she leaned back against the upholstered booth.

Breathe the way you know how.

Years of yoga and she was behaving like this. It was embarrassing, but even the thought of that embarrassment was causing her breathing to quicken, her temples to pulse—

Let it go.

After a while, she opened her eyes.

'I could call for a medic,' said Randolf. 'But you're looking much more relaxed.'

'I am, thank you.'

'Then why don't we take an extended break? The almond cookies here are wonderful, if you want something light. And some more honeyed tea.'

His kindness made her want to cry.

'Yes, please,' she said.

They talked about Singapore and a little about Randolf's upbringing in Germany. They drank tea and ate croissants as well as cookies. It was an hour before he said: 'Bittersweet will be worrying about you, you know. She has a caring personality.'

Rekka blinked.

'I thought no one else had noticed.'

'Because you've been working so hard.'

'Oh.'

'So how are you getting on,' he said, 'with finding a place?'

Her hotel was upmarket. On first arrival, as soon as she had walked through the entrance, she had received a cool drink from a pretty young staff member, while the inbuilt system registered her automatically and a porter came to take her bags. But that had been six weeks ago, and she had two more left before UNSA would stop paying the bill.

'I've not really been . . . looking.'

Because she had planned on viewing properties with Simon, at least with him on the other end of a real time link. Because in trying to forget that, she had immersed herself in work to the extent of making herself ill.

'Come to dinner tonight. My wife will be able to offer advice.'

'Oh.' The invitation surprised her. 'I . . . would love to come. Thank you.'

'So.' Randolf held up his infostrand and tapped it, causing her strand to chime. 'You have my details, and everything is organized.'

'*Alles in Ordnung?*' It was one of the few phrases Rekka knew. 'Did I get that right?'

'Exactly correct.' He smiled. 'Time to get back to our inscrutable friends.'

'Not so inscrutable,' said Rekka.

Rekka rode up in one of twelve lifts that followed helical paths through the braided tower, where apartments were stacked like corn-on-the-cob given a twist. She wondered whether she could live here, if there were vacancies, and how much it would cost.

Imagined herself living alone.

No. It's just the pressure, making him act weird.

If she could suffer from shaking hypertension, why would Simon be immune?

According to the text-and-map Randolf had sent, his wife's name was Angela. Rekka had assumed, with her basic knowledge of German, that the name would have a hard *g*, pronounced *An-gay-la*. But the woman who opened the door was oriental, and when she introduced herself as Angela it was in the English fashion.

Over dinner, Rekka learned that Angela was native Singaporean, that she had met Randolf in an art gallery during his first week here – he had been a researcher at the University of Singapore before getting a post at UNSA – and that Randolf laughed a lot in Angela's presence.

'Come sightseeing on Saturday,' said Angela. 'Randolf will be hanging out with his old colleagues on campus.'

He seemed to belong here, with connections that extended beyond the closed world of UNSA.

'Definitely,' said Rekka.

On Saturday, they sat in a pavilion in Stanley Park; explored the resurrected Raffles Hotel with its airy white corridors and ceiling fans and Sikh doormen; saw the harbour and the sea-lion statues and, in another park, a group practising in the designated 'tai-chi area'; and watched shoppers buying smartfabric and biotech off the stalls in Chinatown. There, Angela frowned as a young oriental couple walked off with a new configurator, smiling, while the proprietor was blank-faced.

'What's wrong?' said Rekka.

'If you want anything here, let me buy it, and give me the money afterwards.'

'Because ...?'

'There's such a thing as preferential pricing. I'd pay less. You'd pay more, but not as much as those two.'

She meant the young couple.

'Why would they be charged more?'

Angela shrugged.

'They're Japanese.'

Afterwards they took the mag-lev to Changi station, transferred to a bus, and travelled along white-paved streets through an upmarket residential area: gardens an explosion of tropical colour, scarlet blossoms bigger than Rekka's head, the ubiquitous palm trees surrounding beautiful homes. When they got off at the stop, it was just the two of them. As they walked, to their right rose a tall fortified wall with razor wire rotating non-stop, coated with neurotoxin nanovectors according to

Angela. The establishment was Changi Prison, and its security was the best that modern tech could provide.

'Let's carry on,' said Angela.

There was a white one-storey building outside the prison wall.

'During World War II, that building would have been inside' – Angela pointed – 'because it's one of the original prison buildings. The Japanese treatment of prisoners was notorious, that's European prisoners as well us.'

Rekka noted the pronoun – *us* – and wondered why events of two centuries earlier should be so manifest in the present.

They went inside, to see the exhibits and to experience the dark claustrophobia of a cell – Rekka thought that perhaps ultrasonics magnified the effect – and return to the display cases. Angela pointed to a diary whose entries, in twentieth-century handwriting, were hard to make out.

'"We thought the Europeans to be superior,"' she read aloud, '"yet they seemed as lost and bewildered as we were." That's a world-view being shattered, right there.'

No history buff, Rekka was intrigued.

'At school we learned that white people used to think themselves superior.' She looked down at her dark hands, then up at Angela. 'I hadn't realized that the rest of us agreed with them.'

'Disquieting, isn't it?'

As they left, Rekka wondered what negative beliefs she might subconsciously hold, constraining her life now as people two centuries ago had limited theirs.

Simon. Why don't you call?

Waiting for the return bus, Angela asked: 'What about your family, Rekka? Were you born in India?'

'Born, yes.' She tried to tell it objectively. 'My father fell victim to the Changeling Plague when I was a baby. Maybe even while my mother was pregnant with me. And with so many people starving in those days . . . She took me to a Suttee Pavilion – you know about those? – for a last wonderful meal and music and all the rest, intending to kill me along with herself.'

'Oh, my God.'

Rekka had not talked about this so openly with Simon. Perhaps because Angela was a near-stranger – or a brand-new friend with no shared history between them – the facts had been easier to verbalize.

'My adoptive parents were Canadian. Pulled me out of the Pavilion before the flames went up. They took care of me. Took me with them when they left India.'

Angela's eyes were wet.

'Oh, Rekka. That's ... But good for them. Good work.'

'Yes.'

Not knowing why Angela was so affected, Rekka patted her shoulder.

'We ...' Angela stopped, stared down the street, then looked at Rekka. 'We can't have kids, Randolf and I. We've been talking about adopting, and your story ...'

She pulled out a tissue and blew her nose.

'Sorry,' she added.

Rekka shook her head, then hugged Angela.

It was three in the morning when Amber called. In the grey semi-darkness, wrenching herself out of sleep, Rekka blurted: 'Simon?'

Silver metallic sockets in place of eyes. Not Simon.

'Rekka, what time is it with you? I'm sorry.'

'Amber, no.' Rekka rubbed her face. 'Are you all right? How's Jared?'

At four months old, he would still be a worry. When did a mother start taking her child for granted? Ever? A real, caring mother, that was. Not like—

'He's ... Oh, shit. He's OK.'

'Well,' said Rekka. 'Good.'

She was still trying to pull her faculties together. Amber was in a bad state and not saying why.

'How have you been coping, Rekka?'

'Me? Er, working hard. Too many hours to leave time for thinking.'

'Enough to forget the bastard? You do it, girl.'

This felt like Rekka's first night in Singapore, with the timelag messing up her perceptions, the world appearing off-balance when really it was herself out of kilter.

'I hate them,' said Amber. 'I hate them for leaving me no choice, even if it's the right one for Jared.'

'Oh. UNSA.' Rekka was beginning to understand. 'You're going back to UNSA, to your ship. And sending Jared to an UNSA school?'

But he was only four months old.

'I don't have tear ducts, you know that? Well of course you do.' Amber shook her head. 'Makes it worse. Maybe it makes me a worse person, too. Maybe if I could cry, I'd still have a partner and so would you.'

What?

Rekka tried to ask: 'P-partner?'

'Fucking Mary,' said Amber. 'Fucking Mary fucking fucking Simon, that's the problem, isn't it? And vice versa. Shit, I hate them.'

Rekka coughed as if punched.

'I ... Rekka?' In the image, Amber reached up with one hand. 'You knew, didn't you?'

'N-no.'

Mary. Simon and Mary.

'Simon didn't call you? Didn't ...? Oh, God, Rekka.'

Six thousand miles apart, linked only by technology, the two women bawled; and for the next twenty minutes, Rekka produced enough burning tears for them both.

FORTY-NINE

MOLSIN 2603 AD

He ought to kill Hansen, assuming he found her.

I want to. I really want to.

Roger knew he could kill. Or perhaps he only *thought* he knew. Maybe he had the emotional toughness, or whatever you called it, but lacked the physical ability. After all, Helsen had got away with so much already. She had killed an entire world.

Rhianna was staring at him, her black Pilot eyes glittering.

'Maybe I can't,' he told her.

'What's stopping you?' she asked.

It was a classic question from neurorhetoric studies, and she must have known it would trigger the traditional counterpart: *What would it be like if you could?*

'Helsen can alter your thoughts,' he said. 'Make you see things that aren't really there.'

'*My* thoughts?'

'Well, mine, I guess. But—'

'How do you know? What evidence do you have?'

Her eyes were vast, deep-space obsidian.

'The medics who failed to see her walk past them. The, the ...'

In his mind he saw enthralled men in brownshirt uniforms staring at collective visions of helmed warriors wielding blood-axes and war-hammers, and a one-eyed poet casting armed men into confusion as they slew one of their own, a young man tied by leather ropes to a longhall's entrance-post, crying out as tumbling axes chopped into his body, butchery ended only by the casting of a mercy-spear, releasing the poor man's—

'. . . deeper and deeper,' came Rhianna's voice, 'into this relaxed and dreaming state, and my voice will go with you as you sink ever . . .'

—shade to be borne on dread *Naglfar*, Hel's vast ship formed of corpses' fingernails – such a multitude of the dead – to the realm of Niflheim, unless by chance the Death-Choosers of Óthinn had taken Jarl to train among the bravest of warriors, to prepare for the distant future when Ragnarök would be upon them—

'. . . because your unconscious now can keep you safe as you find the trance inside the trance to go deeper than you ever have before your eyes can close again, that's right . . .'

—and they would fight, the warriors of living crystal, those who led from the high command established on an airless moon, while in the night sky there shone the homeworld of humankind, banded now with crimson and silver, once thought to be the entirety of the Middle World – of the nine worlds, the only one to support living humanity – while it seemed now that baryonic matter was the true Midgarth, while the danger came from the realm of, of—

'. . . all right, everything is fine, and you can relax your breathing because all is well and here, now, everything is safe as you are safe and let it go . . .'

—and she was there, the only woman he would ever love for true, long dead and not yet living, his Gavi, his most beautiful Gavi with the crystal smile that grew as he—

'. . . rising up to become fully awake as I count five, four, three . . .'

—cried out as the visions twisted away, dispelling—

'. . . two, one. Now.'

—as Roger blinked, shuddering into wakefulness.

There were tears on Rhianna's face.

Afterwards, as they sipped daistral, Rhianna explained: 'I was in a deeply altered state myself, in full sympathy with you. It's the fastest way to get someone to relax far into trance.'

'I didn't figure you for the kind of person to cry easily,' said Roger. 'And I was a bit surprised. But why crying, exactly? Did I tell you something sad?'

His memories of trance had faded. He could feel them waiting, tucked around some corner in his mind, retrievable perhaps in time, not now.

'That depends,' she said, 'on whether you were being metaphorical or literal. What you told me was far more ... wide-ranging than I expected to hear.'

'Er, do you want to explain that more clearly?'

'No,' she said.

'Oh.'

'But I will teach you how to induce trance in useful ways. You already know how to pitch words within sentences so they act as covert commands. So let's add to that. Use your peripheral vision to watch my breathing. Do it now.'

Roger directed his gaze at her face, his attention on the tiny motions of her shoulders.

'OK.'

'Now synchronize your breathing with mine, and if your commands correspond to the deepest part of my exhalation, so much the better. Try it now.'

'Er ...'

'Just feel confident in what you're doing.'

'All right,' said Roger. 'So relax the muscles around your eyes ...'

That night, Roger dined alone in a small restaurant called The Single Helix. Rhianna was off being her public self ... and for all he knew, conducting high-level espionage at the same time. It would have been nice to fly back to Barbour to spend time with – to make sensuous love to – his wonderful Leeja. But then there would be no excuse to return here to Deltaville, where Rhianna had effectively begun a crash course in being an intelligence officer, with an eclectic syllabus geared towards his needs, at least as she perceived them.

A woman of about his age was eating by herself at a table in front of him. She was not facing him directly, but at a shallow angle: she would be aware of him from peripheral vision. It seemed a good opportunity to practise the non-verbal aspects of the routine that Rhianna had taught him, so he synchronized his respiration with hers, and in various ways altered his body language, forming a resonance between them.

Her eyelids fluttered and closed. Her head tilted forward, chin down.

Oh, shit.

Was this stuff really so powerful? Were the words not even necessary?

'Great food,' he called to a human waiter across the room. 'It's made me *come awake*. Fully alert.'

The woman jerked up, blinked twice, and continued to eat.

That's just so cool.

He grinned, leaned back in his chair, and wondered what other mischief he could get up to.

FIFTY

EARTH, 1942 AD

This was what Gavriela wrote in her diary: *Today I gave birth.*

It was a small collection of words for oceanic waves of pain, for eighteen century-like hours of waiting and effort, of things tearing inside her, her own core come to frightening, would-be-independent life and rearing to burst free, to rend its way into the world amid the stink of piss and blood, of amniotic fluid, shit and disinfectant. And then, the living form itself: shrunken, with blood-red monkey features, a tiny shock of black, spiky hair, the rubbery limbs, and the raucous wailing as the midwife said: 'He's a boy.'

In her arms then, the most beautiful creation in the universe, her son, and the pain inside her lost the edge of its fullness, beginning its backward ebb into the past, into the has-been. Into forgetfulness.

Today I gave birth.

Dividing her life into two: before and after the Moment.

Over the coming days, neither Brian nor Rupert called on her, but they sent separate congratulatory notes – no sense of ownership or responsibility in Brian's, no emotional intimacy in either – along with baskets of fruit and even chocolate: black-market goods that no one, in a maternity ward, would pay attention to.

She was in the Radcliffe Infirmary, and once released she would be living with Mrs Wilson, in her temporary digs from those first few nights in Oxford. The arrangements were Rupert's doing, and would suffice – he had said in writing – until she returned to work.

'What's our handsome boy going to be called?' asked one of the night nurses.

Gavriela, in the midst of suckling, looked up.

'I don't know,' she said. 'What do you think?'

Perhaps it was the aftermath of birth, of that massive effort, but she was finding it hard to be creative in her second language. All the names that occurred to her were German, therefore anathema.

'I like Tyrone,' called out an Irish nurse.

'Or Clark,' said the first nurse. 'Like Clark Gable, you know?'

'How about Winston?' That was the Irish nurse again. 'Or Eamon.'

After Churchill or de Valera, presumably.

'Maybe.' Gavriela smiled at them. 'Maybe.'

When they finally released her from hospital, a friend of Mrs Wilson's drove Gavriela and her blanket-wrapped treasure to the house, where Mrs Wilson fell in love with the baby on sight. It was a feeling that would only strengthen, for within days he was sleeping through the night and crying only when necessary, never for long.

'If only my Peter had been like that,' Mrs Wilson would say.

Her son, friend to Rupert during their schooldays, was serving in North Africa. Occasionally he would send a photograph of a camel or people in Bedouin dress, trying for light-heartedness, his letters unmarked by the censors because he steered away from military details.

'Have you decided yet?' Mrs Wilson would ask each morning at the end of breakfast.

'Sorry.' Gavriela would smile.

The question of the baby's name was beginning to vex her visitors: two of the Radcliffe nurses, who sometimes popped in as they came off duty; once, Rosie, who came by train all the way from Bletchley; and a nervous young Balliol man called Stafford, who on his first visit brought a letter that served obliquely as an introduction, straightforwardly as an explanation of the books and papers he had lugged from college for Gavriela to read.

Perhaps you might like to keep your mind exercised. I know I would, in your circumstances.

Best,

AMT

For a codes-and-ciphers expert, it took a too-long second to realize it was from Turing.

'He's from the other place,' said Stafford, 'but we've met at conferences and so on, becoming . . . friends.'

The other place meaning Cambridge. Learning English had been one thing, but Oxford had a culture all of its own, one that intrigued Gavriela but did not entirely attract her.

'Thank you,' she told him. 'My brain seems to have melted. These will help me mend it.'

Stafford blushed, as though even this indirect mention of childbirth was unseemly.

'Let's look at what we've got,' she added. 'Does Alan realize I'm no mathematician?'

It was a logician's treasure-trove: papers on symbolic logic, lambda calculus, abstract groups, and quantum mechanics; while among the books were the Russell and Whitehead *Principia*, commentaries of Gödel's work, and Karl Popper's *Logik der Forschung*. Only in Oxford could someone carry a German book without raising suspicion. Slightly less challenging were Russell's *Why I Don't Believe*, H.G. Wells' *A Short History of the World*, something by Dorothy Sayers, and a first edition of *The History of Mr Polly*, a Wells novel she had never read.

'The Gödel material,' said Stafford, 'is not entirely irrelevant to Alan's disposal of the deep *Entscheidungsproblem*.'

Gavriela felt a wide grin spread across her face.

'Thank you,' she said.

'Whatever for?'

'For assuming I have a brain capable of more than baby talk.'

Stafford blushed again.

'One takes it for granted,' he said.

His *Entscheidungsproblem* remark pointed out the relationship between Gödel's proof that some truths cannot be proven and Turing's proof that the computability of some problems cannot be decided in advance of working the problem through. Neither those proofs nor any of the material here was classified, but no matter. This was challenging enough: her brain could cope with more than baby talk, but not much more, not yet.

With a grin, Stafford added: 'In the other place, they still don't allow women to graduate, did you know that?'

'I presume they consider themselves the last bastion of civilization.'

'Last bastion of a broken empire,' he said, 'along with ourselves. And that's assuming we survive the war. An empire that fails to defend itself *without assistance* is doomed. Continuing to groom young men to rule such an empire is going to become, well, irrelevant.'

'An empire spanning the globe, and containing a quarter of it,' said Gavriela. 'Surely rebuilding is possible.'

'That's what everyone seems to think. Personally, I believe Hitler's done what Communism and economic depression failed to achieve: begun the dismantling of our rotten class system.'

'But ...' Gavriela wanted to point out his patrician accent and manner, but in some way that would not offend.

'Oh, I'm as rotten as the rest of them.' Stafford's laugh was both girlish and self-deprecating. 'Believe me, I'm aware of it.'

He rose then, and promised he would come again next week. Gavriela said she would look forward to it, and meant it.

When Stafford was gone, Mrs Wilson took the baby for a walk around the house, meaning she carried and rocked him as she perambulated, humming and talking softly, then came back, and said: 'He's told me he wants to be called Algernon.'

Gavriela smiled.

'Really,' she said.

Twenty miles into his prayer run, Kanazawa's mind was as close to *mu-shin*, to no-mind, as he could achieve at his current level. The heavy straw sandals slapped at the stones of the winding path as he came out of the woods and onto a clear stretch of high wall overlooking the valley. Behind him rose the slopes of Mount Hiei, the clean lines of the temple buildings obscured by the mountain's bulk.

He accelerated past a tiny pond into which water dripped from a bamboo pipe.

The world ripples.

The water is still.

Every stride of his run was a prayer of deep devotion, just as much as the ritual words recited at every shrine en route. His spiritual discipline was now twenty-seven miles of daily running in his gathered-up white robes, this being the thirteenth consecutive day. The paradox was this: in freeing his mind of thought, he was following a path that was his alone, not laid out for him by superiors in school then the Navy, not even by his parents. Even though the other monks followed the same rituals, it was different from the enforced uniformity of his earlier life.

It was his parents who had first shown him the mountain monks running their devotions, though they were arguably modernists: Father had been among the first volunteers to have the top-knot shorn. But Mother and Father had liked to watch the monks, as had so many others. Today, though, few spectators waited along on the route: times were different.

Something rippled among the treetops below.

No.

Something dark.

Let the thoughts go.

It was something he had glimpsed before: a symptom of his earlier wrongheaded life. But if anything the illusion was stronger now that he was following the spiritual path.

Keep to the path.

Yet reality was an illusion that the Buddha called *maya*, while his true path was not a physical route but something deeper. He would have thought it should lead away from darkness; but something told him he needed to descend towards it, the enemy. Pine needles and soft soil meant his approach was soundless. The thickness of the trees was enough, perhaps, to hide his robes.

'—to you, Moscow is safe.'

'Not thanks to me, but Dmitri. He's off doing something else now.'

The voices were Russian, only just comprehensible.

'And you're the most important part of the network.'

Moving to catch sight of the men, Kanazawa understood his mistake. The darkness, twisting and rippling, had been something associated with the other *gaijin* of the pair, the two westerners he had spent time with – including the day he witnessed the dojo death that changed everything. One of those two *gaijin* was here; but it was the assistant, the judo man. Perhaps contaminated by his master, he showed touches of the darkness now. But it was the other, his contact, who manifested the greater abomination: twisting black, impossible perspectives.

My path is devotion.

He stepped out from the trees, still upslope from the two men.

'What's this? A monk?'

'Looks like ... I think I know him. Is that you, Kanazawa-san?'

Their faces were a blur, though they were only ten paces below him, maybe less.

'But he's like us. Like Dmitri.'

'What do you mean?'

'Or maybe' – the man pulled out a pistol – 'I should say he's our mirror image. He can see it but he does not hear. Does not *feel*.'

More words followed, but they were faint, as though pulled

off into a great distance. Beyond the men, beyond the abrupt drop and far downslope, a mountain stream – perhaps the same one that fed a trickle into the pond above – shone white and fierce in its descent.

The way is peace.

And then he ran, as he was born to do, the discipline becoming him and he the discipline, hurtling downslope.

'—him, you fool!'

Accelerating. Arms outstretched as if to embrace, and the impact against their torsos.

Yes.

The world ripples.

Taking them with him beyond the edge.

The water is still.

Into the inviting void.

In Gavriela's dream, she spoke in vacuum to a man of living crystal.

—*If you had a son, what would you call him?*

—*I've never thought about it, Gavi.*

—*Could you think about it now, for me?*

Light refracted strangely through his features.

—*I'd name him after my father, I guess.*

The airless hall and moonscape melted away with the ending of the dream.

She had decided that today was the day. Mrs Wilson and Stafford accompanied her to register the birth. The registrar was too young for his brush moustache and round glasses. If he found the delay in registering to be procedurally lax, he did not reveal his thoughts. Instead, as Gavriela sat down in front of the mahogany desk, he asked: 'And what is the baby's name?'

Mrs Wilson craned her neck to look at Gavriela; even Stafford looked interested, intrigued not by the naming but the mystery: Gavriela had given no hints what it might be.

'His name is Carl,' she said. 'Carl Woods.'

The registrar held his pen at the ready.

'That's a little ... Teutonic, Mrs Woods.'

'Spelt with a "c",' she said.

'Hmm, well. If it's good enough for the king's bodyguard ...'

'I beg your pardon?'

'King Harold's carls, don't you know. Viking bodyguards to help him fight the Norse invasion. Then back down south to fight the Normans, of course. More Northmen, when it boils down to it.'

Stafford smiled. So did Mrs Wilson.

'And the father?'

Thinking of Rosie's fiancé, she said: 'Jack Woods, deceased.'

'Oh, I'm very sorry.'

There were a lot of widowed mothers these days, not to mention unmarried mothers assuming the guise of widowhood to avoid pariah status for themselves and their bastard children. In her case, Rupert could create a full fictitious biography, should it ever become necessary.

The registrar filled in the names, first and last, writing in a careful, clear script, making it final.

FIFTY-ONE

It did not begin as a hellflight, the pursuit, but that was how it ended: with Max-and-ship tearing along the most extreme of geodesics deep into golden void, while his nine pursuers pushed hard, one of them faltering at the edge of a crimson nebula, spinning away, all control lost. Max could not tell if recovery was possible. It was perhaps the first fatality.

I can't lose them all.

The point was to keep the leaders with him, close enough so they believed his capture to be possible – so they would not give up – while ensuring he remained ahead of them and free.

Lightning spat past his hull.

Take me if you can.

Ship-and-Max screamed through a Koch cluster of black, infinitely branching stars, then twisted onto another geodesic, equally hard, the shift itself causing wrenching vibration, and another pursuer fell away.

Seven ships pursuing him.

Better.

He increased acceleration yet again.

Jed's nerves were howling, a voice in his head screaming the question: why was he doing this? But Davey Golwyn was flying alongside even more recklessly, and the whole thing had become a challenge Jed could not set aside. Mulling things over was not an option: a lapse in concentration would mean losing the fugitive's trace. It was a binary choice: follow or give up.

Another ship dropped out.

Six of us left.

If they caught Gould soon, it would be enough.

A discontinuity plane threw off all of their trajectories, a message flaring among the pursuers—

I'm sorry

—all of them suffering as they were reduced to five, their sanity as at risk as their hulls, with no time to wonder how an older Pilot could stay ahead of them, swinging through a sequence of appalling shifts and breaks, the most chaotic of hellflights—

Transition, everybody!

—as Davey Golwyn's message saved them, hauling through a tight geodesic after Gould, straight into the exiting transition, all of them expecting black space sprinkled with stars because that was the usual realspace reality, and they had been too busy to figure out where Gould's insane trajectory had led: realspace, but not as they were used to.

All five Pilots were stunned at the blazing light of a billion suns surrounding them, dangerous in its massive magnificence, impressive and immense.

The heart of the galaxy, or near enough.

Close to the core.

Gould's ship was behind them: some last-second shift placing them at a disadvantage, but not much. The rearmost three vessels flipped around, conjoining their communications, one of the Pilots forming the words that blasted along the high-intensity signal.

SURRENDER OR WE OPEN—

But something moved across the shining light of all those stars. Jed saw it, but once again it was Davey Golwyn who reacted fastest, understanding the situation.

If you want to live, break off!

He threw his vessel into a hard, curving trajectory; and Jed did likewise, noting that Gould was doing the same: his dark, white-webbed vessel powering in a new direction at about .9*c*, an immense speed in realspace.

Then a tightbeam message sounded in Jed's ears.

This is Max Gould. I am not the enemy. Follow me, you two.

Jed tried to work out why Gould had said two, not five; but the mirage-like twisting of starlight intensified, and Jed-and-ship threw themselves aside then hurtled along a new path, following Gould, powered by fear because three of their number were doomed.

The trio of ships blew up.

Drifting in the braided rings of a gas giant, Jed remained silent, emitting no broadcasts. Passive visual observation showed Davey's vessel likewise hiding. Somewhere nearby, Max Gould's ship also floated, but out of sight.

Waiting for the enemy, whatever it was, to pass.

Max had three more deaths on his hands: not just innocents, but arguably heroes, trying to apprehend someone they thought was a criminal. Perhaps it was four deaths or more, for at least one of the pursuers in mu-space had broken off the chase during dangerous manoeuvres.

I'll get you home.

Was that her thought or his? The ship surrounding him was infinitely comforting.

I know you will.

Perhaps they were each making the same promise to the other. Then it was time to tightbeam a signal to the two survivors.

Follow me now. Minimal acceleration, passive sensors only.

They were smart, given that they were still here, but he made his instructions explicit all the same. Both Pilots blipped back acknowledgements.

And now.

Slowly, slowly, he drifted up from the concealing planetary ring.

*

From this place of blazing starlight, one direction shone even more brightly, with radiation from the core itself . . . and there, pointing radially into shining space, the long narrow-looking line of a galactic jet, blasting its away outwards. And hanging between the jet and the three mu-space vessels, a vast space station of what looked like human construction, around which a flotilla of strange ships floated.

Several of the ships turned around.

We've been spotted.

That was Gould.

All three Pilots threw their vessels into arcing escape trajectories; then Davey Golwyn changed direction again, and lightning played across his ship's hull as all his weapon systems powered up.

Get the hell away!

Whether the yell was meant for the enemy or his fellow Pilots, neither Jed nor Max would ever work out. All they could focus on was the need to fly fast and smart, away from the danger behind them.

But they saw the explosion that killed Davey even as they made their transition into mu-space.

FIFTY-TWO

The war had disrupted the university's teaching, but Oxford retained its traditions and procedures. A new year meant the start of Hilary Term, and it was in the fifth week that Gavriela gave her first physics lecture. It was a one-off, and followed from her debriefing with the local atomic bomb developers, sharing what little she had learned in Los Alamos. She had a strong sense that the English programme lagged behind the American effort; by how far, she could not tell.

At tea following that debriefing, discussions of atomic structure and strategies for producing chain reactions naturally gravitated to college politics – though the programme was removed from academia, and its personnel included graduates of the redbrick universities – and then to general matters. A large, walrus-moustached man called Braithwaite delivered his opinion that Oxford would remain free of devastation, not because Hitler wanted to hold back from bombing the venerable sandstone architecture, but because the Luftwaffe's aeroplanes and Rommel's tanks were built by German women rather than their menfolk.

Stafford looked at Gavriela, and she found herself speaking.

'Actually,' she said, her voice mimicking the languid, fluting arrogance of the men, 'you'll find that the well-off German *Hausfrau* maintains her household with the aid of her maid-servants, meaning the women are either presiding over drudges or working as such. That's why they'll *lose* the war, because Englishwomen are constructing the Wellington bombers that will blow the Wehrmacht war machine to bits.'

'Well said, my dear.' That was a narrow-featured man called

Sanders, whose unlit pipe perched vertically in his breast pocket like a periscope, as if his unseen heart was peeking at the world. 'And once the war is won, what do you expect to do? You personally.'

'Teach physics, I suppose.' Gavriela blinked. 'I really haven't really been thinking about life afterwards.'

At that, Braithwaite snorted and coughed out a *huh*: a walrus-like, barking sound to match his moustache. Afterwards, Gavriela thought that if he had not been so rude, Sanders would not have felt impelled to offer her the opportunity to speak to undergraduates, such few as remained studying while the war continued. Stafford said it was an excellent idea, effectively seconding and carrying the motion.

On the day of the lecture, she was in the room first, ahead of the students. The blackboard was one of the new kind: a tall loop of rubberized canvas stretched over horizontal rollers at ceiling height and floor. She would be able to present an extended train of argument without wiping clear the previous steps. Chalk in hand, she drew a diagram so that it would be ready before she spoke.

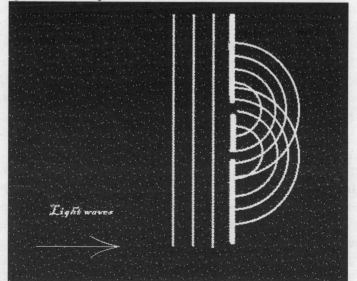

It represented linear wavefronts coming from the left, hitting a barrier with two holes in it, and propagating onwards as two sets of semicircular waves. She would have preferred to back it up with a demonstration, using a water tank with a strong light to illuminate the wave crests, but Sanders had balked when she suggested it. It was too bad, because thinking back to her first day at the ETH in Zürich, Professor Möller's demonstration of the rubbish-basket Faraday cage had formed a spectacular memory that would be with her always.

When her audience had filed in and sat, she said, 'Good afternoon, gentlemen. Dr Sanders tells me that you recently discussed wave-particle duality, at which point everyone's head fell right off.'

She used her most patrician pronunciation – *awf* – and the students laughed.

'So you'll know about the double slit experiment' – she gestured at the diagram – 'and you see that wherever the semicircular wavefronts cross, two wave-crests are reinforcing each other. If we had a row of little fishing-floats on water waves, you can imagine them bobbing up and down strongly at those points.'

Nodding her head as she mentioned bobbing, she saw the students unconsciously nod in time.

'In the mid-points between the maximum bobbing, we have places where a wave crest from one gap always meets the bottom of a wave from the other gap, cancelling out. So some of our imaginary fishing-floats remain calm, not bobbing at all.'

Again the nods: they were with her.

'If this were light waves, and the gaps were narrow slits at right angles to the board' – she gestured, moving her hand in towards the board, then out – 'then instead of bobbing floats, we'd have lines of light interspersed with shadow, agreed?'

Nods, still.

'That is an experimental fact, observed of course by Young in the nineteenth century, and thousands of times since. So the puzzle is, if light is a stream of particles as demonstrated by Einstein among others, then each individual photon can surely go through only one slit. So how does it know about the other slit? In particular, how does it know *never* to go where the two *imaginary* wavefronts cancel out?'

Fewer nods, but they were still with her, because this was in the realm of what they knew but did not understand.

Them and everybody else.

Gavriela pushed that thought behind her, and focused on the faces, so young-looking.

'Now Professor Bohr says that reality behaves like either waves or particles, according to which kind of observation we choose to make. In this, he's factually correct, but only because he's using the words *behaves like* in a very technical sense. In everyday terms, you *do* get wave and particle behaviour together, and I'm going to show you how.'

She turned to the board and drew an X at random.

'If we shine light through slits onto a piece of card or a blank wall, we get a series of vertical bright lines. But replace the card or wall with an array of photomultipliers, and we detect exactly where each photon lands.' She drew another X. 'And that seems pretty particle-like to me.'

Moving apparently at random from right to left across the board, she drew some four dozen Xs in total. A pattern was emerging, and so was comprehension on the students' faces.

'As we keep track of the points' – she drew two more – 'we see that they gradually build up the vertical lines of light that we expect. Wave behaviour grows from the particle behaviour, while the particles followed wavelike constraints.'

It was time to explore the Schrödinger equation, which would lead to discussing the difference between electromagnetic waves and the ψ waves that the equation dealt with: a varying quantity specified by two numbers, like longitude and latitude combining to give a map location, from which a probability could be worked out. But before that, she needed to ensure her audience was with her psychologically.

'I hope I've thrown some light on the subject' – she waited for the smiles and groans – 'and leave you to consider later how new patterns arise from increasing observations, and how, for the Sherlock Holmes devotees among you, it's the places where the light may *not* shine that define the pattern, making it depart most strongly from classical reality, so that ... that ...'

She shivered, hearing nine discordant notes, but only in memory, not in the moment; and knew that her words meant more than intended.

'... the darkness defines the light.'

After a moment, she was able to continue, but not without awareness of a strange, unfocused image lurking at the back of her mind.

Dmitri travelled in civilian clothes, not uniform, but his papers identified him as a member of the SS. His biography was well established in the Berlin archives, planted there by a V-man who was in fact a double agent: embedded in the Reich's intelligence hierarchy but run from Moscow. Dmitri's orders were to rendezvous with a contact in Kreisau, then decide on his own initiative whether to attempt an infiltration of the group in question.

The preliminary intelligence was that local high-ranking officers intended to attempt assassinating Hitler. Dmitri's cynicism noted that such sentiment was rising now that the Wehrmacht no longer seemed unstoppable: not just their faltering against Moscow, but their destroying less than fifty Allied ships in the North Atlantic during the previous three months, in contrast to the six and a quarter million tonnes of shipping sunk in the prior year.

He knew those figures were accurate. He had purloined them himself via an asset among Admiral Canaris's staff, and passed them on via courier to Moscow.

The German theatre of operations was where he belonged. His linguistic expertise and cultural knowledge meant that he should never have been sent to Japan; except that it had been a fortuitous posting, far from internal politics: his former superior, Colonel Yavorski, was no more. That had been the gossip from the case officer running the Frankfurt network and engaged in courier work on the side, hence his meeting with Dmitri.

The compartment door rattled open.

'Ihre Papiere, bitte.'

Dmitri had no qualms as he handed over his ID for inspection. He could fit in here. If Germany won the war, he intended to become part of the establishment; meanwhile, he would continue to perform for his Soviet masters. While the more he quelled his desire for murder and the taste of human meat, the less hold his *other* master seemed to have on him. Or perhaps it did not care to direct him any more.

Perhaps, by his nature, he furthered its purpose no matter which side he took in humanity's ephemeral, parochial affairs.

They worked in caverns below ground, a legion of the lost, each of them in the process of being broken down by workload and cold and starvation, each man a unit to be replaced: corpses were one of the waste products of Peenemünde; and Erik Wolf was just one more temporary component among the damned.

He did not believe in the concept of life force, of an *élan vital*; but there was a shining thought that kept him from death for now, and it was the conviction that Ilse had got away, using the loft that ran through to the house next door, before the Gestapo had come pouring in. There were no illusions: for him, it was only the work-gang and suffering, with death at the end.

But it lasted longer than he had expected, moving from

digging and rail-laying to work that demanded more nimble fingers: fastening components inside metal casings of what looked like huge finned torpedoes, designed for flight. The insides had the clunky functionality of refrigerators or cars, robust and inelegant.

'What is *Vergeltungswaffen*?' muttered one of the other prisoners, a Russian.

They could get away with mumbled conversation from time to time, provided they remained bent over their work and did not stop assembling the hardware.

'You understand "revenge"?' said Dmitri.

'Sure. *Mest*. I understand.'

'Weapon of revenge, then.'

The Russian, his face lined and collapsed like everyone else's, became even more grim.

'Aeroplane bomb without pilot,' he said.

'Yes.'

The missiles were to be called reprisal-weapons, propaganda for the people at home who were suffering now as Allied bombers encroached on the Reich's airspace, the name a joke to any non-Nazi. But the weapons themselves were deadly, urban populations their target.

Overhead on the catwalk, the guards were talking among themselves, paying no attention to their charges below. Escape was impossible for the prisoners, and overseers would check the assembly work before the final part of the casing was fastened in place, so why should they bother spending every second watching sub-humans at work?

Erik was dehydrated but not fully, and he could feel it in his bladder now.

'Tell me,' he said to the Russian, 'if the guards turn this way.'

'What? Yes.'

Pulling at his ragged trousers, Erik shuffled so he was pressing up against the exposed guidance system.

I'll show you reprisal.

A thin stream of urine trickled out. All around him, expressions altered, just a little.

Try guiding yourself after this.

It would evaporate, and the overseers would never know.

'Now,' said the Russian.

Erik was at work again by the time the guards looked down. And the prisoners had a weapon of their own, a final riposte before their coming death.

FIFTY-THREE

Rhianna was clad in a tight jumpsuit, matching Roger's. All around, the quickglass chamber was set to a malleable softness, for their protection.

'In the old days,' said Rhianna, 'when the first Pilots were created by nanosurgery and their eyes were removed—'

Roger shuddered.

'—they learnt aikido,' Rhianna continued, 'along with other bodywork systems to enhance their somatic awareness. So let's do the traditional unbendable arm trick.'

'Er . . .'

'Place your left hand palm-up on my right shoulder.'

He did so.

'Now,' Rhianna went on, 'stop me bending it.'

She clasped her hands atop his biceps, close to his elbow, and hauled down. Her own elbows travelled close to her body, the strongest form of pulling motion. He tried to fight it, but was already failing. His arm bent at the elbow, despite the tension in his muscles.

'All right.' She released him. 'Try again. This time, extend your arm fully as you visualize your fingers reaching to the far wall. Imagine energy flowing down your arm and out of your fingertips, that's right, and see what happens . . .'

She hauled down on his hyperextended arm to zero effect.

'Cool,' he said.

'Isn't it?' Rhianna stepped back. 'The visualization is just that, although imaginary *ki* or *chi* flow often maps to neuro-peptide movement in the body.'

'Er, right.'

'But mainly, the hyper-rotation has deactivated your biceps and triceps, and effectively screwed your joint into position, held by elastic tension in the rotator cuff. It's because your upper arm *can't* tense that I have nothing to work with when pulling down, because the use of your strength tends to bend your own elbow.'

Roger put his proprioreceptive awareness into his arm, remembering the position.

'The triceps,' he said, 'was hanging there loose. The biceps was stretched right out, which means ... the Golgi reflex kicked in. Of course.'

The same reflex that activates when someone loses an arm-wrestling match: the sudden switching off of all tension, the limb going floppy in order to protect muscles from tearing.

'Well done,' said Rhianna. 'Well done. Now for fighting under extreme conditions, you really don't want the Golgi reflex to work, because the other fucker will kill you in that moment.'

Roger blinked at the strong language, so different from her normal speech.

'So I'm going to teach you,' Rhianna went on, 'to disengage the reflex. Attack me.'

'What kind of—?'

The slap against his face was shocking.

'Just fucking *fight!*' she yelled.

He went for it.

Holy shit.

The ceiling whipped past his vision, something massive hammered into his entire back – the floor – and her legs were across his chest and throat, his left arm extended and caught in her grip as she leaned back, pain flaring as the armbar technique hyperextended everything.

He tapped twice, the traditional signal to acknowledge an inescapable hold was on, that he could not release himself short of allowing his arm to snap.

'I didn't say give up!' she shouted. 'I said fight!'

'Holy . . . fuck.'

He worked at it.

'Put the pain aside,' she said. 'Leave it for later.'

'I . . .'

'Just fight!'

A loud crack sounded as his forearm broke—

Holy shit!

—but his limb was no longer trapped, the armbar depending on the forearm's integrity. He squirmed around and hit her in the jaw. She twisted away.

'Good.' She spat blood. 'Good.'

Rolling further, she made distance and rose to her feet.

'Stand up,' she said.

He came up ready, covered in sweat, a predator about to kill.

'And relax, Roger. Let's take a look at that arm.'

Blowing out a breath, he shuddered, stepped back, and regained control.

Fuck, it hurts.

Something told him this was *not* the most painful lesson she had lined up.

Darkness, and the movement within it.

Now.

She was close behind him and he whipped back, an elbow-uppercut to the rear, using his good arm – *contact* – then his kidneys exploded with pain. They went down together, Rhianna and he, squirming on the floor until her legs scissored around his throat, his right arm caught between her thighs but not helping him, because his own shoulder, pressed into his carotid artery, enhanced the triangle technique. And then he was asleep.

The lights were bright when she brought him awake.

The ninth time, he gave as good as he got. Afterwards, Rhianna smiled a red-and-white smile, and pulled out the tooth his elbow-strike had broken. She stared at the quickglass wall, causing it to pucker then create a small alcove. She placed the tooth inside, and returned to the room's centre as the wall sealed up.

Rhianna's going to make me pay for that.

His pain was everywhere, but he would not let it matter.

Here goes.

Scarlet light blazed, and massive, thunderous vibrations drove through him – battlefield simulation – and Rhianna came for him at incredible speed.

Fuck.

He spun away growling and the fight was on.

Again.

FIFTY-FOUR

THE WORLD, 5568 AD

For two thousand nights and more, he Sought. Across the Sere Wastes and the Shattered Range, he followed Ideas, sharing those he captured with the villagers he came across, always receiving hospitality, always bidden farewell with relief: his difference was both useful and unsettling.

Once, he skirted a settlement where a flux storm combined with a buried crystal lode had induced foam-mouthed insanity. They were raving and armed, too dangerous to approach. He wondered, sometimes, how long they had lasted before death took them. But most of the adults he met were normal, with names and remembered childhoods, so unlike him; for he was Seeker, and that was all he could be.

Sometimes he walked past dawn, the rising sun shining red upon his burnished skin; but only if he was sure of shelter before the conditions grew deadly. There was some kind of enjoyment in not having the constraints that ruled villagers' lives; but the true joy was finding Ideas like the one captured yesterday, swirling in his mind:

Vacuum is a phase of spacetime as ice is a phase of water. The properties of a vacuum are emergent, just as the properties of solids – the existence and hardness of surfaces – arise independently of the quantum attributes of constituent molecules.

Tonight, as he walked beneath the light of Magnus and Minissimus, both of them full-orbed, he wondered if this region harboured a Theme. Yesternight's Idea resonated with one he had captured two nights earlier, and with another he had received in trade from a fellow Seeker on one of those rare occasions when two paths of Seeking crossed.

This was the Idea that the other Seeker had given him:

Emergence is more obvious the wider one travels. It is rare to find two worlds whose organisms use the same molecule or group of molecules (the latter tending to feature one or more autocatalytic reactions) as the basis for replication. No planet besides Earth has ever shown evidence of DNA. Yet evolution occurs similarly in every biosphere, producing predator-prey relationships alongside symbiosis.

It was an old Idea, long-held in some crystal lode; but the one he had snagged himself two nights before featured even more archaic references, linkages to other deep Ideas that might or might not be lost to time, broken apart into random flux perhaps generations before Seeker's birth.

Poor mad, suicidal Boltzmann correctly derived the behaviour of gases by considering their molecules to be small, hard, miniature billiard balls flying about at random. His ideal gas law is a decent fit to observed behaviour; while adding the concept of electrical charge gives the 'real' gas law, an even better match. This remains true even though molecules are clouds of probabilistic vibration, not billiard balls at all.

So much in common, with such tantalizing gaps, suggesting missing Ideas whose absence cried out for discovery. He was thinking these things as something bright arced meteor-like across the night and landed, or appeared to land, somewhere among the rippling ridges that lay ahead.

The next day, he sheltered – having pushed himself too long into the hours of heat – close to a lode bearing an energetic Idea, but not close enough for him to catch it. Hunkered down, he ached with the need to take it, unable to sleep as it called to him. Finally, daring to move before dusk, he pulled the complex, twisting flux inside himself.

'Phase transition' and 'symmetry breaking' are synonymous terms, though it may not be obvious. In the very early universe, the electroweak force was singular. When it shivered apart, spacetime itself entered a new phase.

Unusually, the flux had tangled with a tenuous strand, leading him to a linked Idea embedded in the same lode. After a moment, Seeker realized it had been a single Idea broken in two, and a sense of rightness filled him as he pulled the second half inside himself.

Faster-than-light travel was long thought to destroy causality, allowing travel outside the light-cone. However, relativistic lightspeed performs two functions: the speed on which all observers agree, and the universal speed limit for motion. Finite FTL breaks this symmetry – different observers will not agree on an FTL flight's duration – and causality is indeed distorted from the Newtonian paradigm, but not to randomness, no more than distance and duration are destroyed by Lorentz-Fitzgerald transformations.

If this region did in fact contain a lost Theme, he should notify as many people as he could, in the hope that more Seekers would learn of it. But he was drawn by something else: the sight of that meteor, which lay a night's journey ahead of him, or so he thought.

In fact it was two nights later when he peered over a ridge and saw the strange, massive, shining craft on the sands below, with its soft-fleshed but human-shaped crew and their metallic, dragon-like companion, and the silver-skinned prisoner, bound and kneeling.

It was the other Seeker, whom he had met so recently.

There was a niche to hide in, though buried seams contained tangled flux – powerful but random, therefore dangerous – but he had to do it, to secrete himself and think, to work out what to do. He was terrified, that was the thing: too scared to imagine courses of action, never mind carry them out. They had overwhelmed the other Seeker; they could do the same to him.

Vibrating in his hiding-place, he managed to form two questions: where had the awful-looking things come from? And why had they landed where they did?

It was a craft, the huge device below; and as he thought of

it – without having the courage to risk another look – the outside had been damaged, blackened and torn, much as the other Seeker's skin would turn in daylight if they kept him out there. While from below the sand he had caught a sense of something archaic and huge, buried very deep, in place for a long time – many generations, maybe even fifty or more.

A howl of agonized flux spun this away.

They were torturing their prisoner.

FIFTY-FIVE

EARTH, 2033 AD

Portrait of a scared physicist, one Lucas Woods, hiding out in a damp-smelling budget hotel room for which he had paid cash (no questions asked, this being the dodgy end of Bayswater), working on a fake-ID qPad likewise bought for cash (this time with raised eyebrows but acceptance, in a small Tottenham Court Road establishment), dividing his time between reading and thinking and puking up with fear in the en suite, before reading once more:

It was nine years since a young, British-born researcher called Gus Calzonni – her legal name being Augusta – made her controversial discovery in Caltech. A laser beam that appeared broken, non-existent along part of its length, was significant in itself; but Calzonni's claim was that the beam in fact remained continuous, with a segment inside another spacetime continuum that she named mu-space. What gave the claim some credibility was that she had calculated the transition requirements in advance, based on the fractal geometry of a hypothetical ur-continuum, and designed the experiment afterwards. However, it remained an open question: just because the beam behaved *as if* it had entered mu-space did not guarantee it actually had.

The webAnts and webAgents that Lucas set loose returned an interesting picture, more high-tech entrepeneur (or *entrepeneuse* as several journal sites had it) than researcher. There was a small tradition of Oxford, where she had taken her first degree and DPhil both, producing academics who grew rich from spin-off companies; but Calzonni appeared to have a greater, un-English (or un-English-academic) drive for wealth.

A mathematical prodigy, she had also studied a near-forgotten non-academic system called neurolinguistic programming, which she claimed produced useful psychological techniques and skills for business people, even as she denounced the system's community as New Age schizoid delusional, with minimal knowledge of neurology, linguistics or software engineering, unable to see past their dogmatic constraints or test themselves with scientific rigour. Lucas removed the latter set of findings from his workspace – they seemed strident about an irrelevance – so he could concentrate on the physics.

What he had set the ants and agents to search for had been the triplet of variables and values in the postscript of the note he had dug up from his floor, ruining the parquet: the note that appeared to have been secreted by his grandmother decades ago.

You will see three. You will be wrong.
G
P.S. Pass it on! $\kappa_\infty = 9.42$; $\lambda_\infty = 2.703 \times 10^{23}$; $\mu_\infty = .02289$

The values had no specified units and returned no significant matches from the web, but the triplet of variable names was distinctive: kappa, lambda and mu, each with an infinity sign as subscript. The webAgents found a match in Calzonni's published papers, being three of the nine key parameters that she had set for the beam's insertion into mu-space ... if that was what she had achieved.

Interestingly, despite the insertion parameter μ (as in mew like a pussycat), Calzonni intended mu-space to be named after the Japanese concept of *mu* (like a cow, not a cat). Physicists still failed to agree whether 'quark' rhymed with dark or dork, Lucas following the latter. But regarding mu-space, he decided he had been using the wrong pronunciation.

As a child, during the evenings while her mother worked as an office cleaner, Gus Calzonni had taught herself logic by coding in Java. She wrote: *Storing data in value objects, such as Strings and Booleans, was immensely valuable. It meant that if*

I declared a variable b *of type Boolean, evaluating* b.booleanValue( ) *gave me three possible outcomes:* true, false *or* NullPointerException. *This made it natural for me to recast discrete mathematics as trinary logic when I began to* ...

The Japanese *mu*, it seemed, could mean boundless or nothingness or neither/nor: concepts not normally synonymous in Western minds, but apparently in Calzonni's.

She was also an expert in something called jeet kune do. Rich, brilliant, masterful, and no one to argue with. The thought of meeting someone like that, especially a woman, was appalling.

But then there was that note from Grandma – apparently – and the triple gamma-ray burster event, observed by separate astronomical set-ups, but deleted from them all via simultaneous worm attacks. That had been three days ago, and still he had not told anyone about the data he had copied to his memory flake, an offline replica of the destroyed Cloud data.

Nor had he returned home, or seen Maria, because whenever he thought of her attitude as the mysterious message arrived on his holoterminal, the more he became afraid.

Why would a musically talented, nympho beauty hang around with a geek scientist like me?

Perhaps his low self-esteem was illusion; but he thought it was more likely realistic. And perhaps Maria's calculating manner was just part of her personality – but what if she was only with him for a deliberate reason?

The qPad had few of the facilities available to Imperial's holoterminals, so before looking at the data again, Lucas used low-level reflection and introspection hacks, pulling open the component structures, before running data-projection extracts, retrieving subsets suitable for 2-D rendering. That initial dissection turned out to be fortuitous, for hidden inside the nested object aggregates were worm vectors, lying in wait and ready to go wild.

'You little bastards,' Lucas told them.

As he popped up a flat still image containing the three shining dots among the stars, he remembered something from seeing the real time data as it arrived: in a subsidiary panel showing numeric data, two values were in familiar territory: the right ascension close to 6 hours, the declination close to +40°.

A second image, with lower resolution – showing the triplet as a single unresolved dot, but with a greater visible area of sky – confirmed that the gamma ray bursters shone from a little to the left of β Aurigae, at the bottom of the distorted hexagon that was the Auriga constellation.

From the direction of the galactic anti-centre.

'So it has to be a hoax,' he said aloud. 'Has to be.'

While the scared voice inside his head told him it was real.

In the morning he travelled to Heathrow via a roundabout route: Victoria to Hounslow by coach, on to Slough by bus, then a second bus to the airport, paying via the touristToken he had bought for cash. Only at Terminal 7 did he revert to his legal identity, waiting as long as he dared before buying a seat on the next flight to Los Angeles.

She won't even see me.

Perhaps it was better if he did not try. From all accounts, a copy of her original apparatus – or an early generation among variations – remained in the Caltech laboratory where she had constructed it, guaranteed a safe place due to her financial endowments. If he had to break into someplace, a university would surely be less challenging than some corporate head-quarters.

Grandma, I'm scared shitless.

Had she ever been afraid like this?

FIFTY-SIX

EARTH, 1948 AD

Gavriela's war ended like so many others: in anti-climax, forbidden to discuss her work, without guarantees of the future. Only the continuing support from Rupert on Brian's behalf – Rupert being rather better off – gave her any feeling of security in the colourless desolation that followed victorious national euphoria. How many years would it be before the ubiquitous urban bomb sites were replaced with new buildings? Ten years? Twenty? Industries were slow to regain a peacetime footing. Among ordinary people, initial talk of the end of rationing faded soon.

But then there was Carl, the miracle of having a son.

Carl started school today, she wrote in her diary. *My boy is a schoolboy!*

She left no written record of her tears, of the wrench caused by his easy acceptance of the schoolyard, the difficulty of her walking away.

Her own work was not what she had expected, and yet it provided both income and challenge: teaching physics at a 1930s-built redbrick grammar school for boys that was trying to come to terms with its changing identity. The pupils were almost entirely middle class – being so much better prepared for the Eleven Plus, the national IQ test for eleven-year-olds that was supposed to be impartial – but the working-class entrants were more numerous than before, and some of them had been *de facto* socially elevated during the evacuation years, living among rural foster families. They were often troubled by living once more with parents they had half (or wholly) forgotten; and when it came to fathers, that applied to other boys besides the returned evacuees: changed men coming home to changed wives, if they came back at all.

An older generation of teachers was struggling with this newness. The ones who accepted Gavriela were the minority, but they were enough; and she came to care for the boys as much as for the science that she taught them. So this was survival, therefore victory, if not the life she had dreamed of.

Carl was in bed, and she was reading the new C.P. Snow, *The Light and the Dark*, when a triplet of knocks sounded from the front door of the flat, peremptory and recognizable.

'What are *you* doing here?' she asked the empty room, putting down her book.

When she let Rupert in, he sauntered through to the small sitting-room and sat down on the burgundy two-seater, before crossing his legs and greeting her.

'I'm really glad to see you again,' he said. 'Dear Gavi.'

His Oxonian drawl, to some ears, might have belied the surface meaning; but Gavriela thought, with surprise, that he meant it.

'I'll make some tea,' she said.

'No sugar, that'd be splendid.'

She came back with tea and bourbon creams; and they made a start on both before continuing their talk, preamble to whatever it was that Rupert wanted.

'I'm known as Gabrielle these days,' she said. 'Gabby was a little too informal.'

'One needs a smidgen or more of gravitas among the brats, I suppose. How *is* the world of teaching?'

'I don't need to use the cane more than twenty times a day.' She looked at him. 'That was a joke.'

'My old school's motto was: *So many thrashings, so little time*. At least that was how we translated the Latin.'

'Ours is *ad astra*.' She smiled. 'I point out that the RAF adds *per ardua*, because if you dream of reaching the stars, you have to put in the work.'

'Hmm.'

'So why have you ventured out among the struggling classes, dear Rupert?'

They smiled more or less together, in a harmony that was new.

'This and that,' he said. 'I've a couple of photographs to show you, but that's not why I'm here. May I?'

'If you like.'

They were in an envelope; he slid them out and handed over the first.

'Do you recognize the older gentleman?' he said. 'Either of them, really.'

'Sorry. They're standing like father and son. Or ...'

Rupert's smile was more sad than cold.

'Or two men with a relationship they dare not speak of? The former, in fact. The older gentleman is Max Planck, which is a name I gather you are bound to know.'

'Of course.' She laid a hand on the book she had put down. 'Doesn't everyone?'

'Neither Virgil nor Homer wrote much about quantum mechanics,' said Rupert. 'It's a little outside my purview.'

'And the younger man?' she said. 'Is he significant?'

'To Planck, certainly. It's his son Erwin, or rather was. The Nazis hanged him in '45.'

'Oh.'

'For trying to kill Hitler in fact, which makes me think rather highly of the chap. Take a look at this.'

The second photograph showed the younger Planck standing with a man in suit and overcoat. Blurred though the background was, the black hooked cross was obvious: a *Hakenkreuz*, centre of a hanging Swastika. Wartime Germany or occupied Europe was the photograph's setting. She had no problem recognizing the other man.

'When I met him before the war,' she said, 'he told me his name was Dmitri Shtemenko, though he introduced himself to everyone else as ... Jürgen. Oh, what was ...? Jürgen Schäffer-Braun, that was it. He was ... But you know what he was, don't you?'

'I do.' Rupert re-crossed his legs, elegant as always. 'When you debriefed in Baker Street to Brian' – he paused, just a little – 'that night we apprehended those two darkness-driven men in Trafalgar Square . . . You gave those names then, Shtemenko and Schäffer-Braun, when you talked about your past.'

'Well, then.'

It was a way of asking him to explain.

'There was an incident in Berlin last month,' he said. 'During de-Nazification procedures, someone made an accusation against our man here.' He tapped the picture of Dmitri. 'He'd resurrected the Schäffer-Braun identity, presumably in a hurry, which is how he got flagged up. He featured in Berlin Station's reports because of the rather unusual way he slipped out of their grasp.'

'Using something like hypnotism,' said Gavriela.

'Exactly.'

She handed him back the photographs.

'But this wasn't why you came here?'

'No, I just wanted confirmation of our slippery friend's identity. In case he reappears someday.'

'All right.'

'Er . . . Would you mind if I use the little boy's room?'

'Go ahead.'

She cleared the cups and plates while he was gone. There was a thump – Rupert had pulled the chain unnecessarily hard – and he waited with the door closed before the sound of flushing diminished – how very like him – before exiting the lavatory and going in to the bathroom to wash his hands.

Gavriela checked on Carl: asleep, tired out by his day.

She went back to the sitting-room and sat down, knowing that Rupert on his return was going to come to the point.

Afterwards, for all her resolution against it, she went back into Carl's room and woke him.

'Sorry,' she said. 'I couldn't help it.'

'Ugh ... That's all right, Mummy.' Sleepy smile, trusting eyes. 'All right.'

'I wondered ... How would you like to live in a new place? Go to a new school?'

Carl frowned. School *was* new. What else could it be?

'I mean a different new school,' Gavriela added.

But Carl was blinking, yawning.

'Go back to sleep,' she told him. 'Go on now. Mummy's sorry. Sleep now.'

She used the voice tone she had read about in D.A.R. Greene's book on mesmerism, but it was probably exhaustion that dropped her tired son back into sleep.

Four weeks later, she took a bus then walked along a drab street in Eastcote, the sooty air typical of Middlesex, or north-west London if one preferred. After tomorrow, there would be special transport she could ride on, so she had been told: a grey-painted coach that looked like a factory bus for ferrying workers to its site; and that had a certain accuracy.

Am I doing the right thing?

She would miss the boys, but she knew what she was good at, and here she could achieve so much more, if it was anything like she imagined.

'There's a list of names, old thing,' Rupert had told her, 'of those who worked at BP. It won't be published for thirty years, of course, under the usual rules.'

Three decades was too long to worry about. The annual declassification of thirty-year-old secrets was nothing that could concern her.

'And of course, there are quite a few chaps with clearance to read the list right now,' added Rupert. 'You'd expect that, naturally.'

'I suppose so,' she had said.

'The thing is, if one compares the number of names on the list with the known complement of the Park, well, there's something of a shortfall. A four-digit shortfall.'

Perhaps it was the reference to numbers or the hint of a mystery, but that was the moment she had become interested.

'What happened to them all?' she asked.

'They never left, of course.'

'But Bletchley Park—'

'The site's been decommissioned, but it's not the location that's important, is it?'

'No, of course not.' Now she understood the decision he was after. 'Did you think I might say no? So long as you realize I don't speak Russian.'

'I'm sure you can learn, old girl.'

Now, she arrived at a gateway between a wall and a brick building with barred windows. In the courtyard beyond, a single-storey whitewashed affair stood before a two-storey backdrop, the whole site looking like the headquarters for one of the big dairy companies or some such, except that here no fleet of milk-carts would be setting out at dawn for the door-steps of Middlesex. Overt signs of armed guards were absent; but the men at the gate had the relaxed, joking, watchful manner of grizzled NCOs, fazed by nothing.

'It's my first day,' she said, as they checked her name off a list in the security hut. 'I suppose someone needs to meet me.'

'Too true, lass,' replied a heavyset guard.

'Aye 'appen,' said someone else, aping the Yorkshire accent. 'Lucky I'm here, then.'

It was Brian, of course. The suit was of better cut than she had seen him in last; the empty left sleeve was tucked in to the pocket as if sewn in place and ironed flat. When he looked at her, no emotional spark leapt between them.

Good.

There had been nothing to worry about.

And when he added, 'Welcome to GCHQ. Or rather, welcome back,' his tone was only marginally warmer than neutral, mildly marking her re-entrance to the covert world.

FIFTY-SEVEN

The maths was more painful than the fighting.

'I can't do this.' Roger minimized the holo display. 'Really, I can't.'

They were sitting cross-legged on the quickglass floor, facing each other. Without the holo phase space and subsidiary equations glowing in mid-air, their mutual view was unobstructed.

'It's only a form of fear that holds you back,' she said. 'Are you open to a motivational technique?'

'What kind of technique?' he asked.

'There are all sorts of mental states we can usefully distinguish.' Reflected lights slid across Rhianna's polished-jet eyes. 'Being lost in a holodrama – very trance-like – or fascinated by abstract geometry or fearfully aware of physical danger. They're all useful states in context, all worth triggering when appropriate. Agreed?'

'Er, yes.'

Roger had grown wary of agreeing with her. It seemed to indicate a short path to a situation he was not going to like.

'So here's my psychological technique,' said Rhianna, 'for encouraging you to become fascinated with maths. All right?'

'Um, OK.'

'You're ready for this technique?'

Saliva was doing odd things inside his throat.

'I . . . Right.'

'Brace yourself. Here it is.'

He held himself ready.

'If you don't solve the Lockwood equations,' said Rhianna, 'I will beat the fucking shit out of you.'

'Er . . .'

Her knuckles cracked as she made fists.

'Are we motivated yet?'

They were four days into the training. Roger checked through the inverse-power-law high-connection web that modelled the surveillance network Rhianna was tapped into – not just in Deltaville and Barbour, but in other sky-cities. It was a robust set-up, and he told her so.

'But we haven't caught sight of Helsen, have we?' said Rhianna. 'What do you think that means?'

'That she's not stupid. Specifically' – he knew Rhianna would want an explanation – 'she's done the same kind of analysis, matching surveillance coverage to connectedness, and exploited the, er, dark areas. The places no one watches.'

He had come to another conclusion. Rhianna had helped ensure that no Zajinets or other Pilots remained on Molsin, thereby isolating Helsen and Ranulph, confining them to this world. It was better for the risk to be here, known and imminent, than on some other planet, unknown to those who lived there.

Roger did not want to die, but beyond that, he would have hesitated rather than risk Leeja's life, even Tannier's. Rhianna would have understood precisely what was going on; and he was sure that she would commit suicide before allowing darkness-controlled people to seize her ship . . . assuming she had one. Perhaps she was one of the Shipless (he dared not ask), requiring others to transport her. If anything, it might make her a better agent-in-place than Dad had been, always pining for his own ship.

Just as Roger missed *his* ship, child though she was, not big enough to fly for real.

'We'll make a true Pilot out of you,' said Rhianna. 'Back in Labyrinth, when this is over.'

He was getting used to her spooky manner of deducing thoughts. Then he processed the plural pronoun.

'But you're . . .' Roger thought about it. 'Dad was in place for decades. On Fulgor, I mean.'

'I have to consider myself compromised.' Rhianna popped open several holovolumes. 'Tannier is a good man, and I'm sure his superiors are good people. But someone will talk, even if the immediate group choose to protect me. Which I doubt.'

'Not even if you move to another sky-city?'

'Ah.' Rhianna smiled. 'I rather fancy living on Yukawa. But I think I'm done here.'

'My fault.'

'No, it's the nature of the job. As you well know, and well done for keeping control of the conversation.'

'What do you mean?'

'I mean' – Rhianna caused the holos to grow and brighten – 'you're trying to avoid more maths.'

Roger smiled. 'Maybe.'

'Yeah, well. Start by telling me what these pictures have in common. Keep it easy and conceptual, and we'll get to the hairy equations shortly.'

That suited him. One by one he checked the holos: fireflies pulsing in a forest, wind-rays billowing and brightening above paramagnetic sands, the planet Mercury and Earth's moon in their respective orbits, a swaying rope bridge as a party of tourists marched along it—

'Resonance,' he said, without examining the rest. 'Synchronization caused by feedback.'

It was a universal property in so many contexts, from the quantum realm to entire worlds, like Mercury whose orbit and axial rotation were phase-locked, its year and day identical. Put two pendulum clocks together and they alter their swings until they are in opposite lock-step. Let the same effect occur in cardiac cells and you have a heart that knows how to beat in rhythm.

'Give me some more examples of negative feedback adjusting towards resonance.'

'Well, there's—'

'With equations now,' said Rhianna. 'Come on.'

'Oh. Right.'

Later they stared at a holo depicting Fulgor.

'Here be dragons,' said Rhianna. 'The place no ship dares to approach.'

'Shouldn't we be doing some modelling?' asked Roger. 'You know, maths? Those equations I love to formulate?'

'Feeling more confident, are we? Well, good enough. Cheek your elders and betters, why don't you.'

The more Roger grew used to her bullying, the less she seemed to do it.

'We don't know how far the Anomaly can reach through the hyperdimensions,' he said. 'Is that it? We haven't got a critical parameter for the model.'

'Maximum range is of the order of tens of kilometres in the main three dimensions.' Rhianna enlarged the holo. 'No doubt the Admiralty will have posted ships beyond that range. And other observers at successive distances further out, just in case we got it wrong.'

Cold-blooded but sensible.

'So we're safe,' said Roger, 'as long as we quarantine the planet.'

'Molsin was under quarantine, but the bastard Zajinets still appeared.'

'They hate the darkness more than we do.'

'Maybe they're not the problem, though I hate to say so.'

Alone and with time to think, Roger pondered while flexing his hand. The forearm felt intact, thanks to Rhianna's ministrations after her armbar technique had snapped the bone through. Long-molecule arrays formed of smartatoms were aggregated into a lattice that held everything in place, promoting and directing the healing process. As the new cells formed, the smartatoms would pull away, dissolving themselves.

Resonance, global synchrony from local feedback, enabled the aggregated arrays to work as if collectively intelligent. Whether the Anomaly functioned like that, resonating from one component to another like pendulums in step, no one knew for sure. But reasoning from mathematical principles, it seemed likely.

Can you use maths that way?

The history of computation had been an odd subject, taught in Fulgidi schools at age twelve standard. Centuries ago, early software had been cobbled together more than mathematically designed, even though symbolic logic and set theory were well understood long before the mathematics of cohenstewart discontinuities and other forms of emergent phenomena. It was a wonder the old systems had ever worked at all.

And while AI had been a success for more than a century, it became subsumed in other technology – such as quickglass – and largely forgotten (while a part of Roger's mind noted that Ai had been the forefather of the race of serfs, just as Fathir and Mothir had produced the noble-born). Nowadays system studies tended towards the descriptiveness of ecoscience as much as the prescriptiveness of engineering disciplines.

What the Fulgidi educational system did not address was the study of war.

Labyrinth must be different.

Because the Aeternal word for *tactic* had structural similarities to the words *schema* and *process*, while *military engagement* had overtones of *network* and *parallel sequential-process interactions*. The word for *war* was almost identical to the term for *global system architecture*.

Warfare as a branch of mathematics.

For a moment it did not sit right with him, this notion. But that was the old Roger, the innocent whose world had not yet been torn to shreds. Now, nothing could be more important than revenge, to take the fight to the enemy.

For the first time, maths came totally to life in his mind.

*

Some three hours later, Rhianna looked over the phase-spaces, schemata, proof-trees and system diagrams, hanging in holos like a small orchard of tree-images, rich and complex and structured, artistic in its overall configuration.

'I think I might have underestimated you, my young friend.'

'No,' said Roger. 'You gave me motivation. And thank you.'

Rhianna nodded, but her face was grim.

It doesn't matter.

As if she could see the changes taking place inside him, and wished there were another way for him to grow as a person.

Not your fault.

Helsen, and the darkness she allowed to control her, had created whatever he was becoming.

And they will regret it.

That was a promise.

Mum. Dad.

A promise to the loved ones the darkness had killed.

FIFTY-EIGHT

EARTH, 2147 AD

'It's not just the money,' said Amber, her voice desperate, her expression of conflict and anguish clear, despite the metal eye-sockets that so often made her hard to read. 'I mean, it's not the *economic* need to work, or I'd find something on, on ...'

'Something on Earth,' said Rekka. 'In realspace.'

'Yes. Thank you.'

Beyond the restaurant window was the shopper's paradise of Orchard Road, and the outdoor-sauna air. Rekka sat next to Amber, facing Angela and Randolf, whose voices were very careful, their conscious sympathy focused on Amber.

I'm hurting too.

But today was not about the betrayal as such. Rekka had been wrenched through her core, as if her whole body had sheared along a transverse plane to split her organs, when she learned that Simon had moved in with Mary. Amber's reaction could only be worse, because of her situation: baby Jared, months old, natural-born Pilot unknown to UNSA; and Amber herself, a Pilot of the original kind, eyeless and blind in realspace, coming alive only in another universe, flying an UNSA ship configured precisely for her.

They ate a meal of sorts as the discussion proceeded; afterwards, Rekka would not remember the dishes nor even who paid.

'In mu-space,' Randolf said at one point, 'you're in your element. Playing devil's advocate against myself, what would it be like if you never saw mu-space again? I mean surely you could in fact cope.'

Even with her eyes replaced with I/O sockets, Amber could project a feeling of emptiness without a word.

'That's the thing, isn't it?' she said after some moments. 'Maybe I'm a junkie, and our lords and masters in UNSA are the only ones who can provide my fix. Maybe I can't cope without it.'

'You're being too harsh on yourself,' said Angela. 'If we ... if we were to raise Jared, you could visit us ...' She turned to Randolf. 'Right?'

'There would be visits,' he said. 'Of course there would. He'll be glad to have, have ...'

'Two mothers.' Rekka put her hand on Amber's. 'Two mothers to share the load, and twice the fun when you're all out having a good time together.'

Randolf's voice went very soft.

'Two mothers to love him,' he said.

With her hand still on Amber's, Rekka could feel the change in muscle tone, in that moment when Randolf's words persuaded her.

The next day, Rekka went to work.

She would have liked to oversee the whole thing, the handing over of baby Jared, the legal completion in a notary booth – online processing took seconds, but procedures like adoption required full DNA identification and diffractive quark brain-imaging along with blood analysis to verify the absence of coercion – but this was their day, Randolf and Angela's, Jared's, and in a different way, Amber's.

On the ground floor, strips of red carpet adorned the reception area, clear sign of bigwigs paying a visit. No doubt they would think the carpet a compliment, if they even noticed – if they had not seen such things so often they failed to register it – while Rekka thought the real intent was to signal everybody else to behave appropriately.

Signals and communication were all she could think of these days, besides the emotional vortex that was her private life.

Riding up in the lift, she used her hatha yoga breathing to induce a modicum of calm. In theory, human-to-Haxigoji communication consisted only of voice-translated-to-airborne molecules by the technology; in practice, she knew they could read her emotional state with a sniff. Only the rational words needed translation.

Instead of Bittersweet, it was a male called Redolent Mint with whom she spent the morning conversing. Rekka suspected that Bittersweet had ordered the males to buck up and take an interest in the linguistics, but she did not share that analysis with anyone else. If Rekka was right in reading intentions and motives, then Bittersweet was trying to make the six males appear less like a bodyguard team and more like fellow ambassadors. And that meant the males were here for Bittersweet's protection because they thought she needed it.

Sharp was so different.

He had possessed no defensiveness on Earth, had shown no negative reactions at all, apart from the day he had seen the UN senators, the Higashionna cousins. (*Do you not taste their evil?* he had asked. *Can you not smell dark nothing?*) Perhaps it was something to do with his masculinity; yet Bittersweet seemed, if anything, more confident than her male companions.

At lunchtime, Rekka delayed long enough for her colleagues to finish eating – of course Randolf was not here today – before going down to the staff restaurant, intending to eat alone. But after two mouthfuls of noodles, here came Google Li, tray in hand, popping it down opposite Rekka, then taking a seat.

'Lovely to see you, Rekka,' she said. 'I hear your work's going wonderfully. Oh and, rumour-wise, that a certain missing Pilot has been back in touch, talking about getting back in harness. Wonderful news.'

'Sure.'

An absence of threats was no reason for Rekka to think of this as sudden friendship.

'As for the VIPs,' Google said, 'I hear they'll be dropping in unexpectedly at around four o'clock. Just so you know.'

'Thanks for telling me.'

The afternoon session was all about Bittersweet and Rekka exploring the boundaries of verb tenses. Rekka was aiming for the future pluperfect – 'I will have had smelled him,' she said into the translator – and getting replies back that did not quite match, hinting at some form of parallelism, some innate Haxigoji sense of multiple subjective time experiences considered at, well, the same time. Was this pushing the boundaries of their subjective compatibility? Or was it a constant factor, unrecognized before now, which called in question all their apparent understanding of Haxigoji language and psychology?

Staring at Bittersweet, Rekka was aware of the moment that the Haxigoji stiffened. Among the males, ranged around the lab, there was a faint new scent that Rekka had never experienced. A translation unit with a visual display was reading: *Unknown referent.*

Five slow seconds later, the facility's doors whisked open, and the dignitaries came in: senior managers in their best suits, forming an approximate U around two visitors at the front.

Bittersweet looked at Rekka and winked.

What?

No one had ever observed such a gesture from the Haxijogi.

The female senator, Luisa Higashionna, approached. She was slender and glamorous, and Rekka felt unlovely as she listened to the question: 'Is their pheromone-based language really as detailed as ours?'

A faint, complex scent indicated that the technology had done its work, allowing Bittersweet to understand syntactical, semantic and tonal content: condescending sneers translated perfectly well, in full. But she did not react, though her six-strong bodyguard made minute adjustments of posture that Rekka could read. One of the other researchers, Diane Chiang, looked around the room: she had picked it up too.

'Perhaps not quite as complex,' Rekka lied, her tone implying simplicity.

'Ah. Well, carry on.'

There were other questions from the visitors, but senior management fielded them all, including the usual explanation of smell in humans: how the receptors in the nose did not respond to molecular shapes so much as energy levels, a resonance effect. Finally the group left, and everyone but the six Haxigoji males relaxed.

'Jesus Christ,' said Harry, junior member of the team.

'I know what you mean,' said Diane. 'Though he is pretty sexy, isn't he?'

'Who is?'

'Senator Roberto Higashionna. Sort of glows with charisma, don't you think? He can analyse my lexical patterns any time. Every component.'

Harry's reply was a blush.

'I'm sorry,' said Rekka, turning back to Bittersweet.

For putting down her species, she meant. For denying the richness of their communication.

'Thank you.'

Bittersweet reached out and squeezed Rekka's hand with two gentle thumbs. The gesture made Rekka realize her own motivation for belittling the Haxigoji language to the senator: it is always good for an enemy to underestimate you.

For the next thirty minutes they continued their work, until Rekka's infostrand beeped with a priority personal call.

'It's Amber. We're downstairs in reception, all four of us. I've got to go, catch a shuttle flight to Xi'an airport. My ship's at ShaanxiTwo.'

'Down in thirty seconds.'

It took nearer two minutes for Rekka to descend, swirling with poignant elation, hoping her friends had created the framework for a good life, one to withstand the strains that would surely come in the future, with Amber disappearing into mu-space and then coming back into Jared's life, or more precisely Angela's and Randolf's lives. Then the door slid open, and she almost ran out across the polished floor and the red carpet not intended for her, reaching the trio of smiling adults and baby Jared, shawl-wrapped in Amber's arms.

'So it's all done,' said Randolf.

Rekka hugged Amber-and-Jared first, then Angela, then Randolf. Returning her attention to Jared – his eyelids, drooping with sleepiness, not concealing his glossily opaque, obsidian eyes – she kissed his forehead, then looked up at the parents, all three of them.

'Congratulations, all of you. Except . . .' – with a glance around the glass-dominated reception – 'I didn't expect to see Jared here.'

Amber was in a rush to leave, either because of UNSA orders, now she was back in touch, or because she thought it best for Randolf and Angela to have time alone with Jared for bonding to commence. Rekka understood that much, but not their openness in this place.

'We registered him officially,' said Amber, cuddling Jared.

'Yes, we did.' Angela tickled Jared. 'Didn't we?'

Randolf said: 'We've nothing to hide, none of us. No one's taking Jared to an UNSA boarding school. He's ours, you see.' Nodding to Amber. 'All of ours. He'll have the kind of home he deserves.'

There were tears in Rekka's eyes.

'He's very lucky to have you all.'

That was when another lift opened, and a group of well-dressed men and women came out, and a familiar tone said: 'Oh, look. A baby, and isn't he sweet?'

Luisa Higashionna, elegant and tall, swept across with the handsome Roberto beside her. Both senators kissed little Jared in turn, while Rekka stepped back, confused by the smiles on her friends' faces, realizing after a second that the abhorrence was hers alone.

Senior management looked on, their self-serving smiles benign, happy for the official visit to end with an emotional high note, a photo opportunity that could not have been bettered had it been choreographed. If Bittersweet had been here, she would have emitted a faint but deliberate smell of excrement.

'A fine young Pilot.' Roberto Higashionna tickled him under the chin. 'And what's the brave lad's name?'

'Jared,' said Amber, then turned her blind eyes towards Angela, who completed the naming: 'Jared Schenck.'

Luisa Higashionna tucked her finger inside Jared's tiny grasp.

'Pleased to meet you, Pilot Schenck.'

When she looked at her cousin, perhaps it was only Rekka who processed that glance as reptilian. As the delegates left, the neurochemical tide of hatred began to sink inside her, to dissipate; but still she had little to say as Angela, Randolf and Amber exchanged more farewells and promises, until it was time for Jared to be taken into Angela's arms.

While the emptiness left by Rekka's hatred filled up with fear, though she could not have delineated the reasons in a logical manner of the kind Simon would have demanded were he here.

Fear for baby Jared.

FIFTY-NINE

They floated side by side in a crimson nebula, Jed in his silver-and-bronze ship, Max in his vessel of black and midnight blue with white-webbed wings. Hanging there, they conferred, getting to know each other, discussing the dangers of reappearing when Max was legally a fugitive.

I might be Labyrinth's most-wanted criminal. Or they might have buried public knowledge of me.

Jed did not want to admit the extent to which Labyrinthine internal politics could turn rotten; but he knew what he had seen at the galactic core in realspace.

That space station was human-built.

It was.

He thought about Davey Golwyn's death, and the others'.

We should fly in side by side, Commodore. With me broadcasting the all-OK.

Agreed.

They moved out of cover, into golden nothingness.

In a wide café overlooking Borges Boulevard, a lean-faced Pilot jerked in his seat. A cup of daistral, freshly ordered, rose through the tabletop; but he ignored it. Instead he stared into space, then muttered: 'I'll be right there.'

He got up from his seat, found a clear area, and summoned a fastpath rotation. It whirled into place, he stepped inside, and then he was gone.

That was when three other diners, scattered around the café, looked up from their meals. They rose, walked carefully among the tables, and met as if by chance at the spot where the first

Pilot had exited. Almost as one, they tapped their prepared turings, which began to glow.

'All right,' said one of them.

Together, they brought a fastpath into existence. Had any of the innocent clientele possessed the means and ability to analyse the rotation's geometric precision, they would have found it identical to the previous manifestation, set for the same destination, capable of transporting three Pilots at once.

They stepped inside.

After a moment, another diner, a young Pilot just off a long shift at the Med Centre, looked up from her omelette, trying to work out what was odd about the departure she had peripherally seen. She stared, then shook her head, and returned her attention to her food.

Had she realized that a thousand similar events were taking place throughout Labyrinth, she might have taken notice.

Into the vast docking space they floated. An immensity of distant wall lay in every direction, forming an approximate hollow sphere that was kilometres across in mean-geodesic units. Their progress was slow, the two ships; and they separated as they neared one of the great promenades, each docking sideways on, so a wingtip touched with kiss-like gentleness.

Max, sleeves pushed up from his huge forearms as always, stepped on to a powerful wing of black, deepest blue and white. Off to one side, Jed was exiting in parallel; but the danger, if it came, would be focused on Max Gould, commodore, former senior intelligence officer, now enemy of Labyrinth.

=Welcome back.=

Enemy of those who claimed to represent Labyrinth, more precisely.

On the promenade, walkers stopped, looking not at Max but at their surroundings, puzzled by what they were sensing.

Some of them, more perceptive or survival-oriented, began to hurry away. A few tried to summon fastpath rotations, but the nascent activity made this difficult, as if spacetime were becoming turgid and viscous, impossible to handle.

Here they come.

Hundreds of Pilots rippled into existence, all along the promenade, and upon the various floating platforms that serviced the docks, and other vantage points which had one thing in common: all provided a view of their common target, him. The full complement, once they rotated into place, numbered a thousand, give or take a handful.

Ionization rendered the air heady, pleasant unless you realized it was due to so many weapons emitting spill-over radiation, their resonant energies desperate to spurt forth.

In the centre of them all, a uniformed man rotated onto the promenade.

'Garber,' called out Max. 'How loathsome to see you, Colonel.'

Even from this distance, Garber's cold smile sent a message: *fuck off*. Beside him, a larger rotation spun then dissipated, leaving five more figures, including one who wore ceremonial brocade, as if he had been interrupted in official duties, or considered the capture of one renegade commodore to be a state occasion in itself.

'Admiral Schenck,' said Max. 'How unusual to see you down among the working Pilots.'

Not that the innocent were here in numbers: they had cleared the promenade and most of the dock space, some to watch from what they hoped were safe positions, most to flee deeper inside Labyrinth. Only a handful tried to alert the authorities; the others already knew this was some kind of official action. Perhaps that was why they took it for granted that their ships were safe. It was not an assumption Max would have made.

Schenck looked at Garber.

'Commodore Maximilian Gould,' Garber recited, 'you are

being detained on a charge of treasonous homicide, the victim being Admiral Adrienne Kaltberg, with additional counts of—'

'Never mind,' said Schenck. 'Do the legal niceties once this bastard's in a cell.'

If this was being recorded, his performance would go down well. He pointed, and two Pilots made their way towards Max, careful with the spinning infinity-symbol-shaped brightness they caused to move ahead of them: a topology bracelet, unbreakable.

'Stand right there.' Garber gestured at the hundreds of Pilots all around. 'You can see how many people we have. Enough to destroy your ship as well as you. I assume you're enough of a Pilot to care about that.'

His personal staff were behind him, stone-faced to reinforce their superior officer's intent. Of the group, Clara James stood furthest to the left.

'Raise your hands, sir,' said one of the Pilots controlling the restraint.

It glowed brighter, the twisted infinity that Max dared not place his hands inside.

'You're attempting to execute an illegal order,' he said. 'Hold back.'

'Don't be stupid,' called Garber. 'You've no choice.'

Max's barrel chest expanded with preparatory inhalation.

'No choice,' he said, 'but to take you bastards down.'

He slammed his big hands together and twisted, squinting against the fluorescence in his eyes, snarling with the effort of rotating the stuff of spacetime in this fashion, but doing it. In time with his hands, the infinity symbol rotated, then snapped outwards, ripping through the Pilots who thought they controlled it. One fell sideways, with a scream that came straight from the abattoir, while the other's head bounced on the promenade, arterial blood spraying from his collapsed body.

'Kill—' Garber's voice strangled shut.

Clara James stood between Garber and Schenck, her body cruciform: one extended fist pointed at Colonel Garber's neck, the other at Admiral Schenck's. Both fists were glowing scarlet.

'No,' she said.

Schenck's lip turned up.

'I've a thousand officers here,' he said. 'You have precisely—'

Those Pilots had been focused on the present danger, or they might have sensed it a second earlier: the twisting and shimmering of air around their positions, wherever they were.

'Considerably more,' said Clara.

Some three thousand Pilots stepped out of fastpath rotations, each with aimed fists, rings shimmering with the potential for devastation.

'You thought it was time to move openly, after all those years of planning,' called Max. 'You were wrong.'

He stared up at the ceiling, for want of a better place to look.

'How many of them can hear you?'

=Not so many.=

Perhaps being in the minority who could hear the city itself meant you were less likely to fall prey to Schenck's type of treasonous conspiracy.

'Tell them anyway.'

He waited, then gave a start as the words came through with full intensity, directed at everyone capable of perceiving them:

=Gould is correct. Schenck is a traitor.=

Here and there among the massed Pilots, individuals flinched. After a moment, those who had been part of Schenck's force powered down their weapons. A few looked about to snarl: whether angry with themselves for being duped, or the city for not warning them, Max could not tell.

'Kill them!' yelled Schenck.

Max threw himself sideways – *the moron* – reacting even though he had expected Schenck to surrender – *it's insane* – and he dropped to one knee, looking up at Schenck, in time to see the Admiral clap his hands and implode in blackness, disappearing.

What was that?

On the promenade and all around, isolated firefights flared

amid screaming, while others threw themselves flat, but that was not the strangest thing: here and there, Pilots were coming to attention and clapping their hands, each disappearing in blackness.

Then around the dock space, ships were pulling clear, heading for the portal, accelerating at dangerous levels but with no collisions: streaming for the exit.

Max craned his neck back.

'Stop them!'

The reply – directed at him, not generally – resonated through his body.

=I will not risk the damage.=

One by one, the Pilots most deeply immersed in conspiracy were fleeing Labyrinth, heading out into mu-space.

'How many?' said Max.

=Hundreds. Not just from your location.=

Meaning that, from other docks inside the city, and in ships that floated outside, Schenck's people were getting away, still powerful, with their long-term intent unknown.

But it had a positive outcome: on the promenade, most of those who had been serving Schenck's cause – thinking it legitimate – were surrendering. There was still fighting, but in some twenty isolated pockets, not spreading.

Max looked up at Clara. Her fist still glowed at Colonel Garber's neck. The colonel's face had manifested a layer of slick sweat, like transparent grease.

'I don't . . .'

He stopped, clearly not knowing what to say. Max had no reply, either. He was too far away to deliver a kick to the balls.

'We've stopped you bastards,' said Clara.

Her shoulder exploded, spray spattering Max's face and Garber's.

They met in the Admiralty Council Chamber: Max, Pavel Karelin, and several other Pilots, male and female, whom Jed did not know. Quite why he, Jed Goran, was here, no one said. They sat around the big conference table, and Jed was not the only one to be checking out the simple yet lustrous surroundings, unchanged from the Council's founding after the first Admiral, Ro McNamara, stepped aside centuries before. Max, Jed noted, took a seat to the left of the empty chair at the table's head. Opposite him, the right-hand seat was also vacant, while Pavel took the next one down.

'Ladies and gentlemen,' said Max. 'I'm here to prevent a treasonous coup, not perpetrate one. My intention is *not* to hold control. I sincerely hope that this is the only time I will sit at this table.'

There were nods from all around, though a few touched the richness of the tabletop. Perhaps they did have ambitions of returning here – hopefully by legitimate career advancement.

'Our intention,' Max added, 'was that Admiral Asai run this session. His death was not as natural as official reports indicated, as some of you know. It was in fact one of the triggers for moving our counter-coup to the final stages.'

He looked around.

'I would like to invite Admiral Whitwell and Admiral Zajac to take their seats, please.'

The black doors opened, and the two men entered, their physiques very different – Whitwell slender, Zajac stocky – but with similarly tightened body language. Jed assumed that they had not been part of Max's covert campaign; the lack of friendly looks from those seated confirmed it.

Zajac's face was blotched as he sat down at the table's head. He did not look at Whitwell lowering himself into the seat at his right; instead he stared at one face and then the next face among the others: memorizing them in sequence, recognizing some.

'Let us watch some footage first,' suggested Max. 'Because neither of you, gentlemen, saw what happened at the dock.'

Growling deep in his larynx, Zajac looked about to swing a punch. Then he said: 'Agreed.'

The holovolume was of the highest resolution, while every

chair offered its occupant the option of additional copies to be manipulated and explored at will. Everyone watched as the events played out once more. Jed found it odd to see himself, and embarrassing to see that he had done nothing but watch; but then, he had not known what was happening. Nor did he feel he had much grasp of the situation now.

'What was that manifestation?' asked Whitwell finally, with the vocal precision that Jed associated with academics. 'Schenck's escape mechanism at the end, along with his ... cohort.'

Zajac, his face still blotched, took in a breath as if about to let loose verbally; then he stopped himself.

'We don't know,' said Max. 'Something like a fastpath rotation, clearly. But with the number of people and fastpaths in place, he should not have been able to summon an exit. The best we can think' – he nodded to some Pilots further down the table – 'is a sort of permanent spacetime fracture, rather than something that needs to be created as it's used. An escape route that's always in place.'

'He used an unknown technique,' said Zajac, 'to escape a larger hostile force. Nothing in that constitutes treason.'

Jed, staring at the now-still holo, had a different question to ask.

'What happened to Clara?' he said.

Frowns came from all sides; but she was one of the few people involved here that he actually knew, and he liked her.

'In the Med Centre,' said Pavel. 'With Clayton guarding over her.'

'Well, good. Sorry.'

Max gestured, and the holoview was replenished. For a moment, Jed thought it was a replay, because it showed the same docking space. But this was an earlier time, with fewer ships at dock, and after a moment he recognized one of them. It was distinctive: black and powerful, banded with red. Configured for unusual work, since it clearly lacked cargo space.

'That's Carl Blackstone's ship,' he said. 'I saw it on Fulgor.'

Several people looked at him. Everyone knew who Black-stone had been, and the story of his hellflight sacrifice, coming here to raise the alarm.

'You're right,' said Max. 'And the city will verify what you'll see if you zoom in on her hull. Admiral Zajac, you have control.'

'What?'

'Of the image, sir. Please go ahead.'

'Hmm. Right.'

The black-and-red ship expanded in the display, and the scoring became obvious: gashes in her hull only just beginning to heal and scar.

'That's not realspace weapon fire,' said Whitwell.

Max smiled, as if he had placed a bet with himself about who would spot it first, and had won.

'Are you fucking serious?' Zajac's voice boomed around the majestic chamber. 'You're saying that one of Schenck's people tried to kill Carl Blackstone? Tried to stop him raising the alarm regarding Fulgor?'

'That's right,' said Max. 'That's what fucking Schenck did.'

Matching Zajac's profanity had no noticeable effect.

Whitwell said, 'More than one, I think. A prolonged engage-ment could leave similar traces, but I think there were multiple attackers, perhaps an ambush.'

'Ambush?' said Zajac. 'You mean you believe these bastards?'

'I don't know. Perhaps I do.'

Zajac turned on Max.

'You'd better have more than this.'

'Of course I do,' said Max. 'When Schenck began to move openly, we had the final confirmation on who was part of his coup. Our surveillance has been years in the construction, you understand. Recruiting the counter-strike force and keeping it secret, that was Pavel's work. He saved us, gentlemen, in case you haven't got that yet.'

'So you have the details of all Schenck's . . . co-conspirators, is that it?'

'One of whom' – Max nodded to Whitwell – 'was your aide-de-camp, Admiral. I'm sorry to say that she was killed ... on her way to assassinate you.'

'What? You've got ... evidence. Of course you have.'

'Yes. Sorry. While you, sir,' Max said to Zajac, 'Schenck thought safe to leave in place. It gave us suspicions about you, but he simply thought he could use your ... ebullience ... to his advantage, at least in the early days of assuming total control.'

Jed thought: for ebullience read belligerence.

'What's more, um, rarefied,' added Max, 'is that we have some people capable of detecting a sort of malign influence that ... Schenck is not normal, and he broadcasts some kind of signs of that. Our people haven't determined its nature, but every sensitive individual detects the same phenomena under the same double-blind circumstances. Call it an evil aura.'

'Is this some form of mysticism?' said Zajac.

'Not to me. Maybe to Schenck. The point is, Carl Blackstone was one of the sensitives, and so is his son.' Max looked at Jed. 'Currently in hiding, and I think someone should fetch him back, don't you?'

'Er ... Yes, sir.' Jed started to shift forward, the chair reconfiguring to help him stand.

'Not right this moment. Stay now, for pity's sake,' said Max. 'Your testimony is possibly the most important part of what we're discussing today.'

Confusion twisted vortex-like inside Jed.

'Me?'

Max sighed.

'Everyone, this footage I'm about to show you is from my ship. You'll see Jed Goran's ship appearing in it. The point is, since he was there with me, he'll have similar footage from his own vessel's memory. Not to mention, he can verify what he saw himself.'

Jed both understood and did not. Everything had been massively strange since the moment he gave chase to Max

Gould; only now could he see that it had been two insane episodes, not one: the events at the galactic core, then here on the docks.

This time the holoview showed realspace, but blazing so brightly that someone had to ask: 'Where is this, exactly?'

'It's near the heart of the galaxy,' said Max. 'There's a phenomenon that I've known of for some time, but had not witnessed myself. Unlike Carl Blackstone.'

Jed did not know what to make of that.

'I was there,' he said. 'Following the commodore.'

The image swung, revealing the linear spike from the galaxy's core, like a needle thrust into a shining ball.

'Galactic jet,' said Whitwell. 'In our galaxy. I didn't know, but what is the point?'

Everything was in slow motion. They watched as the space station swung into view, saw the five mu-space vessels that were Max's pursuers, and the ripple in reality that preceded the triple explosion destroying three of the ships. Jed looked away, not wanting to see Davey's death again.

'Let's reset.' Max gestured, and the galactic jet was visible once more, the image frozen. 'And take a look at the geometry, will you, everyone?'

Numeric data glowed.

'The ascension and declination look familiar,' said Zajac. 'I mean, tracing the jet's path, the way it's pointing . . .'

'Earth,' said Whitwell. 'The jet is pointed radially out of the core, directly at Earth.'

That was when the air above the table began to ripple.

'Holo, out!' commanded Max.

Without the image, the distortion was obvious, and growing bigger. People began pushing themselves back from the conference table, getting to their feet.

'Evacuate,' said Max. 'Everybody get—'

A hole in reality appeared, and a small white-and-red object fell out, hit the tabletop and bounced. Then spacetime wriggled back to normalcy, and the phenomenon was past.

Everyone looked to Admiral Whitwell for the answer – he had a reputation for immense eclectic knowledge, and his observations on the holo footage had been perceptive and incisive – but he shook his head, mouth downturned.

'I think I know what it is,' said a Pilot who looked too young to be part of this. 'I'm a history buff, and my dad was a – he flew a large-distortion geodesic before I was born, see. With the time dilation, he remembers visiting Earth centuries ago. So I've always been interested in artefacts, and . . . Can I?'

Max took hold of the small object, remained still for a moment – nothing happened – then slid it along the table.

'Oh, yeah.' The young man picked it up. 'This is great. Fantastic specimen. You'd think it was made yesterday instead of—'

Zajac growled.

'Oh. Er . . . Sorry. It's a graphene flake.'

'What's a graphene flake?'

With a blush: 'Graphene was the miracle material of the twenty-first century. They called it a metamaterial, effectively a two-dimensional solid.'

To a roomful of Pilots, this was quaint, unimpressive stuff.

'Get on with,' said Max. 'What use is a flake of material?'

'Oh, didn't I . . .? It's a memory flake, almost indestructible. Data storage device. No one's used anything like this for five hundred years.' And, with a wondering look: 'If there's any data on here, it would be like a message from the past, wouldn't it?'

Zajac looked at Max.

'Your doing?'

'No, sir.'

Jed wondered if everyone was as confused as he was.

SIXTY

EARTH, 2033 AD

So here it was: Los Angeles. White-top freeways, crowded and stinking, and sun-glitter everywhere. The airport pick-up had no air-con, and the hot draught did little to help the seven passengers breathe. No one talked to the driver. Two British couples started comparing cynical notes, popping up local news sites on their qPads and pointing out the lack of international reportage. One of them muttered about parochialism. Lucas stared out the window as if he spoke no English, only occasionally glancing at the driver whose frown deepened by the mile.

They pulled up by the awning over the hotel entrance. The driver got out first, to unload the luggage from the side compartment. Lucas, whose bag came out last, slipped the driver a ten-dollar coin. Perhaps the tip-your-service-provider meme kept cash in existence here; back home, it was cultural inertia.

As the pick-up bus pulled away, Lucas scanned the sky and busy road before looking back at the entrance. There was a doorman, but he was helping one of the couples. Lucas might not be a trained spy or criminal, and he had flown on his passport because he had no idea how one might get a forgery; but he had been to the States before, and knew there was something unknown to the urban culture, a blind spot that might allow him to slip surveillance.

It was called walking; or perhaps he was relying too much on perceived gross differences. But so much of the city area was devoid of footpaths, designed only to be driven through.

His bag could be worn as a backpack, and after he had left

the immediate environs of the hotel, he adjusted the strapping and slipped it over his shoulders, then tightened it up without breaking stride. As he walked, he thought back to the Indian mathematician Srinivasa Ramanujan, and his sojourn in England before the First World War. It was G.H. Hardy in Cambridge, renowned in the mathematical world, who had spotted the self-educated genius – had Ramunajan been a painter, he would have been called a primitive – and brought him over from southern India.

For about a mile, Lucas continued in the absence of a path or track. In England one walks on the pavement; in the States pavement is for driving on. He could imagine the British couples making snotty remarks. Finally he was back on a real pavement – sidewalk – passing a row of single-storey businesses.

One of the things about Ramanujan – Lucas resumed his meditation – was his vegetarianism. Him and Gandhi both, Lucas recalled. The thing was, Edwardian cooking had no notion of balanced meatless diets: between the lack of nourishment, the damp cold, and his customary lack of exercise, Ramanujan's health plummeted; and back in India he suffered a grim and painful death at the edge of thirty-two.

Now Lucas was in a residential area, the streets laid out in a geometric grid with empty sidewalks. It was mid-morning and the place looked empty. Again, there was the contrast to every other country he had been in: the rectilinear layout, streets labelled by numbers rather than names: practical yet subtly oppressive. Perhaps that was due to his sense of enemies watching from everywhere, because arrival in the States usually perked him up, straightening his spine as he resonated with a sense of confidence and self-determination so lacking in his usual life.

His colleague Arne did have confidence: strapping and muscular, strictly vegetarian, fond of the occasional lager but a fanatic about physical conditioning. He had a second dan black belt in Brazilian Jiu Jitsu, and had previously competed in powerlifting, while these days his strength training consisted mostly of exercises from India, traditionally used by wrestlers: yoga-like, strenuous callisthenics called dands and bethaks. Once, he had demonstrated the movements in the Imperial bar, to the joy of his colleagues, Lucas included.

Bethaks, it turned out, were deep knee-bends, while dands were cat-lick push-ups that looked like the motion of a tireless male porn star – 'He's forgotten to put a woman underneath him,' Jim had said – after which they had given Arne a new name: Captain Carpet Shagger.

In Edwardian Cambridge, where Town and Gown remained disparate, the well-off took a four-hour walk every afternoon, while impoverished working men spent the same amount of time walking to and from their jobs – and their wives would make the same journey in the middle of the day, fetching lunch to their husbands. It was a contrast to the self-taught mathematical genius who remained shut up in his rooms to work amid gloomy days and dark unlit nights, with Cambridge blacked out in case of Zeppelin attack.

Arne followed a Hindu-inspired lifestyle that gave him enormous vitality; poor Ramanujan had dwindled to skin and bones for the same reason.

When he reached the next shopping area, Lucas went into a diner and ordered steak and eggs, OJ and coffee. Ongoing free refills of juice and coffee: another difference from home. He took alternating sips from glass and cup as he powered up his qPad and checked the route to Caltech. The jet lag was catching up with him, but if he could stay awake for a full Californian day, he would avoid the danger of checking into a hotel where they might ask for ID. Or was that paranoid thinking?

They deleted data from Palo Alto and LongWatch.

Secure systems both. From the Chinese astrophysics community, there had been no mention of a triple gamma-ray burster event, no joining in with international discussion. Perhaps that absence meant their systems, too, had fallen victim to worms.

When the steak and eggs came, Lucas slathered ketchup over everything, and ate. It was a taste explosion, just wonderful.

While eating, he revisited his material on Gus Calzonni. In interviews, her tone was occasionally sarcastic, with comments that Lucas found funny. *Since Ramanujan died back in 1920 or whenever*, he read, *mathematicians and scientists have been raiding his work for good stuff. He had this intuition, you see, like nobody else. Without partition theory and modular forms, I would never have discovered mu-space. Of course, that meant disproving string theory, also inspired by Ramanujan's theorems, but them's the breaks, string-kiddies.*

Perhaps this was why so much dispute remained about the nature of mu-space: physically real continuum or mathematical device.

'It better be sodding real.' He realized a waitress was looking at him. 'Sorry.'

'Hey, no problem.'

A few seconds later, the waitress was behind the counter with her colleague, stage-whispering: 'Oh, I just *love* his accent.'

Lucas rubbed his face and shut down his qPad.

Night-time in Pasadena was orange, with palm-trees. A profusion of sodium-vapour streetlamps, warm un-English air, a sense of un-European space between buildings that would have been austere without the advertising. It was not the darkness that Lucas had envisioned creeping through like a ninja; but he could see that no one was lying in wait, no black-garbed snatch team ready to truss him up and remove him from the everyday world.

Once on campus, he solved the security problem in the usual way: walking in behind someone else, in this case a dark-skinned young woman with ferociously intelligent eyes who held the door open for him.

'That's very kind of you,' he said. 'Thank you very much.'

'Oh, you're British.' She giggled. 'You're welcome.'

When she turned left at the first corridor, Lucas turned right. From behind, he heard her give a small, disappointed sigh.

For God's sake.

But he was in, and that was all that counted. Following the route he had planned from online diagrams, he tried to project a sense of belonging here, in case some security guard was watching internal surveillance views. Twice, he nodded to a white-coated person walking the opposite way. Scientists do not always work nine-to-five.

The door lock on the lab was the real barrier, with a redfang sensor expecting a digital code. But this was the technology that Lucas had expected to come up against – zooming in on students' Facebook photos – and before leaving London, he had returned to Tottenham Court Road for one last piece of shopping.

All sorts of covert surveillance devices were on sale in several of the electronics shops, not always the dingy ones. It had surprised Lucas the first time he went there as an undergraduate, and so he had checked online: it was the use, not ownership, of pen cameras and the like that was illegal. In the event, he bought the app from the man who had sold him the qPad; it came on a memory flake in a small cardboard box labelled *For entertainment purposes only*. Lucas's hand shook when he took it, but the shopkeeper looked calm. Buying it here seemed safer than downloading from online, not knowing which agency might have the download site under surveillance.

He cranked it up now. The qPad showed no visible output, but it must have finally redfanged the correct pass-code because the lock clicked; and when Lucas pushed, the door swung in.

Holy crap, I'm doing it.

As he went inside, the door swung shut behind him. His surroundings were gloomy at first, then lights began to flicker on – motion sensors, hopefully not linked to a security system – and shadows became benches and equipment, over there a vertical torus, and to the other side—

'Bloody hell.'

A woman was standing there.

'Too bleeding right,' she said.

Agony exploded in Lucas's thigh, and he was down on one knee as if genuflecting, with his arm wrenched up behind him, leverage and pain somehow combining to immobilize his whole body. Even his neck could only turn through a degree or two.

'You're English,' the woman added.

From her, there was no giggling.

'Yeah, you— Christ!' The hold had tightened. 'You too. I'm not a criminal.'

'Actually you are.'

'Shit. Yes. But I wasn't until thirty seconds ago. I'm Lucas Woods from Imperial College.'

'What, come to steal results? You won't find any in here. Nothing unpublished.'

'Yeah, I know . . .'

There was no way to explain his breaking in.

'Or was it the apparatus you were planning to steal?'

'No, I . . . I was going to borrow it.' Something wrenched, and the pain level rocketed. 'No, not borrow! I mean I was going to use it.'

The hold relaxed, by some tiny quantum of torture.

'Use what apparatus for what purpose, specifically?'

'I need to . . .' He tried to clear saliva from his throat. 'I need to send something through to mu-space.'

'You need to what? Member of some kind of cult, are you?'

'No, I'm a fucking *physicist*.' Despite the pain, he turned his head enough to look up at her. 'Much like yourself, Dr Calzonni.'

With repeated backtracking and filling-in of skipped details, he told her everything. From his pocket, he took out the black-and-white photograph of his grandmother, and the note he had found with it.

You will see three. You will be wrong.

   G

P.S. Pass it on! $\kappa_\infty = 9.42$; $\lambda_\infty = 2.703 \times 10^{23}$; $\mu_\infty = .02289$

And they talked about the gamma-ray burster event. Throughout the conversation, Calzonni had been watchful, ready to strike him down again – this time she would break something, she had promised, then beat him unconscious – but when he ran through the events of that day, she relaxed a little. When he said he had a copy of some LongWatch data, she looked excited.

Lucas wondered why she had been sitting alone in the dark, brooding over her most notable scientific achievement, but dismissed the idea of asking her, on the grounds that she might beat the shit out of him.

'The full outer component is compromised,' he said. 'There are private members in inner objects, even initialization blocks, designed to bootstrap worms. Luckily I dissected the thing instead of trying to load it whole.'

Calzonni gave the first hint of a smile.

'You're not the only one who took a data copy,' she said. 'But you're the first one to still have it, as far as I know. Well done.'

'Er, thank you.'

He showed her the snapshots of the astronomical event. Three dots shining to the east of β Aurigae, the triangle perfectly equilateral, its centre corresponding to the galactic anti-centre.

'Draw a line from that through Earth,' said Calzonni, 'and you'd reach the galactic core. It can't be natural.'

'I got that note from my grandmother' – Lucas pointed – 'several hours *before* the burster event. Don't talk to me about natural.'

'I don't believe in ghosts, gods or magic.'

Lucas said: 'Me neither. You know Hardy once had a list of New Year resolutions that included, find an argument for the non-existence of God which shall convince the general public?'

'Hardy who?'

'The one who mentored Ramanujan. As in modal forms, infinities, and just possibly travel into mu-space, Dr Calzonni.'

'Right.'

'Mind you,' said Lucas, grinning, 'other items on the list included assassinating Mussolini and becoming Communist president of Britain and Germany.'

Calzonni stared at him.

'Tell me again what you wanted to do here.'

'It's the note.' Again he pointed, this time specifically at the postscript. 'She told me to pass it on. I think' – gesturing at the burster event data – 'that's *what* I'm supposed to pass on. And I think the parameter values tell me *where* to pass it to.'

'Totally insane,' she said.

'Like thinking it took some conspiracy to wipe out all that data with a worm attack. That's parallel worm attacks on separate systems you'd expect to be secure, with massive redundancy in the Cloud.'

'Yeah.' She tapped her finger on the note. 'There are nine insertion parameters. But for all my early experiments, I fixed six of the values, varying only these three.'

'Which is how I made the connection, scanning papers for those variable names.'

'You mean you didn't know my work by heart?' Again, the partial smile. 'So if we're going to send this data, how are we going to do it? Not the qPad, surely.'

Lucas processed the *we* in her sentence.

'You're going to help?'

'If it's a delusion, what's the harm? And if it isn't . . . Too bad we'll never know how it turns out.'

'I suppose.'

He fished inside his pocket and pulled out the payload: a white-and-red memory flake.

'Graphene,' said Calzonni. 'Fair enough.'

She went over to the torus, and started the equipment up.

SIXTY-ONE

As always, before Rhianna and Roger began training, they checked the surveillance nets they had tapped into. The local equivalents of netAgents were set up as realtime observers, ready to report the instant they saw something; but the point was this: the patterns might have been subverted, the registration links of view-source (normally an area of quickglass wall in some convenient location) to watcher (a conglomerate of software agents active elsewhere in the architecture) destroyed or redirected. They had countermeasures in place, but Helsen and Ranulph might be smart enough to avoid them. The setup-check was necessary.

'Intact,' said Rhianna. 'I almost wish it wasn't.'

Because at least something would have happened. Roger understood. The negative result could mean anything, even that Helsen and Ranulph had escaped offworld, though the mu-space quarantine should have prevented that.

'So what's the agenda today?' asked Roger.

It was the fifth day of training, and he had passed through exhaustion to a kind of flow state, everything happening automatically because he was too fatigued for self-critical thought, too tired to get in his own way. Ancient samurai called this state *mu-shin*, the derivation identical to that of mu-space; and they strove to reach it always.

'Metacognition,' said Rhianna in local Spanalian, then repeated it in Aeternum.

Roger blinked at the semantic resonance of the Aeternal term.

'You've got to be kidding me.'

'In what way?' asked Rhianna.

'We can't do it in realspace.'

'Really? Trust me.' She smiled. 'I've done this before.'

All around, the quickglass chamber reconfigured into shapes that would have looked bizarrely angular to a normal observer, here spiky with fractal complexity, there distorted into visual paradoxes of impossible polygons, of straight edges that appeared to spiral, of static lattices that seemed to twist into and around themselves.

To a Pilot, it meant more: the shadow of a reflection, the hint of different geometry.

A soupçon of mu-space.

'Now relax deeply.' Her voice appeared to pulse and wash in tidal waves. 'And deeper still . . .'

His awareness fell deep inside himself, though his eyes remained open, assisting the illusion that he was plunging into a different universe, the continuum where he and all his kind came wonderfully alive. But now it was more than that.

Roger split apart.

The mind that had been Roger Blackstone became a scale-free forest of neural cliques and groups, miniature gestalten with their own brand of self-awareness: a community, a population of cognitive daemons aware of and communicating with each other. Those groups, freed of the old patterns, began to explore new ways of joining together, of running in parallel, trying new architecture as suggested by the decoded linguistic input – he/they/all of him were aware of the processing in his language centres, the auditory computation, the words originating from the other being whose designation was Rhianna Chiang, signposting this process of change but not controlling it, because that task was his/theirs/all components' responsibility – and some self-aware cliques combined to form a fleeting thought: Was this how the Anomaly experienced itself?

Change continued.

By the timeflow of realspace thermodynamics in the location

that his body occupied, some three standard hours passed while this process of metacomputational reorganization continued in Roger's central nervous system. But no one, not even a Pilot, could remain in this state for ever. Not in this universe. So he began, under Rhianna's measured direction, to come out of it.

Rebuilding his mind, piece by piece, as he did so.

Talk about multi-tasking.

He understood, as he reintegrated, how different things would be in future – and how wildly marvellous they would be in mu-space, back where he belonged. Summoning a Labyrinthine fastpath no longer seemed impossible, rather a trivial application of inductive projection, of the neural and quasi-neural flows that all Pilots were capable of, no matter where they had been raised.

How incredible the world is.

Every pore of Rhianna's facial skin, every tiny feature of the quickglass surroundings, glowed with an inner light it had always possessed. Every sound – all the vibration that washed over and through his skin during every second he was alive – became rich and crisp and wonderfully complex. Rhianna's pride in his change was obvious from the airborne molecules that every human being could atavistically sense, but not bring into conscious awareness the way he could now.

Metaconsciousness was his.

Who could have believed it might be like this?

He was a multitude of shifting personalities – as he had always been, as everyone was – with a new qualitative awareness, and the ability to be many people at once: the observer scanning the surroundings constantly for danger; the mathematician and the artist appreciating the world and the ideal forms beyond; the caring, empathising lover of all people, who understood everyone and forgave them their weaknesses; and the binding personality, the one who emerged and might in emergency control the others: the new core Roger, if there was such a thing.

'I'm sorry,' said Rhianna.

She sensed it, and he knew that: the feedback between them was a pulsing bidirectional blizzard of non-verbal signals, from pheromones to micromuscle twitches.

'I'm not,' he said.

Because there was only one word that suited his coordinating self, a single name that matched perfectly: an old word that resonated down the centuries from its roots among the followers of Thórr and Óthinn.

Wolf.

He smiled, a rictus appropriately lupine.

'That's right,' he told Rhianna. 'You understand.'

She turned away, broadcasting regret.

But it's all right.

He had become the Wolf.

SIXTY-TWO

EARTH, 778 AD

Shingle crunched beneath Ulfr's feet. Ahead on the shore rose the rotting hulk of a sea-monster, of the kind known as whale. Much meat had been hacked from it. Farther along, around a bonfire upon the beach, men, women and children were feasting. Out on the waves, a sea-going longship was at anchor with sail furled. Only a few men were aboard, as far as Ulfr could see.

Kolr followed, his reins in Ulfr's left hand. Brandr, most faithful of war-hounds, trotted at Ulfr's side. They were all he needed. Chief Folkvar and the village were far behind him now.

Ulfr had thought he was setting out to hunt, but that had been many days ago, and he still did not know what manner of prey he was after. There had been rabbits but no deer; nuts and berries but no fruit. The journey had lasted long enough for the two wolf hides to cure: wind-dried and rubbed with bitter earth as the women used back home. The preserved hides were tied in a roll at the back of Kolr's saddle.

'Ho, stranger.' It was a woman, clad in scarlet wool, her apron blue as her eyes. 'You are welcome to join us.'

'I will, and thank you.'

He hobbled Kolr and strode on with Brandr.

'Where are you from?' asked a bearded man, handing over a chunk of well-cooked whale meat.

'I am Ulfr Ulfrsson, and I hail from Dark Lake, where Folkvar Grímsson is chief.'

'Then we are more than well met, for I am named Grímr, though I am not your chief's father. As far as I know, that is. But a man's seed spreads far.'

'Not unless you sired a child,' said Ulfr, 'when you were two years old. Is everyone here so manly?'

There were roars of laughter, redoubled when the woman in red said: 'I'm not.'

'I still wouldn't argue with you, Ása,' said Grímr.

She was beautiful, and there was something in the way she looked at Ulfr; but the crackling of the bonfire reminded him of a funeral pyre, the burning of Eira's shrouded remains. He continued to eat, splitting his food with Brandr, but only because he knew he should replenish his body at every chance. Enjoyment had dissipated, like rising smoke.

Still he talked, because courtesy demanded it. Some of the group were from the ship's crew; all were from the same settlement, a considerable walk north. They had used the longship, rowing hard when the wind was against them, to force the whale to beach, frightening it with war-yells and clashing weapons, being careful not to lose the oars.

'It was well done,' Ulfr told them.

So even monsters of the sea feared armed warriors. It was a good thing to know.

Afterwards he left them, despite their offers of hospitality – despite the inviting thought of sleeping in a longhall instead of outdoors – and headed upslope on foot, into forest land, Brandr at his side and leading Kolr as before. They saw no people before dusk, at which point he tethered Kolr to a pine-tree, then planted a short, slender branch in the ground and hunkered beside it, stretching his cloak over it to form a tent, while Brandr crawled in next to him.

Woodsmoke woke him before dawn.

When he found the other campsite, it was deserted, the fire still smouldering. Poor discipline: it should have been buried or put out with water. The men – he was sure it was a reaver-band – had left a clear path through the forest: heading towards the sea.

'No. I will not let this happen.'

Ása and Grímr and the rest . . . they were good people, tough but not necessarily prepared to fend off a reaver-band's sneak attack.

There was a limit to how fast he could go, on foot or on Kolr, for the descent was in darkness, even after dawn must have broken, thanks to the multitude of trees all around. At the least the ground was soft, deadening sound, so with luck the rearmost warriors would not hear him.

But tiny, distant screams sounded when he was still deep inside the forest.

No.

They moved faster, Ulfr and his stallion and hound, but when they reached the beach, the scattered bonfire was as dead as the people, with no sign of the longship off shore.

Her red robe was torn, made brown where the blood was beginning to dry.

'Damn you.' He looked north. 'This was ill done.'

But vengeance on a reaver-band? What was he thinking?

Among the other bodies lay bluff Grímr who had made Ulfr welcome. He was weaponless – the reavers had stolen his sword – but his shield lay face-down on the shingle near his hand. Ulfr crouched down and turned it over. The design was a wolf's head, all in red.

So.

He hated the Norns, the three dread sisters – Fate, Being and Necessity – who played pitiless games with human lives. But sometimes their messages were clear.

From behind Kolr's saddle, he cut loose the two wolf skins. The male's head and upper jaw remained attached to one; this, he drew over his head like a helm, fastening the forearms around his throat, outside his cloak. The female's skin he wrapped around his body but underneath the cloak. Then using the male's claws, he drew three parallel cuts beneath his left cheekbone, three more beneath the right, and three across his forehead.

Now we'll see.

Taking up the wolf shield, he vaulted onto Kolr's back, while Brandr gave a bark. Then they moved off, heading north.

The first people he came to were four in number, on foot. Ulfr slipped down from the saddle, shield still on his left forearm – he had been getting a feel for it as he rode – but with his right hand held clear of his body, palm forward.

'Are you from the settlement where Grímr and Ása lived?' he said.

'We might be. Who are you?'

'Reavers caught them on the beach. I was—'

One of the men was pointing at him.

'That's Grímr's shield.'

'Look, I'm a traveller and they offered hospitality. I didn't—'

'Wolf skins, war-cuts and a stolen shield. *Traveller*. You think we're stupid?'

Ulfr took a step back.

'Please don't do this. Just listen.'

Blades scraped free of scabbards.

'Hear that? Next sound will be you squealing, wolf-man.'

They came for him, and all was blood.

Damn you all.

Shield-edge to throat and clawing for eyes, spinning with a kick to the liver, elbow whipped to jaw, stripping the sword from a weakened grip, left, right, slice the ankle tendon, jump, blast through with heavy blows, knocking everything aside and smashing the bastards down, down into mud, wet mud soaked with blood—

Bastards.

—then stepping back, breath sawing, snarling at the four ripped corpses, staring at the sword in his hand though his own was still sheathed. Then he looked at the shield on his left arm and nodded, for it had served well.

Brandr was spattered with blood, not his own.

Good.

Ulfr tipped back his head and howled.

*

The next day, far ahead, he saw a man moving amid forest cover. Ulfr dismounted, pointed at Brandr to sit, then placed the ends of Kolr's reins between the war-hound's teeth.

'Come if I whistle, brave Brandr.'

Dark eyes stared at him with love. The only good thing left in the Middle World, when even those you tried to help did nothing but attempt to kill you. He had tried to help the thralls, and he had tried to help the local villagers, and all it brought was blades thrusting at him. And the only time he came to life was in the storm of battle-sea, of spear's torrent. Of blood.

'Good boy.'

Ulfr drew his sword – his own blade, rune-inscribed with his name – but left the shield hanging on Kolr's saddle. He still wore the wolf skins. Then he loped after the lone man, hoping this was what he thought.

Silent, his run.

A left-hand punch to the kidneys, hooking in front of the bastard's shin with the sword blade, and he went down face-first, Ulfr following, dropping his weight down to sit on the bastard's back; but said bastard was on elbows and knees, still in the fight. Ulfr slammed both feet back, kicking the thighs to straighten the man out. Flattened, there was no way for him to resist as Ulfr sat on his back and pulled his head back, using his left hand, then angled the sword to nick his throat.

'Are you with the reavers? I swear by Sif's thighs, I won't cut your throat if you talk.'

'Fuck you.'

'Tell me.' Ulfr hauled back left-handed, cranking the neck. 'Now.'

'Reavers, if you want to ... call us ... that.'

'And who is your chief? Your leader?'

The man's face worked, then:

'Magnús, damn you! Magnús the Carver.'

'I take it it's not wood he carves?'

Movement, but not laughter.

'He carves man-meat. So, I've talked.'

'More. How did this Magnús become your leader?'

'What?'

'You heard. How?'

Ulfr pulled back harder.

'It doesn't— He fought! Challenged old Arnkell. Killed ... him.'

'Good.'

He let the pressure off a little.

'You swore you wouldn't ... cut my throat.'

'I won't.'

'Oh. Good. Can you—'

Ulfr dropped the sword, clamped his right hand over his left against the man's forehead, and bared his teeth as he wrenched back, revelling in the crack of sound.

'Maybe you were right, Vermundr,' he said to the big man who was not there. 'You and Chief Folkvar. Or maybe you were very wrong.'

He stripped the dead man of weapons and food.

It took another day to circle around ahead of the band, work out where they were likely to camp – there was a deep dell, cupped from a hill, with good vantage points for guards at the top, and he knew from observing the previous nights that this Magnús chose the sites well, however poor his reavers' camp discipline might be – and then he made his preparations.

Alone, with Brandr and Kolr at a distant hiding-place, because their presence would give everything away.

The reavers threw wood onto the remains of someone else's fire. One began striking flint, trying to get the first dried leaves to light. Finally their leader, Magnús, strode down from where he had been placing look-outs, and examined the struggling flame.

'Is this what you call a fire? Why don't you—?'

Something erupted from the pile of wood, spewing charcoal

and ash from the previous remains, roaring upwards and throwing its arms wide.

'Demon!'

Magnús stepped back, pulling free his sword.

'Wolf,' said someone.

The figure smiled beneath his wolf skin. His arms were outstretched, his hands empty, though a sheathed sword was at his side.

'I am what he said.' Ulfr's voice was calm. 'And I challenge you for leadership.'

'*What?*'

'You heard.'

There was a conjoined roar as both men closed, Ulfr not drawing his sword, stepping inside the swing of Magnús's cut, right hand clamping the back of his neck, face heading for the throat like a lover, but Ulfr's mouth was wide and he clamped his teeth deep, aiming true, wanting the windpipe – not the blood vessels – and crushing it in his bite, then ripping back. Magnús croaked, falling. Left-handed, Ulfr snatched Magnús's sword, then plunged it into its owner's heart.

He kept the tableau like this so the reavers could see their leader's fate; then he thrust with his foot to push the corpse clear of the blade. In the frozen quiet, the wet sucking sound was clear. Then Ulfr drew his own sword, spat, and stood with both blades unsheathed. Around him in the dell were some fifty men, maybe more, all staring this way.

'Any questions?' he said.

At least a dozen reavers looked at each other and snarled, turned back to Ulfr and yelled as they ran at him, drawing swords and swinging axes to the ready, in one case a long-handled war-hammer.

Óthinn's shit.

Time for the blood-rage once more.

Glimpses: chopped fingers, hammer falling from the riven hand as his other blade took out an eye; hilt into face on the backswing, rebound forward into another's throat, while his other sword chopped down, and someone roared; spinning, using the ground, their headlong sprint working for him as he deflected one man into another, and then again; fingers tingling as he lost a sword but grabbed testicles, howling as he ripped upwards and the man went down, tripping two more; turned another right around, the back of his neck fresh and clear like a girl's, his scream like an animal's as blade severed vertebrae; tearing an axe loose from a dead man's hand; two-handed once more, screaming as he plunged into a group of five, six men and chopped down with strength that could not be deflected; split a face vertically in two.

And clicked it off, the rage.

Soaked with sweat and blood, he took in the twisted wounded and the dead, strewn across the bottom of the dell. Then he looked up at the others, the three dozen who had stood back. They were staring at him, afraid but not of the violence or even the rage, for they were reavers, used to blood and battle. What they had never seen was someone who could enter and exit *berserkrgangr* at will.

Good. So you understand.

He turned in a circle, checking them all, not ignoring the danger from those he had wounded without killing.

'Any more questions, anyone?'

Suddenly, someone laughed.

Thank Loki for that.

Others began to laugh, then beat their weapons against their shields, while the wounded looked up at them as though they were insane.

'Give us your name,' a reaver called, 'if it please you, good Chief.'

The new leader put down his axe, then raised his sword. Runes were carved on it, the first six newer and cruder than the final four, but making sense all the same to those reavers who could read.

*

ᚠᛖᚾᚱᛁ·ᚢᛚᚠᚱ

'I am Fenrisulfr!' he cried. 'And with a hell-wolf at your head, who can stand against you, against *us*, my brave and bloody reavers?'

There was a pause, then a roar, weapons shaking, not at him but at their prey, all the weak of the Middle World.

'I promise you blood and gold and death!'

Far away, with Kolr's reins between his teeth, sitting by the ash-tree where he had been commanded, Brandr whimpered.

SIXTY-THREE

EARTH, 1953 AD

Seven years since the war's end. Gavriela, with time to spare before the meeting, stood staring at a rubble-strewn bomb site. Boys in short trousers were kicking a football, innocent of the events that created their playground – the deaths and screaming, the flames and collapse – and she could not tell whether it meant hope or despair: moving on from the past, or failing to learn its lessons. They would grow up as individuals; but what of the species?

Some said the end of rationing was only a year away. Food, intact housing, and family safe: that was all that mattered. You had to deal with the rest only because ignoring it placed the fundamentals in jeopardy. Hence, by sequences of faultless logic leading to insane conclusions, the mutual fear between Soviets and the West. They said that not a single Russian family had made it through the war with everyone living; now they reached for the uranium, created missiles in readiness, so that more devastation like this could be brought into being; except there would be no children playing in the ruins.

According to a mole in Washington, plans for something called the Atlas ICBM were being drawn up; the mole's opinion was that once proposed in final form, the programme would be initiated. But it was the thinking more than the hardware that worried Gavriela; Turing's transatlantic counterpart, von Neumann, was recommending a first-strike all-out nuclear attack against the USSR, on the basis of rigorous mathematical analysis.

Both of these reports had crossed her desk in the context of signals intelligence; the first because the radio relay was a joint Section VIII-GCHQ operation, while the second was a composite analysis arising from a series of intercepts: SIS's eavesdropping on the Cousins (the new term for American spooks) had expanded to included the RAND corporation, think-tank to White House and Pentagon alike.

One of the boys had fallen over. After some thirty seconds, he got up and continued to play, receiving the ball and dribbling it with aplomb across the broken ground, heedless of the red streak starting at his knee.

Gavriela blew out a breath then walked away.

King's Cross was close by, and the queue at the taxi rank was short: only six people. She joined it, alert for anyone following, and climbed into the fifth taxi – two had shared – and told the driver Charing Cross. No one struck as her odd when she climbed out at her destination – 'Thank you, missus,' said the driver, checking his tip – and from there she went on foot, past Trafalgar Square and along Flea Spotter Alley, tradename for the static counter-surveillance setup where the eponymous fleaspotters would check to see whether she had picked up anything untoward, most likely with Slavic features.

The entry protocol took the usual length of time, not least because there were visitors ahead of her, including a large group with American accents – she gave a tiny nod to an NSA officer who had spent time at Eastcote; he returned the nod but no more – but finally she was through, with an escort to lead her upstairs. His name was Price, and she had met him before but knew nothing about him, except that he looked hard around the edges, meaning he probably got here via SIS's absorption of SOE. At Rupert's office he knocked and opened the door for her, then closed it behind her as she went in.

'Sit down, old thing,' said Rupert. 'I'll be Mum.'

There was a tray ready, the porcelain tea-pot with a gaudy cosy. Rupert poured strong-looking tea through a sterling silver strainer. He added the milk for her, just a soupçon, and handed it over without sugar. Trust him to remember how she took it.

'How's Brian?' she asked.

'Shivering in Trondheim.'

Which could mean frying in Tangiers or sitting downstairs at a desk: his once-temporary transfer to SIS had long ago turned permanent. He had never attempted to be Carl's father, which was just as well: everyone knew that Carl had been sired by Jack Woods, Lieutenant RN, deceased.

For spinster read widow.

'I wondered' – with her, Rupert rarely spun things out – 'whether you had seen much of AMT lately.'

His voice sounded languid, but the signals he transmitted were always what he wanted others to read. The real Rupert Forrester was buttoned up inside; she wondered if Brian ever saw that man.

'I've been to Manchester a few times,' she said. 'The Colossus there, even the Pilot ACE, are far behind the Eastcote setup, but we're starting to struggle. You know that the Americans are going to dominate the computer world if you don't let civilian BP veterans talk about it. In a couple of years, we'll have lost our lead. Plus,' she added, 'we need Alan full time, not the short-term visits he's been putting in.'

Turing had been GCHQ's chief liaison to the Americans.

'You're singing to the choir, Gabby. Our lords and masters don't agree.'

'Right. And?'

'And what, precisely?'

'Come on, Rupert. It's a travesty. Alan's no security risk. He was totally open with the police when he reported the theft. That's how his homosexuality landed him in court, but that's precisely why he was never open to blackmail in the first place.'

Unspoken: Rupert of all people had to sympathize.

'Men like ... Alan,' he said, 'are accepted more than ever these days, by ordinary people, though that's not saying much. Accepted by men who served alongside queers in the war.'

The pejorative had an ugly tone in his mouth, immediately covered up.

'But there's paranoia blowing through the corridors of Whitehall' – he gestured at the door – 'and he damn well should have known better, the stupid bastard. I can't do anything for him.'

'If you can't, then who will?'

'No one, that's the point. You probably won't know this, but your senior directors—'

'Offered him a permanent post,' she said. 'Five thousand a year, cheap at the price and academia's loss. So for God's sake, why can't we have him?'

'Because the world's insane, which is why you and I have jobs in the first place.' He stared at the window, and asked it: 'Have you read Forster?'

'Captain Hornblower? One of Carl's favourites.'

'I meant E.M.' He faced her again. 'As you well know. He said he hoped to have the strength to betray his country before his friends. Ignore the abstract in favour of the tangible, I expect he meant.'

'So I take it RO never considered him,' she said, meaning the Recruitment Office.

'Unlikely. I was hoping you'd do a courier job for me. Be my legman.' He smiled his Etonian smile. 'Legwoman.'

From a drawer he took a cream-coloured envelope. Only the best stationery for the privileged few.

'It looks thin,' she said.

'There's a cheque inside, farewell payment for services rendered. Drawn,' he said, 'from a slush fund that does not exist as far as the grannies are concerned.'

For grannies read accountants.

'Made out to whom?'

'To A. M. Turing, old girl. To the man who did more than any other individual, apart from maybe Winnie, to save this bloody country from the jackboot.'

The envelope was light in her hand.

'Is there a message to go with that?'

'Yes.' Just for a moment, something burned in Rupert's eyes;

then the glacial mantle was back in place. 'Tell him, we hope he enjoyed his holiday in Norway.'

The Lyons Tea House establishments were ubiquitous, and while Rupert these days would not be seen dead in one, Gavriela rather liked them: warm and moist, with steam escaping from the polished urns, the chatter of young mothers taking their children out for a treat – a glass of orange squash, a soft round doughnut crunchy with sugar – and men of all sorts reading newspapers while they drank their tea. Also, the company had designed and built their own computer, the LEO, operational for the past two years, which made them smart people, or so Gavriela thought.

On her way here, she had seen no mobile spotters; but a watcher already in place would be hard to detect, except by being too good: an absence of vibration from someone who looked capable. She sat waiting and watching, tea in front of her, picking up nothing untoward.

Alan came at the appointed time, bought tea and McVitie's at the counter, and brought his tray over. His eyes, the same shade of startling blue as Oppenheimer's, remained fastened on her as he sat, scraping the wooden chair into place.

'Nice to see you again, Gabby.'

'Likewise. Have you been following the news from Japan?'

'Mesons? Yes, interesting, isn't it?' With an almost-smile: 'Even I know you're not here to talk physics.' He pulled his jacket down, tight against his chest. 'What do you think? Am I developing gorgeous teats or what?'

He let go, and his clothing fell normally, making his bust less obvious.

'God, Alan. I . . . Oh, God.'

Not calling on the divine, but expressing inarticulate sympathy.

'Organotherapy, they call it,' he said. 'Sounds so scientific, doesn't it?'

'Like eugenics.' She was trying not to cry. 'And about as palatable.'

People like him had gone to the gas chambers, alongside people like her.

'Everything is subject to causal laws,' he said. 'By definition of being inside the light-cone of creation. Vacuum being weightless, you see, it must expand at lightspeed.'

'I thought we weren't going to discuss physics.'

'I'm just trying to make sense of people.'

'Talk about lost causes,' she said. 'Listen ... The message is, hope you enjoyed your holiday in Norway. Spoken by someone who looked like he was chewing a lemon, by the way.'

'I don't need a computer to decode that one.'

'Oh.'

'The terms of my sentence are quite explicit. If I'm abroad with a friend, outside the borders of this country, certain restrictions on my behaviour do not apply. Except that my body remains filled with oestrogen, not conducive to romance, shall we say.'

'But it means they're keeping you under surveillance,' she said. 'I'm sorry. I didn't get the significance.'

She was careful passing the envelope, not knowing who might be watching now.

'Call it recompense from a friend,' she added.

Terming it an apology would be insulting. This was bad enough.

'I saw some runes over there,' he said.

'Ruins?'

'Runes, in Norway. In a museum. Saw a buckle with your name on, like this.'

He took a propelling pencil from his inside pocket, and drew on the envelope:

ᚾᚠᛁᛏ

Gavriela had never studied the archaic symbols, never learned them as far as she could remember; and yet the word made sense.

'How did you know?' she said.

She had been Dr Woods, not Wolf, at Bletchley Park.

'I've seen so much. Maybe I really am a security risk, the way they say.' He slipped the envelope inside his pocket, as if it had been there all along, with his pencil. It was nicely done. 'I probably won't see you around, will I?'

'Probably not.'

She let him go first, then headed for the ladies room. There, stairs led down to a side entrance; she let herself out, walked past a stack of crates, and checked the alleyway. No one expected her to be a field operative; but the annual streetcraft course was mandatory, and her memory of wartime Berlin always made the exercises vivid.

By the time she crossed the High Road and doubled around the block, her expectation had been that Alan would have disappeared. But he had stopped to chat with an Evening Standard vendor under the Tube overhang – KILBURN STATION rendered in white against blue – and as he went inside, just for a moment Gavriela thought she saw a shadow within shadows, a darkness descending to follow her lost friend; but the memory that made her shiver went all the way back to a graveyard in Berlin, to the man who saved her then met her family, but terrified her whenever she remembered.

'You know, Jürgen,' Ilse had said that night. 'Never mind Erik. *You* and Gavriela could be brother and sister.'

Perhaps it was the situation, the senseless official sadism visited on Alan.

He can't be here.

She went into the Tube station, bought a ticket, and went down. But the sucking, dust-laden wind was the aftermath of a departing train, and the platform was empty.

For Jürgen read Dmitri. Or paranoid imagination.

SIXTY-FOUR

THE WORLD, 5568 AD

It was coming, the storm. Down below, where the strange, damaged craft with its soft-skinned inhabitants interrogated that other Seeker – now unconscious – they did not seem to understand the build-up of flux all around, to levels that Seeker had never experienced.

He wished he could formulate a rescue, snatch the one like him from these alien things – so like people, yet with skins so soft and squishy instead of shining silver – but he was one person and they had weapons: witness the captive's fate. That other being, with wings and carapace of metal, had crept inside the craft, trembling and clacking as it moved. Seeker thought that the natural flux levels were affecting it; surely, then, it could sense the disturbance hurtling this way at immense velocity?

Perhaps the blackened craft was too damaged to move. Though he had never seen such a thing, Seeker had experienced the Idea of one; observing it in reality was nothing special.

Closer now, the coming chaos.

His shelter was as secure as he could manage: overhang, rock on one side, a small boulder on the other, which he had been able to push and tug to a more snug position. Soon it would be here, flux raging strong enough to tear apart minds, flinging grains of ferrous sand with force enough to strip flesh, to flense ordinary people, never mind the soft intruders below.

But they had their prisoner, that other Seeker, blackened and wounded.

Almost on them, the edge of it.

Yet something was happening, something that tore and twisted at ambient flux in ways that had nothing to do with the advancing storm; so Seeker dragged himself out of the shelter and peeked over the ridge, hoping they were too busy to spot him.

Light of sapphire blue shone from their eyes – impossible, for light entering the eyes is how people see – but it was happening. And now the glow became lines, stretching towards the captive Seeker, heading for his eyes; and then they made contact, those blue arcs converging; and then their prisoner shivered and the blueness snapped out of existence.

This was abomination.

Seeker could not sense the aliens' thoughts, sentient though they looked; but his fellow Seeker down below was resonating with strangeness, with vortices of incompleteness whirling through his skull. It was the non-thoughts, the aspects of cognition missing from his radiating mind, that stood out for Seeker. For those partially formed thoughts needed to be complete in order to exist, as surely as flux must always loop; and if they did not complete in the captive Seeker's mind, they must complete elsewhere: in the minds of his soft-skinned captors.

A single mind existing in a formation of bodies.

Appalled, Seeker could only hunker down, hoping that the new conglomerate could not sense him – he had not tried to mask himself from the captive's perceptions – then realized his concern was irrelevant, because glittering sand was spraying against surrounding rock, and the edge of the storm was upon them. He hid beneath the overhang, cowering, hands over forehead and eyes squeezed shut.

I cannot.

Twisting flux tore the thought out of him; yet the intention remained.

Another Seeker needed him.

He had experienced only Ideas of heroism, never the actuality. Then he pushed that thought aside – a ridiculous flux-knot, torn away by the storm – and told himself to do what was necessary. Skin hurting with sand-spatter, he pulled himself up to the top of the ridge as before, already finding it hard to think, here at the storm's edge; then he squinted his eyes open, staring into the sand-blizzard and trying to see.

They had fallen back, the soft-skinned ones: ripped red by the flensing sand.

Good.

While that abomination, the Seeker-that-was, struggled against the storm, pulling himself finger's length by finger's length towards the vessel's hatch. It was hard to watch, and Seeker did not try. Instead he hauled himself forward, pulling against the storm's force, crawling downwards with all the exertion of an upward climb, fingers digging into sand that thumped and rippled with inductive effects, skin burning with the wash of flying grains.

Down below, the Seeker-that-was had spotted him.

Incoherent flux tumbled this way. Torn by storm vortices or distorted from human thought because of what they had done to him, Seeker could not tell. The Seeker-that-was had been weakened by his violent capture or subsequent torture; and while he raised his arms to try controlling the storm-flux, to use it as a weapon, he was too weak and the vortices spun past, barely grazing Seeker's skin.

And then he was close enough to act.

Storm-smash and vortex-tear.

Spin in. Hold in!

All his strength to fight against the rage.

Hold in, damn you!

Fight against the hammering flux, tidal waves of chaos strong enough to lift them up, to throw them far, but he had to hold it, control, and force the other to do so too.

Curl it in!

Pulling back the flux; repairing the vortices of thought;

closing them off and making them whole within themselves, not running through others.

Tighten the curl, that's right.

A tiny light of humanity amid the pain.

That's right! Fight it. Haul it in.

The captive began to fight back, with part of his mind at least: joining his strength to Seeker's instead of opposing it. Still the flux remanence, induced by the aliens in the captive's mind, was strong; Seeker concentrated, howling with effort to direct the hysteresis, pushing it, restoring the mind to what it was; and then some critical point was reached and they broke apart, falling to the ground.

Whirlwind sand all around.

Cutting sharp, battering hard.

Which way?

Climb there.

Together, helping each other, neither sure of who he was, knowing only that this chaos required their joint escape, they heaved and screamed and struggled like primitive animals, climbing to shelter from the storm. And then they were out of it, the worst of it, staring at each other and laughing.

Seeker.

Yes, Seeker.

They clasped forearms, then squeezed further into the shelter, because the storm was still intensifying, with stronger flux to come.

They retained consciousness long enough to sense what happened to the alien craft. Making no attempt to rescue the humanoid crew exposed on the ground – cut by the storm, surely they were dead already – the metal-winged alien (and any others that might have been on board all along, not revealing themselves) caused the damaged craft to come to life, its powerful engines thrusting down, rising up into the vortex of the storm.

Rising . . .

And then the full power of flux fell upon it, flinging the craft against a ferrimagnetic cliff, smashing the alien thing to shreds. Both Seekers could sense the shards flying through the storm; then random chaos heightened to maximum strength, and holding on to their own thoughts was near impossible, all distant perceptions closed off by the storm.

Finally, finally, it was past.

Thank you, Seeker.

The one who had been captive passed out. Wounded but freed, Seeker thought he would recover. Perhaps they would both return to explore beneath the sands, for surely this other Seeker also had sensed what lay beneath, incarcerated for so many generations.

Then Seeker, too, slipped into sleep, and dreamed with flux curled up inside his head, inducing no resonance in his companion: a very private dream, and a strange one. For in that dream his body was transparent, like living glass; and he was on a world that was not this one; yet he was not afraid.

SIXTY-FIVE

MOLSIN, 2603 AD

Closer and closer, the sky-cities moved to Conjunction, their trajectories coming together despite the vagaries of air currents, even the occasional macro-vortex. The strengthening or loosening of political ties and commercial interests were as important to the final configuration as the altitude of laminar flows or the lift capacity of this city compared to that. Not counting D-2 and a handful of other urban babies, nine hundred and twenty-seven cities were coming together high above the Amber Spot.

Condensing from a planet-ranging patternless spread to a globular formation, shrinking inwards to a predetermined centre, they came at leisurely, controlled velocities. There would be no single city at the configuration's heart. Instead, the core must form itself first; then the other cities could begin to attach themselves, building the formation outwards in concentric shells.

Gaggles and flocks of cities, drawing together.

First Popper, Dubrovnik and Dalton formed a horizontal triangle, extruding vast, thick spars to join themselves together. They would be the middle tier. Later the spars would hollow out, granting intercity access; but while the joining was in progress, they remained solid.

Above them, another triangle formed, these three pulling themselves closer together, creating a tighter, smaller shape. Then Cohenville-Feynmanton-Gaussburg floated into place, above Popper-Dubrovnik-Dalton, and rotated to a forty-degree offset. Spars grew at angles to fasten the two triangles together. Soon after that was done and tests confirmed the structural integrity, the Whitton-Strossville-Aéroparis formation floated underneath, rotated into position, and fastened itself to the cities above.

Two small triangles, above and below a larger triangle: the hub was done.

The first hollow, spherical shell was a five-layer grouping, with varying numbers of cities at each level. From top to bottom, once the shell was complete, the layers were: on top, Kakujing by itself; then Sakharovgorod-Penrose-Pneumos-Bernersley-Neumannstadt forming the second layer down; with Franklin2-Hodgekinston-Yukawa-Darwin9-Melville-Newton-IrEinstein forming the central 'ring'. Below that was Lahore2.0-Reynoldston-Gödelburg-Emelianenkogorod-Dennettminster; while the singular Cantorℵ (which everyone but lawyers called The Big Aleph) formed the lowest point.

Twenty-eight cities in place; only eight hundred and ninety-nine (plus babies) to go.

Five careful days later, after a flurry of final checking, a single message propagated through every corridor and hall, every private dwelling and public space:

Conjunction achieved.

The tunnel-surfers were the worst: kids with superb intuitive control of quickglass, chasing each other whooping through the crowds. They sailed just over other people's heads, propelling themselves by flicking strands of quickglass, or whipped along centimetres below the ceilings, hanging from fast-flowing strips. Falls were rare but frequent enough to jeopardize the innocent.

Roger saw one such fall – a teenage girl dropping as she failed to swing from one extruded handle to another – but Rhianna gestured, flinging up floor-tendrils to catch the girl and lower her feet-first. 'Thanks,' the girl called, forming a slideway that carried her along the mall floor to a clear area, where she embedded her fists and feet in the wall and caused it to carry her upwards once more. There were smiles among the thronging adults, which Roger took to mean that such sports were nothing new, evoking youthful memories.

'It's Conjunction,' said Rhianna. 'Everyone needs to go a little wild on occasion.'

'Even so . . .'

He was approximately his old self, and she was reacting as if he were the unchanged Roger. But they both knew he could dig deeper, and react faster and differently compared to a mere six standard days before.

'Better inside,' she said, 'than out on the hull. *That's* what the law clamps down on.'

'Are they from Deltaville, do you think?' Roger gestured at another group hurtling past overhead. 'Or passing through from elsewhere?'

'Doesn't matter. Right now, there's only one titanic city called Conjunction, and that's it.'

All of Molsin's humanity in one massive place. There was no need to point out the strategic implications; Rhianna had been way ahead of him, declaring that this was the flashpoint if Helsen was about to do something.

'I've got assets from other cities as well as Deltaville,' she said now, 'and they're all spacing themselves out, passing through as much of Conjunction as they can.'

Helsen had stolen an autodoc capable of altering her features and her DNA signature. None of Rhianna's assets – for asset read agent – were likely to sense the darkness that warped Helsen and perhaps controlled her.

'It's impossible. Spotting Helsen, I mean.'

'Not as much as you think.' Rhianna pointed at his tu-ring. 'You've a few little extras in there, haven't you?'

'Maybe.' But keeping secrets from your director in the field, when they could affect operational effectiveness, was a no-no. Commodore Gould had suggested Roger was a natural; so perhaps he should act as if he were already an intelligence officer, and Rhianna was local-controlling him. 'Meaning yes.

I've a massive amount still to explore. As far as I can tell, Dad dumped a copy of everything he had into here.'

'Good to know. There are some tricks available to us' – she wobbled her hand, tu-ring in front of Roger's face – 'which you'll learn. There's a range of possible alterations to Helsen's DNA, but not an infinite range, certainly not if she planned on avoiding a lengthy time in coma. Likewise the grosser physical work: she won't have altered her limb length and gait, unless she was willing to compromise her ability to run and dodge.'

'Oh.'

'Just because the cities don't like to spy on their inhabitants' – Rhianna's smile momentarily showed innocent joy, mirroring the teenage girl earlier – 'doesn't mean they can't. Quickglass is quickglass, and my people will make use of it.'

If Dad's work on Fulgor had included running a network of agents, he had never hinted at it. Roger wondered what psychological mastery was required to recruit someone and be certain that you were not betraying yourself to the authorities.

'You could do your socialite thing again.' Roger pointed at her functional clothing and practical hairstyle. 'Get recognized, get on the newscasts with me standing beside you.'

'When Helsen attacked before, she was expecting you to be a softer target, and she didn't expect me at all. I don't think the Judas goat thing will work a second time. She's either going to carry on with her operation if there is one, or go deep into hiding.'

'Marvellous. So is there any point in being here in Deltaville in particular?'

Rhianna looked at him.

'You want to go back to Barbour to see Leeja Rigelle?'

'Er, no ...' He had not thought of Leeja for two days or more. 'I didn't realize you knew about her.'

'Backtracking your details wasn't hard,' said Rhianna. 'Pity Helsen's proving less– Oh, hello. It's the new observers.' She blinked as her smartlenses flickered. 'We have three possible sightings from urban surveillance. In three different cities.'

The lenses cleared.

'Let's have nice a cup of daistral,' she said.

It was not what he expected, but it made sense: inside a cocoon of quickglass – privacy booth, less noticeable than usual, this being a festive occasion – Rhianna brought up a sequence of real-holo images, tiny dots glowing inside transparent city-representations. She had been dumping new observer-agents in place, with wider parameters. A sheaf of sighting possibilities had arrived before Rhianna shut off all outside comms, indicating twenty-three possible locations, each annotated in subsidiary holovolumes. Some were multiple sightings of the same individual; but there were seven different people involved, and potentially none of them was Helsen: none of the probabilities quite reached seventy per cent.

Still, it was new data.

'That's probabilities based on our expanded search profile,' said Rhianna. 'Which is purely physical: gait, DNA, so forth. If I filter that through tactical analysis, we might get a narrower– There.'

Five locations remained.

'Using what criteria?' asked Roger.

'Destructive potential,' said Rhianna, 'based on current physical position within Conjunction or on normal cultural influence. Think highly connected networks: there's a small number of cities which, if they undergo some catastrophe, would affect a large number of others.'

'What kind of catastrophe?'

'Any kind. Disease, you name it.'

But of course she must be thinking of the Fulgor Anomaly, and the possibility that Helsen could create another such abomination here, through some mechanism neither of them had thought of.

'So how do we narrow it down?'

Information sprang up all around him. History and news related to the likely locations.

'Read everything,' she said. 'Run any inference engines you can construct, and remember to use the one that's right behind your eyes.'

From the table, daistral and sandwiches rose up.

'Expect it to take time,' she added.

Which was tough advice, given the incoming tide of urgency and fear, and the possibility that another world might die.

Afterwards, it was difficult to work out which of them had spotted it. For sure it was Roger's unconscious flinch that formed the immediate trigger; but if Rhianna had not noticed his reaction then he might not have followed up the topic of *FULGOR SURVIVORS' REUNION*, and seen what they did.

Capturing a real time view, they swung in on a holo banner over rows of banquet-laden tables:

<– Survivors of Fulgor: WELCOME –>

Rhianna shook her head as they moved the viewpoint, while a dozen more holovolumes showed results from scanning constructs coursing through the quickglass systems: constructs locally injected by one of her agents. Reading Roger's body language before he could speak, she directed a zoom-in to see a young woman greeting other survivors, looking shell-shocked rather than weeping. All sorts of reactions were on display.

'That's Alisha,' said Roger.

'All right.' Rhianna directed the viewpoint to spin away. 'Let's see if we can find—'

They did not see the first one: the phenomenon had already begun to manifest when they spotted it.

'Oh, shit.' Roger tried to point. 'It's—'

'I've got it.' Everything swung then sharpened. 'Son of a bitch.'

Blue glows were extending from one pair of eyes to another, and another and another: a network, expanding person by person as others stumbled back, beginning to notice. Soon there would be a stampede.

'Anomaly,' he said.

Alisha was there. Alisha who no longer knew him. He had rescued her once but this time it was impossible.

'Dubrovnik,' said Rhianna. 'Right in the fucking centre, and wouldn't you know it.'

Deltaville was six layers out. There was no way to get there in the next few seconds; and nothing that could be done to fight a second Anomaly, any more than they had the first: victory had consisted in getting clear.

'We have to sound an evacuation,' said Roger. 'There's no other way. Break up the Conjunction and spread the cities out.'

If Rhianna could subvert urban systems, perhaps she could broadcast an official-looking—

'That's not an Anomaly,' said Rhianna.

'*What?*'

'The body language is all wrong. Listen to me.' She pointed, hand inside the image. 'I've seen the footage from Fulgor: real time external views from the ships, and surveillance data they remotely captured. I've pored over the victims' behaviour and this isn't it.'

Those unaffected were beginning their panicked escape: knots of people banging into each other, here and there a head disappearing as someone fell beneath rushing feet.

Rhianna shut the holos down.

'These victims look,' she said, 'as if they're in a trance.'

'Helsen.'

'Yes.'

It rushed past him on every side, the quickglass. His arms were clamped against his ribs, fingers down as if at attention, legs squeezed together and toes pointed, and from someone else's viewpoint he must have looked like a torpedo speeding through a fluid medium; but for him it was a hellride, his body

banged and shaken, tearing through city-stuff –
floor/ceiling/wall, it made no difference; and perhaps conjoining spars – he thought he had left Deltaville behind but
there was no way to tell.

He could not see Rhianna, keeping pace alongside; could
not have said how he knew she was there.

We have to go faster.

As if Rhianna knew his thought, the vibration intensified,
acceleration heightening as the world roared past in torrential
flow.

Torpedo, heading for the fight.

Once inside the apartment, Jed looked around, liking the
place – liking the woman too, though she was older than him,
therefore older again compared to Roger.

'He's not been here for a few days,' she said.

'I'm sorry. They gave me this as Roger's official address.
Known address, I mean.'

It had taken six days of bureaucratic negotiation to get this
far; and he reckoned he was lucky it had only taken that long,
given the privacy-obsessed culture. Although, on a world the
size of Molsin, you would have thought there would be a
Pilots' Sanctuary to provide assistance – or if not, at least
undercover spooks in place, people that Max Gould could have
given him the means to get in touch with. Perhaps it had just
slipped everyone's mind – that weird memory flake, popping
into existence above the conference table, had stirred everything up.

Or it might be that there were spooks on Molsin, but they
worked for Schenck and his mob: the ones that had been
defeated in Labyrinth, but what about the realspace worlds?
For all Jed knew, every Pilot spook in realspace might be acting
for the enemy, knowingly or not.

Best to keep things low-key and solo, then.

'—daistral?' she was saying.

'Er, no thanks, Ms Rigelle. I don't suppose you know where

Roger is now, or even better, how to contact him?'

His comms code did not function, possibly because Conjunction changed everything, nearly a thousand cities merging their comms systems while shutting out the rest. Either that, or Roger was deliberately out of contact.

'He was on Deltaville, even before Conjunction, because he—'

Soft redness flickered through walls, floor and ceiling, then again.

'What's that?' said Jed.

A deep moan began to sound: everything vibrating all around.

'General alarm. We're taught about it school, but I've never—' She gestured a holo into being. It showed an image of people in a crowd, their eyes joined by a criss-crossed web of glowing blue light. 'Oh, no.'

'Fucking hell.' Jed grabbed her. 'With me, now. Leave everything.'

Her eyes sparkled with tears and fright.

'All right.'

'Fucking, fucking shit,' said Jed.

SIXTY-SIX

LABYRINTH, 2603 AD (REALSPACE-EQUIVALENT)

It glowed above Max's flowmetal desk – newly extruded in his new office – watched by Pavel, Clayton, Clara with a rebuild-cast large and clunky around her shoulder, and an addition to their inner circle: white-haired Kelvin Stanier, Head of Records and older than the cosmos, who not only remembered more than the combined memories of everyone else present, but assumed the right to criticize Max Gould as though he were a schoolboy. Right now, riding high on a wave of triumph – although the countercoup's nature and extent were unknown to most of Labyrinth: political circles being rife with waves of disinformation planted by Max's senior officers, while Pilots at large knew nothing – Max needed someone like Kelvin to keep him on track. Some of the service's officers, especially the younger ones, looked at Max with new-minted awe. Kelvin would have none of that, which meant if Max made a mistake, there would be at least one adviser to tell him so.

Pavel did raise a concern which they would have to return to: what to do with the realspace intelligence networks. Between Max's long-term counter-surveillance and Pavel's own operations, there were some agents in place known to be compromised. But they were aware also, from the mass debriefing that was already underway, that the majority of Schenck's people knew nothing of the darkness; if they thought anything about the internal struggle for power, it had simply been that: the extension of politics by covert means, therefore business as usual.

'This is clearly long term.' Pavel gestured at the holo. 'I mean, think of the timescales we know about. It's not like we need to solve the problem before lunch.'

Kelvin, his lined face unreadable, gave a slow headshake that could have meant anything; but they already knew his views: that semantics betrayed their collective parochialism.

At the beginning of the twentieth century, 'galaxy' and 'universe' had been synonyms, though within decades that had changed. What remained constant for nearly six centuries afterwards was that the galaxy containing Earth remained simply 'the galaxy' while others gained names and M-numbers. It said something not just about realspace humanity's perspective, but also that of the Pilots who thought they held themselves apart by living here in Labyrinth.

'Should we have explored more?' said Max, gesturing at the holo. 'As a species, I mean.'

'A matter of scale,' answered Pavel. 'Like I said. We're doing all right.'

But to Max's eyes, the image denied that proposition. The faint needle of light from the galactic centre, pointing not just to the spiral arm containing Earth, but to Earth precisely; and continuing that line, the observation – deciphered from the centuries-old memory flake dropped into their collective lap – of a mystery beyond a cosmic void, something lined up.

'No, I want to follow this up.' Max looked at Kelvin. 'You know what I mean.'

'Suicide missions.'

'What?' Clayton looked at them both. 'What the hell?'

'A series of observation flights,' said Max. 'I want to set distance intervals of a hundred-and-fifty million lightyears. The first to appear here' – he pointed on the notional line – 'the next here, and so on.'

The steps were huge, equal to the galactic radius, each destination farther out from the galactic core.

'So they're very long observation flights,' said Pavel. 'What's suicidal about that?'

'Because' – Max slid his finger along the line – 'at some

point, one of the observers is going to meet something nasty coming the other way.'

'And that Pilot,' said Kelvin, in case anyone failed to grasp the point, 'won't come back. So I'll have someone else's identity to expunge from Records.'

'Or not.' Max looked at him. 'Things have changed. Any officer who falls, deserves to be honoured.'

Clara shrugged her good shoulder.

'If the timescales are as Pavel says, then by the time . . . it . . . arrives, won't Earth have rotated far away from your pretty line here?'

Max looked at them, one by one, as though deciding what they were up to hearing.

'I don't think Earth is the target,' he said. 'I think it formed a convenient recruiting station.'

'Recruits?' said Pavel.

'For whichever force' – Max pointed into the galactic core – 'has established this bridgehead, ready and waiting for the main enemy to come.'

All of them stared at the holo.

'Well,' said Clayton finally, 'at least there's one good thing.'

Their stares transferred to him.

'Irreverent humour,' said Kelvin, 'is hardly what we need.'

'No, but' – Clayton gestured – 'it's what we're good at, isn't it? Us as a species, Max.'

'Good at what?'

'Good at warfare. Because that's what this is, isn't it?'

In the holo, the spiral galaxy looked serene and eternal, destined never to change; and during any human lifetime, that illusion held true. Only on longer timescales, as Pavel had said, did the picture change, as the galaxy became a fragile-looking thing, small in the immensity of surrounding darkness, already altered at its heart, ripe perhaps for sundering apart.

SIXTY-SEVEN

MOLSIN, 2603 AD

They burst from the quickglass floor, erupting upwards: Rhianna and Roger both. All around were screaming people, running but bypassing them, as Rhianna gestured a thick, curved, rising barrier into place. Beyond the panicked mob, the others were simply standing, the blue web of light joining their eyes.

'We need to get through!' yelled Rhianna. 'Show everyone what this is.'

Roger nodded. He jumped onto the top of the barrier, and she followed.

'Ready?' she said.

'Yeah.'

It threw them over the mob, pulsing and lengthening beneath their feet, propelling them high, then arcing down. They jumped clear less than two metres above the floor. Roger broke the momentum with a shoulder roll, feeling momentarily good about that; but Rhianna had been less spectacular in her landing, taking the impact by ordinary knee-bend, and she was first at the group of people: some fifty Fulgidi refugees, no more, frozen in place with the blue glow that terrified everyone.

'It's holo,' she said, waving her tu-ring. 'A simple holo illusion.'

'Shit.'

Rhianna did something, and the blueness simply faded out of existence. The people remained standing, still in whatever trance Helsen had induced.

Roger took in a deep breath.

'She was here,' he said. 'Helsen.'

'You can *smell* her?'

'Don't ask me to explain. I think she went that way.' He pointed to an exit behind Rhianna. 'But I don't think she's close.'

It was faint, the spoor: the evil he could taste more than smell. The combined roar of running people would not have buried the familiar discordant nine notes, not if the sound had been present; but there was no trace of it.

Then waves of orange and black strobed across the hall's high, neo-Baroque ceiling, its intricate walls and polished floor.

'Bug out,' said Rhianna. 'Bug out now.'

Quickglass began to boom, again and again, sounding a tocsin.

'Why?'

After all their breakneck rush to get here.

'Seppuku bomb,' she said. 'They're sacrificing the city.'

No wonder there were no police officers present. The official response to a burgeoning new Anomaly would have to be all-out, to have a chance of being effective. Had the threat here been real, it was probably the one course of action likely to succeed: stand off and take out the danger, hard.

'But I can't leave Alisha,' said Roger.

'I can.'

She stepped close, pressed her body against him, and kissed him.

What?

He heard from far away: 'Sorry.'

Bands of something bound him to her, close as if lovers; but her lips had delivered anaesthesia, not passion. Soft and melting, then: not her, but the floor beneath them.

Dropping now.

From a distance, but only from a distance, Emergency Disjunction was a beautiful process: cities propelled outward from cities, like some globular blossom dissipating seeds in all dir-

413

ections. Spars dissolved as sky-cities flew, attaining velocities they had never attempted before, pulling apart before it could happen.

White, incandescent, the sphere of explosion at the centre.

But the expansion was not fast enough: four more of the inner nine were caught in the seppuku bomb's devastation: Popper, Dalton, Gaussburg and Whitton, all damaged and already dying.

In control rooms, senior officers let out sighs or curses as the case might be: five cities lost, therefore nine hundred and twenty-two – plus babies – saved. For several minutes, the emergency proper appeared to be over, traumatic though the coming aftermath would be: the cleanup, the relocation of people in cities not their own, the re-establishment of order.

Then flame licked across the hulls of Penrose and The Big Aleph, and the news came in: more Anomalous centres were appearing, in cities where the authorities no longer had time to evacuate and order urban suicide. Only one response remained: sky-city after sky-city activated energy-weapon systems they had never used in anger, not before.

Now, they let loose.

Soon the warfare was all-out, or even worse than war: for each city fired upon every other city nearby, no longer knowing who the enemy was, therefore assuming all.

Only the baby cities, unable to fight, floated clear of the conflagration.

For a second, dropping through the toxic air, Roger had come round – Dubrovnik's lower hull was receding overhead – and then a gold-and-cobalt-blue ship was underneath them, a dorsal opening appeared a second before they fell inside, then whatever had bound him to Rhianna was gone. But the impact against the control cabin floor was hard, knocking him into a state where he could not see though hearing remained. Perhaps for a few seconds he was out of it entirely.

And then transition.

Waking up to amber-tinted air, and the deep knowledge in every cell of his body that this was mu-space, and he and Rhianna were safe.

Friss Reejan, in her quickglass bubble, fell clear of the awfulness above. As Lady Mayor of Deltaville, she had been the officers' first priority in the evacuation process, getting her to the city's edge where she toppled clear, encased in quickglass. Dry-eyed because she had to be, she commanded the extrusion of glider-wings, bringing the bubble's flight under some kind of control. Soon her trajectory flattened out, at an altitude far lower than the lowest point of Conjunction.

When she looked back, flames and dropping debris were all she could see.

'My God. Oh, sweet God.'

She looked at her hand. How incongruous: holding a bowl of orgasmousse from the fresh consignment, so much better than any other food. The officers had snatched her clear of a banquet, and she had not even let go.

Behind her, the cities were gone.

'Oh, God.'

Using her fingers, she spooned all of the orgasmousse into her mouth. Immediate pleasure flooded through her, more intense than she had never known, wave after wave of sheerest joy. Eyes closed, whimpering, she formed control gestures.

The wings melted back into the quickglass as it formed a vertical bullet-shape, driving straight down to the hydrofluoric acid ocean.

Tannier hit Helsen with a hooking palm-heel, smashing her sideways.

'You think we're all fucking amateurs, bitch?'

She was down on one knee. Most men would have been in coma.

I'm going to kill you, Helsen.

He was a professional, and he had picked up her trail through a tour de force of surveillance hacking that he would never be able to share with anyone; and he had intercepted her here, in a lonely chamber just inside the hull of Pneumos, too late to prevent the cascade of violence she had kicked off. Too late for normal procedures of arrest and detention then: just time for him to be the executioner.

'Piss off,' she said.

The floor ripped apart between them: a gap widening very fast. Already they were separated by a chasm too wide to jump across. He stared around, raising his arms to summon quickglass tendrils; but a rush of wind indicated the outer hull was splitting open, and then he was choking as Molsin's toxic atmosphere mixed with city air.

Shit.

He saw Helsen throw herself out through the gap – *good, she's suicided* – but then a shining hull told of something very different: a mu-space ship, and Helsen's being dropped inside by a city tendril before the ship's opening sealed up.

It turned away, silver and red its colours; then it slammed out of existence.

Escaped.

He could choke here, throw himself out, or run back inside the city to prolong his end; but whichever way it went, this was it.

It's all too soon. Maura, I should never have—

Then scarlet light was blazing.

<<Man, with us.>>

<<Ending is.>>

<<Now now now.>>

<<Death not death.>>

Sapphire blue, as the surroundings changed. A cabin, with air that did not choke him; and three more traceries of living light.

'Wait,' he managed. 'I can't survive in mu-space.'

Not conscious, anyhow. But they did not seem to hear him.

Oh, frigging God.

416

He stood up, stared at the metal bulkhead, then crouched.
Oh, Maura.
And lunged headfirst against the—

SIXTY-EIGHT

Piet Gunnarsson and his ship were basking in the golden void, meditating on the distant strings of black fractal stars, glad to be back in the universe where they belonged. It was a rest period, and he had already slept. Here, strictly, they had nothing to do.

In realspace there had been Fulgor to watch over, from what they had hoped was a safe distance. However deadly the possibility of attack from the planet-locked Anomaly, there was always a tedium to hanging in realspace. Here, the opposite was true: simply relaxing involved a resonance with mu-space energies that made him-and-ship fully alive.

Far off, Alice's ship floated, and beyond her the others from their shift. A replacement sequence of ships was hanging in realspace to observe the hellworld of Fulgor.

Someone's in a hurry.

That was Alice.

I see them.

No ID signals were evident, but the ship was flying hard – her hull silver and scarlet, translated to realspace colours. Not a vessel that Piet recognized. It would be past them in seconds.

Another signal came in from Alice.

No response to hails and pings.

On this geodesic, the newcomer could transit into realspace and pop out close to Fulgor. Piet's stomach churned as he sank into ship-interface, and he-and-ship powered up their weapon systems.

You can't be serious.

Alice again, but ship-and-Piet did not reply, because they

knew how ferocious was the intent behind their orders: to let nothing leave or approach the realspace hellworld.

**$\Sigma \; \Gamma \; 7 \; \Xi \; \Psi \; 9$ **

Piet-and-ship felt the signal activate their recognition module. Entanglement collapsed to reveal the corresponding eigenmessage:

Priority Aleph. Admiral on board.

He-and-ship allowed their weaponry to relax as the other ship sped past, flared with light, and disappeared from the golden void.

Ours not to reason why, Piet.

Nobody tells us nothing.

In Aeternum, the double negative implied an infinite mutual recursion akin to paradox, while the counter-rhythm of the nouns formed a twisted pun. It was enough for Alice to transmit a chuckle without words.

But Piet was not amused by his own joke, because he could see no reason why a lone admiral would fly straight towards the most unpredictable of danger zones.

On the other hand, Piet had his orders.

I'm not going to fail in my duty.

If he had been more alert days earlier, he would have followed the evacuation fleet to Fulgor and helped refugees get clear before the Anomaly took over. Then, he had not been civic-minded, and the shame would remain for ever.

So I'll do what I'm told.

In a subjective hour, he would be back in realspace, on watch once more.

Observing the enemy.

Because when it boiled down to it, the Anomaly was simply that.

The enemy.

SIXTY-NINE

FULGOR, 2603 AD

It had evolved. It continued to evolve.

Its billions of constituent, pinpoint components, had once been independent minds. Buried deep inside were flimsy theories from Its ancestral species, such as: in the absence of a vast plurality, evolution could not progress: a solitary, unitary organism could only grow. Yet It continued to change in ways tiny life-forms could not contemplate, unable to fully grasp the strong coupling between emergent resonance and natural selection. It spread across the face of Its world. Soon, It would become Its world; only solitude was necessary.

And then, something disturbed Its isolation.

The ship that landed was silver and scarlet. Using archaic, ancestral communication modes, it broadcast this message:

We wish to help. We wish to help you spread.

For many nanoseconds, It contemplated the primitive semantics; then it received a further signal.

Give us some of your people, and we will take them with us.

This needed no thought. It would miss a handful of internal components no more than a human might regret a shed skin-cell. Using a level of detailed control It had not needed for some time, It directed several of Its human components to walk towards the waiting ship.

An opening melted in the hull, and a ramp flowed out. In single file, Its components ascended and went inside.

We give our word.

There was no need for It to answer.

SEVENTY

LABYRINTH, 2603 AD (REALSPACE-EQUIVALENT)

Jed and Rhianna were with him, but he could hardly perceive their presence. Even before the wall melted open, he could sense her inside, and knew how much had changed, how much he had missed by being away on Molsin.

I'm here.

The space was as vast as ever, but now she seemed to fill it. Stately in a way she could never have managed before, she floated closer: magnificent and huge and beautiful: black and webbed with both scarlet and gold, all power and manoeuvrability. Roger touched her lower hull with his hand.

You're so beautiful.

And I'm yours.

Tears blurred everything.

Yes.

A tendril came down, ready to lift him aloft, to take him inside her for the maiden flight.

I'm ready.

For the flight?

And the rest.

The moment stretched out as the tendril took hold of him around the waist.

Rest?

I have my mother's memories.

Oh.

She lifted him up.

ACKNOWLEDGMENTS

This stanza, which I've quoted in chapter 35, is from one of the Hávamál collection of poems as translated by R.I. Page, and printed in Page [1995]. Though the verses were not gathered until the late Viking Age, many date from earlier times.

> *Medium wise should a man be,*
> *Never too wise.*
> *No man should know his fate in advance;*
> *His heart will be the freer of care.*

Many thanks to the volunteer staff at Bletchley Park and others who have told me more than I can use here. Massive gratitude to Andrew Jenkins, Mark Williamson and James Winters for encouraging feedback. And infinite love and thanks, as always, to Yvonne for getting me through it.

BIBLIOGRAPHY

Barnes, M., *A New Introduction to Old Norse*, Viking Society for Northern Research, University College London, 3rd Edition, 2008

Copeland, B.J. et al., *Colossus: The Secrets of Bletchley Park's Code-breaking Computers*, Oxford University Press, 2006

Crossley-Holland, K., *The Norse Myths*, Pantheon Books, 1980

Fairbairn, Capt. W.E., *Get Tough!*, Paladin Press, 1979 (original pub. 1942)

Fölsing, A., *Albert Einstein*, Penguin Books, 1998

Hawkins, J., *On Intelligence*, Holt, 2004

Hodges, A., *Alan Turing: the Enigma*, Vintage, 1992

Jeffery, K., *MI6: The History of the Secret Intelligence Service*, Bloomsbury, 2010

Kanigel, R., *The Man Who Knew Infinity*, Abacus, 1991

Laughlin, R.B., *A Different Universe*, Basic Books, 2005

Law, M., *The Pyjama Game*, Aurum, 2007

Navarro, J., *What Every Body Is Saying*, HarperCollins, 2008

Ornstein, R., *The Right Mind*, Harcourt Brace, 1997

Page, R.I., *Chronicles of the Vikings*, The British Museum Press, 1995

Page, R.I., *Runes*, The British Museum Press, 1987

Parker, A., *Seven Deadly Colours*, Free Press, 2005

Reid, J.M., *The Atomic Nucleus*, Penguin Books, 1972

Poundstone, W., *Prisoner's Dilemma*, Oxford University Press, 1993

Rhodes, R., *The Making of the Atomic Bomb*, Penguin Books, 1988

Sanmark, A., Sundman, F., *The Vikings*, Lyxo, 2008

Shirer, William L., *The Rise and Fall of the Third Reich*, Arrow Books, 1998

Strogatz, S., *SYNC*, Hyperion, 2003

Taylor, P.B., Auden, W.H., *The Elder Edda*, Faber and Faber, 1969

West, N., *GCHQ: The Secret Wireless War 1900–86*, Coronet, 1987

Yourgrau, P., *A World Without Time*, Basic Books, 2005

Articles on Telegraphy and on World War II in the 1956 edition of the *Encyclopædia Britannica* were also helpful.